# Out of the Snare

*Thank you for allowing me to use the words of your tract. May this be a blessing and entertaining!*

*Pamela Bush*
*Ps. 124:7+8*

tompambush48@yahoo.com
pambush.blogspot.com

# Out of the Snare

**PAMELA BUSH**

TATE PUBLISHING & *Enterprises*

*Out of the Snare*
Copyright © 2009 by Pamela Bush. All rights reserved.

This title is also available as a Tate Out Loud product. Visit www.tatepublishing.com for more information.

No part of this publication may be reproduced, stored in a retrieval system or transmitted in any way by any means, electronic, mechanical, photocopy, recording or otherwise without the prior permission of the author except as provided by USA copyright law.

Scripture taken from the *New King James Version*®. Copyright © 1982 by Thomas Nelson, Inc. Used by permission. All rights reserved.

Moyer, Larry. May I Ask You A Question? Copyright © 2004 by EvanTell, Inc. Used by permission.

This novel is a work of fiction. Names, descriptions, entities, and incidents included in the story are products of the author's imagination. Any resemblance to actual persons, events, and entities is entirely coincidental.

The opinions expressed by the author are not necessarily those of Tate Publishing, LLC.

Published by Tate Publishing & Enterprises, LLC
127 E. Trade Center Terrace | Mustang, Oklahoma 73064 USA
1.888.361.9473 | www.tatepublishing.com

Tate Publishing is committed to excellence in the publishing industry. The company reflects the philosophy established by the founders, based on Psalm 68:11,
*"The Lord gave the word and great was the company of those who published it."*

Book design copyright © 2009 by Tate Publishing, LLC. All rights reserved.
*Cover design by Tyler Evans*
*Interior design by Nathan Harmony*

Published in the United States of America

ISBN: 978-1-61566-298-2
1. Fiction: Christian: Suspense
1. Fiction: Christian: Romance
09.10.27

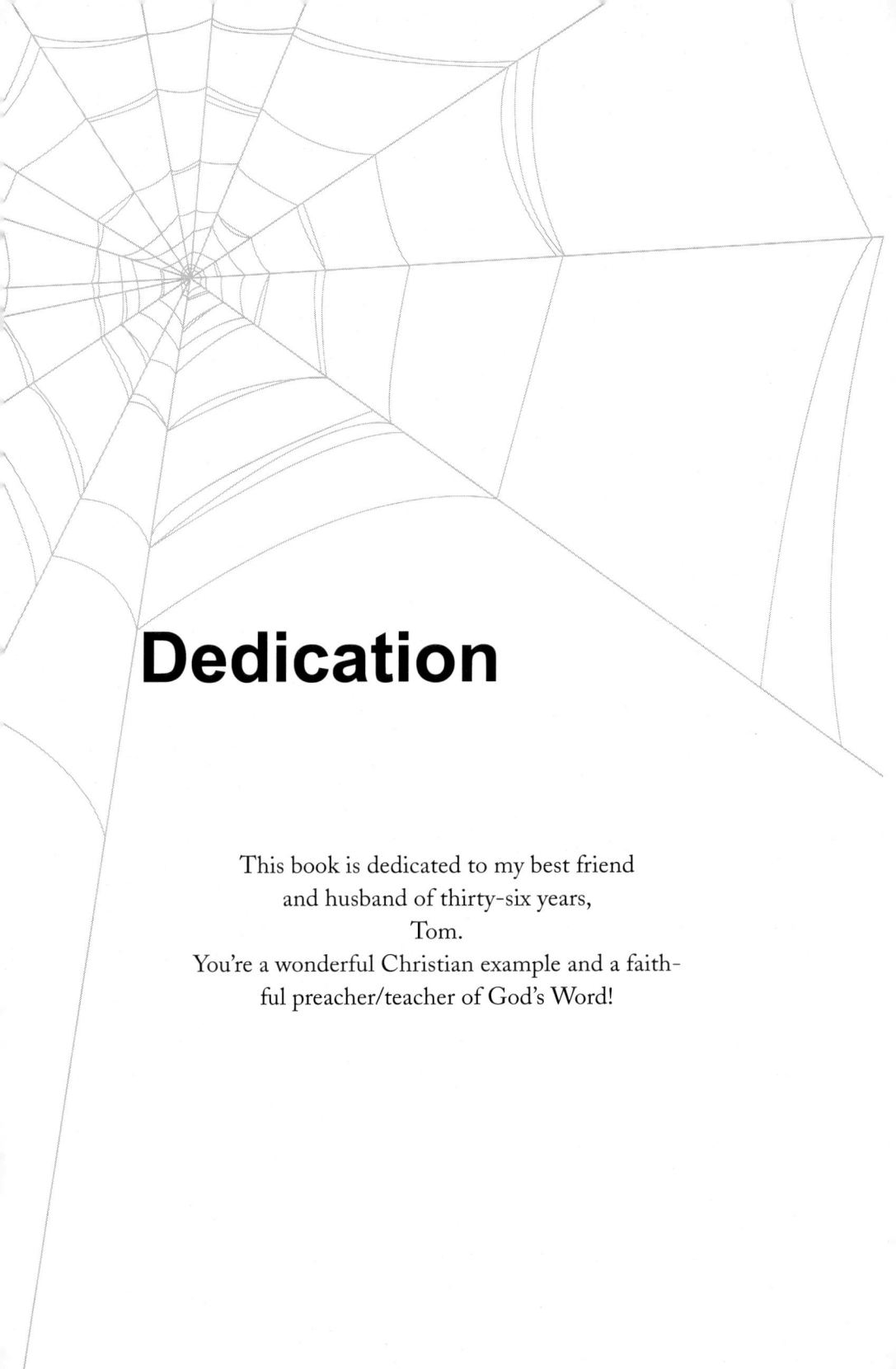

# Dedication

This book is dedicated to my best friend
and husband of thirty-six years,
Tom.
You're a wonderful Christian example and a faithful preacher/teacher of God's Word!

# Acknowledgments

First and foremost, I desire to thank my Lord and Savior, Jesus Christ, who willingly died on the cross for me. As with my first novel, *Out of the Whirlwind,* my main goal is for Jesus to receive all the honor, glory, and praise.

A large thank you goes to my beloved husband, Tom, and daughter, Rhonda, for the hours of help I received. You faithfully read every word and offered suggestions when I couldn't see my way through a section. Thank you! I couldn't have done it without your time and encouragement. Also, thank you to my son-in-law, Edward, for giving up precious time with Rhonda in order for us to have phone time.

To my son, Paul; husband, Tom; and the Michigan State Police troopers George and Connie Haw: thank you for letting me pick your brains about weapons, ammunition, two-way radios, etc.

Special thanks goes to Larry Moyer for his kind, encouraging words and for permission to use one of his Gospel tracts in Chapter 25. EvanTell Inc. has a tremendous outreach ministry that we've prayerfully supported for years.

A special thanks goes to my team at Tate Publishing, especially Jaime. Your insights and suggestions were a learning experience for me. Tyler, your creative genius helped me look beyond the normal for a cover. I've greatly enjoyed working with all of you, and with possible future writing projects.

To the people of Langston Church, thank you for your constant interest and encouragement. I greatly appreciate your prayers on my behalf.

Finally, I wish to thank all the people who read *Out of the Whirlwind*. Being my first novel, I wondered how it would be received. I've been overwhelmed by your response and enthusiasm! Hearing repeatedly that you couldn't put it down and constantly being asked when the sequel would be out were huge motivators. Thank you!

To God, I say thank you for giving me the ability to do something I really enjoy—write! Unfortunately, it took me over forty years to gain the confidence I needed to accomplish this dream. I trust others will not give up on their own dreams.

Trust God. His timing is always perfect.

And that they may come to their senses
And escape the snare of the devil,
Having been taken captive
By him to do his will.
II Timothy 2:26

# Prologue

"Where is she?"

Vince Edgar shuddered as he heard the demanding question over the phone line. Being head accountant for a prestigious corporation, the power this man wielded irritated him. A sinister, unnamed man who pulled all the strings, and Vince feared him. It was this fear fueled by resentment that had prompted Vince to purchase a virtually undetectable phone recorder. Having the presence of mind to quietly click it on, Vince found his voice. "She's up in northern lower Michigan in a small city called Petoskey."

"How are you keeping tabs on her?"

"I hired a local Petoskey man. He reports back every couple weeks.

She's working in a women's clothing store, and get this..." Warming to his subject, Vince actually chuckled. "She's pretending to be religious and has gotten herself connected with a church in the area." He chuckled again but was shortly snapped back to attention.

"Spare me the details! As long as she keeps to the plan and keeps her mouth shut, I don't care what else she does!" The voice fell silent and then demanded, "Do you have a contingency plan if she doesn't keep her mouth shut?"

Vince grew very quiet as chills ran up his spine.

"Well, have you?"

"I'm...m...m working on it."

"See that you do! She makes me nervous, and I don't like being nervous! We may need to come up with a different solution just for my own peace of mind."

Vince heard what he assumed to be a high pitched female voice on the other end of the line, which was quickly muffled. Picking up his gold letter opener, he nervously tapped it on his leather desk pad. This situation was becoming more and more uncomfortable. He jumped when the voice suddenly barked, "What name is she using?"

"Syd... Sydney Larsen, but..." He went to say more, but the phone line went dead.

Shutting the recorder off, Vince sat motionless for a second as frustrated rage filled his being. Without thinking, he hurled the opener at the nearest wall. The point imbedded itself. Staring blindly at it, Vince replayed the recent decisions he'd impulsively made. He did them out of self-preservation, but now he fully realized what the ramifications could be to him and his family. He also realized that his own life was in a precarious position.

Suddenly Vince jumped as a voice came over the phone—the one that he still held in his hand. Had he been wrong about the man hanging up? Vince's heart flew to his throat as he frantically tried to recall if he'd just mumbled anything out loud. Vince pulled the phone closer to his ear and heard a recorded message telling him to hang the receiver up. Relief flooded him, and he was able to breathe more normally again. Gently pushing the *off* button, he set the phone down. Sighing, he stated to the air, "We can't dispose of Syd. I've turned her into a key player, and so far no one knows that but me!"

Vince placed his elbows on the desk, dropped his head into his hands, and groaned. "What am I going to do? What have I done?"

Corey Drake ignored the woman vying for his attention as he stared at the cell phone still in his hand. Something was bothering him. *Vince's voice didn't sound right. He was more nervous than usual.* For a moment he wondered out loud, "Could he possibly have been recording me?" Dismissing that as being far too inventive for his partner, Corey still couldn't shake the idea that he was up to something. But what? *What could you be up to that I don't know about, Vince?*

As the woman continued calling seductively to him, Corey came to a decision. His current job had him located several states away, but as soon as he was able, it was time to head back to Louisville, Kentucky.

After setting the phone down, he mumbled under his breath, "I think it's time you and I had a face to face, Vince Edgar."

Corey stood tall, shook his shoulders as if to shake the foreboding away, and then turned to the woman impatiently waiting for him.

# Chapter 1

Quaid Williams, Pierce Matthews, and Pastor Jim were seated in Jim's study trying to solve a problem, namely Sydney Larsen.

"She's gone too far this time, and I have to do something about it!" Pierce was very upset. Coming to his feet he began to pace.

"Pierce, it's not like you to be so worked up," Pastor Jim observed. "Calm down and tell us what happened. Start at the beginning."

Pierce stopped behind the tall wing-backed chair and leaned his arms on it. "She paid Hope a visit the other night and…"

Raising his hand, Pastor Jim forestalled any more words. "Let me catch up here. Who's Hope?"

Quaid entered the conversation. "She's the nanny Pierce brought to Petoskey from the Grand Rapids area to care for his daughter, Sarah." Leaning slightly forward, he asked with interest, "Why'd she go see Hope?"

"It seems to warn her to maintain a strict boss/employee relationship with me. Sydney even went so far as to tell Hope that I already belonged to her!" Pierce shook his head out of frustration. "I personally think she's certifiable. I had a hard enough time getting Hope to northern Michigan in the first place, and I've never given Sydney any reason to think I belonged to her or anyone else for that matter." Leaning heavily on the chair back, he added, "Why on earth would I? It's been less than a year since I lost my Vicki."

Sighing, Pierce turned his head toward Pastor Jim, but before he could speak, Quaid quietly yet firmly asserted, "Sydney's not certifiable as you suggest. Instead, I think she may be desperate."

"Desperate or not, I'm not going to stand by while she threatens every woman I may talk to!"

At his words, Quaid came to full alert. "What do you mean she threatened her? How?"

Pierce paused to stare at him with one raised eyebrow. Quaid was an undercover detective for the Michigan State Police, and Pierce knew he had access to information—private information—about people. Seeing Quaid's obvious attention, Pierce asked, "Why the interest? Is something else going on here?"

Quaid looked from Pierce to Pastor Jim then down to the floor. Sorting out just how much he could reveal, he straightened and said, "Shortly after Sydney arrived in Petoskey, we received a heads up that she was a suspect in an embezzlement scam in Louisville, Kentucky. We've had our eye on her ever since."

"Embezzlement! You've got to be kidding!" Pierce came from around the chair he'd been leaning on and sat down. "So...is she involved? Could she go to jail?"

"Just this afternoon the evidence came through, and we're to arrest her." Seeing both the men ready to hit him with more questions, Quaid forestalled them with a raised hand. "Let me finish. My boss and I did some fast talking, and the Feds agreed to let us country boys handle it. We're offering her a deal."

Pastor Jim sat straighter in his chair. "What kind of deal?"

"Sydney has to pay back a large portion, plus agree to name *and* testify against her partners. We believe there's at least two, maybe more. If she's willing, she'll be under three year's probation, and all charges will be dropped."

Leaning forward in his seat, Pierce asked, "And if she doesn't agree?"

"Then she'll go to prison for however long the judge decides."

Sadly shaking his head, Pastor Jim asked, "How much money did they take?"

"Upwards of $750,000."

Silently the men mulled over the ramifications. Finally Pierce spoke. "When you mentioned that Sydney was desperate, what did you mean? Had she purposely singled me out? If so, why me?" He then froze as an alarmed look crossed his face. "She doesn't know who I really am, does she?"

Up until that moment, Pierce had been confident the two men with him were the only ones in Petoskey who knew that in reality he was a multimillionaire. Years earlier he had quietly walked away from the business world, letting competent CEOs and his board handle the affairs, calling him in occasionally when needed. Pierce had wanted to get as far away from that life as possible. Winding up in Petoskey, he got his contractor's license, formed his own business, and purchased a large cabin in a wooded section outside of the city. Now he was concerned that his idyllic life could be disrupted by Sydney.

Seeing all this play across Pierce's face, Quaid confidently stated, "No, Pierce. I'm convinced your secret is still safe. Sydney probably zeroed in on you because you're your own boss, drive an impressive four-door hemi, and in her mind, available." Tossing in a bit of levity, he added, "Even though you're not quite as good-looking as me, I suppose that may have factored in too." Growing serious again, he continued. "Sydney probably thought your grief over Vicki's death made you a prime target for her to step in and soothe away your hurt. She wasn't counting on you being a believer in Christ and that you actually lived like one. Plus, I'm sure she wasn't planning on your hiring a nanny either." Here Quaid paused then thoughtfully stated, "A very pretty one, at that."

All grew silent again, and then the pastor inquired, "What are the odds she has enough money to pay what the judge decides? How much time do you think they will give her to come up with it if she doesn't?"

Quaid stood and began pacing in front of the two men. "I highly doubt she's been allowed near the bulk of the money. I would imagine she was given a hefty sum to get her started someplace new and to ensure she keeps her mouth shut. Usually in situations like this, the perpetrators set up a plan to divide the money at a later date when they figure things have cooled down enough." Rubbing the back of his neck, he added, "The judge will decide Monday how much she'll have to pay back. The Feds stipulated three months as the limit for the payback. Plus, since she's a flight risk, I'm to place her under house arrest, but she'll spend the first few days in the county lockup where the tether will be put on her ankle."

For the first time since the conversation started, Quaid actually smiled. "Usually house arrest means nowhere but home and work, but I was able to squeeze in church attendance too. I thought it couldn't hurt under the circumstances, but it makes me more responsible for her."

Once again the room grew quiet as the three men absorbed all that had just been discussed.

Pierce broke the silence. "A couple nights ago, I finally got Hope to confess about Sydney's visit. I had been building up her trust in me; then suddenly all that stopped, and she grew testy and distant. I knew something was drastically wrong, but she was afraid to tell me. Anyway, after talking it out, we prayed together for God's wisdom on how best to show Sydney his love. We both have a desire to help Sydney see the need of the Lord Jesus in her life. Now that I know there's so much more involved, I'm not sure what our roles should be."

Pastor Jim turned to Quaid. "When are you going to arrest her?"

"First thing tomorrow morning."

Standing, Pastor Jim walked to the front of his oak study desk. "Guys, we need to pray for God's wisdom and leading in dealing with Sydney and her situation, that God may have the ultimate glory and victory in all this."

Later, as the men prepared to go their separate ways, Quaid briefly placed his hand on Pierce's shoulder. "If you don't mind, I was hoping you'd come along in the morning. Since Sydney is keen on you, the chief and I thought you might be able to help persuade her to be smart and give us the names we need. Are you available?"

"What time and where should we meet?"

"My partner, Paul Statham, will be at my house at 7:30 a.m. Come at the same time, and we'll drive my car to her place."

"I'll be there."

Quaid turned to leave when Pierce stalled him with one more question. "Since Hope is kind of involved in this, do you mind if I share some of what you told us with her?"

"If you trust her to keep quiet about it, then go ahead."

After assuring him he did, Pierce left the room. Quaid followed shortly. Pastor Jim sat back down to pray for the situation again. He had much heaviness over what might lie ahead for Sydney Larsen.

The next morning the sun came streaming in the window hitting Quaid full in the face. He was tempted to pull the covers up and ignore it, but he'd been awake too long already. Sleep was long gone. In spite of the sun's warm beckoning, he had a feeling it wasn't going to be one of his better days.

Sydney Larsen. For the last half hour, she'd been strongly on his mind. The woman was a bundle of trouble, and Quaid knew it.

She'd been involved in much more than just stealing. That just happened to be the latest incident they had finally gotten evidence on her about. According to her rap sheet, Sydney's turn to the wrong road started back when she was in her early teens. Over the years, she'd been hauled in for petty thefts, sniffing glue, and soliciting. This latest incident had the ability to put her away for several years. Quaid had honestly been surprised when the Feds had agreed with a possible three-month time period if she gave up the names. It saddened Quaid to see the road she was determined to head down, and he wished there was something he could do. Once she began attending church, he'd thought like everyone else that she was a true believer in Christ, but apparently not.

Throwing the covers back, Quaid swung his muscular legs to the floor while flexing his shoulder and neck muscles. Sydney might have made some bad decisions over the years, but one thing Quaid knew for sure—she wasn't the brains of this operation. Somehow he and Pierce needed to convince Sydney it was in her best interest to give up the names of her partners. If he had to press the realities of prison to her, then so be it.

Quaid sighed and got to his feet. Deep down he had a feeling she wouldn't cooperate. He'd seen it too many times. She'd start out being arrogant and cocky; then the reality of what repercussions could happen from the unnamed partners would sink in, and fear would take over. She'd probably clam up while defensively stating she wanted to speak to a lawyer.

Disgust rippled through Quaid as he walked to the heavily built white oak dresser. Before pulling a drawer out, he paused to study his bedroom. He'd taken great pleasure and care in remodeling this home, starting with this room. The dresser matched the floor-to-ceiling headboard of the king-size bed. Quaid chose the headboard for all its nooks and crannies. Being an avid outdoorsman on his days off, he could display his wildlife figurines and knife collection in all the cubbyholes. The whole room spoke woodsy nature. Quaid slowly spun on his heel to take it all in before pulling clean underwear from the dresser and heading to the adjoining bathroom.

Moments later, he opened the shower door to step into a steaming hot spray of water. Allowing it to wash over him, Quaid's mind wandered back to all the Sydneys he'd dealt with before. Most of them grew up on the streets with little to no parental guidance. Quaid knew these women did what was needed to survive, which usually led to breaking the law and jail.

As his mind replayed the various women he'd arrested over the years, similar characteristics stood out: tight, revealing clothes; foul mouths; toughness; and too much makeup, especially around the eyes. Their stories were all different, and yet, the desperate hopelessness shone out of all their eyes. At times, Quaid had caught the same look in Sydney's. No understanding of morals and ethics. No knowledge of pure love. No hope. The word *hope* caused Quaid to think on Hope Montgomery, Pierce's nanny. Like her name, she'd found true hope in Jesus Christ. From there, his thoughts went to his buddy Pierce. Pierce had struggled spiritually over the sudden death of his wife, Vicki, in childbirth, even to the point of initially rejecting his beautiful newborn daughter. Quaid had prayed much for them during that time. Now he thought about the struggles of Pierce attempting to raise his daughter with the help of this transplanted nanny. To keep all things above board, the nanny and baby Sarah were living in a much smaller nearby cabin, but Quaid surmised that his friend would love to have his baby even closer.

With steaming water still falling all around him, Quaid said to the air, "I know some people would frown if Pierce started dating when it's been less than a year since Vicki's death, but surely Sarah's need of a mother and her being with her father should allow leniency in what people think is a proper time of mourning." But then, so far his friend hadn't shown any desire to look for a new mother. This brought his thoughts to his own lonely lifestyle.

Like an old cancer raising its ugly head, Quaid's private battle with loneliness came surging forward. Being an undercover detective was a job that required his full-time attention. He had to be mobile and walk into dangerous situations. It wasn't a job that lent itself to building relationships with women. Not that he'd met all that many that interested him. The majority who crossed his path were clones of Sydney—messed up women. Being in his mid-thirties, Quaid had long ago formulated what constituted a good girl and a bad one. Sydney definitely fell in the latter.

Even though their first meeting was in church, Sydney had an air about her that sent off his *Beware!* alarms. Then as time went on and he saw the numerous ways she openly flirted with Pierce, other men, and himself, Quaid knew she was the type of woman he wanted to avoid at all cost. True, once one got beyond the heavy makeup, she had the potential of being a beautiful woman, but she wore clothes too tight and revealing. Even so, what bothered Quaid the most was what he kept getting glimpses of in her eyes. There was an inner hardness coated with an unresolved bitterness. All of those spelled trouble with a capital *T*.

Stepping from the shower, Quaid grabbed a large, dark brown towel while reflecting on what he valued most in a woman. Faith in Christ was top on his list, closely followed by honesty and integrity. Women like Sydney lacked all those things. As his thoughts wandered back to Pierce's nanny, for a moment he couldn't help but wish that he could get to know her better. Loneliness surged over him again, and for the first time, he wondered if maybe it was getting time to think about a career change.

"Something I can do that will be compatible with a wife and possible future kids," he said to his mirror. The whole issue was a big struggle to Quaid because he loved the adrenaline involved with his job. He liked outthinking the bad guys, and he was good at it.

A short time later, with the towel draped around his neck, Quaid walked back into his bedroom and sighed. Being alone all the time was getting old. He prayed that God would help him have peace and wisdom for a career change if that was the Lord's choosing, but until then he needed his mind strengthened and alert for the job at hand. He had a woman to arrest this morning.

Mentally ready for the day, Quaid finished dressing. Snapping his watch in place, he noted the time. Paul and Pierce would be arriving soon. The more Quaid thought about Pierce coming along, the better he liked it. Combing his thick black hair into place, Quaid took a moment to study his overall appearance in the mirror. Turning sideways, Quaid flexed his arm and studied his tall, solid build. He took pride in his athletic ability and the fact he could literally run down the best of them if it came to a foot race. Speed and quick reflexes were a must in his line of work. Nodding his head at the mirrored reflection, he turned away while thinking again that possibly Pierce could get Sydney to talk about her partners.

Quaid picked up his shoulder holster, slipped the gun out, and had just strapped the holster on when he heard the doorbell peal. Picking up his 9mm Glock, he checked the full clip. Snapping it into the pistol, he loaded one into the chamber. Strapping it in the holster, he walked out to the hall where two more bedrooms were evident and went down the stairs, through the living room to the front door.

Through the glass, Quaid saw Pierce standing there, so he twisted the deadbolt and swung the door open. He then noted Paul climbing out of his vehicle. "Good timing, guys. Come on in." Noting Pierce's hands were full, Quaid swung the door wide while motioning for Paul to come in. Instead, he saw his partner lean against the nearest vehicle. "Okay, we'll be out soon," Quaid said before following Pierce into the house.

Once inside, Pierce handed Quaid a steaming cup of coffee. "Since I was out and about first, I took the liberty. It's black, no cream, and no sugar. Just the way you like it." Taking a sip, he added, "And here are a couple sausage and cheese McMuffins. I figured you wouldn't take the time to eat this morning. Am I right?"

Quaid took a sip of coffee and a large bite of the sandwich before replying, "You know me too well." Lifting the sandwich in the air, he added, "Thanks. I owe you."

"As I was leaving the house, my cell phone rang. It was Pastor Jim with a prayer request. It seems one of the older people of the church passed away last night. I guess it was one of those situations where he'd suffered a long time and the family was ready to let him go. Not like…" Staring at the floor, Pierce's words trailed off.

Studying his dear friend whose heart was still aching, Quaid quietly stated, "I know losing Vicki the way you did was shocking. I'm praying that over time the pain will ease, and you'll be comforted through your precious little girl, Sarah."

With an effort, Pierce pushed away the pain trying to surge and focused on something else instead. "While we're en route to Sydney's, I'd like to talk with you and Paul about an idea Hope had."

As Pierce talked, Quaid picked up a jacket lying on the chair arm and buttoned it on over his weapon.

For the first time, Pierce noticed the gun. "Isn't the gun a bit much? Sydney's only one woman, and we're all physically fit, strong men."

"That may be. But I'm going in an official capacity, and I learned long ago not to overlook things. We never know how people will respond when they're cornered, not even beautiful, seemingly harmless women."

Quaid checked his watch then clipped a badge to the right side of his belt. Picking up his remaining sandwich and coffee, he said, "Let's go."

# Chapter 2

Walking out the front door, Quaid introduced the two men. Extending his hand, Paul smiled and said, "I've heard lots about you and am glad to finally meet you."

The two men briefly sized each other up. Paul might have been a few inches shorter, but Pierce could tell by his handshake that size didn't reflect strength. Another thing he noted was Paul's demeanor. He had a deceptively relaxed, easygoing manner, but from what little bit Quaid had mentioned of his partner, Pierce knew this man was fast and could be lethal. "It's good to meet you too. I know how much Quaid trusts you, and I'm prepared to do the same." In that moment, the two men silently acknowledged their mutual respect for Quaid and therefore each other as they climbed into the vehicle.

Once the three men were seated in Quaid's black Humvee, Quaid turned in his seat to better see Pierce beside him and Paul in the back left. "Pierce, I've decided to let you ring the doorbell. She's more apt to open the door for you without any question than me. Paul, you go around back just in case she tries to be stupid and run. I'll position myself out of sight to Pierce's left and show myself once the door's all the way open."

Up to this point, Paul had been quiet, just nodding his head in agreement to the plan. Now he stated, "Give me a couple minutes to get in position."

"I'll let you out a few houses down from hers." Swinging his attention back to the steering wheel, Quaid added, "Once we're inside, I'll take over, and Pierce, you let Paul in from the back." Starting the engine, Quaid backed the powerful vehicle out of the driveway onto the main road.

The men drove a mile or so before Paul piped up from the back, "Pierce, did Quaid tell you her real name isn't Sydney Larsen?"

Quaid glanced sideways in time to note the surprised look on Pierce's face. "No, I hadn't told him yet."

"What is her name?"

"Abigail Turner," Paul stated.

After letting that settle in a moment, Quaid thoughtfully added, "Actually, her middle name is Sydney. So her present name isn't entirely false."

"Abigail Sydney Turner." Pierce slowly said it back while shaking his head sadly.

The two passengers grew silent again while Quaid called headquarters and reported his destination, objective, and ETA.

A few moments later, Pierce began talking. "I almost forgot. I wanted to talk to you about Hope's idea."

For Paul's information, Quaid supplied, "That's Pierce's nanny from the Grand Rapids area. He brought her here to care for his baby, Sarah." He then nodded for Pierce to continue.

"Well, last night I mentioned to Hope about what's going on with Sydney or Abigail. Anyway, Hope suddenly exclaimed that she knew what she was supposed to do with her crystal." Shaking his head, Pierce's voice was full of wonder. "She's quite the woman!" He then became lost in his own thoughts.

Briefly glancing his way, Quaid arched his eyebrows and then smiled. "Okay, buddy. Obviously the lady impresses you, but what was her idea? You wandered off on us here."

An embarrassed Pierce chuckled. "I did, didn't I? Sorry. At first, I didn't have a clue what she was talking about. But it seems Hope has a box of expensive crystal. Her idea is to auction the crystal pieces and give the money to Sydney to help her pay back the debt she owes."

Amazement coated Quaid's words as he said, "But she hardly knows her, and how could a box of crystal even come close to giving Sydney what she needs?"

"Apparently the crystal is top grade, quality stuff, and very valuable. She expects it could auction off for thousands of dollars."

Silence hit the vehicle as the men thought the idea over. Houses were becoming more plentiful as Quaid drove toward Sydney's home. It puzzled Quaid how a nanny ended up with a box full of expensive crystal. Obviously there was a story there, one the detective in him wanted to investigate, but out loud he stated, "What a nice, giving gesture!" He paused then impulsively asked, "Are you sure the crystal is really hers to auction off? After all, how well do you know her? She is just a nanny."

"Actually, she isn't a nanny at all, at least not professionally. She had a high paying job at a bank until there was a merger and her job was eliminated. Plus, I understand that her husband had been a well-to-do man."

Jumping into the conversation, Paul asked, "If that's true, how on earth did she jump from well-to-do to a nanny living in a small cabin? And what happened to her husband?" Seeing Pierce stiffen, he quickly added, "Not that I'm accusing her of anything. The detective in me is curious. That's all."

After an awkward silence, Pierce said, "I don't know the whole story, but I was at Vicki's parents when a man brought the box of crystal to Hope. I heard him say that it had been stolen from his auction house and then mysteriously showed up just before I moved her here." He paused. With a touch of frustration tinting his voice, he added, "Actually, the details aren't important. What we need to decide is whether or not we want to mention this to Sydney."

"Let me think about it. Since we're on our way to arrest her, I suppose we could do a little detour before taking her to the station. That way the two women could meet and talk. Otherwise, Hope would need to come to Sydney because she won't be allowed to go out of town once she's under house arrest."

Quaid turned onto a side street and slowed the speed as he studied the area around Sydney's duplex more intently. Two-storied homes with well-kept yards lined the first part of the street. Farther in, the men could see a series of duplexes. These yards were mowed but not well trimmed. Windows boasted flower boxes, but being mid-summer, many were empty or full of dried-up flowers.

Pointing forward, Quaid said, "Sydney's in the last duplex on the far left side of the street."

Paul leaned forward to better assess the situation. Seeing the duplex garages were situated in the middle with an adjoining single level home on each end, he said, "There's probably a side door leading from the kitchen into the garage, plus back-patio sliders."

Quaid slowed the Hummer to a crawl as he inched the vehicle forward. The men continued surveying the layout. Sydney's duplex looked exactly like the others, with a ground level porch starting from the far right and ending at the protruding garage at the left. Besides the door, the front of the house contained a large picture window with attached smaller side ones that the men noticed were open.

"I was hoping they wouldn't have huge picture windows in the front, but I guess that's out of the question," Quaid stated. "We'll just have to pray she doesn't look out the window when we pull up."

"The neighborhood still seems to be indoors," Paul observed. "I don't see any children playing outside yet."

As Quaid brought the car to a stop, Paul moved to exit the vehicle, when he had one last question: "Does she by chance have a dog?"

The two detectives turned to Pierce.

With a raised eyebrow, he responded, "I don't think so. I've never heard her mention one before."

"Okay, well, I guess we'll soon find out for sure. Give me a few minutes to get in position." So saying, Paul slipped out the door to rapidly move across the street. He disappeared from sight before Quaid started moving the Hummer once more.

Just before turning into the drive, Quaid slipped the car into neutral and coasted to the closed garage door. Shutting the engine off, he turned to Pierce, saying, "I've been thinking about the crystal. Today's the only time I can legally take her out to your place, so we'll do it before heading to the jail."

The two men stared quietly out the car windows. They both knew in the next few minutes, Sydney Larsen's, or rather Abigail Sydney Turner's, life was going to change drastically.

Quaid broke the silence. "I think Paul's probably in position by now."

They both sighed and then exited the vehicle as smoothly and quietly as they could.

Sydney was finishing her makeup in the bathroom. That morning she'd woken up in high spirits. Lazily she had stretched in her rusting brass bed and then thrown back the covers. She had then flipped on the kitchen radio, cranked it up, and headed for the shower while humming along with the music.

After the refreshing shower, she selected pants and a T-shirt then headed back to the kitchen to put a cup of water in the microwave for coffee. While waiting, she lit a cigarette then scanned her meager surroundings. So far, all she'd managed to buy were a kitchen table with a couple metal chairs, a worn sofa, a mismatched stuffed chair needing to be recovered, and one end table. The walls were still bare except for one ornate mirror hanging in the small hall to the bedroom.

Pushing herself away from the kitchen counter, Sydney walked to the mirror. Her plans were to have one in every room. She saw once in a magazine that it was the fashionable thing to do. This one had cost her a whole paycheck, but she didn't care. Running her hand over the gold scrolled frame, Sydney imagined how nice a home she'd be living in once Vince released the money.

She turned to smile at her reflection. "Just a little more time and I'll be living like a queen!"

The microwave bell sounded, effectively bringing her back to the present. Walking to the kitchen, Sydney extinguished the cigarette and lifted out the hot cup of water. Then she flipped open the cupboard, taking out instant coffee. Feeling quite pleased with herself, she reached for a spoon from the drainer. Tapping it against her cheek, Sydney's mind temporarily wandered to Pierce's friend Quaid.

She narrowed her eyes as past encounters with the man came to mind. Something about him unsettled her. For one thing, what he did for a living was a mystery. Sydney had tried discreetly to find out, but people either answered in vague general ways or truly didn't know. *It'd be my luck that he's with the FBI or something.*

Sydney finished putting the instant coffee into her cup then stirred it as a malicious thought entered her mind. *Why not go for both of them?*

She pondered that a bit then decided she was being silly. Picking up the cup, she walked to the bathroom. "Not that you couldn't do it, Syd, but... No. I'll stick with Pierce. Better to leave Quaid alone until

I find out what he really does for a living." Picking up her bottle of foundation, she added, "Besides, he's probably a chef or a store clerk."

As she began lathering on the heavy makeup she so enjoyed wearing, Sydney's mind traveled back to her talk with Pierce's nanny, Hope. She told her reflection, "She may be pretty, but what man would choose her over me? No backbones! She sat right there and let me threaten her!" Sydney finished applying thick black eyeliner and mascara while plotting how best to make her next move on Pierce.

Setting her mascara brush down, Sydney admitted to herself that it wasn't just Pierce's looks and possible money that attracted her. There was something genuine about his belief in God and his Christian walk that puzzled yet intrigued her. Also, she hadn't run across men with his obvious manly physique who weren't players. He honestly didn't seem to notice her, which went beyond Sydney's realm of experience.

For the first time, she had met some truly good men. Pierce and Quaid were two of them. They actually looked at her with courtesy and respect, not lust. It piqued her interest. Perversely, part of her wanted to bring them down to her level. Yet another part of her wanted to be deserving of that respect. For just a moment, Sydney allowed herself to think how much different her life could have been if men like them had crossed her path years ago. She sighed heavily and stared unseeing into the mirror.

Growing frustrated with herself, Sydney chided her reflection, "Snap out of it, Syd! You're a beautiful woman with a near perfect body! In just a few more months, you're going to have oodles of money to play with as you choose. It's a great, sunny day with all kinds of good things in store. All you have to do is go out and grab them!" Sydney smiled at her reflection, picked up her now cold coffee, and headed out to storm her world.

Right then, the front doorbell rang.

# Chapter 3

"Eight days! It's only been eight days, and already I'm sick of it!"

Sydney threw down the book she'd been attempting to read. She was bored. Restlessly her eyes scanned the living room that used to be such a delight to her. She glared at the police tether attached to her right ankle and grimaced. For a brief moment, she contemplated seeing if it could be cut off. Deciding that would land her in a boatload of more trouble, she focused instead on the day the judge had ordered it put on, the day she was placed on house arrest.

There were only four other people in the room—the judge, her court-appointed attorney, Quaid, and a stranger that she assumed was her new probation officer. As her mind transported her back to the scene, she remembered tuning out the legal jargon going on between the attorney and judge; instead, she focused her attention on the attorney. His name was Mr. Gobel; that's all he would tell her, which immediately put him in the snooty category. He was kind of rotund. Sydney marked that down as his way of letting people know he had plenty of money. He also wore a fancy suit that was expertly tailored.

Sydney's eyes had wandered on to Quaid, who was studying the judge. He was slouched in the chair, but Sydney didn't let that fool her. She'd seen how quickly he could react if need be. Her eyes caught the slight bulge at his left shoulder. Frowning, she remembered the thoughts she'd had that Saturday morning of his being an FBI agent and laughed off. Turns out, she wasn't too far off.

At that moment, Quaid had turned his brown eyes to hers and raised one eyebrow. Instantly, Sydney adopted a haughty look. Shooting daggers at him, she squared her shoulders and turned her attention forward while purposely flipping her long blonde ponytail backward. It angered her that he seemed oblivious to her womanly attributes. Bringing her mind back to the day he'd arrested her, her memories continued.

After Quaid had brought her in on Saturday, he left, and she went through all the paperwork, a strip search, and a clothes change. She soon landed in a community cell with a couple of scantily clad prostitutes and a younger girl with purple streaked hair. Sydney ignored the other two but openly studied the girl. She had been the only one to show any interest when Sydney had walked into the cell. What parts of her were seeable were covered with tattoos of snakes and cobwebs. She had tattered shorts on but wore a long sleeved shirt. It took Sydney about five seconds to figure out what she was in for. Shaking her head, Sydney found an empty bunk and settled in—thankful that she'd only dabbled in drugs and had never been caught up in it. Before leaving, Quaid had said she'd be seeing the judge on Monday, so these were to be her roommates for a couple of nights.

On Sunday morning a policeman had taken her to a small room

where she met her attorney. Without much preliminary, he plopped his casually dressed body in the chair and stated he was taking her on out of the goodness of his heart. Sydney hadn't believed him for a moment. She knew the judge had appointed him. The whole talk didn't take long, for Mr. Gobel seemed in a hurry as he kept checking his Rolex. Sydney considered telling him to get lost, that she'd represent herself, but thought better of it. But as she sat next to him in the somber courtroom, she wondered if she'd made the right decision after all. He wasted no time with fancy talk but got right to the heart of things.

Chiding herself that she best pay attention, Sydney tuned in to hear her lawyer say, "Agreed to pay back a portion of the money, but she doesn't have any family still living to help her. We're asking the judge's leniency. With the help of Detective Williams and her probation officer, Mr. Barton, we're asking for three months of house arrest with the understanding that the amount you designate be due at that time. Otherwise, she understands the house confinement could be extended, or she'd be interred." Before the judge could respond, he hurriedly added, "After all, Judge, this is her first major offense."

The judge's eyes narrowed at his last words, and Sydney almost kicked him under the table. The judge stared at Sydney for a long moment before turning to Quaid and the parole officer. Out of the corner of her eye, Sydney noted Quaid straightening up in his chair and becoming all business for the judge. After a few questions and answers were bantered back and forth, the judge refocused on Sydney.

"Miss Turner, I'm setting your payback amount at $100,000."

"$100,000! But Judge ..." Sydney clamped her mouth shut when the judge openly glared at her.

"Young woman, consider yourself lucky! I have half a mind to toss you right back in jail since you're not willing to cooperate with us by giving us names! Instead, out of my respect for Detective Williams, we're going to try the house arrest route for a minimum of three months, at which time the full amount will be due!"

Once again Sydney started to speak, even lifting off her seat, but stopped when the judge stated, "Mr. Gobel, get your client under control, or we're going to have words!"

Grabbing her arm, Mr. Gobel forced her back in the seat while hissing under his breath, "Shut your mouth unless you'd rather be in jail! Either way, I'm washing my hands of you once this is over! Now be quiet!"

They exchanged glares until the judge continued what he was saying. "The conditions of your house detention are the following: you will be allowed privileges to work your job, to grocery shop at a designated store, and at the urging of Detective Williams—which I concur can't hurt—to attend morning worship at a pre-approved church. Mr. Barton and Detective Williams will be held responsible for monitoring your activities. Do you understand all that I've explained?"

Sydney said through gritted teeth, "Yes, Your Honor."

"Good. Court adjourned."

The next hour was a blur as she met with Mr. Barton and Quaid. The probation officer explained the rules and restrictions as a police woman fastened the monitor on her ankle.

Mr. Barton had momentarily left the room, so Sydney turned to Quaid, who'd been silently standing by watching. She deeply resented his presence and blamed him for all her current troubles. "So what's your role in all this? Will you be camped out on my living room sofa?"

Raising one eyebrow, Quaid replied, "No, but I plan on being around. We'd still appreciate your telling us the names of your accomplices." He paused, allowing her time to reconsider. When she glared, he changed the subject. "I was informed you didn't choose to call anyone after you were arrested. Surely there was someone you could have contacted about your whereabouts and your…current situation."

Dropping her eyes to the monitor now resting just above her ankle, she bitterly replied, "There's no one!" She was saved from any further comments as Mr. Barton stepped back into the room.

That had been eight days earlier, and Quaid's question still rankled. She had purposely waited to call Vince until after returning home. That way, the call couldn't be overheard, but so far she hadn't been able to contact him. He wasn't returning her calls.

A feeling of frustration surged through her, and she had nowhere to vent it. Little by little it unreasonably seeped into her being that the real culprit in all this trouble was Quaid. If he'd kept his nose to himself, none of this would be happening. Thinking back to the Saturday of her arrest, she found herself fuming while declaring to the room around her, "He's going to pay!"

When she had opened the door that fateful Saturday morning, Sydney was surprised to see Pierce standing there. When Quaid stepped into her view, that surprise turned to alarm. His whole demeanor shouted *official*—his stance, his eyes, and his determined look. In those first seconds, time stood still, and every detail became sharp, especially the badge clipped to his belt and the telltale bulge at his left shoulder.

With her eyes widened, Sydney moved to take a step backward but checked herself. She contemplated making a run for the back. Darting her eyes sideways toward the opened Venetian blinds, Sydney was startled to see a man standing there observing her every move. In mounting fear, Sydney sought an alternative plan and resorted to an old habit, flirting.

Focusing her attention back on the two men, she slowly and deliberately scanned them from head to toe. Smiling, Sydney placed her hand on Pierce's arm. Stepping back, she swung her other arm backward, inviting them into her home. "How did you know I was just thinking about you two handsome men?"

Once they entered, Quaid took a post by the shut front door while Pierce went to let Paul in. Quaid then began reciting the Miranda rights while Paul stood sentry-like at the back door, and Pierce walked back into the center of the living room.

At first, Sydney played dumb and surprised while various emotions raced through her being—panic, blame, vanity, fear, sadness, then pride, arrogance, and denial. She tried every trick in her arsenal of words and body language, but the men weren't buying any of it. In the end, she settled on defiance and silence while plopping unceremoniously into a nearby chair.

As these memories came flooding back, Sydney began pacing. "I guess I should be thankful that Quaid didn't march me out with handcuffs in front of all my neighbors." As she paced, the tether chaffed her skin, and Sydney's resentment toward Quaid grew.

Then her eyes fell on the beautiful crystal cross resting on the windowsill. She'd placed it there to catch the morning rays, which sent myriads of rainbow prisms dancing around the room. Sydney walked to it and carefully lifted it up to examine the exquisite detail. Her mind traveled back to that same Saturday.

The three men had spent much time talking to her about the supposed evidence, trying to get her to tell them the names of others who might be involved. She adamantly denied any knowledge of any money or knowledge of the company in Louisville that she'd supposedly helped embezzle from. After a long time, the men gave up, and she was taken out to the vehicle with Detective Statham sitting in the back with her. Once seated, she'd heard the ominous lockout button being pushed by Quaid to stop any thought of escape while en route to the jail.

Then Quaid had done a couple of strange things. First, he went through a fast food drive-thru. She didn't eat much, but they all devoured theirs. She turned her head away in disgust and tried to appear uninterested while staring out the window.

On the road once again, Quaid further surprised her by announcing they were making a short detour and headed the Hummer out of town. Frowning, Sydney stiffened when he turned into Pierce's drive.

"What's going on? How come we're going to Pierce's cabin?"

"Actually, we're not. I'm taking you to see Hope Montgomery."

At Hope's name, Sydney tensed and grew angry. "I have no interest in seeing her. Just take me to the jail and be done with it!"

Totally ignoring her request, Quaid drove up to the little cabin and stopped the vehicle.

Forcing herself to relax, Sydney assumed the indifferent attitude once more. Shrugging, she stated, "Whatever!" Quaid unlocked the doors; then the three men took her inside.

Still holding the crystal cross, Sydney continued her walk down the lane of memories from that fateful day.

Once inside Hope's cabin, Paul remained at attention by the front door while the other three took seats. Then the show was turned over to Hope. To Sydney's consternation and boredom, Hope began a long discourse about her life back in Grand Rapids. She belabored the points about her trials and miseries. Even now, Sydney remembered vividly her frustration over why she was being subjected to this other woman's problems. Most of it she was trying to tune out as she studied the interior of the small cabin. What she saw was a neat, orderly home with greenery in abundance. A small potted tree stood in the corner just to the side of Sydney's chair. She was tempted to see if it was real but refrained. Another thing she noticed was the furniture. She could see it was solid, quality stuff. She resented the fact that it didn't come from Goodwill like hers. Sydney's eyes had narrowed as she wondered how a nanny could afford such furniture. Deciding it must all belong to Pierce, Sydney let her eyes go to him.

As she studied his handsome face, her brows had knit together in a frown. Cocking her head, Sydney's long blonde hair fell forward over her shoulder. Hearing Hope's word become hesitant, Sydney figured it was because she wasn't paying attention. Ignoring her, she continued looking at Pierce. He was seated at an angle from her, but Sydney could still see his face, especially his eyes, clearly. She started getting irritated that he never looked her way once. Instead, his full attention was on Hope. Sydney saw open admiration, which made her jealous. Deciding it was time to study her competition a little better, Sydney focused back on the petite woman seated directly in front of her.

Once eye contact was made, Hope smiled. At that moment,

a sunbeam had come through the window, highlighting Hope's shoulder-length auburn hair. It created a golden sheen that made Hope's blue eyes deepen. Sydney noted that Hope didn't wear much makeup, yet in that moment Sydney had to grudgingly admit that Hope had a natural beauty about her. Feeling the jealousy surge once more, Sydney began fidgeting. She was fast becoming bored with the topic of Hope Montgomery.

That was until Hope mentioned the loss of her unborn child.

Without warning, inner feelings of her own aborted baby came rushing to the forefront of Sydney's mind, memories she'd thought were locked behind steel doors in her heart. Feigning boredom and disgust, Sydney stood, announcing she'd heard enough and wanted to leave. Immediately, Quaid was at her elbow commanding her to sit down. "Hope isn't done yet!"

Defiantly, Sydney glared at Quaid, but something in his eyes told her he meant business. She slumped back into the recliner more determined than ever to ignore the drama that was being played out in the little cabin. She tried shutting Hope's continuing words out; then the crystal was mentioned. Sitting up straighter, Sydney couldn't believe her ears. Had the woman just stated that God was prompting her to give a box full of expensive crystal to Sydney? As Sydney thought about how she could pawn it and use the money, she almost missed the next statements.

Pierce was speaking. "I think the box of crystal should be held by Quaid until an auction date can be set up and the pieces sold. That way, Hope is out of it."

Liking the idea, three of them agreed. Paul remained silent, vigilantly watching. Once again, Sydney briefly centered on the fact that Quaid was coming between her and something she wanted.

Bile began building in Sydney's stomach as her growing bitterness toward Quaid brought her back to the present. Her thoughts swirled toward an unjust world and people like Quaid, Pierce, and Hope. Carrying the crystal cross to her one living room chair, Sydney sat and let her head drop. "I wish I'd been born to different parents somewhere else, if only..."

Eventually, her mind wandered back to the events at Hope's cabin. The significance of the box full of crystal presented itself to Sydney, and she couldn't believe there wasn't a catch. People didn't give away stuff like that without a reason! But Hope had insisted there wasn't. All she wanted was an opportunity to be a friend to Sydney. A friend? This was something she didn't know how to deal with. So instead, she chose to focus on the crystal and how it could help repay her so called debt to society. Eagerly Sydney agreed to accept the crystal.

Quaid's partner, Paul, and Pierce then brought the heavy box into the small living room so Hope could show her some of the pieces. Quaid and Pierce stepped out to the front porch while Paul made a point to walk out the kitchen side door. Bitterly, Sydney watched the move, realizing anew that this wasn't a pleasure trip. She would soon be on her way to the lockup.

The quality of the crystal was apparent with the first piece unwrapped, and Sydney couldn't help but be intrigued. She'd never seen or held such beautiful stuff. It baffled her even more that someone—a near stranger—would willingly give this crystal to help her. Under cover of long mascara-heavy eyelashes, Sydney had studied Hope with a frown. A long past memory tried wandering into her mind, but she pushed it back as Hope unwrapped more pieces. After freeing them from the special wrap, Hope handed each piece to Sydney for inspection. She thoroughly enjoyed the feel of them in her hands.

For a moment, resentment had surged. She'd never been able to acquire that level of lifestyle before Vince, and now it was being taken away. As Sydney's thoughts flowed, the resentment turned to sadness. Then as Sydney thought about her lack of beautiful things and injustices in her growing up world, sadness turned to bitterness. This bitterness threatened to overwhelm her as thoughts of jail, judges, and other criminals coursed through her.

Sydney knew that wanting nice things had been what had prompted her to steal with Vince in the first place. After a little waiting period, she would have been able to have most anything she'd wanted. Now that too was being taken away from her. As bitterness surged, Sydney had glanced out Hope's front window to glare at Quaid leaning next to the railing. As if sensing her glare, Quaid had turned to look directly into her eyes. They held for a long, poignant, hate-filled minute before Sydney broke the contact to gaze back at the crystal on the floor around her.

That's when Hope handed her a wrapped piece, encouraging her to get involved and open one. Still thinking bad thoughts toward Quaid, Sydney unwrapped a crystal cross positioned in the middle of a small hill. Ironically, the sight of it had sent her back to a dingy apartment full of pain, yelling, and abuse. Long-buried mental scars threatened to surface. The cross also brought back a second memory of another cross and a woman—a Christian woman—who had done something nice for a bedraggled little street girl. Unaware of her actions, Sydney had lovingly run her hand over the sparkling crystal piece.

Noting the emotional struggle on Sydney's face, Hope said, "Tell you what. Let's not sell this one with the rest. You keep it for yourself. I make it a present to you. May it always remind you that Jesus loves you, and he wants to be a part of your life. May it also remind you that we're all your friends, and we'll be praying for you."

For the first time in a long, long time, Sydney allowed herself to hope that there really could be good people like that in the world—that there really could be a God up there somewhere who might even care for someone like her. And for the first time in an even longer time, Sydney felt tears come to her eyes at the generosity and kindness of another woman who called herself a Christian.

The memory of all these emotions now tugged at Sydney's heart and mind as her eyes stared at the tether so indicative of lost freedom. Lifting the cross, she held it in the sun's rays while her eyes followed the rainbows it created. A sigh escaped once more. Resting her head on the back of her chair, Sydney did something rare; she unlocked that inner door of pain and allowed this particular memory to flow out.

Her mom and stepfather were having a terrible fight, and nine-year-old Abigail Sydney Turner was afraid. Sometimes the fights would escalate, and she would become a victim too. So she quickly made a decision to vacate the low-income apartment and go for a walk. She remembered thinking at the time how thankful she was that her older sister, Alicia, had left the neighborhood a year earlier. Not that she and Allie didn't have their moments—after all, they shared the same small bedroom. Plus, Allie was eight years older. The two girls didn't even have fathers in common. About two years earlier, their mother had remarried again, and her husband wasn't a good man to them or their mother.

Heading to the street, Abby feared the night far less than she'd feared the temper of her stepfather. Having lived in the poor section of Louisville all her young life, Abby knew the area very well. Not only had she learned safe places in back alleys, but she also knew which restaurant back doors would be good for an occasional handout. Being hungry, she made her way to one of them. A few minutes later with a chicken leg in one hand and a piece of warm bread in the other, she moved down the sidewalk. Deciding not to look up her normal street buddies, she went instead a couple blocks over to the Open Door Mission. She never knew why the mission house drew her other than the fact that she liked to hear the music and singing. It strangely calmed her fears and helped her forget how bad it was at home.

This particular evening it was chilly, and she had left the house in such a hurry that she hadn't grabbed a coat. It didn't matter much. The coat was thin and had holes. Tossing her finished chicken bone, Abby munched on the bread as she rounded the corner near the mission. Usually she stayed well away from the front door, but this night the warmth inside beckoned her to come closer. Being drawn to the bright lights and warm music flowing from within, she walked right up to the front steps. Huddling down near them, she no sooner got situated than the door opened and a well-dressed woman stepped out.

Instinctively, Abby moved to flee but hesitated. Something about the woman held her where she was. At first the woman hadn't noticed her as she stood buttoning her coat, but then Abby drew farther back into the shadows. It must have caught the woman's attention. Leaning over the rail, she said, "Who's there? Please step out and let me see you."

Again to Abby's own surprise, instead of fleeing, she slowly moved toward the warm, friendly voice. As she timidly stepped out, the woman smiled and came down the steps. She invited her to come in out of the cold, but Abby declined, stammering that she really should be getting home. The woman looked Abby over in the light of the street lamp. Her action made Abby woefully aware of the shabbiness of her clothes. Unconsciously she tried smoothing her rumpled shirt and torn pants.

Then the woman did something totally unexpected. "I bet you don't get very many pretty things, do you?" She gently leaned forward to brush long blonde bangs out of Abigail's eyes. Abby instinctively pulled her face back, and the woman paused before slowly moving her hand forward again. For the third time, Abby did a surprising thing and held perfectly still. She marveled at the gentle touch of the beautiful woman.

After a few moments, the woman straightened to do a shocking thing. She unclasped the necklace around her neck. Taking Abby's cold hand in hers, she slowly lowered the necklace in it. "Here, take this. Your parents can sell it to buy you some clothes and food. May the necklace remind you that Jesus loves you and wants to be a part of your life." She then curled Abby's fingers around the still warm necklace.

For a moment, Abby froze in place; then it all became more than she could handle. Fearing the woman might change her mind, she clutched the necklace close, whirled, and ran quickly down the street.

Thinking back on it now, Sydney was saddened that she hadn't even told the woman thank you. Then a new thought presented itself. Sitting up, Sydney realized for the first time that the woman and Hope had said almost the same words to her in regards to their gifts: "May it remind you that Jesus loves you and wants to be a part of your life." Not ready to start acknowledging if God existed or not, Sydney leaned back. Closing her eyes, she forced her mind to complete the long ago memory.

Finally gaining a safe place in the stairwell of her apartment building, Abigail caught her breath then opened her still tightly clenched hand. In the dull light, she gasped as she gazed upon a beautiful, jeweled silver cross on a delicate silver chain. She was so engrossed in her wonderful gift that she didn't hear her stepfather coming down the stairs until it was too late.

"What've you got there?"

Abby curled her fingers around the necklace while scrambling to her feet. Tucking her hand behind her, she replied, "Nothing."

Seconds later, a resounding slap knocked her against the wall; her stepfather angrily grabbed her arm and pulled it forward while yelling, "Don't lie to me, you worthless child. I saw something shiny in your hand!"

She tried with all her might to keep her fist closed but wasn't any match for him. Soon the beautiful silver necklace dangled in front of her nose as her stepfather sneered. "Where'd you steal this?"

Abby had tried explaining about the nice woman, but her stepfather had raised his hand to strike again; so she cowered in silence.

He studied the necklace in the light and then said, "You done good, girl! This ought to get me a lot of cash, enough to keep me in booze for a long while!" He then slapped her face hard. Bringing his eyes to her level, he fiercely warned, "Don't you ever try hiding stuff like this from me again."

Abby shrunk against the wall as he laughed wickedly and then headed down the stairs and out the front door. As she massaged her aching cheek, Abigail Sydney Turner vowed to do whatever she needed to better her life and to look down on her stepfather. Bringing her mind back to the present, Sydney fought the feelings of hatred that she still harbored toward her now dead stepfather.

Sydney considered the crystal cross still in her hand, rose, and walked to the window. Her voice soon broke the silence in the air. "You didn't get this one... did you?"

Sydney hugged the cross close then gently placed it back on the windowsill. A cloud momentarily covered the sun as the long ago memories evaporated from her mind, and the present situation came surging back.

# Chapter 4

It had been almost thirty days since Quaid Williams arrested Sydney, and Quaid wasn't very happy. Sydney had steadfastly refused to tell him the names of her accomplices and, according to her probation officer, was getting seriously bored with home confinement. He was concerned she might consider doing something stupid. He'd seen it many times before.

Walking into his living room, Quaid balanced a hot plate of supper in one hand as he reached for the remote to his flat screen TV then changed his mind. Turning, he walked back to the walnut pedestal dining room table. Pulling out one of the matching wooden spindle back chairs, he sat down. Silently munching his meal, Quaid took a moment to appreciate his open kitchen-living room area.

When he'd bought the home, every room was separate and needed work. His first project was his bedroom, and then he had moved to the downstairs. The carpet throughout the house was torn up, the wall between the kitchen and living room was removed, and hardwood floors were laid. Next, he knocked a couple holes in the outside walls for more windows and then replaced all the old windows with aluminum double-paned ones. The house still needed much work, but Quaid wasn't in a hurry. He and Pierce Matthews worked on it as time permitted and when Quaid knew what he wanted done.

Sitting there at the table, Quaid decided the next project would be to replace all the electrical outlets and switch plates to antiqued brass ones and put in a brass kitchen faucet set.

The thought of brass made him think about brass locks, then jail, and soon Sydney was foremost on his mind once again. He couldn't seem to get the woman out of his head. Something was bothering him, but so far he hadn't been able to put his finger on what.

Sydney's early years were pretty much blank, as it seemed this was her first major brush with the law. Even so, it puzzled him—her unwillingness to tell the names of her partners even though she knew it could make things easier for her. Were they holding something over her? She had willingly said there were two others—one she knew personally, the other she'd never met. When the other one had been mentioned, Quaid noticed Sydney's voice tinged with fear.

On and on his thoughts went.

Quaid finished his supper then set the plate in the sink. His stomach now full, Quaid walked to the large L-shaped, leather sectional sofa. Placing a throw pillow in a convenient place for his head, Quaid went to lay down when he caught his reflection on the plasma screen. It revealed a man wearing a black T-shirt with a few evident tears in sight. The well-worn shorts weren't really shorts at all. They were a pair of comfortable, slightly ragged boxer-style swim trunks. Sandals completed the picture. Smiling at his comfortable-looking reflection, Quaid kicked off the sandals and plopped full length on the sofa.

As soon as his head hit the pillow, the issue of Abigail Sydney Turner surged to the forefront of his mind once more, only this time it was a replay of the Saturday morning when the three men had shown up at Sydney's door. Closing his eyes, Quaid replayed the morning of Sydney's arrest.

Once they'd all acquired their desired positions, Quaid willed his tense body to relax before giving Pierce the go ahead to push the doorbell. Whenever Quaid was heading into some form of legal action, his muscles involuntarily tensed up. It didn't matter what the job entailed—Quaid was trained to be sharp, and that day had been no different. Finally achieving a relaxed demeanor, he nodded for Pierce to step forward and press the doorbell.

As they both figured, Sydney was surprised when she swung the door open to see Pierce standing there but expertly hid it as she smoothly moved to invite him in. That's when she'd caught sight of Quaid, and that pleasure changed quickly. A frown flitted across her face, but Quaid had to give her credit. Like a chameleon, she once again recovered well. Too well, in fact.

"Isn't this a surprise," she said warmly while stepping closer to Pierce. Placing a possessive hand on his arm yet still not acknowledging Quaid, she added, "Now how did you know I was just thinking about you two handsome men?" She then had walked Pierce into the house with Quaid following close behind. Once inside, she insisted they take a seat, but Quaid had other plans. He soon took over the situation.

Since that morning, the only time Quaid had seen her indifferent, cool manner change was when he made eye contact with her. The strong emotion of hate she glared at him didn't surprise him. Quaid had seen that attitude many times before. Always, the caught criminals wanted to blame him for their current problems instead of admitting they'd brought it upon themselves. Thinking over the scene now, Quaid's thoughts wandered to Hope. He coupled those thoughts with Sydney's current restlessness, and an idea formed. Without further hesitation, he picked up his cell phone to call Pierce for Hope's unlisted number.

Hope Montgomery flipped her cell phone shut. Quaid had just asked her to consider taking baby Sarah to visit Sydney. His words still stuck in her head. "It's been thirty days, and she's getting really antsy. Maybe this is a good time for you to start working on that friendship you talked to her about."

Ever since giving Sydney the crystal cross, Hope had daily prayed for opportunities to build a trust and friendship with her. So far, Sydney hadn't returned a single one of Hope's calls. She expressed this to Quaid, but he seemed to think Sydney might be bored enough to want company, any company.

Before dialing the number, Hope thought on the crystal and what an adventure the pieces had already been through. She had tried to sell the box of crystal back in her hometown of Grand Rapids when she herself needed money badly. In fact, hours before Dean's tragic auto accident, Hope had been notified that her job was being terminated due to a bank merger. She had soon found herself in a financial bind. There was nothing she could do except sell their beautiful condo and most of her possessions, and move into the basement of a dear church friend. It ended up that the friend was Pierce Matthews's mother-in-law, and so their lives began to intertwine even though it was months before the two actually met.

On the day of the sale, Hope had visited the auction house to check the display of her worldly goods. She noticed the crystal was missing. All of it! The auctioneer was very upset, but there wasn't anything he could do. It had mysteriously disappeared. Being extremely distraught over everything happening in her life, Hope had opted not to notify the police. It would have meant moving the auction to another day, and she just wanted the sale done and over with. Weeks later, a few days before Hope was due to head north with Pierce to be baby Sarah's nanny, the auctioneer showed up with the missing crystal. Hope was amazed to find only a couple pieces missing. She took that as a sign that the crystal was to move north with her, but until she heard Sydney's situation, she hadn't known why.

Since her earlier trials, Hope had learned to daily commit her situations to her Heavenly Father. So when she felt prompted to give the crystal for Sydney's debt, Hope didn't hesitate. Even when the idea was presented to Pierce and he had concerns, Hope remained steadfast and at peace with the decision. Now she was once again being prompted in regards to Sydney.

Hope dialed her number. After the second ring, Sydney's voice came over the line. Hope greeted her and then came right to the point. "Sarah and I are planning a trip to town tomorrow morning and thought we'd stop in for a visit." Silence met her suggestion, so Hope patiently waited for a reply.

Finally, "Sure, whatever," came over the line. Sydney then added in a sarcastic voice, "I don't really have much to say in the matter, do I?"

Trying to sound upbeat and cheerful, Hope decided to ignore the comment. "Good! The Lord willing, we'll see you around ten tomorrow morning."

Slowly closing her cell phone, Hope whispered, "Okay, Lord. The door's open a crack, so I'm walking through it."

Sarah chose that moment to toss something out of the play yard; hearing it hit the floor, Hope went to investigate.

*The Lord willing! As if he cares about me and what I do!* When Abigail had first come to Petoskey, she decided to appear completely opposite of what she normally was. So, changing her name to Sydney Larsen, she began attending a local church. It didn't take much acting on her part to assume the role of a believer. The church people were very accepting... and gullible. They believed whatever lies she told them. She'd also been adept at avoiding the pastor. Sydney didn't want him asking her spiritual questions. As Sydney thought back on it now, a couple of the church people hadn't been as accepting and trusting as the others—Pierce Matthews and his buddy Quaid Williams.

As she dwelt on the two men, Sydney grudgingly admitted to herself what was so attractive about them. Their good looks and muscular bodies helped, but it was more than that. Pierce and Quaid were honest, good men who knew how to treat women, not like men from her past or Vince and their unnamed partner. For just a second, Sydney regretted ever willfully stepping into the snare that had now caught her.

Her mind roamed back. It was a late night party in Louisville after the famous Kentucky Derby. Sydney had been invited by a girlfriend to an exclusive party. "We're to be companions to men with plenty of money, looking for a good time."

Normally, Sydney's extra income had come from cheap one night stands with lowlifes who had some money. She was willing to help them spend it, even taking it from a few who were too drugged up to know the difference. Never before had she been privy to high rollers, so she found herself eagerly agreeing, especially after her friend enticed her with the amount she could earn.

Once she'd been introduced to Vince Edgar—a high paid accountant with a firm located in one of the taller buildings in the city—Sydney latched on to him for the rest of the night. He was a married man with kids, but Sydney didn't care. As long as they both had a good time, what harm would one night be?

The more Vince drank, the more he bragged about how high his IQ was. "I can outthink seven out of every ten men," he stated over and over again.

Growing tired of the repetition, Sydney challenged him. "If you're so smart, could you get away with money from your company without being caught?" She figured that would shut him up.

Instead, he grew deep in thought. He then slowly but firmly stated, "I could do that."

It seemed to be a new idea to him, one that grew in interest as he mulled it over in his head. Staring Sydney right in the eye, he restated more firmly, "I could do that, and no one would ever know. I could invent a fictitious corporation and start billing my company for products purchased. I'd start out small at first; then as the 'business' grew, I could increase the amount paid." His voice had grown excited as the plan evolved in his mind. "I could build a large nest egg in say a couple years or so." He then laughed outright, almost falling out of his chair. Since Sydney was occupying his lap, the action caused her to spill some of her drink down her fancy dress. The next day she'd thrown the dress away. Periodically, Vince would mention another idea about the plan, but as he grew drunker, he began focusing on other things.

Early the next morning, Sydney lay beside him staring at the ceiling, thinking about his words. Slowly, a plan began emerging. So that morning she threatened to tell Vince's wife and kids about their night together if he didn't follow through with his bragging and make her his partner.

Even now, Sydney could clearly recall how pale his face had become. He had stammered while vehemently protesting. "But... but I was drunk! I didn't mean anything by it!"

But Sydney liked the idea and wasn't backing down. She vocalized all kinds of things she would do to make his life miserable and wore him down. Reluctantly, he finally agreed and thus began a period of frequent liaisons and the siphoning of monies from the company.

At first Sydney desired money from him every week, but then he became adamant about not touching the bulk of the money to allow it to gain interest, which would permit the funds to grow even faster. She relented when he agreed to continue paying her from his private account. Over the next couple years, she made him pay dearly for the pleasure of her short, late-night visits. This went on smoothly for three and a half years until all of a sudden the unknown man came into the picture.

About that same time, Vince heard rumors that the company might be under investigation, and a major audit was to be done. Immediately, he stopped rigging the books by having the fake company appear to file bankruptcy; by that time, he'd been able to accumulate over $750,000 in an offshore account.

Now, smiling to herself, Sydney had to admit the man truly was brilliant. She regretted not being able to spend more of the money, but if Vince was to be believed, the money was still safe. No one could get at it except Vince. Sydney's smile faded as she remembered signing some important looking papers—papers Vince had shrugged away while mumbling about the bank needing her signature for something or other. Then her mind wandered to the unknown person. According to Vince, this mystery person soon began calling the shots, and Vince would never explain why.

It was this person who had wanted Sydney to move away and change her name, so Vince had given her a large sum of money and told her to leave the state. "Don't contact me until you've relocated under a new identity. When you do want to reach me, always use my private phone line or cell phone, not the company line!"

Off Sydney had gone. She traveled around until deciding to tour the Great Lakes surrounding Michigan. One day driving into Petoskey, Sydney fell in love with the quaint city on the shores of Lake Michigan and decided to stay. She'd contacted former forger friends in Louisville and soon changed her name from Abigail to Sydney.

Sydney pulled the front window curtain back to better observe the sunny day as she recalled all the recent calls she'd made to Vince—calls he hadn't returned. "What a mess I'm in, and Vince isn't returning my calls." Sydney blew cigarette smoke toward the ceiling and scowled. "How come you're not returning my calls, Vince? What are you up to?"

Sydney turned away from the window so didn't notice the neighbor's dog barking at the man casually leaning against a tree slightly down from her home.

Picking up her phone, she decided to try Vince once more, this time on the company line.

Vince stared at the caller ID displayed on his office phone. It read "Sydney." Running a hand through his thinning hair, he sighed. He'd been trying to avoid her, but obviously something was up for her to call him using all the numbers in her arsenal. Making sure his office door was closed, Vince sighed and picked up the receiver. "Hello, Ab, uh, Syd. I thought we agreed you wouldn't call me unless it was an emergency. Are you calling for money again?"

"It's about time you answered, and it is an emergency! I'm in trouble, Vince, and I need your help!"

Alarm coursed through his body. Raising his voice, he demanded, "What kind of trouble?"

"I was arrested for suspicion of money embezzling from your company!" Sydney suddenly grew quiet then asked suspiciously, "Now that I think about it, how come you haven't been arrested too?"

At her words, Vince came to his feet. A kaleidoscope of things flashed through his mind. Ignoring her question, he practically shouted into the phone, "Are you calling me from jail? What are you thinking? Do the police know you're talking to me? What have you told them?"

"Stop shouting and calm down! Didn't my name come up on your caller ID? Man, for being so smart, sometimes you brainiacs can be so dumb! I can only answer one question at a time, so let me do it. I spent two nights in jail, and then the judge released me under house arrest. I'm confined to my home with a lovely bracelet attached to my ankle. The reason I'm calling is for $100,000. That's what the judge says I owe, and it has to be paid in three months. That was a month ago, Vince! You need to get me the money!"

Trying to absorb all she was saying, Vince calmed his racing heart while trying to think. Ignoring her heated words, Vince finally said, "For one thing, how would it look if you suddenly appeared with all that money able to pay? It's not going to happen. They'd trace it back to me in a moment! Secondly, just what do the police know about me?" Raising his voice, he repeated, "What do they know?"

"Nothing! I've told them nothing! Although I did kind of imply that I might tell the names of my accomplices. It helped the judge decide to let me come home." Sydney could hear Vince stuttering on the other end of the line, so she quickly added, "I haven't told them anything... yet. But I might if you don't get me that money!"

Vince breathed a sigh of relief and then collapsed back into his chair. His mind was racing. For all he knew, Sydney's home phone could be bugged. He had to get her off the line.

"Listen, Syd. We can't talk over the phone. Are you allowed visitors?"

"Yes, but..."

"Any time day or night?"

"Yes, but..."

"Then look for me, say..." Vince quickly scanned his appointment book. "Look for me late Thursday night of next week. I'll come to you. We'll talk then, so don't call me!"

Hanging up the receiver, Vince leaned forward, placing his head in his hands. Taking big gulps of air, he tried to still his racing heart and scattered thoughts. Knowing Sydney was too far away to drive, the first thing he did was request his secretary to purchase a private charter flight to Petoskey, Michigan, and then asked not to be disturbed. Growing steadier, he stood and walked to the large window overlooking the Ohio River. Down below him on the edge of the river was a picnic water park. Memories of fun days spent there with his family floated past his eyes then stopped on one in particular.

It was a beautiful, warm Sunday afternoon in August, when his three boys were still in grade school. That day a picnic was packed and bathing suits were worn under shirts and shorts. Upon their arrival, the boys made short work of shedding their outer clothes and running to join their friends in the fountains of water sporadically bursting from the large cement play area that gently sloped down to a landing at the river. Vince and Stephanie had found a picnic table within sight and hearing of the boys. They had sat with shoulders touching to watch the boys' antics.

Suddenly, one of the boys had yelled, "Dad, come join us."

Vince remembered how he had frowned and shaken his head. The boys knew perfectly well he didn't have swim trunks on under his clothes.

Then another son's voice had rung out. "Dad, please. Come join us. Other dads are!"

Feeling an elbow in his rib, Vince had turned to Stephanie. She smiled and said, "I remember a guy who didn't let lack of swimming trunks stop him from joining in the fun." She then had added wistfully, "I haven't seen that guy for a while."

Vince had joined his boys that day, and the memory of it made him smile sadly at his reflection in the window glass. As Stephanie had been trying to warn him, that fun, family-oriented Vince was now long gone.

Staring back at the dark, muddy river, Vince groaned from deep inside. He wasn't sure how long he stood there staring into nothingness, but eventually his erratic heartbeats slowed and clearer thoughts began formulating. Then his private phone line chimed, which caused him to jump.

Slowly walking to the phone, his heart sank when the caller ID read *Restricted*. He knew who it was. Forcing himself to steady his voice, he quickly clicked on the recorder then answered.

"I'm in town, and we need to talk!"

A sudden feeling of superiority surged, prompting Vince to state, "You're right. We do need to talk. Sydney just phoned. She's in big trouble!"

"I know. That's another reason why I've decided this needs to be face to face and not over the phone."

At his words, all of Vince's previous bravado fled out the window. *He already knows about Sydney? How is that possible?* Vince stared at the phone in his hand.

The voice abruptly said, "This is what I want you to do. Tell everyone—your wife, secretary, whomever—that you'll be working late next Tuesday evening. I'll come to your office at 10:00 p.m. sharp. Leave a message with downstairs security that a Mr. Clark will be coming for a late business appointment. Don't mess with me, Vince. Be there and don't think about contacting any authorities. Right now, I'm your best friend and worst enemy. Remember that!"

The line went dead.

Vince slowly lowered the phone and turned off the recorder. For the first time, Vince knew there was only one reason why the unknown person was willing to expose his identity to Vince. It wouldn't matter! He knew Vince wouldn't be telling anyone anything. He'd be dead!

Vince walked back to the window and river. Work and rubbing shoulders with the right people had become his gods. It soon became important to be accepted by these same people, and pleasing them was of more value than family time. Overnight, it seemed his boys had grown up and left home. In the midst of that time, he and Stephanie had become strangers. It had been just a small step to turn to mistresses and then, Sydney. Despair and hopelessness assailed Vince's senses as he felt the snare of his own making tighten around him. *Maybe the best solution lies down there in the river. I'm on the tenth floor. Isn't that high enough to do the job?* He even went so far as to study the window, but it wasn't the kind that opened and breaking it was out of the question. Then thoughts of his wife and family came surging in, and he began to grieve.

Leaning his head into the window, tears formed in his eyes. He stood this way for a long time as plans began forming themselves in his distraught mind. Standing straight, he withdrew keys from his pocket then unlocked the bottom left drawer of his desk.

Inside were some legal documents and a mini-cassette tape. He set the items on his desk and then went in search of a large manila envelope. Sitting back at his desk, he pulled out his personal address book. Once an envelope was properly addressed to a particularly trustworthy friend, he slipped the tape and documents inside. Then on impulse, he popped out the tape currently in the machine and added it to the envelope. He quickly wrote a brief note to Sydney. Placing it inside as well, Vince securely sealed the envelope. He then put the now full envelope back in the bottom drawer and locked it, pulling the handle to make sure.

He slipped the keys in his pocket and then walked once more to the large window. He sighed heavily. "I need to spend more time with my family. This job has consumed too much of my life over the last few years." With a determined look, he walked to his desk and buzzed his secretary, telling her he was taking the rest of the day off.

Vince scanned his neat desk and then picked up his briefcase. His eyes went to the locked drawer, which he stared at for a long time. Deciding to put it in the mail Tuesday morning, Vince sighed heavily once more, put a new cassette in the phone recorder, and then left for home.

# Chapter 5

Hope Montgomery stared at herself in the bedroom mirror. In spite of the miscarriage of her first baby only six short months earlier, she was pleased at how healthy her almost thirty-year-old body looked. Leaning slightly forward, she studied her lightly freckled face and blue eyes. "Yup, no doubt about it, you're in love!" A silly smile broke out on the reflection as stars danced in her eyes. She still couldn't believe everything that had happened just a short week ago on Labor Day evening. Pierce's former in-laws, Frank and Helen, had come for a weekend visit, bringing along Lisa, Hope's friend from her former job at the bank.

Back in May so much had happened. Pierce had decided to move baby Sarah home with him to Petoskey, and Hope had finally agreed to go along to be her nanny. At the same time, Helen was undergoing uterine cancer surgery, and Lisa had taken vacation time to be there when Helen returned home. The surgery had gone well, and Helen recovered quickly and so far remained cancer free. The three had traveled north for the extended weekend and had been staying at Pierce's larger cabin near Hope and Sarah's smaller cabin, both of which were nestled in the forest outside Petoskey.

Hope continued looking past her reflection into the memories of that night.

They had all been sitting around Pierce's comfortable living room chatting when Hope had remembered a frozen dessert she'd placed in the freezer earlier. Jumping up, she stopped to speak with baby Sarah sitting in the middle of the floor playing when the baby suddenly smiled grandly, raised her little arms, and said, "Mommy." Hope had frozen and then panicked. Turning, she ran from the room out the front door with Pierce soon following.

She was halfway to the smaller cabin before he caught her, and an argument had ensued. Then, as the other adults watched from the window, their attitudes had gradually changed. Standing outside under the moonlight, she and Pierce recognized their mutual love for baby Sarah and for each other. The reality had taken them both by surprise.

As Hope remembered that first intimate hug with Pierce, a beautiful blush was reflected in the mirror. Lowering her eyes, she also noticed the picture frame by her hand. Growing sober, she slowly raised the photo up of Dean's and her wedding day. Sadness crowded the growing joy as she gazed at Dean, her best friend and lover, who was now in heaven with their premature baby girl. Memories of Dean's auto accident and her miscarriage three months later came flooding in, threatening her senses, until a sound came from the next room. It was the sound of a ten-month-old baby cooing and playing in her crib.

Hope's mind jumped back to the present, and she smiled once more. Sarah was awake. Hope loved the fact that she almost always woke in a happy mood; greeting her stuffed animal friends that shared her crib was the first business of the day. But usually that lasted only a few minutes, and then she'd start fussing for human attention.

Still holding the picture frame in her hands, Hope drew her eyes back to her face in the mirror. What a time Pierce and she had had less than a year ago! Pierce's wife, Vicki, had died in childbirth, leaving him with a daughter. In his sorrow and anger, he had rejected the unseen baby. Giving her to his in-laws, he had walked out of the hospital, not looking back. He didn't want anything to do with her. Helen and Frank had taken Sarah home to East Grand Rapids to raise.

Hope's trials and tragedies began flashing across the mirror blotting out her face; what she saw was how Helen had become a huge mental and spiritual help during that time. Through Helen's friendship and need of assistance with Sarah, Hope became more and more involved with the rejected baby. Resentment had built toward the man who wouldn't even visit his precious daughter.

As Sarah continued cooing, Hope's mind fast-forwarded through the many circumstances that ended up bringing her north to be Sarah's live-in nanny. Having strong Christian principles, she refused to live in the same home as the single father, so residence was set up in the nearby cabin, which had previously been a vacation spot for Frank and Helen when they came to visit their only daughter. Over time and constant exposure, Hope's and Pierce's pain began healing, and their mutual love for baby Sarah opened a whole new world of feelings for each other, something that was still very new and hard to deal with especially since neither of them had been widowed a year yet.

The night that Sarah called her Mommy, Hope had decided she couldn't handle the situation any longer and needed to leave. That was the same night Pierce asked her to be his wife and Sarah's full-time mom.

"Lord, you truly do work in mysterious ways!" Hope stated as she lowered her eyes to the wedding photo once more.

"Dean, I'll always love you. You were my first true love." Running her finger over his photo, she added, "I didn't think I'd ever feel again. My heart grew so hard and bitter after losing you and then our baby, but God had other plans." Sarah's cooing changed to sounds of impatience for Hope's attention. Gently setting the frame back on the dresser top, Hope whispered, "I miss you. Someday, I'll see you again." Hope blew him a kiss as she turned toward the now crying baby.

Just before leaving the room, Hope frowned as she realized deep down there were still some major issues of sorrow that she and Pierce needed to work through. Forcing the thought aside until she had more time to dwell on it, Hope walked into Sarah's room. "Okay, baby girl, let's get up. We're going to visit Sydney this morning."

Sydney's attitude was evident the moment Hope and Sarah walked through the door. Sighing heavily, Hope set Sarah on the floor while unloading her arms of baby paraphernalia. She had to move swiftly, for Sarah was already crawling toward a breakable object of interest.

"Whoa there, little girl. Let's get your sweater off." Having accomplished that task, Hope pulled some toys from the bag, placing them like a barrier around the baby, all the while aware of Sydney watching her every move but saying nothing.

"There. That should occupy her for say ... a good five or ten minutes." Smiling, Hope turned her attention to Sydney. "So how are you doing?"

Sydney flopped unladylike in the overstuffed chair while stating with disgust, "I hate it! I hate the loss of my freedom! And I hate this bracelet!"

Hope almost reminded Sydney that she'd brought it all on herself but refrained. Instead, she cheerfully stated, "Well, since we're stuck here, what do you have for entertainment? Any puzzles? We could work on one together."

At the suggestion, a look of total amazement crossed Sydney's face, and she rolled her eyes. "You're kidding, right? Do I look like the puzzle type?"

Redness crept across Hope's face as the insult slammed home. *Okay, Lord. I need some help here.* "Okay. What would you like to do?" She then waited. All sorts of recriminating thoughts raced through her mind as a silent argument ensued. *I don't need this! She's not even trying to be likeable. Pick up Sarah and go home!* But then another voice would say, *Come on, Hope. It wasn't all that long ago when you weren't so nice either, even to the point of being rude to others and bitter toward God.* Then a still small voice quietly stated to her mind, *Relax and trust me. She needs you as a friend.*

Hope's rambling thoughts were brought back to the room when Sydney stated, "I don't know what to do with myself. I've tried reading books, but I get bored quickly." Sydney pushed herself out of the chair and walked to the kitchen to light up a cigarette.

Hope watched her movements and then gently asked, "Uh, I know this is your home, but would you mind not smoking around the baby?" For a moment, Sydney considered lighting one anyway then refrained and stuffed the cigarette back in the pack. "Thanks. I appreciate it."

Sydney pulled out a couple glasses from the cupboard while stating, "I could use a good drink. What's your flavor? Vodka? Gin? A little wine?"

"Actually, I don't drink." Seeing an argument brewing on Sydney's face, Hope hurriedly added, "But a glass of tea or ice water sounds great!"

After dumping some ice in the glasses, Sydney pulled some Evian water from the fridge. She paused and then with deliberation opened a cupboard that housed multiple bottles of liquor. Selecting one, she poured another glass half full of the amber stuff. With an expert twist of her wrist, the cap secured back on. Lifting challenging eyes to her visitor, Sydney picked up the bottle of water and two glasses. Maintaining eye contact, she walked back to Hope.

Hope's face crept with a blush, but she held her tongue. It was becoming increasingly difficult. As sincerely as she could, Hope thanked Sydney for the water and glass of ice.

With a smirk, Sydney held her glass up in a toast then took a long, deliberate drink. A heavy silence ensued as the two women turned their attentions toward the baby playing on the floor in front of them.

Hope felt a feeling of despair course through her. *Lord, please help me reach this woman for you!* She prayed over and over again.

Then baby Sarah did something fairly foreign for her. Getting on all fours, she crawled to Sydney. Plopping on her butt in front of Sydney's legs, Sarah raised her arms to be lifted up. Shaking her head, Sydney visibly pulled back. "I...I don't do babies."

Not daunted by her tone, Sarah began smiling and blowing bubbles at Sydney, still extending her arms forward.

Panic laced Sydney's voice as she repeated, "Really! This isn't my thing. Would you come get her?"

*Lord, you certainly have a sense of humor and work in mysterious ways!* Not moving, Hope asked, "Have you ever held a baby?"

"Never!"

"Don't you have brothers or sisters?"

Not taking her eyes off Sarah, Sydney responded, "I have one older sister."

"Then maybe it's time you learned how to hold a baby."

Aware of Hope's tone, Sydney turned startled eyes her way as Hope rose from her seat. In one swift move, she hefted Sarah from the floor and sat her in Sydney's lap.

Sydney immediately stiffened, but when Sarah began leaning backward, her arm instinctively reached out to steady her. Hope smiled and took a step back.

Once Sarah was in her lap, Sydney seemed to forget all about Hope. Her full attention was on the baby, and a look of wonder crossed her face. "You're a sturdy little thing, aren't you?" Sarah continued cooing and smiling at Sydney, and little by little Sydney began relaxing. Hope soon took her seat back on the sofa and quietly sipped her water.

Baby Sarah grew more excited about her newfound friend to the point of bouncing up and down. Soon she grabbed the front of Sydney's shirt and pulled herself into a stand. Before the startled Sydney could react, Sarah did a special move usually reserved for her dad or Hope. Pulling her little face close, she touched her forehead to Sydney's. In that moment, an incredibly soft, vulnerable look crossed Sydney's face. She lifted sorrowful eyes to Hope's.

For the first time, Hope saw deep into Sydney's heart. The amount of pain and longing she saw briefly revealed startled her. Sydney closed her eyes and then did something that surprised both the adult women; she wrapped her arms around the baby to hug her close.

After that, the ice between the two women seemed to break a bit, and Hope accepted it cautiously. *Baby steps. This friendship and trust will be built on baby steps.*

About an hour later, Hope and Sarah left, leaving behind a visibly shaken and thoughtful Sydney.

Tuesday morning, Vince Edgar walked into the specialty electronics store. Spying a young man with thick glasses standing near the counter, he walked up.

"I'm looking for a really small recorder of some kind. Something I can preprogram to record … let's say … discreetly."

Pushing his glasses farther up his nose, the clerk eyed him with raised brows and then smiled. He retrieved his keys while stating confidently with a touch of excitement, "It just so happens we recently got in a couple new products that I think are just what you're looking for." As he pulled out the small gadgets, he warned, "But it's going to take some bucks, for these are pricey!"

A short while later, Vince stood in his spacious, plush office looking for the ideal spot to conceal what he held in his hand. The small recorder was about twice the size of a computer flash drive. It partially slid apart revealing a small timer that was now set to turn on at

9:45 p.m. The recorder only lasted an hour, and Vince didn't want to take any chances of telltale sounds alerting his coming visitor.

With a frown pasted on his face, Vince did a slow spin on his heels. If he hid it too well, the possible evidence it might contain might never be found. On the other hand, he didn't want the wrong person finding it either. Slowly his eye focused on an object resting on his desktop. Stepping closer, Vince picked it up to study the possibilities. Perfect!

A few minutes later, a satisfied Vince pushed away a feeling of fatalism as he buzzed for his secretary.

"Yes, Mr. Edgar."

"Please bring me a priority mail flat rate envelope."

"Right away, Mr. Edgar."

Writing a quick note of instructions to his trusted friend, Vince unlocked the bottom drawer pulling out the manila envelope. Slipping it and the note into the stiff white envelope, he addressed it but opted not to add a return on the outside. Pulling the sticky tape off, Vince made sure the top closed securely before walking it out to his secretary with instructions to send it with the morning mail.

As Sydney helped close up shop a few days after speaking with Vince, she was still bothered about how short he'd been with her. *At least he'll be here in a couple days. Hopefully he'll be bringing some money with him!*

As her boss walked with her out the front door, the two exchanged a few words then headed to their cars. Usually Sydney didn't give in to fantasies of a boogeyman lurking in shadows, but Sydney had the feeling she was being watched. As she clipped across the well-lit parking lot in her high heels, Sydney thought she heard footsteps behind her. Part of her wanted to stop and confront whoever might be approaching, but another part said, "Keep moving! Get into your car." So that's what she did.

Before exiting the building, she'd put the keys in her hand. As she drew closer, Sydney pressed the door lock release but almost dropped the keys when she caught movement out of the corner of her eye. Forcing her long legs to move faster, she heard the footsteps pick up speed also.

Finally her hand jerked the car door open when Quaid spoke near her elbow, "Good evening, Sydney."

Fueled with lingering fear, Sydney lashed out angrily, "You scared the snot out of me! Why are you sneaking up on people like that?"

"I didn't sneak. I knew you were closing shop, so I came here purposely to talk about the upcoming auction and see how you're doing."

As she leaned her back against the car, Sydney took a deep breath to slow her rapid heart rate while glaring at his handsome face. She watched his dark eyes narrow as he asked, "Why are you so jumpy? Is there something you're not telling me?"

Flicking imaginary lint from her blouse, Sydney replied, "I'm not jumpy. I don't like a person sneaking up on me; that's all."

"Like I said before, I didn't sneak, and it sure appeared like you were fearful."

Sydney chose not to respond to his statement. "So what's so important that it had to be talked about tonight in person?"

Quaid studied her face. He knew she'd been frightened at his approach, and his instincts told him he should find out why.

"Are you going to stand there staring at me, or are we going to talk?" Sydney checked her watch as if to show she had someplace to be.

Quaid cocked his head and smiled, knowing full well that her only destination was a mandatory trip home. Seeing anger flit to her eyes, he curbed the smile to say, "The crystal auction is to be held this Saturday around 10:00 a.m. As I know you can't attend, afterwards I'll let you know what the final amount is and how much more you'll need to come up with."

"Fine."

Sydney turned to get into her car but paused when Quaid asked, "Are you ready to give us the name or names of your partners?"

Seeing her listening, he added, "Sydney, your giving us their names may seem like a risky thing for you to do, but if doing so could put you in any danger, we'll protect you. You have my word on that."

Straightening up, Sydney whirled around. "Your word? Come on, Quaid! You and I both know you don't care a fig about me. You're just doing your job!"

Quaid started to protest, but Sydney wasn't done. "Forget it! I learned long ago that people can't be trusted, especially men! Now as you know, I'm legally supposed to be home by now." Without another word or looking his direction, she got into her car.

Moving back so she didn't hit him with the door, Quaid frowned when the door slammed, and the lock snapped in place. A few seconds later, the car backed up and spit dirt as she peeled out of the parking lot.

He watched her taillights out of sight and then slowly allowed his eyes to study the surroundings. "What's spooking you, Sydney?" Getting a determined glint in his brown eyes, Quaid pivoted on his heel and walked to his own vehicle. "Whatever it is, you can bet your life I'm getting to the bottom of all of this!"

# Chapter 6

"He didn't show!" Sydney was frantic.

It was now Friday morning, and Vince hadn't come. Sydney had waited up until past midnight. It was highly unusual for Vince to not keep his word.

At one point, Sydney thought he was across the street, leaning against a tree and smoking a cigarette. But then she remembered he didn't smoke, unless it was a new habit for him. When she checked the window again, the man flicked his stub to the road and sauntered off.

As she pondered the man's disappearing back, Sydney vaguely wondered why he was there. She frowned at the thought that she might have noticed him out there before. Shrugging that off as being paranoid about Vince's no-show, Sydney angrily picked up her cell phone to punch in Vince's number. As before, the call went directly to his mailbox. In frustration, she shut the phone and tossed it to the sofa. Sydney picked up a pack of cigarettes and lit one, forgetting all about the one already smoldering in the ashtray.

When the clock showed 1:00 a.m., Sydney finally decided he wasn't coming and didn't appear to be calling to explain why. It worried her. Vince had never intentionally lied to her before as far as she knew. Walking to the bathroom to scrub the makeup layers off, Sydney came to a hard decision. Ignoring the half-clown face reflected in her mirror, she pointed the washcloth at Vince's imaginary face. "As much as I don't want to do this, Vince, you're forcing my hand. If I don't hear anything from you by say ten tomorrow morning, I'm calling Quaid and giving him your info."

Once that was decided, a worried Sydney finished washing her face. Within a couple minutes, a stranger looked at her from the mirror. It always amazed Sydney the extreme contrast she presented in the mirror. Turning her face side to side, Sydney studied her bone structure. Without the makeup, Sydney never seemed to see the natural beauty she was so intent on covering up. Instead, she saw the poor street girl who either stole or begged for money. Once her face was all made up, in Sydney's eye she saw a woman of class, a woman to be noticed and reckoned with. Men always seemed to notice her blue, piercing eyes first and then would roam over the rest of her. These thoughts brought her mind back to Vince and his no-show.

Growing tired of the plain Jane in the mirror, Sydney went to bed. Scrunching the pillow snugly behind her head, she mentally warned, *If I don't hear from Vince, I will call Quaid.*

Her thoughts soon drifted to island paradises and all the money she could ever want. Falling soundly asleep, Sydney had no thoughts of the tall, skinny man she'd seen in the shadows outside her home or the danger that was threatening to come even closer.

The next morning she called Quaid.

State Police Chief Baxter had just received some news from the wire and went in search of Detectives Quaid and Paul. Finding their desks empty, he studied the familiar work area. Both men were quite neat with Quaid a touch more so. He even arranged his pens before vacating the desk. The chief couldn't help but smile. His eyes wandered to Quaid's credenza. Below the upper shelves was mounted a custom made shadow box that housed novelty golf balls.

Stepping around the swivel chair, the chief leaned in closer. Since there were still empty slots in the box, it was becoming a habit to note any new additions. He picked up a small replica of the world. Holding it in his hand, he studied the minute detail more closely before setting it back and pulling out another one. This one Quaid prized and was the best in his collection, at least in Quaid's mind. It was the most controversial one in the mind of the rest of the precinct, for it sported the logo of the New England Patriots. Quaid was an avid Patriots fan in spite of a room full of Detroit Lions fans. He was continually being confronted about his lack of loyalty to Michigan, but it never seemed to faze him. Quaid seemed to strive on adversity.

It was one of the things the chief liked best about these two detectives. They were both confident in who they were and in their abilities. They were especially keen on details, which was evidenced by the neatness of their desks and the fast way they solved crimes. This latest case was stumping them though, which brought the chief back to his purpose of looking for his detectives in the first place. The paper crinkled in his hand as he turned to have them paged. He paused in mid-motion as the two detectives walked through the front door and passed the security desk.

It was shortly after noon when Quaid and Paul walked through the station door. They had spent the last hour at Sydney's, where she'd finally opened up with some information. Vince Edgar was one of her partners in the crime, and he worked for Dison Roselle Inc., located in downtown Louisville, Kentucky. She'd even given them all his phone numbers: private line, company line, and cell phone. The men were excited to have something to go on. Now all they had to do was start researching the guy and get some evidence on him.

One other thing had happened. For the first time, Sydney asked some questions; the men were surprised she hadn't asked before. "How come you arrested me and didn't know about Vince? What evidence did you have on me that didn't include him?"

Neither man was prepared to divulge their information just yet, not until Vince was safely in custody and couldn't be tipped off by Sydney or anyone else. They'd have to move quickly and quietly. Sydney was hopping mad at the man but had grudgingly agreed to give the men three hours. "Do what you have to; then I'm calling him again!"

The chief was standing near their desks when they walked up.

"Hey, men. I think I may have some information for you. I'm not sure it has anything to do with your case or not, but it seems a little too coincidental." Turning, he added, "Let's talk in my office."

En route the men told him what Sydney had divulged. The chief paused just inside his office while absorbing their words. Handing them the single paper in his hand, he then took his desk seat while they scanned the paper from the wire service.

With raised eyebrows, they read, "Top Accountant Found Dead in his Louisville, Kentucky, Office." The article went on to state how Vince Edgar's body had been found by his secretary Wednesday morning. After reading what little bit was there, the men looked back up at the chief with disappointment in their eyes. The two let out sighs of frustration on being too late while they were pulling chairs closer to the chief's desk. An intense discussion followed as to what this meant in regards to their struggling case and Sydney's safety in particular.

"Should we set up a twenty-four-hour detail to watch over her?" Quaid asked.

"It's highly likely that the silent third partner may have gotten wind that Sydney was under house arrest and is taking care of business." Paul added, "If this is that person, I would think Sydney could be in danger."

After about an hour of hashing things back and forth, a plan began to emerge. Paul, state trooper Neal, and a rookie named Jake would set up constant detail around Sydney, whatever she did, while Quaid would make a trip to find out what he could from the authorities in Louisville. Upon his return, they'd have another powwow and decide what their next moves would be.

Standing and stretching, the men looked ready for action, ready for whatever they had to do to resolve this crime and bring people to justice. In that moment, the chief was proud to claim these two particular men as his detectives. He knew they were tenacious and determined. Sydney was in the best hands he could possibly put her in under the circumstances.

As the men went to their desks to make some phone calls and get things rolling, their faces were set. Sydney could be in danger, and nothing was going to happen to her under their watch. So far, they still didn't have any solid lead on the third partner or even know if this person was involved with Vince's murder. It could have been a totally random thing, but Quaid was up to the challenge and rearing to get at it.

By the time he'd packed an overnight bag at his home, the office had called with travel arrangements, and Paul had checked in stating the schedule had been made up for the surveillance team around Sydney. The two men agreed to meet briefly at Sydney's before Quaid headed on to the airport. They were hoping to be the first to break the news to her about Vince.

When Sydney swung the door open, the men noted two things: all pretense of flirting with them was gone, and she was still in a tiff. It was obvious she hadn't heard a thing yet. Swinging the door wide, she silently stepped back while dramatically sweeping her arm backwards for them to enter.

Quaid and Paul exchanged looks. Getting the "you go first" from his partner, Quaid started to talk. "Sydney, we just received some bad news, so you may want to take a seat."

Sydney studied the two detectives' faces for a few seconds. She opted to remain standing but took a defensive posture behind the living room chair.

Shrugging his shoulders, Quaid gently stated, "They found Vince's body in his office Wednesday morning. He'd been shot in the heart at close range."

At the news, Sydney sagged slightly, but when Paul stepped toward her, she straightened and whispered, "What else?"

"There's not much else to tell. His office had been thoroughly ransacked. Someone was obviously looking for something. At this point we're not sure what or if it even has anything to do with our case or you."

"With me?" At that she came around and sagged heavily in the chair. With eyes large as saucers, she asked again, "Do you think it could have something to do with me?" Sydney's hand shakily covered her mouth as she searched the men's eyes for answers and reassurance.

"As I already mentioned, we're not sure; so until we are, things will have to change around here for a while. We'll have men watching you twenty-four-seven with Paul being the point man."

A questioning look came into her eyes, and Paul stepped forward. "What he means is, I'm in charge of your care and safety until Quaid returns."

Sydney swung her eyes to Quaid's. For just a moment he saw a vulnerable side to her he hadn't seen before, a little girl, I-can't-handle-this-alone side, which was verified by her hurried words. "Where are you going, and why you? Why can't Paul go wherever you're going?"

Quaid was startled by a sudden desire to protect her and ease her fear, but that soon disappeared when he saw her transform before him once again.

Realizing she sounded pathetic, Sydney studied her tapered, painted nails. "Not that it matters to me who stays, as long as I'm protected." She tried to sound detached but wasn't quite pulling if off.

The men exchanged an understanding look before Paul continued. "Well, this is how it's going to work. Quaid flies out in an hour to see what he can uncover about our mystery man and if he possibly had anything to do with Vince's murder. Meanwhile, Neal, Jake, and I will take shifts watching you."

"What does that mean exactly? Will you be sitting in cars out front?"

"Part of the time. It also means that if you leave the house one of us will accompany you to work or to the grocery store—at all times."

The pause before the last words caused Sydney to pay closer attention. "Great! So how long will this new form of imprisonment be enforced?"

Anger immediately crossed Quaid's face as he took a couple menacing steps forward. "You don't get it, do you? This is for your protection, not ours. Our protecting you could put us in danger!"

He started to say more when Paul stepped between them. Facing his partner, he cautioned, "Calm down, buddy. This is new for her. We just put some heavy stuff on her."

Before turning away, Quaid stated, "It's attitudes like hers that gets my men killed!" He walked to the window, keeping his back to the offensive woman.

"None of this would have happened if you'd kept your nose out! Vince would still be alive!"

"You don't know that!" Quaid whirled and hurled at her. By now she was on her feet and shaking all over.

Sydney was near a breaking point when Quaid raised a finger and issued an edict. "If this does turn out to be your other partner, you're going to be put in total protection somewhere else! So I guess you'd better appreciate what little freedom you still have, because it could change quickly!"

She started to respond in a raised, angry voice, but Quaid was done with the conversation. Turning to Paul, he stated, "She's your headache now. I'm off to the airport. Good luck. I don't wish her on anyone!" Giving his partner a strong hand grip, he turned to walk out the door, saying, "I'll be in touch."

The last words he heard screamed at him as he slammed the door were, "Who needs you anyway!"

Much later, when Sydney had calmed down, she remembered the man lurking in the shadows but told no one.

Pierce Matthews was just walking into his cabin that Friday afternoon when his phone rang. Since declaring his heart to Hope, he had become increasingly anxious to get cleaned up after work so he could spend as much time with his girls as possible.

Unclipping the phone from his belt, he checked the caller ID before responding. "Hey, Quaid. What's up?"

"I need a favor!"

Immediately Pierce snapped to attention when he heard the urgency in his friend's voice. "Anything! What can I do for you?"

"There's been a serious development with Sydney's case, and I have to go out of town for a while. The auction of Hope's crystal is tomorrow. Would you handle it for me? The crystal was taken to the auction house on Monday, so all you mainly need to do is be there and get any money made."

"Sure. No problem. How serious is this new development?"

"I don't know yet, but pray for her. If my thinking is right, she may be in grave danger. My flight is loading, so I have to run. We'll talk when I get back in a few days."

"Hope and I will be praying, and don't worry about anything at this end. Have a safe trip."

# Chapter 7

After landing in Louisville, it didn't take Quaid long to connect with the murder investigating detective. They compared notes en route to the crime scene.

"Any clues whatsoever on who or why?"

"None, at least not before talking to you. Obviously, it was someone Mr. Edgar knew, and this person was looking for something." The detective paused then added, "The perpetrator covered his tracks well right down to gloves and disguise. Security has a bearded, long-haired man coming in at 9:47 p.m." Checking his notepad, he added, "A Mr. Clark." The detective paused to flash his badge at the local policeman standing near the front of the tall office building.

The two men then walked in. "Mr. Edgar verified the visit, and the guard let him pass on in. The elevator cameras show the man getting on and traveling to the tenth floor. He obviously knew where the cameras were, as he never gave us a good straight-on shot. He must have taken the stairs down because the guard didn't see him exit the building. We've studied the elevator tapes extensively, and our experts believe he was wearing a well-made full-headed mask. Doing digital hair removal gave us nothing solid. The mask was just baggy enough to distort the face structure."

Stepping onto the elevator, Quaid noted the standard hidden camera spot near the ceiling. The men rode in silence. At the tenth floor, Quaid was directed to his left pass several office cubicles to the end of the large room where a better grade desk was positioned just outside an oak door.

"This is where Edgar's secretary sat."

Quaid studied the desk briefly as he walked on into the expansive office beyond. Stopping in the doorway, he then studied the selective mess in general. As his eyes drifted to the work station area, Quaid noted the taped body outline on the floor and that the mess was mainly situated around the mahogany desk and nearby shelves. *Did the perpetrator find what he was looking for?* Quaid's gut told him no.

Stepping closer to the taped area, he stared down at the cold impersonal spot that once represented a living, breathing person. *What a waste!* He didn't spend much time dwelling on what could have been. Quaid knew a fresh pair of eyes sometimes noted things others may have missed, so he began examining the area more intently. After a long while, he asked, "Anything missing?"

"Not according to Mrs. Black, the secretary. The normal things are still here, even petty cash in the middle desk drawer." The detective allowed Quaid to mull that over a moment then added, "This crime scene was thoroughly worked Wednesday and Thursday, so feel free to touch whatever you want."

Checking his watch, he stated, "I'll leave you to it. Arrangements have been made for you to stay just down the block at the Hampton Inn. That way you can come and go as you please. The guards have been instructed to let you in." Handing Quaid his business card, he added, "Give me a call if you come up with something or have more questions." Shaking hands, he turned to leave while saying over his shoulder, "Pete here will stay and help you with whatever you need." He spoke a few words to Pete then left the room.

"Uh, Pete, was there a safe in this room?"

"Yes, we found one under the corner of the rubber floor pad under his desk chair."

Pete picked up the corner to reveal a floor safe underneath.

"I take it it's been opened?"

"Yes, sir. Some cash was inside, but mainly legal documents relating to the company. Oh, and his passport."

"Passport! Has he traveled out of the country lately?"

"Not that we can tell."

Right then Pete's COM link began crackling. "Officer Pete, this is dispatch. Over."

"Pete here. What you got for me? Over."

"We have a gentleman who insists he's got some important info on the Edgar murder. Over."

Quaid and Pete exchanged glances as Pete replied, "Patch him through to my cell phone. Over."

Pete closed the office door just as the phone rang. He pushed the hands-free button. "Detective Peter Greene here. Your name, please?"

Dead silence, then timidly, "Uh, do I have to?"

"It would be helpful toward verifying whatever info you may have."

"Well then, let's go with Bob."

Quaid couldn't help but smile at the obvious lie.

"Okay...*Bob*," Pete purposely emphasized the name. "What do you have for us?"

In a hurried voice he replied, "Tuesday morning your murdered man came in to purchase a very small tape recorder—one he intended on programming *and* concealing. He even had me hide it in the shop so we could see how close and far it picked up voices that could still be understood. Man, it was impressive! The..."

"Bob! Stay on track here! Are you sure it was our man?"

"Yeah, I'm really sure. The recorder is new technology and very pricey, if you know what I mean. He didn't have enough cash on him, so he paid with a credit card."

"Good, Bob. I need you to fax a complete description of the device including a photo. Plus, I need a copy of the receipt. Can you do that for me?"

"Sure, sure. No problem, man!"

Covering the phone, Pete asked Quaid if he had any questions.

"Ask him about what size the recorder was. How small of a hiding space are we talking here?"

The man on the other end replied, "Smaller than an MP3 player but bigger than a computer flash drive."

After hearing him repeatedly state he'd fax the needed items as soon as possible, Pete finally got the excited man off the phone and called the dispatcher. As Pete gave the dispatcher instructions about forwarding the faxes to Edgar's office machine, Quaid started examining the room. "Where would you put a recorder, Vince? Did you know you were in danger? More importantly, did the murderer find it?"

Not having any knowledge of Vince other than what little bit Sydney had shared, Quaid felt at a disadvantage. Holding still, he willed himself to study the décor, trying to feel the personality of the deceased man. All the while, under his breath, Quaid kept repeating, "Talk to me, Vince. Where did you put it? Where would be the best place to pick up any conversation in the room?"

The obvious place seemed to be the desk, which surprisingly wasn't very messed up at all, at least not on the top. The murderer had focused more on the drawers nearby the credenza and the bookcase.

With hands on his hips, Quaid positioned himself in front of the massive desk and studied the contents. In the background he heard the fax machine start whirring and Pete walking to retrieve the incoming information at the wall work station. With papers in hand, Pete walked over to Quaid. The two men glanced at the sheets then turned their focus back to the desktop.

"Does anything look out of place to you? Or that maybe doesn't belong here?" Quaid asked.

The silence grew as the two men studied the desk. Then Pete stepped forward. "What about this?"

Sitting beside the family photo was a mini trophy sporting the sign, "World's Best Dad." It was like a real trophy but flat on the back. Picking it up, Pete said, "It looks like something broke off the front. See this spot?"

"Broke off? Or... maybe it was attached to something bigger," Quaid suggested.

The men systematically eliminated items on the desk—the pen holder, the paperweight, the in-out boxes, and the stapler. Then their eyes landed on the family photo, and Quaid picked it up. "This frame is wider than normal, don't you think?" Turning it sideways, it didn't make sense. The photo was snug to the front glass, and yet the back was a good two inches away from the photo.

"You don't suppose..." Pete still held the little trophy. Moving it to the side of the photo frame, the men could easily see there was sufficient space for it to go inside the frame.

Excitement built in their faces as Quaid turned the frame face down on the desk and flipped the closure tabs holding the black velvet back in place. There, nestled neatly between the photo pushed all the way forward and the velvet back, was a brand new mini recorder.

# Chapter 8

A little after nine thirty Saturday night, Sydney's doorbell rang. It startled her. Sydney cautiously peered out and was relieved to see Pierce silhouetted through the thick diamonded door glass. But then she wondered why he was there again and so late. That wasn't like him. As her hand turned the doorknob, Sydney recalled the earlier visit.

He'd stopped by after the auction to report the crystal had raised $72,400. Sydney was still shocked that the crystal had brought in so much and that it had essentially been a gift from Pierce's nanny, Hope. It rankled that the pretty nanny seemed to have Pierce's eye, and she honestly didn't get it. Sydney had tried flirting with Pierce when he'd stopped by, but he wouldn't even come all the way in.

Turning the deadbolt, Sydney grew excited. Maybe he'd reconsidered! She went to pull the door open, but it wouldn't budge. It was then she remembered that morning Detective Paul had installed a security lock at the top of the door for an added safety measure. Hearing an impatient sigh on the other side of the door, Sydney quickly flipped it open and then threw the door wide. Pasting a seductive smile on her face, Sydney projected her voice forward as she pushed the storm door open. "So did you recon—"

She froze mid-sentence as Sydney realized the man standing before her wasn't Pierce. Narrowing her eyes, Sydney quickly scanned the visitor's profile and noticed a wide scar just off his left eyebrow.

The man slowly turned his full look at Sydney, and there the resemblance stopped. This man's eyes were cold and hard. Dangerous.

Fear shot through her as Sydney moved to shut the door, but she was too late. The stranger easily slid one arm and foot through the doorway while stating, "Now, Syd. Is that any way to greet your partner?"

Partner! Sydney's blood froze in her veins as his words penetrated the thickness of her brain. Her body couldn't seem to move.

Smiling wickedly, the man took his other hand and pushed her backwards while following her into the room. In short order, the door was shut, and Sydney flinched when she heard the deadbolt snap in place.

Involuntarily, Sydney backed further into the living room while the visitor lazily leaned against the door openly studying her. "Wow, Syd! Now that I see you, I can understand how you could convince Vince to do this business in the first place."

One raised eyebrow backed Sydney up another step as she frantically tried to collect her thoughts and decide what to do. All the while she wanted to scream, *Where is my bodyguard?* Having looked into this man's eyes, Sydney had no doubts this was Vince's murderer, and now he stood in her living room, apparently unchecked by anyone from the outside.

Glancing toward the drawn curtain, a new wave of fear hit

Sydney as her visitor's voice said, "Looking for help? There's no one out there. Trust me."

A feeling of helplessness surged through Sydney's body as the security of help was dashed away. Despair threatened to engulf her as she pulled her eyes back to the man still leaning against her front door. For whatever reason he was there, the man didn't seem to be in any hurry or concerned about outside interference. An image of Quaid and safety popped into her mind but vanished quickly as the truth that he was elsewhere chased the comfort away.

Mentally, Sydney tried to regroup. For the first time, the real possibility of death hit her like a blow, and sorrow over her wasted life coursed through her.

Suddenly, the man pushed himself off the door and stretched lazily. "Well, doll, as much as I'd like to get to know you better…" He paused and leered at her, even smiling when he noted a shudder course through her body. "But sadly I don't have the time… this visit," he added ominously.

Sydney looked longingly at the front window once more, but once again, he interrupted her thoughts. "Before we get into why I'm here, I could sure use a drink. Be a good girl and fix me one, okay, baby."

Reluctantly Sydney turned toward the used sideboard a coworker had recently brought her and opened it wide. Trying to appear calm, she waved her hand at the selection but remained quiet.

"I'll take a rum and coke on ice."

Moving to comply, Sydney tried to keep her hands from shaking when she walked the drink to the man now seated on the sofa. As she handed it to him, he patted a spot beside him. "Have a seat."

A part of her wanted to ignore his request, but Sydney knew she'd better obey. Picking up the decorative sofa pillow, she held it defensively in front of her and then sat down with distance between them. Angling into the corner, Sydney noticed her cigarettes nearby and tamped one out. Flicking her lighter, she held out the pack in case he wanted one too, but he declined with, "You know, those are bad for your health." He clinked the ice in his glass before taking another long drink.

Sydney stared at a wall painting off his left shoulder. She'd gotten it at a neighbor's yard sale just the day before. While Sydney exhaled a billow of smoke, she studied the faded gold frame surrounding a beautiful bouquet of roses sitting on a lace tablecloth. Strangely, the action calmed her, and she boldly asked, "Did you kill Vince?"

Sydney hoped the question would rattle him so leveled cool eyes his way at the same time, but she was disappointed.

His dark eyes deepened as he stared her down before replying, "Know about that already, huh? I'm surprised, Sydney. For being in the presence of a possible murderer, you're acting pretty calm. Impressive." He took another substantial drink while maintaining eye contact.

Sydney turned her head away. Memories of her stepfather came storming to the forefront of Sydney's mind, and something hardened within her. She hated mean, dominant men! Taking another long drag of her cigarette, she asked again, "So did you?"

"Let's table that for now. Instead, let's get to why I'm here. I need you to give me all the fictitious corporation papers."

"Corporation papers! What makes you think I have them? Vince took care of all the legal stuff. I don't have them." Sydney frowned in confusion as the man sat straighter to glare at her.

"Don't mess with me, Syd! The papers weren't in his office, and I want them!"

Raising her voice, Sydney restated, "I'm telling you I don't have them! Why on earth did you think I would?"

The man stood and paced while running a hand through his short, almost military looking haircut. Turning, he said in a low, tight voice, "Since you're the sole owner and president, you must have paperwork somewhere."

"President? Owner? I don't know what you're talking about!" Sydney too was on her feet. "I never signed..." Then her voice trailed off as a distant memory came to the forefront of her mind. Pausing, she pictured one late-night visit in Vince's office.

Momentarily forgetting the dangerous man observing her closely, Sydney's mind transported her to a year earlier, a time shortly after the silent partner had become involved. That evening before getting intimate, Vince had hauled out a stack of papers. He said she needed to sign them to get her name on the checkbook. She'd been irritated at his insistence and had tried getting some cash money for her pains, but he'd said it was too soon. Taking his wallet out, he handed her a fifty while saying, "You have to give this more time, Abby."

Guiding her to his desk, he'd pointed out the highlighted spots that required her signature on the legal papers while reminding her to use the Abigail Turner name. Being obsessed with the money that would be accumulating, Sydney hadn't taken the time to read anything. She just did as he'd requested then had promptly forgotten all about it. As she recalled now, that same night they'd argued about the new partner.

Realization dawned, and the man beside her saw it. Vince had obviously had concerns from the start about the man now standing in her living room, and it seemed he had good reason.

Sydney raised sorrowful eyes to the man. "You didn't have to kill him. He was a good man."

"Yeah, a real saint!" he replied sarcastically. Taking a step closer, he said, "You remember signing papers, don't you?"

"I do, but that was more than a year ago, and I haven't seen them since. You have to believe me!" Her voice unintentionally rose on the last words.

Staring at the floor, the man grew quiet and then stated, "If you don't have them, then they must be at his home somewhere. I guess that means a trip back to Louisville." He turned as if to leave.

Startled, Sydney rushed forward, grabbing his arm. "No! Vince wouldn't have done that! He never would have kept the papers where it would possibly bring harm to his family! I know he wouldn't!"

The man pointedly stared at her hand on his arm then flexed the muscle. She pulled her hand away as if burned. He chuckled then asked, "Well then, you tell me. Where does that leave us?"

Remembering the cigarette still burning between her fingers, Sydney hurriedly cupped the long ash until she could knock it off in the nearest ashtray. Rubbing the butt out, she tried to think of a solution, but nothing presented itself. The truth was she didn't have a clue where the papers were.

A heavy silence ensued as the man rubbed the back of his neck.

Sydney knew her life was in danger and felt like she was teetering on the edge of a precipice. She tried to figure out how to alert someone for help, but the man had stated that no one was out there. *Why did the guard leave?* she wondered for the hundredth time. For the first time, a new thought occurred. *Did he kill him too?* Another shudder coursed through Sydney's body as despair threatened to overcome her.

The man watched her reaction and then came to a decision. "This is the way I see it. Since Vince went to all the trouble to make the business and therefore all the money yours, he would have also found a way to get you the paperwork. So…" Walking very close, he looked hard into Sydney's dilated eyes.

When she moved to avert them, his hand clamped on her jaw. "I need you to pay close attention here, doll." The grip tightened as he added, "I believe sometime in the next week or so you're going to be contacted—maybe by phone or mail—about this paperwork." Sydney winced in pain as he warned, "At that time, you will contact me, and we'll talk again. Okay, pumpkin?"

Sydney felt faint with the pain. She was sure he meant to break her jaw to back up his warning. Suddenly, anger surged through her body, and Sydney doubled her fist. The pain in her jaw moved her beyond caring what the consequences might be. Self-preservation was coming to the forefront! Her whole body tensed as she readied herself to slug him in the gut when Sydney suddenly found herself let go. She almost fell onto the sofa behind her.

Gaining her balance, Sydney heard him quietly stress, "Are we clear?"

Unable to find her voice, Sydney nodded her head. She started to raise her trembling hands to gingerly touch her jaw but stopped as he suddenly lashed out, slapping her hard on the left cheek. "Just wanted to make sure you remembered this conversation!"

He smiled wickedly then took a couple steps back while slinging an unnoticed bag from his shoulder.

Not taking her eyes off him, Sydney willed herself to not touch her aching jaw and face as he unzipped the bag and lifted out a mask. Within seconds he'd expertly pulled it over his head and was immediately transformed into a seventies hippie with long hair and a full beard. Snuggling the neck into place, he then reached into his pocket and pulled out a small piece of paper. "Here's the number to a disposable cell phone. Call me the moment the papers come." Sydney flinched as he brought his hand back to her face. But instead of hitting her, he softly caressed the reddened spot. "Don't let me down, Syd. You're too young and pretty to end up like Vince."

He then walked to the back sliding doors. Unlocking them, he peered out into the darkness then moved to slip out. As smooth as silk he said, "Be sure to lock up after me. There are all kinds of dangerous people out there, and we want you to be safe."

With that he disappeared into the night.

Sydney wasn't able to move for a long, long time. Then she slowly walked to the door and clicked it locked. Like a robot, she turned and walked to her bedroom. She stood and looked at the bed before flinging herself across it and crying herself to sleep.

Corey Drake paused on the brick patio, allowing his eyes to adjust before moving into the dark depths of the houses. Making his way around Sydney's duplex, he came to a large clump of bushes and waited. He was puzzled. How come it had been so easy to walk into Sydney's without being challenged? Corey had noticed the man in the car long before he'd walked by, yet the officer had remained in his vehicle. As he walked up the front steps to the door, Corey heard the engine start. Out of the corner of his eye, he'd seen it pull away right when Sydney had opened the door. The car pulling away had been a surprise. Corey knew it wouldn't be that easy next time, so he took the time to study his surroundings more intently.

Right then, a pair of headlights turned onto the street, and he stepped farther into the shadows. He watched the vehicle pull back to the spot of observation and turn off his engine. Corey concluded the officer must be a rookie as he watched him pull out a sandwich and start eating.

Having seen enough, Corey melted back and made his way to the rental car parked one street over. His gut told him Sydney could be moved, and he needed her monitored. Corey pulled his cell phone and punched in the number of Vince's local man. After a terse conversation, Corey drove away.

About half an hour later, another figure appeared on the scene, taking up a position within sight of Sydney's front door but carefully out of the lone officer's line of vision.

# Chapter 9

Quaid Williams was tired but optimistic. Finally they had something to go on, however obscure it might be. After finding the mini recorder, Officer Pete had bagged it, and the two set out for an analysis and listen at the station. The recorder had done its job, picking up Vince and another man's voice, even the soft thud of a silencer and sound of something heavy falling to the floor. From that moment, until the recorder stopped, sounds of a search ensued punctuated with an occasional frustrated expletive.

Once the chip had been copied and safely stowed in Quaid's pocket, he headed to the motel for a few hours of sleep. Later that morning, Quaid reported to the chief then headed back to the Louisville police station to see if anything else had turned up. Disappointed, he went back to Vince's office for one more look and to take some pictures and then was taken to the airport for his flight home. There wasn't anything more he could do at that end; plus, he was developing concerns for Sydney's safety that he'd voiced a few minutes earlier to Paul. Having purchased his ticket, Quaid was pleased to be leaving Louisville within the hour but frustrated with being a last minute add-on, which meant he would have a three-hour layover in Detroit before heading on to Petoskey.

*At least the Louisville police are running a voice check for any known felons. The voice was clear and distinct on the recording, so maybe a match can be found.* Those thoughts were running through his mind when he walked into the Detroit terminal and made his way to the departure gate. Setting his overnight bag nearby, Quaid pulled out his phone and called Officer Pete. A short time later, he was informed a match hadn't been found. "But we're widening the parameters and trying other sources. Something may still turn up," the officer replied.

Being assured he'd be called if anything new turned up, Pete hung up, and Quaid checked his watch—10:20 p.m. Flipping his phone back open, he punched in Paul's number. Quaid knew at eleven Paul was due to relieve Jake and wanted an update. His gut was still telling him something could be wrong.

"Where are you?" his longtime partner asked.

Quaid smiled. No one could ever accuse Paul of being the chit-chatty type. He didn't have time for small talk.

"I'm sitting in the Detroit airport. I've got a three-hour layover. Unless something changes, I won't be landing in Petoskey until close to 2:30 a.m." Quaid and Paul had talked early that morning, but now Quaid filled him in on the first voice match results and what the Louisville police were trying now.

The two men grew thoughtful; then Paul said, "It's been pretty quiet at this end. Jake recently reported that Syd hasn't left the house but did receive two visitors."

"Two?" Quaid sat up in his seat. "When? Did Jake know them?"

"Slow down, partner!" Quaid heard paper rustling as Paul apparently checked his notes. "Let's see... the times were shortly after noon and nine thirty this evening, just a short while ago." Shaking off whatever thoughts were roaming through his head, Paul added, "The interesting thing is both visits were done by Pierce."

"Pierce! Are you sure?"

"Jake confirmed the ID. The first time Pierce stopped and chatted before going on to the house. Jake said he never went in. He just stood outside talking in the doorway."

"And the second? It puzzles me that Pierce returned and at such a late time of night." Quaid began talking to himself. "I imagine the first visit was to report the auction results. But why the second one? That doesn't sound like something Pierce would do, especially with the history he has with Sydney." Pulling his attention back to his partner, Quaid asked, "Did Pierce go inside the second time?"

"Yes, he did."

Alarms began ringing in Quaid's head as he hurriedly asked, "How long did he stay?"

There was no answer at the other end, and for a moment Quaid thought the call had been dropped. "Paul, are you there?"

Emitting a heavy sigh, he said, "Yes, I'm here." He paused again before stating, "Here's where our rookie made a mistake."

Quaid tensed as he waited for his partner to elaborate.

"Jake never saw Pierce come out. He left his post."

"What?"

"I know. I know. According to Jake, he'd needed to visit the bathroom for a while. When he saw Pierce, he thought that was a good time to make a quick run to the nearest gas station. He figured Sydney was safe with him."

Running his hand through his hair, Quaid said in disgust, "I don't believe this!"

"I talked with him about twenty minutes ago, and he says all seems well. I read him the riot act, but it's a little late now. He figures he was gone about twenty minutes, tops."

"So...what did Sydney say about the visit and how long Pierce stayed?"

"That was the rookie's second mistake. He never went to the door to ask her."

Quaid began short paces back and forth in front of the seat he'd just vacated. All the while his mind was racing as he clipped out questions to Paul. "Did Pierce acknowledge Jake before going in like he did the first time? Are her lights still on? Have you tried calling her? For all Jake knows, Pierce or whoever the man is could still be in there with her."

"You're right. He could be," Paul agreed. "Jake didn't mention Pierce's talking to him the second time, but he did say the lights were still on..." Paul's voice tapered off.

"Okay. This is what I want you to do. Go to Sydney's while I call Pierce. This isn't sitting right, and I need you close in case something's wrong. Pierce may be able to explain this all away, and nothing is going on. I'll get back with you shortly."

"I'm already moving!" Paul declared before his phone went dead.

Quaid willed himself to calm down. Taking his seat once more, he took a couple deep breaths then called Pierce.

He answered on the second ring.

"Pierce, buddy, I'm calling to ask if you went to see Sydney twice today."

"Twice?" Quaid could almost hear his head shaking as he added, "No. I only went once. It was shortly after lunch. I wanted to tell her—"

Quaid cut in. "I'm sorry to be rude, but this is important. My man reported that you entered Sydney's home this evening at 9:30 p.m."

"Well, he's wrong. I've spent the whole afternoon and evening right here with Hope and Sarah. It wasn't me."

"Thanks, Pierce. I'm still out of town and can't chat. I'll explain later what this call is all about. Meanwhile, please pray for Sydney. She could be in danger."

"Hope and I will do that right now."

"Thanks."

With his heart racing, Quaid called Paul. "It wasn't Pierce. Proceed with caution, and I'll call for reinforcements and an ambulance just in case."

"Roger. I'm parked right behind Jake, and we'll go investigate. I'll get back with you."

Quaid quickly called the precinct and told them the situation. Help was on its way, and there he sat, helplessly waiting in the airport.

Sydney was sound asleep when her doorbell pealed. It took a moment to realize what was happening and that the bell wasn't stopping. Hauling herself off the bed, she was vaguely aware of still being fully clothed as she stumbled toward the front door. Suddenly, memories of her recent visitor came flooding in, and Sydney came fully awake. She stopped her forward motion. Fear of her visitor returning started to assault her when she heard a siren approaching, and reason took over once more. At that moment, the siren sounded like it was right outside her door.

Raking her hands through her messy hair, Sydney observed all the lights still on as she went to unlock the door and found only the deadbolt was secured. Again memories of her visitor assailed her senses. Chills ran down her spine as she recalled the moment he had locked the door and leaned against it.

Determined to shake the memories from her head, Sydney turned the deadbolt. The doorbell ringer stopped as she swung the door open. She was startled at all the people standing there with the ambulance lights flashing. In the forefront was Detective Paul Statham. He swung the storm door open as he urgently asked, "Are you alone?"

Sydney didn't reply immediately, but when she did, she was angry.

"Yes, I'm alone. Now! No thanks to my great protection! Where were you?" Whirling, she raised her voice as Jake spoke to the EMT men. Paul, with Glock pulled, moved to do a systematic search of the premises. "I thought your job was to protect me! Some protection!"

Making short work of clearing the duplex, Paul walked back to the living room as Jake stepped into the house, shutting the door behind him. The sirens stopped, and Paul noted the ambulance pulling away as he holstered his gun. The two men faced the still ranting female before them.

As it became increasingly clear she was the only one talking, Sydney stopped her pacing to glare at Paul. In a deceptively soft voice, she asked again, "Where were you when I needed you?"

It was then the men got the full view of her face and weren't quite sure how to respond.

Sydney's eyes narrowed at their looks. She walked to the hall mirror and was horrified that her eye makeup had run, making black trails down her cheeks. It gave her a gothic look bordering on comical.

Memory of crying herself to sleep hit her. Squaring her shoulders, Sydney announced, "I need to visit the bathroom." She turned on her heels and walked away.

In her absence, the two men studied the room while Paul called Quaid. "She seems shaken up but okay. At present she's in the bathroom, and I don't see any sign of struggle here. Everything looks neat and in place. As soon as she reappears, I'll ask some questions. Her first words did indicate that she had been in some type of danger, but I don't know what yet."

Having left the bathroom door open a crack, Sydney then heard him snicker while adding, "Other than runny makeup giving her a clown look, she seems to be unharmed."

"Praise the Lord for that. Keep me posted."

When Sydney walked back into the room, the look on the men's faces reflected what she'd hoped to accomplish. Paul's words had so upset her that Sydney decided to go the other extreme. Removing all makeup, she then pulled back her blonde hair into a ponytail. Adopting a defenseless, vulnerable girl demeanor, she walked slowly forward. All the while, she was fully aware that her jaw and neck clearly revealed bruises and a reddish handprint on her left cheek.

Paul stood straight to demand, "What happened, Sydney? How'd you get the bruises? Why did you open the door to him?"

"Why did you let him even get to my front door?" she shot back.

Holding up a hand for calm, Paul quietly started again. "Sydney, I want to get to the bottom of what happened here and who … hurt you. Please take a seat and tell us what happened." Paul knew they both needed to calm down, so he took a seat and waited for her to do the same.

At mention of the bruises, Sydney's hand had involuntarily flown to her cheek. Then in a resigned manner, she sat down and began talking. "I thought it was Pierce. From the side, he looked like Pierce."

Paul shot a look at Jake, who had been staring at the floor in front of him. At her words, his eyes sought Paul's. Paul gave a slight nod but remained silent as Sydney continued.

"It wasn't until the door was all the way open and he turned to fully look at me that I realized my mistake—but then it was too late. I tried shutting the door, but he literally pushed me backwards and stepped in." She then recounted everything that happened: the attitude, the drink, the talk of paperwork, the threat and disguise. All of it right up to the moment he slipped out the back and she cried herself to sleep on the bed.

As she spoke, Paul took notes on a little pad he'd pulled from his pocket while Jake kept fidgeting and changing feet. His restlessness was starting to get on Sydney's nerves, but then she realized that he was the one who in all probability had made the same error of identity that she had. A touch of compassion hit her.

For the most part, Paul had remained quiet, only asking the occasional question for clarity. Now he asked, "Was he wearing gloves?"

Unconsciously rubbing her sore cheek, Sydney shook her head in the negative. She then noted the first sign of excitement she'd ever seen in this man as he restated, "You said he'd wanted a drink. Do you still have the glass he used?"

Sydney replayed the activities done with the man, and her eyes landed on a glass partially hidden by a plant near Paul's elbow. Pointing, she simply said, "There."

Standing, he pulled a handkerchief from his back pocket and carefully picked the glass up by the rim. He then asked, "Do you have a sealable bag I can put this in?"

Sydney went for a Ziploc bag from the kitchen, which Paul lowered the glass into. Once sealed, he was satisfied the evidence had been protected with only Sydney and her evening visitor having touched it with their hands.

Feeling much calmer now that she'd shared her story, Sydney lit a cigarette and asked again, "How did he get this close to me? Where were you?" She glanced from one man to the other wanting answers to her questions.

Paul started to answer, but Jake stepped forward asking if he could do the explaining. He then told her the circumstances of why he'd left his post and apologized. "I promise you this will not happen again on my watch!"

Sydney studied the younger man a long moment before turning her attention back to Paul. "So now what?"

"I'm calling Quaid, and we'll see," was all he volunteered.

As Sydney focused her attention back on Jake, Paul walked a discreet distance from the others to phone Quaid.

Sydney turned to Jake. "Where's Quaid? Will he be here soon?"

"He's at an airport in Detroit but is due to land in Petoskey between two thirty and three this morning."

At Jake's words, relief coursed through Sydney's body. She wouldn't admit it, but she felt safer when Quaid was around.

# Chapter 10

Quaid Williams was frustrated at being stuck in the airport and angered over the brazen behavior of the man he fully believed to be Vince's killer. Every time he thought about the man arrogantly walking right up to Sydney's door in front of a policeman, Quaid's desire to catch him grew.

Finally able to board the small jet headed to Petoskey, he felt his senses sharpen and calm. The jet made good time. Having only a carry-on, Quaid quickly made his way to his vehicle in the parking lot and headed to Sydney's home. After a detailed conference with Paul and being reassured that men were now stationed discreetly all around her home, Quaid took his exhausted body home. Before leaving Detroit, his chief had set up an appointment for the two detectives to meet him for a late lunch the next day.

When Quaid finally rolled into his own bed, it was close to 5:30 a.m. He punched the pillow into shape in preparation for sleep, but it wouldn't come. His mind kept replaying all the events of the last few days. The thought of the man hitting Sydney made his blood boil! She was his responsibility, and he was determined to not let that happen again. Just before falling asleep, Quaid knew it was time to move Sydney to a safer place, and it needed to be done quickly. "The sooner the better," he said softly to the starting dawn as he drifted off to sleep.

Sunday afternoon, a rested Quaid walked into the restaurant ready to take action. Spotting the chief and Paul already seated at a table, he made his way over to them while wondering if his partner had gotten any sleep since he'd last seen him. Taking a seat, he studied Paul's face and was relieved to see his eyes rested and alert. Turning his focus to the chief, Quaid asked about the glass Paul had turned into the lab.

"Darla was able to lift a couple of perfect prints, but so far, no matches have turned up," the chief replied.

"Well, that means he's either not there, or we're not looking in the right place," Quaid observed.

"What do you mean?" Paul inquired as the waitress walked up with her hands full of drinks. Knowing his partner's taste, Paul had ordered Quaid a large root beer. Having handed out the drinks, the waitress stood by waiting for their order. The men suspended talking until orders were placed, and the waitress moved away.

Quaid took a long sip of his cold, frothy mug of root beer then explained. "I'm not sure yet what I mean. But this guy is slick. It's almost like he knew of his resemblance to Pierce. For crying out loud, he walked right up to the house! You can't convince me a man that sharp didn't notice the car sitting there with our man in it. That was a bold move."

## Out of the Snare

"Or dumb luck," Paul offered.

The men drew quiet again as bread and salads arrived. The chief watched his men silently bow their heads to say grace then dive into their salads. Smiling, he asked, "Hungry, boys?" before stating, "Either way, the man's no two-bit operator. I have a feeling we're going to have the run for our money on this one. Look how smoothly he took care of Vince Edgar."

"If you ask me, he's arrogant, and we all know that type gets cocky. Sooner or later they always slip up. Let's pray it's sooner not later this time."

"You're right, Quaid. This man is a murderer, and it's probably not his first time. We'll run the MO and see if there are any similar unsolved ones, but I have a feeling we won't come up with anything. I think this guy adapts his murders to the situation."

"We also need to remember that he still needs Sydney at least for now. He's looking for some paperwork that he's convinced will show up here," Paul thoughtfully replied.

The main meal arrived, and the men grew quiet once more as they sampled their various cuts of meat.

After the waitress walked away, Quaid stated, "In my book, Vince Edgar was one smart man; that's for sure. Imagine him putting everything in Sydney's name! But what did he do with all the paperwork? A whole crew of men, including me, thoroughly went over that office. We found only the recorder and the usual stuff for his type of work, nothing about the bogus company."

"Well, I tend to agree with Miss Turner's visitor. That paperwork will find its way to her sooner or later. We just have to keep an eye out for it," the chief stated.

The three men ate on as the conversation flowed to Sydney's relocation and how to handle it. Little by little a plan evolved, and it was decided that first thing Monday morning the chief would contact the judge. "I'll bring him up to date and ask for the tether to be removed off her ankle. I also think I'll mention bringing in

U.S. Marshals to help if needed in the future. It can't hurt to have that step already taken just in case. But as to the location, that information remains between the judge and the three of us until she's actually in the new location; then we'll let others in the loop on a need-to-know basis."

The men then sifted through places they'd used in the past, but none seemed right. Quaid couldn't explain why, but his gut told him it needed to be someplace not normally used.

He remembered a friend's summer home on Beaver Island. "It's on its own private drive that's way off the main road. In fact, the drive looks like a two-tracking road leading into state owned property. Most people don't even notice it when driving by. The home is beautifully located on a slight bluff with steps leading down to a private beach and dock. It's located on the east side, so the ferry boat is easily seen as it crosses from Charlevoix. There are at least four bedrooms. So there's plenty of space to house those of us watching Sydney, and it's available. My friends just left to spend a couple months in Europe."

The chief liked the idea, so he told him to check into it. Whipping out his cell phone, Quaid got them on the line. Not wanting to reveal Sydney's involvement, Quaid said it was for him to take a much-needed break. A few minutes later, his friends willingly offered their home for Quaid to enjoy a couple months of supposed rest and relaxation.

Once that was settled, the chief turned to Paul and said, "I want you to get the current timetable for the ferry and see if it's possible to make this happen as soon as Tuesday morning."

At the mention of the ferry, Paul's head came up. "Why not fly her in? Why take the chance with the slower mode of the ferry?"

"I don't want her standing out. I plan to send Maria Lopez along to make this a couples' outing—you know—to explore the island and fall colors. Maria is currently between undercover jobs, and she's good. Besides, only the three of us know she's in town. Now, back to why not fly? If we flew her in, it's a much smaller crowd, and someone just might be apt to notice and remember the four of you. We don't want that. You need to blend in with a crowd."

The two detectives looked at each other and then nodded their agreement with the chief's thoughts.

The chief leaned back, let out a satisfied sigh, and took a long sip of hot coffee. Then he looked his two top detectives in the eyes. "Men, our job is to protect Abigail Turner and catch the man who murdered her partner. He's already gotten past us once; I don't want it happening again! Paul, you called me the other night about someone eyeing her place at night. Any more info?"

This was news to Quaid, and he leaned forward with interest.

"One of my PI friends has a bead on a local who does bit jobs on the side. We got his phone records and found several calls coming from Louisville, but they stopped last week. Then last night he received one marked restricted. That usually means an untraceable, disposable phone. We've got eyes on him, but he hasn't gone near her place until last night. I caught sight of him, but I don't think he knows I saw him." He then turned to his partner and quickly added, "Sorry, I meant to catch you up on all this, but it slipped my mind with everything else happening last night."

The chief interrupted with, "Quaid, if this guy's as smart as we think, he's going to enlist more help, probably through this local contact."

"I agree. He's bound to figure us moving her now that he's made contact. He'll need to know where she's taken, and that requires more eyes. We'll get a list of buddies the local guy might bring on board for some easy cash."

"Boys, so far we have a voice and prints that aren't matching any known criminals in our database, which makes this man practically invisible to us. I don't like it! Not only that, he's good with disguises. We've got our work cut out for us, but I have complete confidence that you are the two for this task. Let's catch this guy!"

Standing, the chief pulled out his wallet and tossed a large tip on the table as he prepared to leave. "I've assigned four more men—two on days and two for nights. Paul, let me know the ferry timetable out of Charlevoix. I'll be in touch about the judge."

The chief detained them near the vehicles. "One last thing. Once you're at the safe house, I want Maria on the inside and the two of you taking turns on night detail. Once we get Neal and Jake with you, then you guys set up what feels most comfortable. Something tells me this man's a prowler, more comfortable under cover of night. Abigail's safe for tonight, and I need both of you fresh and ready for whatever may come. Take the rest of today off."

As the three parted ways, Quaid considered the chief's words then headed his Hummer towards Sydney's.

It was Sunday afternoon, and Pierce, Hope, and baby Sarah were coming for a visit. Sydney had mixed feelings about it, but as Quaid had pointed out just a few minutes earlier, "The woman gave you $72,400 worth of crystal! Can't you even be kind enough to thank her in person?"

In spite of trying to appear indifferent to Quaid's presence and criticisms, Sydney had to admit that he looked good—healthy and strong. She had confidence in his ability to watch over her, and that was a great comfort. So, pushing aside any ill feelings toward the upcoming visit, she checked her face in the mirror as she heard Quaid fixing himself a glass of iced tea in the kitchen. He'd relieved the inside man for a few hours and would remain until after the visitors left and Detective Jake came back for the night shift.

Admiring the heavily made-up face staring back at her in the mirror, Sydney smiled and stated softly, "I may have lost out on Pierce, but there are plenty of other fish in the sea." Checking her snug pants and top, she blew a kiss to herself and then turned to walk into the kitchen. Putting on a flirty pout, she whined, "Aren't you going to pour one for me?"

Quaid had been leaning against the counter while sipping his tea. As he went to reply, the doorbell pealed announcing the guests. "Actually, no. But you can be a good little hostess and wait on your guests. I'm sure a nice glass of tea will sound good to them." Chuckling, he went to answer the door as Sydney shot daggers at his retreating back.

The moment the threesome entered, Sydney knew something was different with them. Frowning, she tried to figure out what as she asked them to take a seat. Her eyes narrowed as she observed Pierce touch Hope's elbow. A little while later, she witnessed a lovely blush spread across Hope's cheek as he leaned in to speak in her ear. A fierce feeling of jealousy leapt into Sydney's eyes and face.

After opening Sydney's front door, Quaid sat at the kitchen table. It gave him the advantage of observing all going on in the living room. Knitting his brows, Quaid thoughtfully studied the three adults as an earlier conversation with Pierce came to mind.

Shortly after leaving the restaurant, his cell had gone off. It was Pierce. He was wondering if he and Hope could pay Sydney a visit that afternoon. Pierce had then added, "We think it's time to tell her about Hope and me; plus, the Lord's been prompting Hope to tell Sydney about her namesake in the Bible."

It took Quaid a moment to think that last comment through, as he couldn't recall a Sydney in the Bible. Then, hitting the steering wheel, he had chided himself that her real name was Abigail, not Sydney. Assuring Pierce he thought a visit would be good, Quaid also voiced, "Besides, as far as I know, she hasn't thanked Hope for the generous gift of the money raised from the crystal auction."

"I'm sure Hope isn't coming for that reason," Pierce had quickly replied.

"I know, but Sydney's not a very grateful person. She needs to work on her manners."

Pierce had grown silent then quietly observed, "Hope made a comment the other day that hasn't left me. She said that none of us know what kind of upbringing Sydney had. She could be full of emotional scars and bitterness that led her to the predicament she's in today."

Now, thinking about that conversation and coupling it with the emotions playing on Sydney's face, Quaid tended to agree with Hope's words.

Deciding to take a hand in the situation before it got out of control, Quaid piped up. "Pierce, I understand you have some news for Sydney."

Startled, Sydney flashed a look at Quaid then back to the couple now seated near each other on the sofa. Her eyes narrowed as the two of them exchanged looks, and then Hope extended her left hand. "We're engaged. Pierce proposed to me Labor Day evening."

Sydney froze. Turning toward the stuffed chair nearby, she tried to compose herself. She took a seat and pasted a false smile on her face. "Well, isn't that nice." She then changed the subject. "Did you hear that Vince's murderer paid me a visit last night?"

The shocked look on Hope's face brought a smug look to Sydney's as she became center stage once more.

Hope pulled her hand back as she turned her head toward Quaid. "Is that true?" He nodded, and Hope's attention flew back to Sydney.

At that point, Pierce stood. Picking up baby Sarah, who had been playing in the center of the floor, he said, "Hope, wasn't there something else you wanted to talk to Sydney about?"

With hardened eyes, Sydney watched Pierce pick up Sarah, walk to the kitchen, and then the two men took her outside to the patio. When Hope cleared her throat and took a deep breath, Sydney frowned.

Hope stiffened when Sydney suddenly came to her feet. "If you're going to lecture me about not calling with a thank you, save it!" Here Sydney paused. The next words were harder to utter than she'd expected. Forcing them through stiff lips, she stated, "Thank you."

Sydney plopped unladylike back into the chair she'd recently vacated. An awkward silence filled the room.

Hope cleared her throat once more before saying, "Actually, that wasn't what I was going to talk to you about. But... thank you for acknowledging the gift. Sydney, the crystal honestly doesn't need to be mentioned between us again. The gift was given and sold, and now it's over. Okay?"

Hope looked kindly at Sydney. Other than a slight nod of her head, Sydney said nothing. Gathering her thoughts once more, Hope asked, "Did you know there was an Abigail in the Bible?"

Taken totally off guard, Sydney's face went blank as she asked, "What?"

"In the Old Testament there's a story about a very brave woman, and her name was Abigail. Have you heard it?"

"No."

"May I tell you about her?"

Sydney shrugged her shoulders and sunk deeper into the chair. Studying her nails, she replied indifferently, "Sure."

Hope pulled the nearby diaper bag into her lap and unzipped it. "First off, I wonder. Do you own a Bible?"

Caught off guard again, Sydney slowly shook her head in the negative.

"Well, you do now." Hope pulled a maroon colored leather Bible from the bag and patted the seat beside her. "Pierce and I would love to give you this one. If you don't mind, let's use it to read Abigail's story together."

Sydney wasn't sure how to respond to Hope's enthusiastic, expectant face. The last thing she wanted to do right now was a Bible study with Hope. She considered saying no, but thoughts of Quaid and how he would react came surging into her mind. Darting her eyes toward the back, Sydney sighed then pushed herself out of the chair to sit beside Hope.

For the next half hour, Sydney listened in wonder to a story that stayed with her the remainder of the evening. The story touched Sydney's heart and kept her awake long into the night as the biblical Abigail's bravery and honesty kept replaying in her mind.

# Chapter 11

Abigail was married to a very rich man named Nabal. She was a woman of good understanding and beautiful appearance, but her husband was harsh and evil in his dealings.

One day Abigail was walking through her extensive palace gardens when a young man came running toward her. "Madam, Madam, I must speak with you. It's urgent!" he said breathlessly.

Abigail's long skirt swished as she turned to face the young man.

At that moment, a palace guard latched on to his arm preparing to haul him away, but Abigail waved him back. "Come here, young man. What is it? What has you so distressed?"

## Out of the Snare

With great respect, the young man bowed at her feet. Upon rising, he rapidly told his story.

"His appointed Highness, King David, and his men were visiting our lands for many days. He heard Nabal was shearing sheep during feast time, so he sent ten of his young men to your husband requesting food. I was standing near and heard their words. They reminded your husband how during the days here they hadn't harmed any of your shearers nor taken any of the sheep. In fact, and this I know from personal experience for I was there, David had charged his men to protect us during the night hours from any harm." The young man paused to take a breath.

Abigail had been listening attentively and had a feeling what the man was about to say. Her heart grew anxious as she took a garden seat. Her attendants stood nearby fanning her with palm leaves as Abigail asked the young man to continue.

"Well, Your Ladyship, Nabal rudely refused to give David food and sent his men away! My lady, David is a great man and warrior. This will be an insult, and he will gather his men and come! I fear for this household! I fear for all of us!"

Abigail jumped to her feet as her heart threatened to beat out of her chest. "We must act quickly!" Within seconds several servants came running. "Prepare food! Lots of it!" she commanded. They ran to do her bidding. Turning to her handmaids, she further instructed, "I need my donkey readied and my clothes changed. I must intercede and plead on our behalf!"

As the entourage made their way toward Abigail's private quarters, they pleaded with her, "But my lady, what if he won't listen? What if he kills you and us too?"

"I will go in the name and power of God!" she humbly replied.

Meanwhile, the ten men had returned to David and given their report. He was indeed very angry and ordered four hundred of his best men to grab their swords. David put his on too. They headed toward the palace. Because of Nabal, the king had every intention of killing every man in the city.

Abigail's staff moved quickly, and she soon headed out with the food and with many servants and handmaids. As they rounded a hill, there coming across the valley was David and his army. Fear coursed through Abigail's veins as the two parties drew near to each other.

Then suddenly everything changed in Sydney's dream.

David turned into Sydney's night visitor and brandished a gun, not a sword; her ladyship turned into Sydney! As Sydney drew closer, her helpers all disappeared. She stood alone before the menacing man and his army. Perspiration ran down her cheeks as her inner being yelled, "Don't fight him! Join him! He'll kill you just like he did Vince!"

A snare suddenly appeared at her feet and began coiling like a snake around her ankles. Sydney stared as her feet became unmovable. In horror she sought to break free but couldn't.

The stranger was now very close. He stuck a gun to her temple. "Give me the paperwork, or you die right now!"

Sydney began screaming for her life when in the distance she heard two voices. One was a familiar man's voice yelling, "I'm coming, Sydney!"

The other voice? She wasn't sure if it was a man's or ... God's?

Sydney stopped screaming to listen more intently to the quiet, calm voice, but she lost it when a bright light hit her face. Covering her eyes, Sydney came awake drenched with sweat. It took her a moment to realize she'd been dreaming and that Trooper Jake was standing by her bed with his gun drawn asking if she was all right.

Sydney assured him she was fine. After he left the room, she went to her bathroom for a drink of water and wet washcloth to bathe her face. Calming, she walked back to her bed and straightened the messy blankets before climbing in.

Sydney willed herself to concentrate on the biblical Abigail. The dream had closely followed the story Hope had recently told her. She then remembered how very brave Abigail had been. She had met David and his men coming toward her. Quickly getting off her donkey, Her Ladyship had done something foreign to Sydney—she bowed herself to the ground while pleading mercy for her household and scoundrel husband. Sydney remembered that at this point in the story she'd questioned if the Bible really had used the word *scoundrel*. Hope had then turned the Bible toward Sydney to show her 1 Samuel 25:25; it read *scoundrel husband.*

Unlike Sydney, the biblical Abigail was a woman of many words, but David listened to her long speech and heeded her pleas. Thanking her for coming, he took the food she'd prepared, told her to go in peace, and turned around.

As Sydney's heart slowed back to normal, she recalled what happened next, for this part was something Sydney could relate to.

All that time, Nabal had no clue what his wife was doing. He was partying! In fact, when Abigail got home, she went to tell him but found him drunk and knew he wouldn't remember a word she said. So she waited until the next morning. Nursing a hangover, Nabal listened to his wife's story. When he fully realized how close he'd come to being killed, Nabal suffered a bad heart attack and died ten days later.

When Sydney thought of Nabal, images of her stepfather surfaced along with memories of abuse, bitterness, and anger. Sydney dwelt on this a long time until she remembered there was still more to the story.

When David heard of Nabal's death, he sent servants to propose marriage on his behalf to Abigail. She had risen in haste, got her personal stuff together, and with five handmaids followed David's servants back to become one of his three wives.

Finally growing sleepy once more, Sydney thought about the customs of that day and realized that Abigail probably thought that was a happy ending. As Sydney drifted back to sleep, she mumbled, "Happy endings only happen in fairy tales!"

Early the next morning, Sydney woke to the sound of someone banging on her bedroom door. "Wake up! We have to go see the judge!"

It took her a moment to recognize Quaid's voice. She was surprised to hear it.

Yesterday her visitors had left before 6:30 p.m., and shortly after, Detective Jake made his appearance. The two detectives had exchanged quiet words. Then Jake took over, and Quaid had left.

Sydney's eyes traveled to her clock, and she groaned. Pulling the covers close to her chin, she decided to ignore him.

"Sydney! Get up! I'll give you ten minutes. If you're not out here by then, I'm coming in."

Knowing he meant every word, Sydney threw the covers off. "Fine! I'm up! Give me half an hour to dress and do my makeup."

"No can do. The judge ordered us to have you in his chambers no later than eight fifteen. So move it! I've got Eggos in the toaster. Paul brought coffee. Skip the makeup."

Sydney threw an angry look toward the door while hurrying to her private bathroom. She splashed water in her face then inspected bags under her eyes and the bruises on her jaw.

More pounding hit the door. "You've got six minutes, and then I'm coming in!"

Sydney quickly ran the hairbrush through her hair to gather it back in a ponytail. She next rapidly applied mascara to her lashes. Skipping the eyeliner, she went for her bottled makeup when Quaid's voice sounded once more.

"Four minutes."

Reluctantly setting the makeup down, Sydney reached instead for her watch. Being the bracelet type, she snapped it on her wrist while hurrying back to the closet.

"Time's up!"

As the knob rattled, a fully dressed Sydney grabbed it and flung the door open. After delivering a glare at her tormentor, she arrogantly walked into the living room with Quaid close at her heels.

With her back to him, Sydney missed the anger that had briefly crossed Quaid's face at sight of the bruises.

Paul stood by the front door grinning with two steaming Styrofoam coffees. Handing her one, he glanced over her shoulder. Getting an okay nod from his partner, Paul wheeled to open the door, stepping out first. Sydney followed him with Quaid bringing up the rear of their little parade. He carried his own coffee, napkins, and the warm Eggos.

At precisely 8:12 a.m., the trio walked into the judge's private chambers with Quaid and Paul flanking Sydney's sides, a hand on each of her elbows. Sydney felt like a criminal as she walked in with her two bookends. In spite of the room's rich décor and spaciousness, Sydney felt confined and nervous, which wasn't helped when the door shut behind the trio. Her eyes darted around the room. A massive mahogany desk was situated to the right of a back door. Three large, dark, leather stuffed chairs faced the desk, and Sydney noticed a sizeable space between them and the desk. Into this space, she was led. Sydney moved to take a seat but was kept in a standing position by Quaid and Paul.

A moment later the judge walked in from the back door and took his seat.

Taking a good look at Sydney, he stated, "You look different."

Glancing briefly sideways at Quaid, she tried shaking his hand loose as her face reddened. "I didn't have enough time to put my usual makeup on, Judge."

"Then leave it off!" he stated. "You look much better without it."

Sydney felt the two men beside her nod their agreement with the judge's statement. Thoroughly irritated with all men present, she started to argue but refrained when Quaid gave her arm a subtle squeeze. Sydney stiffened but remained silent.

The judge squinted his eyes and leaned forward to ask, "Did you get those bruises from your night visitor of the other evening?"

"Yes, Your Honor."

Sydney felt Quaid's hand tense at the judge's question but kept her focus forward.

The judge thought about that a moment and then began asking questions of the two men. Much discussion took place between the three before the judge directed his attention back to Sydney.

"Miss Turner, I agree with these men that your life could possibly be in danger. Therefore, I'm setting some protective measures in place. First of all, the tether will be removed before you leave here today. Then tomorrow you'll be taken to an undisclosed location to be guarded around the clock until this situation can be resolved. Hopefully, that won't be long." The judge then began organizing some papers lying on the desk in front of him.

Sydney was starting to grow tired of standing so took turns switching from one foot to the other. That is until she felt a familiar squeeze on her elbow. Resentment coursed through her as she held still while shooting daggers Quaid's direction.

Finally the judge spoke. "Miss Turner, these changes do not negate the financial debt you still owe, but under the circumstances, the deadline will be waived until after this situation is resolved."

For the first time, Sydney smiled and relaxed her stance.

Noting her new attitude, the judge leaned forward to look hard into her eyes. "It may seem to you that I'm going easy on you, but I'm not. You will now be under constant protection, and unless these two men decide otherwise, you won't be allowed any free time alone. And I remind you, you're still under house arrest." Seeing her smile disappear and her body go straighter, the judge decided to push a point home. "Miss Turner, if your life is in danger, then these men are taking risks on your behalf. If you do anything foolish that makes their job more difficult, I will see to it that you regret it! Do you understand me?"

Sydney tensed as the words and warning struck home. For the first time, it actually registered that it wasn't just her life that could be in danger. Glancing at Quaid's profile, she had a sudden fear for his safety. She marveled at how calm he appeared as he stared ahead at the judge.

Forgetting where she was, Sydney jumped when the judge suddenly demanded, "Do you understand me?"

Sydney stammered as she pulled her eyes off Quaid. "Yes ... s ... s, Judge, I understand."

"Good!" Picking up his papers, the judge turned his attention to the two detectives. With obvious respect and approval, he nodded his head while saying, "Go in safety, men."

Lowering his eyes back to his desk, he waved his arm in dismissal. "You may go now. My clerk will see to getting the tether off her ankle."

# Chapter 12

Early Tuesday morning Sydney was headed to an unknown destination with Detectives Quaid, Paul, and a new traveling companion, Officer Maria Lopez. Being a woman who loved center stage, Sydney usually got the upper hand when other women came around, but this one didn't seem in the least intimidated by her. Maria was an obviously tough lady who meant what she said, and it was all packaged in a small, athletic, feminine body. Having arrived during the night while Sydney slept, Maria awoke her well before dawn.

After getting herself around, Sydney was further surprised to find yet another woman in the living room putting on a long blonde wig. Her name was Tressa. The plan was for her to be a decoy, hopefully to fool whoever might be watching into thinking Sydney was still in the home. They all hoped to have a few days lead on Sydney's night visitor, who they now knew had stationed a couple local men in a house just down the street.

Not wanting any lights on, the group worked mainly with the drapes drawn and wide beam flashlights. After a quick cold breakfast, Maria took Sydney back in the bedroom to pack a large suitcase. She was also instructed to pack a small emergency one in case they had to leave the new place quickly. Spying the maroon covered Bible on the dresser, Sydney thought about the story of Abigail. She almost reached to include it but changed her mind. Turning away, she finished packing the suitcases.

Once all were packed, Maria focused on Sydney's disguise. Surveying her critically, she said, "You need to wear something more conservative."

Sydney glanced down at her tight jeans and low-cut top then replied, "What's wrong with this outfit? This is the way I dress, and I'm not changing!"

Maria dropped the subject while pulling a short brown wig from a bag. She soon had it snugly in place with Sydney's ample hair hidden inside. As Sydney moved to put on her makeup, Maria called the men in for a quick conference, and it was decided that less makeup made the better disguise. Glaring suspiciously at Quaid's face, Sydney tried to argue but found herself summarily outvoted. Allowing her only mascara and enough powder and blush to cover her bruises, Sydney grudgingly packed the rest of her makeup in the suitcase.

Once in the living room, Quaid started explaining the plan but paused as he got a better look at Sydney. "You need to go put a different top on, something more conservative."

The two had an ensuing silent war of the eyes. After letting out a disgusted grunt, Sydney wheeled to march back into her bedroom. Finding a shirt, she flung it on over her scooped top. Returning to the living room, she planted herself in front of Quaid before pointedly buttoning it up all the way to her throat.

Quaid further infuriated her by stating, "Good. Now get your coat on while I finish explaining the plan."

Playacting was in order. The four of them would be having a day out as two couples. Then, without warning, Quaid stepped close to Sydney, throwing his arm around her shoulders. Adopting a boyfriend's voice and mannerism, he said, "So, sweetheart, you're my girl for the day."

Stiffening, Sydney tried getting away while retorting, "This isn't going to work. I should be with Paul."

With one raised eyebrow, Quaid flashed a glance at his partner before replying, "Sorry, doll. You're too tall for him. I'm a better fit. Besides…" Here he dropped his arm to walk toward the front door. "You're looking a little too plain for our party boy over here. That pairing would never be convincing."

Sydney was so shocked at being called plain that she couldn't find her voice. She was further humiliated by the smiles on the other two faces. She finally blurted, "Plain! You snob! You arrogant snob!"

Quaid shut his flashlight off and then turned before opening the front door. There was just enough of the morning dawn to outline his torso. His words were serious now. "Sorry for the tease. This really isn't a game. It's essential that anyone we meet see us as normal couples. Can you do that? Your life could depend on it."

The gravity of the situation hit her, and a momentary vision of Vince's dead body floated to the front of her mind. Trying desperately to push the vivid picture away, Sydney focused her frustration on Quaid. With a tight voice, she answered, "Yes, yes I can."

"Good. We'll be taking Maria's car with the two of them in the front, Paul driving. We'll be in the back with you seated behind Paul."

Sydney started to protest when Quaid smoothly interrupted, "Are you going to argue everything with me?" Not allowing her time to respond, he patiently explained as if to a child, "Having you in the backseat makes it harder for anyone to identify you versus you being very visible in the front."

Once the door was open, the foursome moved quickly. Paul took the lead so he could extinguish the car's interior overhead light. The group was soon heading west out of town toward Traverse City on the scenic lakeside road.

Quaid's words about Sydney being plain still chaffed at her, so she ignored any attempt he made with casual conversation. Since the car was headed out of town, the backseat was dark, so Sydney took the opportunity to undo the top three buttons of her shirt. The car was silent for about ten minutes when Sydney's curiosity got the better of her. Through gritted teeth, she asked, "So where's this safe place you're taking me to?"

"Beaver Island," Quaid quietly replied. He then added, "We'll be driving the car right onto the ferry. Once on board, they won't allow us to remain in the vehicle, so we'll have to get out. There won't be any restaurant, just a vending area, so we'll get something to drink and then make our way topside to locate a seat. I'd prefer it to be private yet not reclusive. We don't want to draw attention to ourselves. It's important that we act normal. We're just two normal men out for the day with our girls."

A funny chill ran up Sydney's spine when he said the words *our girls*. Thankful the car was not light enough for him to notice any unnatural redness in her face, Sydney turned her attention to the view outside her window.

Sydney knew that Quaid had doubts that she could pull off pretending to be his girlfriend. Sensing he might be gearing up for another lecture on the point, she asked a question while continuing to stare out her window.

"Where is Beaver Island? How far do we go to get the ferry?"

Quaid leaned forward to ask, "Maria, do you happen to have a Michigan map?"

Maria found one in the glove box. Showing interest, Sydney turned her attention forward. Maria smiled at her when she handed the map back.

Opening it halfway, Quaid leaned toward Sydney. The rising sun made it easy for him to point out a little land mass situated just north. "This is Beaver Island. We board the ferry here." He moved his finger slightly southeast to Charlevoix. "The ride takes about two hours." Turning his dark eyes to hers, he added, "If you let yourself, you might even enjoy the trip. The weather's supposed to be nice, so the water should be calm. Since we're moving into fall when the leaves turn, the scenery on the shoreline should start being colorful."

Satisfied he'd answered her question, Quaid refolded the map, handed it forward, and leaned back in the seat.

Sydney turned her attention back to the window. The sun had now risen, and she was noting some billboards. One in particular caught her attention, *Beware of Satan's Snares!* followed by the name of a church group. The words sent chills up her spine, and she made a mental note to sometime ask Quaid what it meant.

Ten minutes later the silent group drove through Charlevoix to the pier. Vehicles were already stacked up to go aboard, so Paul joined the growing line. As the group inched forward, excitement grew in Sydney as she thought about taking her first boat ride.

Noting her excited expression in the rearview mirror, Paul asked, "Are you prone to motion sickness? We forgot to ask. We may need to get some tablets for you before boarding."

"I've never been on a boat before, but I don't think there will be a problem."

Quaid piped up, "I thought you lived near Louisville. All those beautiful dinner boats cruising the Ohio River and you never ate on one?"

Sydney stared unseeing at the nearby water as she stiffly replied, "They were above my pay grade." Before he could voice anything about her well-paid now-deceased boyfriend, she added, "Vince and I were seldom in public together. I'm sure you can understand why."

Quaid grew thoughtful then asked, "I've been curious about how the silent partner became involved with you two."

"I honestly don't know. It's been a puzzle to me, and I'm wondering why he didn't care that I saw his face the other night."

Quaid knew that usually meant the perpetrator didn't have fears the witness would live to tell anyone his description. Instead of alarming her with the truth, he asked a question. "Sydney, you said you seldom went in public with Vince, but did you a few times?"

"Actually, it was only once, and that was by accident. I came across him eating in an open food court at the mall. He must have been in a hurry, for that wasn't the norm for him. Vince was an expensive place kind of guy. Anyway, he was alone, so I sat down. It didn't make him very happy, and he kept looking around in case he saw someone he knew. That made me mad, and we got in an argument."

"Was anyone sitting nearby?"

"Sure. Lots of people, but I didn't care! I was tired of being the closet girlfriend and wanted him to give me some of the money he'd taken."

"So you talked about the…um…project you two were engaged in?"

"Yeah, we did. It probably wasn't very smart of me."

As the vehicle approached its turn to be driven onto the ferry, Quaid asked one more question. "Can you remember if this happened anytime near the new partner showing up?"

Sydney went quiet as she thought back to the argument and suddenly grew more animated. "Now that you mention it, shortly after that Vince told me he'd been contacted by a stranger who threatened to expose us if we didn't let him in." Temporarily forgetting her animosity, Sydney turned expressive eyes to Quaid's. "How could a stranger know our names and how to contact Vince? After the short argument, Vince rushed me out of there. He didn't go back in. I know because I stood on the sidewalk watching him walk back to his office a couple blocks away." Sadness crept across her face as pictures of the now dead Vince once again played in her mind. Turning vulnerable eyes back to Quaid's, Sydney asked, "Are these questions important?"

"Anything's important if it helps us catch Vince's murderer."

A shiver shook Sydney's body as she sighed heavily and turned to stare blindly out the side window.

The conversation ended as the vehicle pulled on the ferry, but Sydney's questions kept playing in Quaid's mind.

Once on the ferry, the men opened their car doors and got out. Paul walked to Maria's door and opened it for her. Quaid moved to do the same, but Sydney was already standing by the car. His eyes quietly admonished her about the role the two needed to be playing. Lowering her eyes, Sydney defensively stated, "I'm not used to men opening my door. I'll try to remember next time."

Letting the issue drop, Quaid extended his hand. "Shall we go topside?"

Sydney hesitated then slipped her hand into his. Determined to play her part to the hilt, she pasted a dazzling smile on her lips and breathlessly said, "Come on, handsome, let's go join the others."

Quaid studied Sydney's flirty look before leaning in to whisper, "Let's tone it down a notch." Keeping a firm hold of her hand, he expertly guided her to the landing above. Once topside, the foursome purchased drinks then made their way to some benches along the railing so they could enjoy the water once the ferry shoved off.

Observing the other couple with them, Sydney was amazed at how easily Maria and Paul fell into their roles. If she hadn't known better, even she would have thought they were a couple. They seemed totally absorbed with each other but not in a showy, unnatural way. Glancing sideways at Quaid, she noted he was more interested in people boarding and taking positions around the deck than in her seated beside him. She knew he was watching for any suspicious people, but his earlier slur about her looks still rankled. Feeling like stirring up a little trouble, she slid closer to Quaid and deliberately placed her hand on his thigh. A vicious delight coursed through her as she felt his leg muscle tense.

Quickly lifting her hand, Quaid leaned his face down to hers until their foreheads were almost touching. Squeezing her hand, he whispered, "Do that again, and I'll break your finger!" For emphasis he gave her much smaller hand another squeeze before sitting back and letting it go.

Sydney rubbed her sore fingers. "You told me to act like your girlfriend!"

Quaid tilted his head as he pasted a smile on his face. He then reached for her hand once more. To Sydney's consternation, he began gently massaging it while softly saying, "Yes, my sweet. I did. So that means you need to act like a lady, not a hussy!"

Sydney's face grew crimson as she tried pulling her hand from his.

Quaid fueled her evident anger by chuckling. "Sydney, we can have a nice, relaxing time here if you'll just be good."

Taking a deep breath, Sydney started to argue when the boat swayed, throwing her next to Quaid's body. Taking advantage of her nearness, he pulled her hand through the crook of his arm and held her close as the ferry began moving away from the dock. Not realizing what she was doing, Sydney clenched Quaid's arm with her other hand as the excitement of her first ferry ride chased all other thoughts from her mind.

Quaid watched Sydney's unguarded face fill with almost childlike excitement. It caused Quaid to wonder again about her growing up years. He decided to try harder at building a friendship and finding out why Sydney went the path she had. *Maybe I'll even be able to build a bridge toward seriously talking about the reality of Jesus Christ and the Word of God.* But for now, Quaid determined to enjoy what he could of the beautiful fall morning while staying alert to protect Sydney. Glancing Paul's way, the two exchanged looks confirming that no one seemed to be paying them any undue attention.

Relaxing, Quaid stretched his long legs out in front of him, tipped his ball cap slightly down, and rubbed his thumb over Sydney's still captive hand. For all intents and purposes, he looked like a man enjoying a great boat ride with his favorite girl.

"She's gone!"

"What? How long ago?"

"You know that house you rented us on her street worked out great, but... they pulled a fast one on us."

"How long has she been gone?" Corey asked again impatiently.

"Maybe three hours."

The Petoskey man could feel the anger coming across the phone with the next question. "If the police pulled a fast one, how do you know she's gone?"

"That's the lucky part! My friend Buddy just called. He saw her."

"Where?"

"She's on a ferry heading to Beaver Island."

There was a heavy silence then, "Is he sure it's her?"

"Buddy said he didn't recognize her at first, for she's wearing a short brown wig and not much makeup. But then he and his girl walked closer to make sure. It's her all right. Oh, and she's with two men and another woman. He said the other woman looked Latin."

"How does this Buddy know Syd?"

"We've both seen her around town. She's a party girl or was before her house arrest. She liked frequenting the local dives. She never gave us the time of day though, thought she was too good or something, but we noticed her plenty. Sydney likes being noticed, you know. She wore tight, low-cut clothes that revealed a lot... if you know what I mean. It was her all right."

Corey had thought of interrupting but let the guy ramble so he could concentrate on what to do about this latest development. The police had moved her quicker than he'd anticipated. He could kick himself for underestimating the two men guarding her. His research had revealed they were top-notch men who were known to be tough and good at their job. Out loud he asked, "You said they're on a ferry? Where is this Beaver Island? Is a ferry the only way to get there?"

## Out of the Snare

"It's an island in Lake Michigan just north of Charlevoix. It's a two-hour ferry ride, but you can also fly there. I know there's a small airport and possibly a private one too."

"How big is this island? Does it have paved roads?"

"The island is, I'd say, oh, about four to six miles by thirteen miles. There's one main paved road that kind of edges the whole island with a cut-across road halfway down. The majority of houses are on the north and east sides."

By this time, Corey had located an atlas and spotted the island quickly. He grew quiet as the man rambled on.

Not hearing anything, the man asked, "Boss, are you still there?"

"Her getting away from you upsets me, and I don't like being upset! Do you read me?"

"I do, boss. I sure do! What can I do to make you happy again?"

"Call Buddy back. Tell him to follow them and find exactly where they go on the island. He needs to be discreet! These cops are sharp. If I'm happy with his info, I'll make it worthwhile for both of you."

Corey's words met silence. "Are you there? Did you hear me?"

"Yes, boss, but, well, we have a problem." Hearing an exasperated grunt, the man rushed on. "You see, Buddy didn't get there in time to get his car on board the ferry. He and his girl were walk-ons."

"Great! Just great!"

"But boss, I have an idea. A friend of mine works at a marina near the boat dock on Beaver Island. I could give him a call. Maybe he can break free and follow them."

"Get on it! Plus, I want you on that island as soon as possible. I don't care if you have to stay there a month. I want that woman's location found! There's no room for failure here."

"Sure, boss, I'm already packing, but I think there's only one ferry each way this time of year," he lamely replied.

Hardening his voice, Corey stated, "Get there as soon as you can then! Don't disappoint me! I don't handle disappointments well. I tend to take it out on the people responsible."

"No worries, boss. We've got this covered. The woman will be found."

"See to it, and call me as soon as you know something!" The line went dead.

Corey picked up the detailed readout he'd discreetly acquired on Detective Quaid Williams and his partner, Paul Statham. Their skills and tenacity were highly praised on the pages. Corey's adrenaline surged at the thought of outsmarting these two formidable foes. They'd been clever to move so quickly and to bring in a woman. For the moment, she was an unknown, but Corey was confident he'd be able to find out more within the next few days.

Unable to stand still, he began pacing the room as excitement grew. "I imagine she'll stick to Sydney like glue." The challenge fueled Corey's ego. Picking up an almost empty beer can, he easily crunched it with one hand. Grinning, he stated, "So the game is on. This could actually be fun!"

# Chapter 13

Even though he was half asleep, Quaid could feel Sydney's fidgeting body. He wondered how long she'd be content to stay by his side. He figured the novelty of the boat ride would wear off but wasn't ready to give up the warmth of the sun on his face, so he chose to ignore her. That is until she began pulling her arm out of the crook of his.

Opening one eye, he asked, "Planning to go somewhere?"

"Yes, I want to walk and stretch my legs."

Quaid opened both his eyes and smiled as he pulled his legs in to sit up straighter. "Fair enough, let's take a stroll."

Coming to his feet, Quaid pulled her up beside him as he sent an eye signal Paul's way. All still seemed well, which didn't really surprise Quaid. He'd figured they had moved too fast and secretly for the local yokels down the street from Sydney's. It had puzzled him that a man who seemed so meticulous about Vince's murder would use that caliber of men for his surveillance of Sydney. The only thing that made sense was the man had been forced to temporarily use what was available.

He released Sydney's hand in order to eye nearby people under the guise of a stretch. Not sensing any trouble and oblivious to the admiring female looks directed at his lean torso, Quaid smiled and reached for Sydney's hand once more. Instead, he suddenly found her arms wrapped around his neck. She then smoothly planted a kiss squarely on his lips.

Taken momentarily by surprise, Quaid quickly assessed the situation. Even though he knew Sydney was being outrageous, they were supposed to be imitating a couple. Having decided to give Sydney some of her own medicine, Quaid clamped steel arms around her to return the kiss. He wasn't sure why she had decided to kiss him but figured it probably had something to do with showing off. Either way, he knew she hadn't planned on his response, for her body stiffened and tried to back away. Still holding Sydney fast, Quaid lifted his lips to move his mouth close to her ear.

Sydney said in a ragged whisper, "Let me go!"

"Ready to be good?"

Quaid felt her head move in agreement against his face. He slowly released her but stayed close.

Sydney stared at the deck floor. In a tight voice she stated, "I have to use the ladies' room."

Quaid signaled Maria and Paul, so the two walked over hand-in-hand. In a let's-be-friends voice, Maria asked, "Sydney, shall we visit the powder room?"

Looking up quickly, Sydney replied she would, and the two walked off.

## Out of the Snare

With raised eyebrows, Paul asked, "What was that all about, partner? I didn't think you were into women like her."

"Are you kidding? Sydney's trouble from her head to her toes! She keeps trying to goad me, and hopefully my little stunt put a stop to it." Running a hand through his thick black hair, Quaid added, "Next time, you get her!"

"I don't know. Seeing you two together makes me feel all warm and cozy inside—the perfect couple." Paul's partner leveled his eyes on him. He chuckled as Quaid changed the subject.

"Anyone taking undue notice of us?"

"Other than all the jealous women watching that kiss?"

Receiving another glare for response, Paul sobered and stated, "No one that I've seen. I believe we made a clean getaway."

"I'll feel a whole lot better once she's safely in the house. It still angers me the arrogant nerve of this guy walking right up to her front door. Did Sydney give you anything more to go on besides his resemblance to Pierce?"

As the two men conversed, the women made their way down the left side of the boat. The wall signs indicated the restrooms were located at the back of the large glassed-in middle section, which was used to protect people from the elements on bad weather days. Few of the seats were occupied inside. Most everyone was milling around the top deck.

Strangely subdued, Sydney thought about Quaid's kiss when Maria stated, "I know any number of female officers who would give their right arm to be in the situation you were just in."

Sydney wanted to ask if she was one of them but instead retorted, "Tell them to save their arms. It wasn't that great!"

Maria hid a smile while holding the bathroom door for Sydney to precede her in. When the two women stepped out a few minutes later, Sydney almost collided with a couple strolling by close to the door.

Immediately, Maria came alert. The man mumbled his apology as they walked on to benches situated halfway down the room near the glass wall. Selecting one facing the outside, the couple seated themselves with their backs to the women. Seeing the two so absorbed with each other, Maria relaxed. Having her attention focused on the pair, she missed the fleeting look that had crossed Sydney's face.

Sydney stared at the man's retreating back. For a brief moment she thought he'd seemed familiar. Deciding she must be wrong, she dismissed the incident from her mind and walked with Maria out the door to the deck beyond.

Quaid and Paul's discussion turned to the island and how best to protect Sydney. They were just talking about what a potential danger Vince's murderer was to Sydney when Paul saw the women approaching.

The two men came to their feet with welcoming smiles on their faces. Quaid stepped forward to smoothly capture Sydney's hand and walk her to the bench.

Still holding her hand, Quaid sat down and playfully tugged her down beside him. "Are you enjoying your first ferry ride?" Not sure what mood Sydney was in, he was surprised when she joined in the charade.

With an enthusiastic voice, she replied, "I love it! I thought I might get seasick, but the water seems pretty calm today."

There the conversation fizzled. Quaid maintained hold of her hand but directed his attention to the fellow passengers and the scenery, watching and listening.

A short while later, his concentration was interrupted when Sydney blurted, "What does it mean—*Beware of Satan's snares*?"

Surprised, Quaid focused on Sydney's face. Thinking it could be some kind of trap, he cautiously asked, "Why are you asking?"

"I saw it on a billboard on the outskirts of Charlevoix. What does it mean by snares?"

"Snare is another word for trap." Warming to his subject, Quaid said, "I grew up in a farming area down in the middle of Michigan.

When I was young, my dad ran a trap line." Seeing Sydney's confusion, he explained. "A trap line is when men go in the woods or streams and set steel traps to catch animals like beaver, mink, or raccoon. These animals then get skinned, and the furs are sold."

"That's terrible!"

"You may think so, but where do you think all those expensive mink and sable coats come from? Besides, at one time that job helped put food on our table. It's not an easy job either. The trapping happens during the cold of winter when the fur is thickest and nicest. It takes a lot of work to run a trap line. The traps need to be checked every day to get the furs properly taken care of for the buyers."

"I still think it's a terrible thing to do...murdering those poor, innocent animals."

The two grew silent, and then Sydney asked again, "But how does that apply to Satan?"

"Satan sets traps for us—all of us, but he especially delights in tripping up Christians. He wants us to fall into sin; that way we won't be effective for Christ."

Once again, Sydney's expressive face reflected confusion. Turning toward her, Quaid grew more fervent. He was pleased she was asking him spiritual questions and found he really wanted her to understand. "Take you, for instance."

Right away she stiffened. "I'm no Christian! We both know that. Why would Satan bother with me?"

"As hard as this may sound, if you're not a follower of Christ, then you're already in Satan's camp." Seeing her start to protest, Quaid changed tactics. "Sydney, let's look at it this way. If a trapper wants to trap say raccoons, he's not going to study the lifestyle of a squirrel. No, he's going to watch and study a raccoon to see where he goes, what he eats, and what his habits are. That's what Satan does! He studies our habits and sets before us things he knows will tempt us, things that will trip us up and catch us." His voice then softened as he said matter-of-factly, "Like what happened to you and Vince."

Quaid saw that struck a chord, so he let Sydney mull that over a bit.

With wide, sad eyes, Sydney asked in almost a whisper, "Once we're caught in Satan's snare, is it for keeps? Is there hope for us?"

Quaid earnestly replied, "That's the great news of Jesus Christ! There's always hope, at least while we're still on this earth and while we're still alive."

Suddenly, Sydney's attention was drawn to her hand being held by Quaid's.

Quaid saw the direction her mind was heading but wasn't going there with her. Instead, he experienced a strong desire to help her understand just what Christ did for her on the cross, Quaid started to say, "Sydney, Christ died—"

His words were interrupted by the ship's captain announcing their approach to the north end of Beaver Island. As people began standing and moving around, Quaid urgently stated, "Sydney, let's talk about this again."

Sydney stood and said with indifference, "Whatever."

Quaid got to his feet, gave her hand a gentle squeeze, and then let her go.

Relieved to be out of the conversation that was starting to make her nervous, Sydney focused her attention on the approaching land. Craning her neck to look northward, she noted they were approaching a large cove. She then allowed her eyes to travel westward and southward along the shoreline. From where she stood, it was possible to view various large homes looming on the banks overlooking the waters they had just crossed. One in particular stood out. It was a long, sprawling log home with a glassed-in porch running more than half its length. Slightly to the right yet still close to the large log home was a small cottage-type building that threw Sydney into a world of make-believe. She easily could imagine it as the servant quarters from some long ago time.

Letting her imagination run wild, she soon pictured herself and other ladies in long skirts promenading near the beach. Servants walked behind them holding umbrellas to protect the fine gentile ladies from the harsh sun. It wasn't very hard to pick herself out of the crowd. She was the one with the most beautiful deep red dress and the one with several men hovering around. One in particular…

"Sydney, it's time to make our way to the car below deck."

Quaid's voice had effectively brought Sydney back from wherever her mind had been, for an all too familiar frown was leveled at him.

"Whatever you say, warden," she stated in a low voice. Sydney pasted a smile on her face then slipped her arm through his. In a much louder voice dripping with honey, she said, "Come on, handsome. I'm looking forward to spending time alone with you on this lovely island."

Quaid took the lead down the narrow metal flight of stairs when he heard Sydney let out a little yelp as she stumbled behind him. Whirling, he expertly caught her in his arms as she started falling forward.

Being suddenly at eye level with her, Quaid saw Sydney's face blush with embarrassment. For the first time, he caught a vulnerable look in her intense brown eyes. Then Sydney's perfume faintly swirled into his nostrils, which strangely accentuated the feel of her in his arms.

Pulling his mind back to business, Quaid asked, "Are you okay?"

"Yes…yes I am," she replied a little breathlessly.

He smiled and softly stated good as he lowered her to the step. Seeing she was now steady on her feet, he turned and made his way down the rest of the stairs.

Once in the car, Paul and Maria continued their light banter, but the two in the back looked out their respective windows. Within the hour, the foursome had driven off the ferry toward Sydney's temporary home.

About a mile out of town, the airport came into view, and Sydney smiled. Leaning her forehead against the window, she let her imagination spin into the world of Lear jets with plush interiors. Being deep in that pretend world, it was a moment before she realized the car wasn't moving any longer. Pulling herself back to the car's interior, Sydney was surprised to see Quaid out unlocking a chained gate. The two-track beyond looked to lead into the woods. *Where are we going now? It would be just like Quaid to take me to a shack in the middle of the forest.*

Sydney sat up straighter in order to study her surroundings. She didn't see much—only trees, the fence, and the narrow road heading into the woods. Once Quaid had the gate swung wide, Paul drove through then stopped.

*Great! Just great!* Sydney sagged in the seat as Quaid shut the heavy gate and relocked the sturdy chain before getting back into the car.

Noting her rigid attitude, he refrained from talking to her. He did try smiling, but Sydney frowned and turned her face away.

The two-track was long, maybe a mile or so in the trees, until suddenly the trees ended and there stood the house. It was a sprawling single story with a beautifully landscaped lawn. The house appeared to butt up against a sloping beach leading to the lake. The view beyond was wonderful! Straining her neck to take it all in, Sydney saw the drive ended in a circle at the front of the house.

As Paul drove the car into the circle, Sydney saw a small cottage out back near the beach. She grew very excited. She knew this house! It was the one she'd seen from the ferry, the one she'd imagined herself as the owner of. Forgetting her former coolness toward Quaid, Sydney turned excited eyes his way. "What a large, beautiful log home! The builder obviously took great pains to make everything look good with the surroundings. Is this really where I'll be staying?"

"That's right. But until we feel it's safe, you won't be able to leave the house. And you'll have to stay away from the windows, especially at night."

Sydney tuned his words out as Paul stopped directly in front of the massive oak door surrounded by full-length, cut-glass windows. Immediately, she moved to open her door when a steel hand clamped on her arm.

"Stay put!" Maintaining his grip, Quaid instructed Paul and Maria to make sure all was well in the house.

Sydney watched the two pull their guns clear of the holsters then load bullets into the chambers before exiting. Paul unlocked the house door, and the two slowly disappeared inside. Shaking her arm loose, she sat unspeaking while staring at the open front door. *This is so silly! How could anyone know I'd be coming here?*

Sydney jumped as her thoughts were interrupted by a snap to her right. Looking at Quaid, she saw a gun in his hand as he too stepped from the vehicle. In a short while, Maria came out the house door. Leaving Paul standing alertly in the entrance, she made her way to Sydney's door as Quaid walked around the back of the car.

Once again, Sydney had thoughts of opening her door, but the female officer held her body against it until Quaid was standing guard close to her. Annoyed with all the theatrics, Sydney let out a frustrated grunt when Maria stepped aside and opened the door. "Is this really necessary?" Sydney said with disgust as the pair hurried her into the house.

Once the door closed, Maria answered, "We're doing our duty to protect you. Someday you may thank us for taking such good care of you." Holstering her pistol, Maria snapped it down as she turned to stroll from the foyer into the living room.

Still glaring at Maria's back, it took a moment for Sydney to notice the interior of the home. Once she did, a "Wow!" escaped her lips as she stared, then said, "Now this is more like it! Someday I plan to have a house every bit as nice as this!"

She stood in the foyer staring at the open beamed cathedral room spread out before her. In the very middle was a huge chandelier that appeared to hold a million lights. The large room sported a hardwood floor decorated with several braided rugs of various sizes. Directly across from her was a massive floor-to-ceiling, fieldstone fireplace. Double-paned windows went to the peak, allowing natural light to flood the room. To the left of the fireplace, Sydney saw French doors leading to a fully glassed-in porch overlooking the lake.

Quaid stood patiently beside her while Sydney took it all in. Then, placing his hand on her back, he nudged her into the room so Paul could bring in the luggage. "You'll have plenty of time to look the place over, but right now we need to pick you out a bedroom, one that is the easiest for us to keep you safe in."

Just like that, the dream of living in this beautiful home had been cooled by the reminder that someone murdered Vince and could at that very moment be looking for her.

Quaid led her to the right down a long hall with four bedrooms—two to the back facing the lake and two facing the front woods. Sydney was surprised to find that each was very spacious and sported its own private bath. Choosing the first back one, she stepped aside as Paul brought her bags in. He and Quaid then left to pick out their bedrooms while Maria hovered to remind Sydney not to unpack the smaller travel bag. "Remember, if we need to leave quickly, that's the only one you grab; speed may be extremely important for your safety."

Once again the reminder of why she was there sailed to the forefront of Sydney's mind. The irritation of being caught and losing all that money prompted her to reply curtly, "Yeah, yeah, I know. Now can I have some privacy in my cell?"

When Sydney and the three Michigan state detectives had settled in their new location, it was decided that Paul would watch outside during the day and Quaid the night. Sydney's room was on the lakeside closest to the living room with Quaid directly across. Paul was situated in the room beside Quaid's, which was across from Maria's. Sydney was totally surrounded and watched.

A couple days after their arrival, Officers Jake and Neal arrived by airplane, bringing with them Sydney's mail. All were disappointed that paperwork from the deceased Vince still hadn't turned up. The two new arrivals were soon unpacked in the guest cottage located off to the left of the attached two-stall garage.

Jake, being the rookie, worked days with Paul, leaving Neal patrolling the grounds at night with Quaid. The five kept COM links on their person at all times, which Quaid periodically tested to keep them on their toes.

The first couple nights, Neal and Quaid had near scares from wildlife critters like opossums and raccoons, but the two rapidly learned the night sounds and the lay of the land. Everything was becoming quite familiar, which suited Quaid just fine. New sounds would alert them quickly. Shift changes were set up to take place at 6:00 a.m. and 6:00 p.m. It was a long twelve hours but needful with only four men. Once Paul took over, it usually took Quaid a matter of minutes to eat breakfast and then slip quietly into his room to fall fast asleep before the women awoke.

# Chapter 14

They'd been at the log home for three days, and Quaid still thought about his conversation with Sydney on the ferry. Earlier that morning, Paul and he had taken their usual few minutes of transition to discuss where the situation stood. Before coming to their designated meeting spot, Quaid had called the chief for any updates. He was disappointed to tell Paul that it seemed the trail was growing cold.

"Every lead the Louisville people get winds up a dead end. This guy is like a magician! He seems to come and go as he pleases and doesn't leave any evidence."

"I really thought he'd messed up with the glass at Sydney's, but…" Quaid rubbed his tired eyes. It had been a long night. He was more than ready to grab a quick breakfast and sleep. "What was I saying? Oh yes, the prints went nowhere. This man is either very lucky or just plain arrogant. I'm beginning to wonder if your thoughts in the chief's office might not be our next move."

"You mean to start checking former law enforcement… maybe even FBI?"

"Yes, that's what I'm thinking."

Paul frowned. "This isn't going to sit well if this murderer is one of us."

Deciding the best plan was to broach the idea with the chief again, the men soon parted, Paul to patrol and Quaid to sleep.

At least, that was the plan.

Quaid was in bed, but sleep was eluding him. Satan's snares kept running through his mind. Having found it hard to sleep during the daytime, Quaid was happy when darkening drapes had been designed. Quaid's room was now almost totally dark. Sitting up, he turned on the bedside lamp and fluffed the pillow up behind his back.

Over the years, Quaid had learned to trust two weapons that he always had with him, his firearm and his Bible. Reaching for the Bible, he ran his hand over the tooled leather. Turning through the well-worn, gold-tipped pages, Quaid directed his attention to the concordance at the back. Finding the word *snare*, he began looking up the references listed and writing down ones he found. He soon had compiled a small list of verses that he had every intention of giving to Sydney later that day.

Feeling much more at peace, Quaid set his Bible back on the nightstand and turned the light off. He was soon fast asleep.

It had only been three days, but to Sydney it felt like a week. She contemplated skipping the day and staying in bed, but the sun peeking through her drawn drapes was beckoning her. Rising, she walked to the big bay window in her bedroom. She leaned in to pull the drapes back then stilled her hand. Groaning with disgust, she flopped on the window seat. In a childish voice, she mimicked, "No, Sydney! You can't open any drapes! This is a private residence, not the usual safe house. Therefore, the windows aren't bulletproof!" Lowering her voice to Quaid's manly tone, she added, "All you can do is peek out."

Resentment surged toward her protectors, especially Quaid. The man irritated her, and Sydney wasn't used to that. She loved men. It was how she learned to get good things in life. But Quaid? He seemed to be resistant to her obvious charms. She thought on that a long time before pushing his ruggedly handsome image from her mind. "Besides, he's a male chauvinist if I've ever seen one. Before long, he'd probably have me scrubbing floors and liking it."

Her thoughts then moved to the mess she was in. When Vince's face popped into her mind, Sydney stiffened. Unbidden, Quaid's words about snares snuck into her mind.

Standing, Sydney paced the room restlessly. A part of her wanted to ask him more questions, but another part didn't want to appear interested in spiritual things. Sydney walked into her beautifully appointed private bathroom. A short while later, feeling more herself, Sydney peered at her heavily made-up reflection. "Hang in there, beautiful. This will soon be over, and you can move to a big city and find a rich man to take care of you."

Not recognizing her trust in Quaid's ability but liking the plan, Sydney dismissed her earlier thoughts and went to see if Maria had breakfast ready.

Later that afternoon, a fully rested Quaid made his appearance. He paused to study Sydney spread out on the sofa, totally absorbed in a soap opera. Hearing movement in the study located off the foyer near the front door, Quaid went to investigate.

Maria was intently reading book titles as he entered. "Afternoon, Maria. How's it going?"

"Fine, if I don't let her Highness get to me. For some reason, she thinks I'm here as her personal maid."

Quaid strolled on into the room to lean against a large mahogany desk. "You may be new for our post, but I know you've got plenty of experience. Use your discretion on this one. Personally, I'd give her another tour of the house, focusing on the laundry room and kitchen."

Maria turned to smile at him. "Thanks, sir. For now, I'm trying to connect and understand what she's feeling. To be honest, she's a hard read. One moment, she almost comes across like she wants to be a friend; then she'll start ordering me around."

Quaid stood and stated with confidence, "I'm sure you'll learn how best to handle her." Walking closer, he asked, "Did you happen to find any Bibles?"

"Sure did. There's a section right here of several. I don't know why they need so many. One would be sufficient."

"Some people actually like going deeper than just reading the Scriptures. Other translations can help clarify passages. Paraphrases are another matter though. Steer clear of those."

"Why?"

"Paraphrases aren't translations from original texts. They are men's and women's ideas of what they think the Scriptures are trying to say." Changing the subject, Quaid asked, "Are you a believer in Jesus Christ?"

Stiffening, Maria pulled out a book. Hugging it close, she replied, "I grew up attending a Catholic church and school. During that time, I learned all I needed to be a good person."

"Actually, Maria..."

"Excuse me, sir, but my personal beliefs about God aren't part of my job requirements." Sending him a tight smile, she then stated, "Since I'm not into watching soaps, I came here to find a book, which I've done. It's time I got back out there."

Quaid thoughtfully watched her walk from the room then pulled a New King James Bible off the shelf. Glancing at the folded paper in his hand, Quaid said under his breath, "Well, that didn't go so well. Here's hoping I do better with Sydney." Quaid walked to the edge of the living room and was pleased to see a commercial on the TV and that Sydney was now sitting up.

"Afternoon, Sydney." He wondered what her problem could possibly be when all he received in response was a glare and nod.

Standing taller, Quaid walked closer and planted himself between Sydney and the TV. He wanted her full attention. "Sydney, do you remember the conversation we had on the ferry about snares?"

By the look on her face, his words had startled her.

"Yes...yes I do."

"Well, it's been on my mind, so I wrote down a few scriptures from the Bible that mention snares." Without further words, he handed her a folded piece of paper.

Quaid held her gaze with his deep brown eyes as she reached for the paper.

He then handed her a black leather Bible. "I didn't know if you had a Bible, so I borrowed one from the study." He paused and then added, "If you have questions, write them down so you won't forget, and we can talk about them another time."

He turned to walk halfway to the front door before swinging around to state, "By the way, if I were you, I'd rethink the makeup."

Sydney stared at his broad, straight back going out the front door. A red blush crept up her neck and face. Hearing sounds in the kitchen, she had little doubt that Maria heard Quaid's parting words. Sydney tucked the paper inside the Bible and set it on the coffee table.

That night, Sydney carried the still unopened Bible to her bedroom. After dressing for bed, Sydney stared at her made-up face in the mirror. For the first time, her eyes looked too dark and macabre to her. Tilting her head, she then noticed how the layers of foundation gave her face an unnatural sheen. Instead of giving herself a tan look, Sydney saw a face bordering on orange. Taking her fingernail, she dug a trail through the makeup before reaching her skin. Suddenly, unreasonable anger stirred her heart full of sorrow and the beginnings of shame. Scenes of her past flashed across the mirror—scenes of doing whatever was necessary to achieve her goals even to the point of using an abortion as a form of birth control.

Sydney grabbed a washcloth and dampened it. She began scrubbing her face. Once the makeup was off, she kept scrubbing, hoping she could also remove memories that brought pain. Pausing, Sydney leaned her head against the mirror as one particular memory wouldn't be washed away. It was the memory of her enticing Vince to do the embezzling and the image of his murder. Tears streamed down Sydney's raw face. She wanted desperately to turn back the clock and take it all back. Hopelessness coursed through her being. "Why would any nice man look at me? I'm nothing but white trash!"

A long while later, Sydney walked into the main bedroom and pulled open the top dresser drawer. Tucked down underneath was the crystal cross Hope had given her. Pulling it out, an emotionally drained Sydney crawled into bed with the cross still in her hand. Not understanding why it was such a comfort, Sydney ran her fingers over it as she fell asleep.

That night she had a nightmare that her path was full of traps. She could see two figures up ahead beckoning her to come forward—one was tall with a sturdy build; the other was wrapped in a warm glow. Sydney felt a strong desire to reach the two men but didn't see any way around the snares.

The next morning Sydney woke in a bad mood that soon bloomed into a headache. Stepping around the cross that had fallen to the floor during the night, she went to get ready for the day. Seeing puffy eyes and red, sore cheeks in the mirror, she lathered the makeup on heavier than ever. Back in the bedroom, she nudged the now offending cross under the bed. Spying the Bible lying on the dresser, Sydney tossed a shirt over it. Leaving the room, she headed for the kitchen. Since Maria was the one assigned inside duty, Sydney was intent on making her life miserable every chance she could.

"What are you looking at?"

Quaid had just walked in from the outside and met Sydney on her way to the kitchen. Seeing her heavily made-up face, he frowned and paused.

"Well? What compliment do you have for this *clown* today?"

She had a delicious sense of satisfaction when he cringed at her choice of words. With a challenging glare, Sydney leaned in.

Quaid seemed to choose his words carefully before replying. "If you really want to know, I was wondering why you think all that goop makes you look attractive."

At his first word, Sydney opened her mouth to retaliate but clamped it shut in surprise. For a moment she wasn't sure how to respond. Contrary to what she constantly told herself about this man, Sydney was starting to care what he thought.

Quaid continued, but with a softer tone. "Did your mom or maybe a sister..." Realizing he didn't know anything about her family, he asked, "Do you have a sister?"

Looking down at her tight-fitting jeans, Sydney emitted a groan from deep within. Her mind filled with images of her sister. She was nine years older than Sydney and had never looked or acted bold and showy. The fact was, she had always tried being a good example for Sydney. Sydney's attitude drained away.

Looking back up at Quaid, she sadly admitted, "I have one older sister. Since my mom never cared how I looked or what I did, my older sister tried hard to teach me good things." Suddenly a strong need for Quaid to hear some of her upbringing surged to the surface. Stepping forward, Sydney placed a hand on his arm. "May I tell you about her?"

Quaid intently searched her face, which made her regret the request. She saw distrust and caution in his handsome eyes. But then his eyes grew warm as he replied, "Sure." Steering her to the living room, Quaid waited for her to sit in the nearby rocker; then he sat attentively in the easy chair.

Studying her hands clasped in her lap, Sydney raised her head to stare into space while her mind traveled back in time.

Quaid patiently waited.

Sydney cleared her throat then slowly began. "Many times things were bad in our home. Often I'd been able to escape to the street, but sometimes my stepdad wouldn't let me leave. He would confine my sister and me to our small shared room."

Over the next half hour or so, Sydney told Quaid snippets of her life. One was about her sister inventing a game to distract her younger sister. "She called it the *Can You Imagine* game. When we were confined to our room, we would go to our secret stash of old travel magazines found in dumpsters and would choose a page. Once the spot was chosen, we would take turns imagining what our lives would be like if we lived there and what we'd be doing. As we grew older, the beach pictures drew us more and more."

Sydney paused, as the memory became stronger in her mind. After a moment, she wistfully said, "I think it was because those photos were the most different from our world of dirty streets, trash, and no grass."

She raised sad eyes to Quaid's before going on. "We would imagine ourselves with healthy, tan bodies and we'd be waited on by people walking around with trays covered with drinks sporting little umbrellas."

Sydney raised sad eyes to Quaid's. "Have you ever had one of those?" After he nodded affirmative, she went on. "At the time, we didn't know what was in the drinks. We just knew they looked fun, exciting, and probably expensive.

"One evening, my mom and stepdad had a really bad fight, and my sister and I heard her name brought up several times. At that

143

time I was only seven, so I didn't understand what was going on. But something different was happening. My sister turned very pale, and with tears streaming down her cheeks, she pulled me down beside her on the bed. With a shaky voice, she said, 'Abby, I can't live here anymore. I … I can't explain why—you're too young—but as soon as they're asleep, I'm leaving.' I pleaded with her to stay, but all she'd say was, 'He's bad! Stay away from him the best you can. Put a chair up against the doorknob when you go to bed at night.'"

Sydney went on to explain how she hadn't understood what her sister meant and tried to argue with her. "But my sister kept talking over my protests. She repeatedly promised to come back and take me away too. As she rapidly packed her tattered bag, she told me to find safe places in the alleys and with my friends as often as I could.

"Then hugging me close, my sister kissed my forehead and then quietly slipped out the door.

"That night was over eighteen years ago, and I haven't heard from her since." With a catch in her throat, Sydney added, "I don't even know if she's still alive."

As she spoke, Quaid's eyes never left her face, not even when Sydney heard Maria quietly walk from the kitchen to the study, allowing them privacy to talk. Appreciating her kindness, Sydney made a mental note to thank her later.

As her words wound down, Quaid had a question. "What's your sister's name?"

Sydney grew very silent before looking straight into Quaid's eyes. Feeling very vulnerable, she sucked in her breath then exhaled. She sadly replied, "Alicia, but I called her Allie."

"Were there other children?"

"No, just us two."

"Do you have any idea where she might have gone?"

"None." Growing tired of the conversation, Sydney narrowed her eyes. "How come you're so interested?"

"Originally, I came in this morning to ask if you'd been able to read any of the verses yet. But almost running into you and seeing how overdone... that is... I mean your ample makeup... or rather..." Quaid stopped speaking when Sydney visibly stiffened. He finished lamely, "Anyway, I got distracted."

Sydney felt rage filling her veins. She narrowed her eyes and started to stand but sat back down at his next words.

"Honestly, Sydney, does a pretty woman like you really think that looks good?" He swung his hand through the air toward her for emphasis.

Once again, Quaid's words left her unable to respond. Finding her voice, she shrugged while stating, "It's what my friends did, and to be honest, no man has ever complained before."

An awkward silence ensued.

Then Quaid asked, "So did you?"

"Did I what?"

"Did you look up the verses I gave you yesterday?"

Growing uncomfortable, Sydney stood, which brought Quaid also to his feet. Smoothing her top, for the first time Sydney felt indiscreet. Refraining from covering her half-exposed breasts, she made a mental note to go through her clothes for something less revealing. Not wanting to admit it could be because of Quaid, she silently told herself, *Since I'm not leaving the house or seeing other people, I might as well dress comfortably.*

"Sydney? Did you hear me?" Quaid's eyes narrowed then widened again as he added, "Since you have a hard time answering to Sydney, maybe I should start calling you Abigail. That is your real name, right?"

Memory of the biblical Abigail and Abigail's integrity convicted Sydney's heart. Feeling the sudden need to lash out at someone, she raised her voice while punctuating every word. "My... name... is... Sydney. Don't... ever... call... me... Abigail!" Spinning on her heels, Sydney moved to walk away. "As for the verses, I haven't read them yet."

Sydney could feel Quaid's eyes on her back as she retreated to the kitchen. Opening the refrigerator, she peered over in time to see him turn and go to his bedroom.

# Chapter 15

That night Sydney dreamed of a painted lady bowing at a man's feet asking him to spare her husband's life. The man took her hand with kindness and pulled her to her feet. It was then Sydney realized she was the painted woman. Raising her eyes, Sydney was further surprised to see the man was Quaid, but as she blinked, his face suddenly became Pierce's. At least at first it appeared to be him, but peering closer, fear ran through Sydney's body when she recognized Vince's killer instead! The man still held her hand and started tightening his grip. He sneered as Sydney struggled to be free.

Then suddenly her hand was free, and the man bent down. Following him with her eyes, Sydney realized he was setting a large steel-toothed trap at her feet. She soon saw them all around her, and there didn't appear to be any way of escaping them. A moment later, the man stood, and with an evil grin, he triggered the nearest trap. Soon all of them were jumping in the air from slamming shut.

Sydney woke with a start.

Breathing heavily, Sydney wiped sweat from her brow as she tried to figure out the dream. Needing some sense of reality, she threw the covers back and got out of bed. Leaning toward the bedside lamp, she thought to turn it on when her eyes fell upon the shirt-covered Bible still lying on the dresser. Walking up to it, she crossed a thin band of moonlight sneaking across the floor. A strong desire to see the moon caused a new plan to formulate in Sydney's mind.

She walked to the bedroom door and stuffed a shirt under to block any light seeping in from the hallway. Being satisfied, she stood and walked with purpose to the bay window. Pulling the curtain back, Sydney was strangely comforted to see what appeared to be a full moon shining down on the world. Tucking one leg under her, Sydney sat down and stared at it. She was dazzled by the multitude of shining stars blanketed across the sky. The thought of God being somewhere out there just out of her reach caused Sydney to lean her head wearily against the glass. Little by little, her racing heart calmed.

Sydney closed her eyes and tried again to sort out what the dream could mean. She recognized the woman resembling the Abigail that Hope had told her about back in Petoskey. *Oh, how I wish I could be a woman like that.* She remembered that Hope had said the biblical Abigail had thought of others more than herself even to the point of risking her own life. *I've not thought of others since realizing my sister was never returning and I was on my own.* A feeling of bitterness closely followed by sorrow caused a lump to form in Sydney's throat.

Swallowing hard several times, she forced herself to focus on the nightmare once more. The traps made her think of Quaid's words and Satan's snares. Lifting her head, Sydney turned to look at the Bible still lying on the dresser. At that moment, the moonbeam landed squarely on it, causing the gold lettering to look almost luminescent. Sydney was momentarily mesmerized by the sight then remembered the paper nestled inside—the one Quaid had handed her. Coming to a stand, Sydney shook circulation back into her leg before walking to get the Bible. Picking it up, she held it close as many scenes of her life began assailing her mind. Remembering to close the curtain tightly before turning on the lamp, Sydney lowered her now shaking body to the bed.

Images of her humble home life mingled with the taste of nice things offered by Vince. That evolved to his murder mixed with Hope's trying to be her friend by giving her a box full of crystal, very expensive crystal that had been auctioned to help pay her debt to society. An image of the beautiful cross that Hope had given as a gift to Sydney reminded her that it was still under the bed. Setting the Bible on the bed, she knelt to retrieve it and then set it on the stand near the lamp. The light made the cross twinkle brightly.

Sitting once more, Sydney studied the cross as thoughts of Satan's snares invaded to cloud her peaceful thoughts. Soon Quaid's words of criticism over her makeup added to the jumble going on in her head. A deep feeling of hopelessness threatened to consume her. It was then the Bible seemed to remind her of its presence on the bed near her. Reaching for it, Sydney scooted higher in the bed, plumped the pillow behind her back, and pulled the covers up. Laying the Bible in her lap, she opened it to where the paper had been stuck. Sydney unfolded it. As she did, a little booklet fell to the open pages of the Bible. Picking it up, she read on the cover, "May I Ask You a Question?"

She was tempted to read it first but stopped herself. *Not yet, Syd. Do the verses first.*

Setting the booklet aside, she finished unfolding the paper and saw five references written inside. Turning to the index in the front of the Bible, Sydney searched for the first one listed. Finding the listing for 1 Timothy, she turned to the page indicated then found chapter six, verse nine. It read:

> But those who desire to be rich fall into temptation and a snare, and into many foolish and harmful lusts which drown men in destruction and perdition.

"That's what I did!" Sydney stated out loud. "I wanted to be rich and I tempted—actually blackmailed—Vince into stealing. Now he's dead!" Shame filled Sydney's soul as she grieved over Vince's terrible death and how his murderer was probably even now planning the same for her.

She experienced a need to know more about snares so looked up the next one: Job 18:8–9.

> For he is cast into a net by his own feet, and he walks into a snare. The net takes him by the heel, and a snare lays hold of him.

A shiver ran down her spine as she remembered the nightmare. The sound of the traps slamming shut kept playing over and over in her ears. Clamping her hands over them, Sydney whispered fiercely, "No, no! Stop, stop!"

Closing her eyes, she moaned.

A feeling of defeat threatened to engulf her—that is until she remembered Quaid's words telling her it wasn't too late. Eagerly she looked up the next verse, Proverbs 14:27.

> The fear of the Lord is a fountain of life, to turn one away from the snares of death.

Now Sydney was confused. How could fearing the Lord be good? That just meant she'd fear both Satan and the Lord. She knit her brows in a frown. Deciding she needed Quaid to explain, Sydney made a mental note to ask him and then moved to the next verse. It too was in the Old Testament Book of Proverbs. Turning to chapter twenty-nine, verse twenty-five, she read:

> The fear of man brings a snare, but whoever trusts in the Lord shall be safe.

*This verse says to trust the Lord. How can I trust him and also fear him?*

Becoming more confused, Sydney considered forgetting all about the verses but saw there was only one left. Deciding Quaid would probably quiz her about all the verses, she decided to finish. This one was Psalms 91:3.

> Surely He shall deliver you from the snare of the fowler and from the perilous pestilence.

*What's a fowler?* Seeing a tiny number *one* after the word, Sydney searched the page until she found another one. There at the bottom of the page, it read, "That is, one who catches birds in a trap or snare."

She reread the verse. The words, "He shall deliver you," kept playing over and over in Sydney's mind as a tiny spark of hope tried imbedding itself in her doubtful, fearful heart.

A feeling of tiredness and defeat suddenly came upon her. Giving in to the feeling, Sydney decided no one could help her, not even God. "It's my fault Vince is dead! I'm the one who wanted the money and nice things!"

She picked up the little booklet. Not bothering to even open it, she folded it back in the paper and closed the Bible over them both. Sydney placed the Bible on the stand and then climbed wearily in bed. Ignoring the beckoning cross, she shut the light off. Rolling over into the pillow, she sobbed, "It's too late! I'm a terrible person! Satan has me now!"

Her last hopeless thought before crying herself to sleep was, *Vince had two murderers. That awful man ... and ... me!*

# Out of the Snare

The next afternoon an irritated Quaid Williams paced back and forth in front of the seated Sydney. Pausing, he watched her lazily study her nails. Feeling the urge to shake her soundly, he paced some more.

It frustrated him that to his knowledge Sydney still hadn't read the verses he'd given her. Another thing bothering him was their being back at square one in the relationship. He'd hoped since she'd revealed things about her home life and sister there would be a basis of trust, but that hadn't materialized. Now she'd done something to endanger his team.

He knew she was bored, but that didn't allow for what she'd done. It needed to be dealt with. Stopping in front of her once more, he watched Sydney lower her hands docilely to her lap while raising her eyes to his. Once they connected, a malicious smile lit up her face, and Quaid had to control an urge to slap it away. *Lord, please help me with this irritating, immature woman! Give me the words to reach her not only for you but also for the safety of this team.*

As Quaid's face filled with anger, Sydney's smile faded. He saw her stiffen and pull back, as if she expected him to hit her. Not liking how that made him feel, Quaid let out a frustrated grunt then bowed his head and closed his eyes. He needed God's help to handle this issue with Sydney properly.

As Quaid prayed, the Lord reminded him of how trapped Sydney probably felt. Having gone to bed before sunrise, Quaid hadn't been aware of the beautifully warm day until encountering Sydney on the sunny beach. In spite of his initial fear turning to anger, the warm sunshine had invaded his conscious. Now he could admit how it had probably beckoned her to break the security. Feeling God's peace stealing in to take control of his anger and frustration, he then focused his prayer on the team and their safety. With those thoughts now to the forefront of his mind, Quaid felt the need to impress on Sydney once again just what his team was willing to do on her behalf.

Opening his eyes, Quaid raised calm eyes her way.

Fearing she may have pushed him too far, Sydney worked on pretending humbleness when she saw Quaid close his eyes and bow his head. Stunned at the fact that he seemed to be praying right there in front of her, Sydney wondered what he was praying about. Narrowing her eyes, she decided he was probably asking God to remove her from his life and care. Not liking how that made her feel, Sydney tried to pull up her usual arrogant attitude by recalling to mind what had happened after lunch that day.

Sydney had woken with a bad headache and the need to escape her confines. As the morning passed, she had become more and more restless. She'd begun pacing the living room and sneaking peeks out the curtained windows. Then a plan hatched itself in her mind. Sitting down and pretending interest in a book, Sydney waited for an opportunity to implement her plan, which came when Maria walked into the bathroom.

Quickly, she ran to the back patio door. Soundlessly flicking the bolt lock, Sydney had held her breath as she slipped out and down the stairs leading to the sandy beach. In seconds, she'd ditched her shoes and socks. It had been a delight to dig her toes into the sand. Tilting her head skyward, Sydney had closed her eyes to let the sun soak into her face. Her whole being felt rejuvenated from the sun and fresh air.

Unfortunately, it hadn't lasted long. Maria had raised the alarm that Sydney was missing from the house.

Shifting her focus to the still praying Quaid, Sydney ventured a smile as she pictured Maria running through the house vainly searching. Unable to find her, Maria had taken her concern to the sleeping Quaid, who called Paul on the COM link.

*He was sure mad when he marched up to me on the beach.* Memory of the first sight of him stirred her senses. In the midst of all that drama, Sydney had observed Quaid's uncombed hair. She remembered briefly thinking how attractive he looked even in a scruffy

## Out of the Snare

state. Again a smile became prominent on her face as she recalled the beach scene. But then memory of his next words and actions came back, effectively chasing her smile away.

By digging her toes deeper into the warm sand, Sydney had tried ignoring him while standing her ground. At that point, Quaid's hand had clamped on Sydney's arm and swung her roughly around. Clicking the COM link, Quaid stated, "Stand down. We've got her. She wanted some sun. Go back to your positions. Over."

He had then lowered his face to within inches of hers to demand, "Do you have any idea what you've done? What's the matter with you? Do you think we're all here for the fun of it?"

"I needed fresh air! I'm sick of this prison! Vince's murderer has freedom to do what he wants while I'm stuck in this house!"

Twirling her around, Quaid had started pulling her back toward the safety of the house above. Realizing it would be futile to resist, Sydney had bent to retrieve her shoes. Not realizing her intention, Quaid kept walking. Flailing her arms, Sydney lost her balance and started giggling at the vision of him dragging her caveman-style by the arm to the house.

Quaid grunted in disgust while helping Sydney regain her balance. His grunt went so well with the caveman image that Sydney had broken into a belly laugh as she once again bent to pick up the wayward shoes and socks. But the laughter died when Sydney witnessed Quaid running a hand over his tired eyes.

Sighing heavily, Quaid maintained a hand on her arm as he started her toward the stairs once more. "Sydney, you may not think your life is valuable, but I do. Plus, you could have placed all of us in needless danger!"

"Oh, come on! It wasn't that big of a deal. I just—"

She wasn't able to finish as Quaid hurried her up the stairs in front of him. Looking up, Sydney had seen Maria standing at the top with the door open. Her brows had been pulled together in a deep frown. In spite of the constant reminder that these people were here for her protection, Sydney couldn't resist flashing a resentful look her way as Maria stepped back to let Sydney pass.

Once inside, Sydney headed toward the safety of her bedroom, but Quaid's commanding voice forestalled her. "Have a seat, Sydney. Apparently, you're still not getting the gravity of this situation, so we need to go over the rules one more time."

Even now, the memory of those few moments barefoot in the sand made it worth whatever Quaid was about to say. Glancing sideways, Sydney studied Maria. She was standing nearby with her feet about a foot apart and hands held together in front. The bulge of her pistol was evident under her light sweater. Sydney thought she looked like a soldier who had just been told to stand at ease. Maria's face registered no emotion as she kept her eyes on Quaid, waiting just like Sydney.

Then, he raised his head and Sydney was shocked at the obvious change in his whole demeanor. She grappled with what she'd just witnessed as Quaid began speaking.

"First and most important rule—no leaving the house unless accompanied by one of us. We're keeping a close watch on the happenings around the house, but it's impossible to know if there are any spies even now casing this place from a distance. And I repeat, this may seem like a game to you, but I will not—Look at me, Sydney!"

Sydney narrowed her eyes. She thought about studying her nails again but refrained; instead, she lifted angry eyes his way.

Quaid repeated, "I will not allow you to place my people in needless danger! You're acting like an immature girl rather than someone her proper age. Must I remind you of Vince's death? Or of how you've already had one visit from his probable murderer?"

Stiffening, Sydney spat out, "I don't need you to remind me of anything! I just needed some fresh air. Surely there must be some time during the day that one of you can go with me outside, even if it's for five minutes!"

Quaid grew silent as Maria calmly stated, "Sir, if there's a time you feel is safer than others, I don't mind going with her, even if we just sit on the stair steps for a few minutes each day."

For the first time, Maria noted Sydney looking at her with a touch of gratitude.

"Thank you, Maria. I appreciate it." Turning her eyes back to Quaid, she asked, "Well, warden, is that a possibility?"

Lowering his eyes to the floor, Quaid shook his head in a helpless gesture as a heavy sigh escaped his lips. Bringing his eyes back to Maria, he said, "If you're willing to trust her to follow your rules, I'll talk to Paul. We'll find a suitable time when it will be safe."

A happy Sydney made a move to rise from the chair.

"Not so fast! I'm not done with you yet. The other rules still stand—no flinging the curtains back to enjoy fresh air through open windows. You may crack them for peeks out or sit in the dark on the enclosed back porch. Since I now don't trust you, Maria accompanies you whenever you're on the back porch. Any questions?"

"Is it really so dangerous for me to be outside on the beach? You can see for miles across the water! If there was a boat, you'd easily see it."

"I'm not concerned about anything coming by way of the water. It's the woods around us that are the real danger. Someone could get quite close before we saw them. Plus, if they are excellent shots, once they established a clear line of vision, all they have to do is be patient. You cross the line of their scope, and you could be dead!"

A frown creased Sydney's brow as Quaid let that sink in a minute.

Pulling fingers through his still uncombed hair, Quaid sat on the sofa near Sydney's chair. "Sydney, it's important that you fully understand just what our team is willing to do for you. It's our job to protect you; that's what we've sworn to do even to the point of death. What I'm saying is, if that means stepping in front of a bullet to protect you, that's what we will do. But if one of us is going to die in the line of duty, it sure sits better if it isn't for some needless action on the part of the one we're protecting."

"You're telling me that you, Quaid, are willing to die for me?"

"That's what I'm telling you. But it's not just me; that includes Maria here; my partner, Paul; Neal; and Jake."

"Why? Why would you willingly die for me? You yourself said I have a face like a clown and dress like a harlot! I'm no good. It's my fault Vince is dead!"

"Sydney, I never said those things the way you're presenting them, and you're wrong about it being your fault that Vince is dead. He was a grown man making his own choices."

"Yes, but..." A lump of guilt had formed in her throat, and she couldn't go on.

Quaid's hand came forward, and Sydney had the distinct impression he was going to take hold of hers. Instead, he pulled his hand back and said, "Sydney, let's set aside the Vince issue and focus on today and your protection. We don't protect someone because they're good or bad; we do it partly because it's our job but also because we're trying to put men like Vince's killer behind bars. You need to understand the odds that Vince was his first murder are pretty slim. Whoever did it was a professional. He's a bad man, and we want to catch him."

Quaid frowned at the new conflict playing across Sydney's expressive face.

She appreciated the attempt he made to soften his voice. "Sydney, you seem to be wrestling with the thought of a stranger being willing to die for you; but on a much larger scale, that's exactly what Christ did on the cross for each and every one of us. He took our sin—past, present, and future—and paid the penalty for us. He didn't have to. He could have come off that cross anytime he wanted, but he didn't. He stayed up there so you and I might have eternal life. He willingly died for us. Personally, I've surrendered my life to him, and I know that when or if I die in the line of duty I'll be with him in heaven."

As he spoke, Sydney's eyes flew to his face. Fear came and went, but she didn't say a word to interrupt. Out of the corner of her eye, she saw Maria stiffen and then turn to walk toward her bedroom. This puzzled Sydney, but now wasn't the time for her to dwell on it.

Quaid's words were overwhelming her. She was at the point of telling him to stop when he stood.

"Sydney, please think about what I just said. If you have any questions in the spiritual realm, please ask me. But for now, I need you to acknowledge that you understand the seriousness of what we're doing here."

Unable to speak, Sydney nodded her head and then watched Quaid walk to his own bedroom. She figured he was hoping to still get a couple more hours of sleep before relieving Paul.

A few moments later, Sydney knocked on Maria's door. As Sydney waited for her to answer, she heard Quaid's door creak. Maria's door opened, so Sydney ignored the idea of Quaid listening. In a rush she said, "I'm sorry for sneaking out on you, Maria. I wasn't trying to put anyone in danger. I just needed to feel the sand in my toes."

Maria smiled and said, "Thank you for apologizing. To tell you the truth, for a second there, I was afraid someone had somehow gotten to you. That's why I woke Quaid up. I'm glad you're okay."

As the two women chatted a moment longer, Sydney heard Quaid's door softly close.

# Chapter 16

Six days later, in spite of Quaid's lecture, Sydney Larsen was feeling the stirrings of restlessness once again. It was no longer a comfort that she was staying in the home she'd seen from the ferry's deck, the one she'd imagined herself in front of on the beach, wearing a beautiful full-skirted, deep-red, taffeta dress while the other women had worn pale yellow or washed-out cream. The reality was, instead of being pampered and made to feel special, Sydney rankled under the harsh living rules. In rebellion, she'd refused to lift a finger. It surprised her that Maria hadn't said, "You don't help; you don't eat." Instead, she was still waiting on her.

The caution of danger seemed overdone to Sydney, and this morning of the tenth day, she felt especially rebellious. Flopping on the nearest of two recliners situated in the living room, she occupied her mind by daydreaming back to the time she and Quaid had kissed on the ferry. That thought flowed into the near collision with the couple outside the bathroom on the ferry, and Sydney frowned. Once again, it niggled her mind that the man was familiar, someone she'd seen somewhere before. Out of the blue, it came to her that he frequented one of the same taverns she did in Petoskey. As she smiled over finally placing the man, she then recalled how he hadn't shown her any attention. Frowning, Sydney thought on that a while, for she remembered he and his buddies often had tried buying her drinks and she always refused. Finally deciding he wasn't worth wasting time on, she shrugged her shoulders, settled deeper in the recliner, and moved her memory to their arrival on Beaver Island. Sydney purposely forced her mind to skip over the near fall on the ferry steps, specifically the feel of Quaid's arms around her. It bothered Sydney how much the man was on her mind. Suddenly, a realization hit her. *I felt safe in his arms. In fact, I feel safe whenever Quaid's around!*

The thought unsettled Sydney so much that she pushed it from her mind. Instead, she focused on how quickly the vehicles had been unloaded from the ferry. The foursome had soon made their way on land and down the road. Once in the car, Sydney had pointedly ignored Quaid. As they pulled away from the town, she had pasted her nose to the window to observe the passing scenery. For the most part, everyone was quiet except for the occasional comments from the front seat.

Now, sitting in the beautiful large home with all its beautiful furnishings around her, Sydney felt alone. Her mind wandered to the now frequent vision of Vince's death, which played havoc with her already tender mind and emotions.

Then the game her older sister had invented entered her head. It brought with it memories of yelling matches in the other room between their mom and stepdad. Now it occurred to Sydney that her sister had been trying to distract or shield her from the harsh life they shared. Once again a flood of negative thoughts assailed her mind.

Hearing Maria in the kitchen brought Sydney's mind back to the present. Mentally shaking herself, she jumped to her feet. Sydney paced the finely furnished living room while trying to refocus her mind away from the long ago past. In her pacing, she stopped atced the fireplace to study some family photos on the mantel. Everyone seemed so happy and loving. Sydney wondered what that was like.

Growing more and more irritated, she scowled at the photo. "What makes your family so special? I bet you don't always do honest things to get your money! You just haven't been caught!"

Still grumbling, Sydney slowly finished circling the room to land back at the recliner she'd recently vacated. In an unladylike manner, she plopped her body down. Grabbing a nearby magazine, she began flipping through it.

Maria opening and closing the refrigerator caught Sydney's attention. Shifting her weight on the recliner, she smiled. *It must be lunchtime. I wonder what she's making us today.* Feeling relaxed and smug, Sydney realized there had been some advantages to being kept in the house. She hadn't prepared a meal or done any cleaning since their arrival. Maria was doing it all, which suited Sydney just fine.

Since Sydney's trip to the beach, Quaid had been restless, and on the morning of the tenth day, he couldn't sleep. Paul was working the grounds alone that day, as Jake had left the previous morning for the mainland to pick up Sydney's mail and drop in at headquarters. Still tossing back and forth at around 11:00 a.m., Quaid finally gave up and went outside to stroll the grounds with Paul.

Quaid was thankful for his partner. The two of them had been through much over the years, and they trusted each other completely. Now as he tried sneaking up on his partner, Quaid admitted to himself that two things were keeping him from sleep. One

## Out of the Snare

was the lack of another appearance by Vince's murderer. It made no sense that he would just let them walk off with her. Quaid was positive they shouldn't be lulled into a false sense of security. It was only a matter of time before the mystery man found them. Of that Quaid was sure.

Paul and he needed to be extra alert over the next few days. Even the smallest overlooked detail could mean disaster. Slowing his pace, Quaid spied Paul around a bush just ahead. Bending over, he noiselessly worked his way closer. Just before reaching out to touch his partner, Paul spoke. "What are you doing up? I thought you went to bed."

Straightening, Quaid hit his partner's shoulder while smugly stating, "I knew I taught you well."

"What are you talking about? I had you pegged when you came out the front door."

The two bantered back and forth all the while scanning the woods and surrounding area.

"Seriously, though, why are you out here?"

Quaid explained his concern about Vince's murderer and his lack of appearance.

He then grew silent before adding, "The other thing bothering me is the necklace I bought for Sydney. At the time it seemed like a good idea—get something to point her toward Christ. Now I'm having second thoughts. If it's such a harmless gift, why have I hesitated for more than twelve days to give it to her?"

The two men thoughtfully walked the grounds. Then in a soft voice, Quaid observed, "You know, daylight gives a totally different perspective on lines of sight to the house and which windows are more visible. Now that I'm aware of that, maybe we should switch up every other night just to be more efficient?"

Paul agreed and then asked his partner, "Are you trying to change the subject, or do you really want to talk about the necklace you bought Sydney at the Detroit airport?"

As he and Paul walked and talked in low tones, Paul urged Quaid to give the necklace to Sydney but make it as impersonal as possible. "You don't want her to attach any romantic notions with it. She needs to see it as your way of reaching her soul for Christ, nothing else."

Shortly after that, with the necklace already in his pocket, Quaid left to find Sydney.

"Do you mind if I turn on the TV? I'd like to watch the midday news." Noting Maria's hands carried a paper plate full of a sandwich, chips, and even a pickle, Sydney offered a smile and reached for the food. "Sure, and thanks for lunch."

Much to her surprise, Maria walked on by.

Maria hid a smile as she picked up the remote, clicked on the television, and then took a seat on the sofa. Without glancing Sydney's way, she lifted the sandwich to her lips then paused to state, "I didn't make you lunch today. This is mine."

"But, but... where's mine?"

"I suppose in the refrigerator, depending on what you decide to eat."

A surprised Sydney let her feet fall in order to sit up in the recliner. "What do you mean, you suppose?"

Maria chewed before leveling her eyes at Sydney. "I think it's time to remind you that I'm here to protect you, not wait on you. If you're hungry, go make yourself something."

Sydney's jaw dropped as she watched Maria turn her attention to the news and take another bite.

*Of all the...* At that moment, Sydney's tummy growled, reminding her that breakfast had been skipped. Maria's obvious enjoyment of her sandwich was making Sydney hungry. She shot daggers Maria's way, but as she wasn't looking, they evaporated harmlessly in the air. Realizing the conversation was over, Sydney propelled herself from the recliner and huffed. "Fine, I'll do that!" As she turned toward the kitchen, Sydney noticed Quaid leaning against the doorway leading into the fully equipped kitchen.

## Out of the Snare

"What are you smirking at?" she snapped.

When Sydney drew even with him, Quaid pushed himself away from the wall. Noting the deep frown on her brow and glare in her eyes, he stated, "I wasn't smirking. If you ask me, it's about time Maria stopped pampering you."

"No one asked you!" Moving into the kitchen, she opened the refrigerator and scanned the contents. Spying some shredded ham and Swiss cheese, she pulled out other things needed to make a sandwich. Carrying the items to the middle cutting board island, she noted Quaid now seated on one of the stools directly across from her. He was intently watching her every movement.

Sydney tried ignoring him, but Quaid apparently wasn't having it. Hearing him clear his throat a couple times, Sydney stopped what she was doing to study his face. It wasn't like Quaid to stumble about saying something.

Then, totally uncharacteristic of him, Quaid blurted, "Sydney, I bought you something."

Having picked up the knife, Sydney started slathering mayonnaise on the bread.

Startled at his words, Sydney's hand stopped, and her mouth dropped open. A large glob of mayo plopped on the counter. Scooping it with the knife, she managed to get most of it on the bread before saying, "You did what?"

Before replying, Quaid studied her face. Then he said, "When I had that three-hour layover in the Detroit airport, I was walking around and found a gift shop. Not having anything better to do, I impulsively went in and saw something I thought you might like."

As he talked, Sydney kept her eyes centered on the food while thinking, *No one buys me gifts for no reason. There must be a catch!* Realizing Quaid had stopped talking, Sydney assumed he was waiting for some acknowledgment from her. Deliberately taking time to finish the sandwich to remove any telltale emotion from her eyes, Sydney finished the sandwich before looking up.

Quaid maintained eye contact while pulling a box from his pants pocket. Setting it on the counter between them, he took one finger and slid it toward her. "Open it, and then I'll explain."

Staring into his eyes a moment, Sydney reluctantly lowered hers to the small velvet box that looked to hold some form of jewelry. Frowning, she asked, "Why would you buy me a gift? We're practically strangers, and you don't even like me."

"I've never said I didn't like you. When I'm on duty, liking doesn't enter the picture. You're my job, but neither of those statements have anything to do with this gift." Growing a little impatient, he added, "Just open it. Hopefully then you'll understand a little better."

Quaid watched her expressive face go through multiple emotions ranging from embarrassment to frustration, to a form of vulnerability, and then ended with open curiosity. Stubbornly, she still made no move to touch the box. Seeing so much emotion made Quaid frown. *Obviously there's much bad history in her life. I wonder if she's ever really had someone to open up to.*

Quaid reached for the box while gently saying, "Tell you what. Maybe this was a mistake."

Before he could wrap his fingers around it, Sydney snatched it up.

Smiling briefly at his victory, Quaid met flashing indignant eyes as he added, "So I guess you want it. Okay then, this is the deal. You open it and listen to why I bought it. If you don't want the gift, I'll take it back. No harm done. How about that?"

Sydney stared at the box yet still hesitated, and Quaid's patience finally broke. Coming to his feet, he extended his hand. "Okay, Sydney. You either open it or hand it back! It's your choice!"

Sydney drew the box close to her chest while her eyes dared him to try taking it.

In frustration, Quaid ran a hand through his black hair. He wondered how he should respond. *This isn't the way I saw this playing out. I guess I should have picked a better time.*

The two had a stare down, and surprising to Quaid, Sydney backed down first.

Raising vulnerable, sad eyes to him, she tilted her head slightly and softly said, "No one buys me things, not even Vince." She paused then added, "If I got something for Christmas or my birthday, it was because I found discarded stuff in the garbage, or Allie would get me something from the dollar store."

Embarrassed at her sudden confession, anger surged to the forefront. She brought the box forward and snapped it open. As she studied the contents, the sudden anger was replaced with surprise then puzzlement. Bringing her eyes once more to Quaid's, she said, "I don't understand."

Quaid retook his seat before replying, "I didn't think you would. That's why I asked you to look and then said I'd explain. As you can see, it's a tiny Bible locket."

In order to peer more closely at the two-inch pewter book, Sydney pulled her eyes from Quaid's. She ran her finger over a tiny cross etched on the front.

"Open it up. There's a verse imprinted inside. It's Joshua 1:9." He then quoted it from memory as she read along. "Be strong and of good courage; do not be afraid, nor be dismayed, for the Lord your God is with you wherever you go."

She snapped the box lid closed and handed it back. "No, thank you. We both know I'm not a believer like you. I was only pretending to be as part of my cover and to get closer to Pierce Matthews. I'm not interested in your religion." She placed her sandwich on a paper plate and then moved to leave the room as Quaid came to his feet. His next words stopped her.

"I'm not interested in religion either."

"But... you go to church and are different than the guys I know and usually hang around with. I've never heard you swear or seen you in the bars."

"I didn't say I wasn't a believer and follower of Jesus Christ. I said

I wasn't interested in religion." Seeing a frown knit her brows, he hurriedly added, "I'm not trying to confuse you, but religion is man-made with traditions formed by men. Being a Christian is a way of life learned by reading and studying God's Word, the Bible."

Seeing confusion still evident on her face, Quaid picked up the necklace and stepped closer to her. "We can talk about that stuff at a later time. For now, let's get back to why I bought this necklace for you."

Sydney stiffened at his closeness, so Quaid took a step back and softened his voice. "Sydney, we all have times of doubts and fears." Seeing her eyes get mischievous and her lips part to say something, Quaid rushed on. "Even me."

Quaid then paused, for he expected a reply, but all he got was a raised brow. "You're going through a particularly difficult time right now, and I thought the necklace might be a comfort. I also thought it might be a reminder that you're not alone. God's here for you. All you have to do is reach out to his Son, Jesus. He'll give you the strength and courage to face whatever lies ahead... if you will let him."

At his last words, all traces of cuteness disappeared and were replaced by hardness in her eyes and by further stiffening of her body.

Finished, Quaid extended his hand with the box. "It's yours if you'd like it."

More and more uncomfortable with the whole conversation, Sydney couldn't explain why Quaid's words had made her heart race and given her a strong desire to flee the room. As this feeling grew, Sydney snatched the box out of his hand and headed for the doorway with her lunch in the other. She didn't stop until safely behind the closed door of her bedroom.

Leaning against the door, Sydney felt short of air and was surprised at how small the large bedroom suddenly felt. Closing her eyes, she took several deep breaths before walking to the bed. Placing the unopened box down, she sat on the bed. "Why would he do that? Why would he buy me a gift?" Sydney spoke those questions over and over to the room, temporarily forgetting about the still uneaten lunch.

## Out of the Snare

Eventually, her tummy began growling again, and she emotionally calmed down. Sydney picked up her sandwich as her mind moved to a similar gift she'd received long ago from another Christian person, a woman. The image of hiding beside snow-covered steps after fleeing the wrath of her stepfather came to mind.

As Sydney's mind replayed the story, the sandwich remained untouched. Slowly lowering it, Sydney realized that her hatred for her stepfather had evolved into her lack of trust for any man, including Vince and now Quaid.

As her mind whirled between the past and present, Sydney grew tired of the emotional fight. She decided to spend the rest of the day and night in bed. Securing her door so no one could come in, she put on her nightwear and crawled into bed. Repeatedly, she tried to push the two necklaces from her mind and what they tried to spiritually represent to her. Seeing the box on the bedside stand didn't help, so Sydney grabbed it to thrust it under her pillow. *There. Out of sight, out of mind!*

She was snuggling back in bed when her eyes landed on the leather Bible. To date, she still hadn't told Quaid she'd looked up the verses. The fact was she'd read them so often that a couple she could say from memory. Sydney couldn't explain why she didn't tell him. Every time she thought to do so, an unreasonable fear would fill her. She'd then tell herself it was best to wait for a better day.

Quaid's image presented itself strongly in her mind. To her consternation, with it also came a vivid memory of him kissing her on the deck of the ferry. Sydney dreamily entertained the idea of him being her lover and let her imagination run wild with that until sleep overcame her.

Some time later, Maria knocked to tell her supper was ready. Yelling that she wasn't hungry and wouldn't come out, Sydney rolled over and pulled the covers way up with the pillow over her head.

Most of the night, she was haunted by swirling dreams of the kiss mixed with nightmares of Vince being murdered and with the field being full of steel traps. At one point, she awoke in a sweat and reached under the pillow to touch the box. The fact of its presence was a comfort, and she soon fell back asleep.

She might not have slept so soundly if she knew just how close Vince's killer was to finding her.

# Chapter 17

"It's been ten days, and you're telling me you still haven't found her?" Corey Drake was angry. "How hard can it be finding one woman with three people guarding her?" His main man, Jerry, had been clearly instructed that the moment Sydney was found he was to be sent a text message stating "located." Since none came, Corey was more than ready to hear the reason why.

"Boss, it's not like we're not trying! My friend Pete had the perfect idea. He disguised himself as a delivery guy. He even strapped fake pizza boxes on the back of his moped. He sighted Sydney and her group less than a block from the ferry dock. Unfortunately, as they headed past the airport, he had some trouble with his moped.

Not wanting to draw too much attention, he pulled over and pretended a delivery. Before he could get going again, a couple cars got between them." Jerry paused to take a breath then rushed on. "But he could still see the car in the distance. That is until the bend in the road." Here he paused again.

An exasperated Corey practically hollered into his cell phone, "So he lost them?"

"No, boss. That is…not exactly." Before his boss could utter anything, Jerry rushed on. "There's only one new housing development off the straightaway around the bend. Since they disappeared so quickly, Pete believes they're holed up in one of those. The bad news is there are close to fifteen homes in there. Plus, they all have lots of trees and sit back from the road. The good news is most of the people have already left the island for the winter. There are only a few hangers on, so Pete is asking around about what homes are still getting heat, etc."

Corey let out a heavy sigh and then asked, "So what are you geniuses doing? Walking up to the doors and knocking?"

Jerry chuckled. "No, boss. We wouldn't do that."

"So what exactly is my money paying for?"

"Boss, we're working hard here! Every day we talk to shop owners and others, trying to narrow down what people are still here in those houses. I'm happy to tell you we're down to only five possibilities. Yup, that's right, only five. We've been able to rule out ten already. That's good news, isn't it, boss?"

"Ten whole houses ruled out, huh? Let's see…at that rate it'll be close to another week before you find her." Lacing his words with sarcasm, he added, "Unless we get lucky, and she's in the next house!" Before Jerry could respond, Corey said through clenched teeth, "Now you listen to me! I want this girl found in the next couple of days! Short of announcing it over a PA system, find her, or you'll regret knowing me! Get the picture?"

"Sure, boss, sure. We'll find her, you bet. No worries," Jerry hurriedly replied as he heard a heavy click on the other end of the line.

## Out of the Snare

The next morning, Sydney lazily lit a cigarette as she thought about the little jewelry box still under the pillow. Being drawn to it, she clamped her lighter closed then pulled out the velvet box. Sydney wanted to touch the little pewter Bible. She was strongly tempted to put the chain around her neck—that is until she reread the verse on the inside. Taking a deep inhale, Sydney exhaled a heavy cloud of smoke while watching it swirl into the air. As it disappeared, Quaid's words of the afternoon before suddenly came vividly back. "God's here for you. All you have to do is reach out to his Son, Jesus. He'll give you the strength and courage to face whatever lies ahead." With a frown she stared at the glowing end of the cigarette. She suddenly snubbed it out and then wondered why.

Part of her wanted to believe Quaid's words, those of the well-dressed woman outside the mission, or even Hope's. Then past memories of injustices came surging to the forefront of her mind, and her heart hardened. Shutting the box, Sydney put it under her socks in the dresser and got herself ready for another long, boring day, all the while thinking, *Only fools believe in fairy tale gods. What good has one ever done me?*

The following morning before going to bed, Quaid drove to pick up Jake returning on the ferry. Having arrived a few minutes early, he found a bench nearby and watched the local village come alive. While sitting there, a noisy moped sped by loaded with pizza boxes on the back. *That's strange. How many people eat pizza this early in the morning?*

Hearing a little alarm go off in his head, Quaid stood to glance around at the businesses. He was looking for the pizza place. Spying McDonough's Market with a window "pizza" sign, Quaid walked over. The place had an Irish theme on the outside. Opening the door, Quaid walked in like he was looking for something in particular. He

171

was delighted with the interior décor as well as the fact that the place sold just about everything anyone would need. Seeing a man near the counter, Quaid walked over. "I see you have pizza. Do you deliver?"

"No, you'll need to come pick it up," the man replied with a slight Irish accent.

A puzzled Quaid stated, "That's strange. I thought for sure I'd seen a moped around the area delivering pizza."

The man broke into laughter. "Oh, you're talking about Pete. He loves his moped!" Shaking his head, the talkative man added, "We all know it's Pete long before we see him. He's the only one still using a moped on the island, and it's noisy!" Here he paused and grew thoughtful. "But lately he's been acting strange... like pretending he's a pizza delivery guy. I don't know why he has pizza boxes on his moped, but they certainly aren't full of pizzas. He works at the marina, and I know they don't sell pizza."

Pleased with the information he was receiving, Quaid engaged the man in more small talk about Pete and other local people. Before long the man volunteered, "Actually, now that I think of it, Pete started acting strange when his two friends arrived here from the mainland. Shortly after that, they started asking too many questions if you ask me."

"What kind of questions?"

"Things like: Who's still living on the island? Are any new people staying in the houses located south of the airport?"

In hopes of finding out more information, Quaid patiently chatted on. "Was one of them tall, say six-foot-two or three with wavy dark hair? Quite well built?"

Again the clerk laughed. "Are you kidding? These guys are kind of seedy and look like throwbacks from the seventies if you know what I mean. Not that I think they're bad!" He then added, "Actually, I think they're just easygoing guys not concerned about working a career." Then for the first time, he narrowed his eyes and asked, "Say, why all the questions? Are you looking for someone?"

## Out of the Snare

"No," Quaid quickly assured. "They sound like some guys I know from Petoskey, and I wondered if my friend was with them." Feeling he'd asked enough questions, Quaid did a little more small talk then purchased a newspaper. Walking out, he flipped open his cell phone as he strolled back to the dock. Quaid waited for Paul to answer. His senses now in full alert, Quaid noted everything around him, including the approaching ferry bringing Jake. As Quaid waited near the dock, his insides were screaming, *They're here and closing in*, yet his demeanor remained calm and in control.

On the second ring, Paul answered. "What did you forget? Want me to ask the girls for a grocery list?"

Not wasting any time, Quaid stated, "They're here! It's time for the evacuation plan. Wake up Neal and get the girls moving!"

"I'm moving as we speak and almost to his door. Fill me in."

"The main thing is that three men are combing the area looking for new people on the island. I don't believe they've located us yet. Get the pilot on the horn. Jake is docking as we speak, and we'll be there soon. I want to leave within the hour. Once we're airborne, I'll fill you in with the details." As Quaid went to hang up, his last words were, "Keep an eye and ear out for a noisy moped. It's the only one currently being used on the island. And I believe it's being driven by someone hired to find us."

"Boss! We think we finally got a break! Pete was on his way back to town when he saw something!" Jerry could hardly contain his excitement. Taking a breath, he rushed on. "Pete's moped broke down just after he left cruising around that new housing area. Anyway, he pulled off the road right beside a locked gate with a two-track leading deep into the woods. He normally wouldn't have paid attention, but he could see recent tire tracks leading in and out. When he got back to town, he asked around, and there's a home back there. A nice big one! We think it's a good possibility that Sydney is there!"

Corey's heart surged with adrenaline, and his palms grew sweaty with excitement that his prey might be near. He said, "This is what I want you boys to do. Make sure whether or not the owners of the house are still on the island. Then, after dark, get as close as you can to the house. For goodness sakes, be quiet about it! There are at least three detectives guarding her. They're sharp, so don't do anything stupid. Just see if there are lights on and then get out of there. This sounds like the perfect place for her to be, so I don't want you boys alerting them. If you see lights, get out of there before giving me a call. I don't want them hearing you. When you call back, I'll give you more information about what to do next."

"Okay, boss. We'll see what we can find out, and don't worry—we'll be invisible. They won't know a thing."

*Yeah right! As if I believe that!* Out loud he said, "Just get in and out; then call me."

Hanging up, Corey rapidly made plans. If this was even a remote possibility, he needed to get to that island as fast as possible. Turning to his computer, he started checking into chartering a private jet for a late-night flight.

That evening, Pierce Matthews was having a personal struggle and wasn't sure how to deal with it. Baby Sarah's one year birthday was coming up, and Hope was planning a party. The dilemma? It was also the first year anniversary of Vicki's death. Part of him wanted to talk about it with Hope, especially since the two of them were contemplating marriage in January or February. But a stronger part of him wanted to be alone with his grief. He wanted to take out all the special memories of the great life he and Vicki had shared especially at the last when they were preparing for their first child. The memories were his and Vicki's. Hope had never met her, so how could she possibly be a comfort?

At this point in his thinking, Pierce would start having an inner struggle, for he knew deep down that Hope could relate. After all, Dean's death in an auto accident had been just as sudden. As his thoughts played back and forth, Pierce leaned back in his recliner and groaned. "Lord, it's not that I want to shut Hope out of this part of my life, but there's still so much I need to deal with."

Multiple arguments flowed through his mind. *I need to let her in. But then won't her grief get muddled in with mine? Maybe it's best to hash out my grieving alone between me and God and Vicki's memories. But Hope may not understand. It may hurt her feelings or even make her think I don't truly love her. Lord, I do love her. In fact, the more I'm around her, the more I see things to love! She's sweet, giving, tender with baby Sarah and me.*

Then the thoughts of Sarah would bring Pierce back to the hospital and Vicki's sudden death in childbirth, and the circle would start all over again.

Grabbing the recliner lever to lower his feet down, Pierce leaned forward to cover his head with work-worn hands and groaned. "Oh, Lord, what should I do? Do I include Hope in this struggle? How should I handle this? Please give me wisdom to help me and Hope through this time."

After a long moment, Pierce rose and walked to his bedroom where a photo of Vicki sat on the dresser. Picking it up, Pierce lovingly ran his finger over her face while softly saying, "I miss you, darling. Our little girl will soon be one year old. She looks a lot like you. She has your eyes, hair, and she's already taking her first steps."

As he lowered himself on the bed, Pierce held the photo close to his heart. "Oh, Vicki. We were so excited about our first baby. Your parents were here, and we had made plans to celebrate. But then...but then God had other plans, and you suddenly left to be with him."

Sighing heavily, Pierce closed his eyes as a couple tears emerged and slid down his tan, rugged cheeks. As he sat there hugging the photo, more followed, then more. Soon great sobs tore at the air and at his heart as Pierce struggled to remember if Vicki had lived long enough to know their baby was a little girl.

Hope Montgomery sat on her porch swing and studied the night sky. Pierce had left for his nearby cabin shortly after Sarah had been put to bed, which was unusual for him. Hope had wanted to talk to him about a couple things.

One was the remodeling of the wonderful engagement gift he'd given her. Even now, she found it hard to believe that she was engaged to a multimillionaire and that he'd bought her a very large stone-turreted home that they were making into a bed and breakfast. Working at Bev's Bed and Breakfast down in East Grand Rapids had been very therapeutic in helping her get over some of the hardships the Lord had allowed to cross her path after Dean's sudden death. Now Hope had a desire to help others the same way, and Pierce was giving her the opportunity. There were many decisions needing to be made, but Pierce wasn't in the mood. He asked her to talk about it another day.

The other thing she'd wanted to discuss was Sarah's upcoming birthday party, but again Pierce had put her off with "Not tonight, Hope. I'm tired. We'll talk about it tomorrow." He kissed Hope lightly, hugged her for a long time, and then left.

Now, still seeing his lights on, Hope wondered out loud to the crisp November air. "If he was so tired, how come he's still up?"

Pulling her jacket tighter, Hope realized she should have grabbed her winter coat instead. Ignoring the chill creeping up her arms, she felt a strong need to pray. Instead of bowing her head as usual, Hope raised her blue eyes toward the heavens and said, "Lord, there's something bothering Pierce, and I don't know what. Please help him to find the peace that surpasses all understanding. I believe you brought me into Pierce's and Sarah's lives for a reason. The fact that we fell in love is an almost overwhelming surprise. I love them both dearly, which is something six months ago I never thought I'd be able to say again, ever! You did all that, Lord! Oh, the pain and suffering I'd been through with losing my job just minutes before learning of Dean's death in a car accident. A month later, I found myself with financial problems, which led to my losing our condo and ending up living in a very small basement apartment."

Here she paused as the memory of her next heartache came surging to the forefront of her mind—the premature birth and death of her and Dean's baby. Before Hope could go on, a sob escaped. The memory of bitterness and the feeling of being rejected by God humbled Hope.

She stood and walked to the porch railing. At that moment, her beagle puppy of six months came running up wanting attention. Hope stooped to scratch his head and ears. The puppy soon ran off again chasing some imaginary foe. Straightening back up, Hope placed her hands on the railing and looked at Pierce's cabin once more.

It slowly began seeping into her mind that since the anniversary of Vicki's death coincided with Sarah's birthday, Pierce might be struggling with past memories.

Hope's thoughts grew into a conviction that she now knew what Pierce's problem was. Bowing her head, she earnestly prayed they'd both learn how to handle their memories and pain and that they'd both learn how to go on and do it in an emotionally healthy and spiritual way.

Hope's thoughts then flowed to Sydney. "Lord, we have no idea where she is, but she's in trouble. Please keep her and the people protecting her safe. Help the police find whoever killed Sydney's partner, Vince. But more importantly, please draw her to yourself. Help Syd see the need of you in her life. Thank you, Jesus, that I can freely bring all these things before you, knowing that you hear and care. Amen."

Opening her eyes, Hope watched Pierce's lights go out one by one. Turning to go inside, she whispered one more quick prayer.

"Help us both have a peace-filled, restful night's sleep."

# Chapter 18

The moment Quaid entered the front door, Sydney rushed from her bedroom. Meeting him in the middle of the living room, she anxiously wrapped her hands around Quaid's bicep. "Is he here? Did you see him? What are we going to do? Where are we going?"

Checking his forward progress, Quaid looked into her wide, dilated eyes. He noticed she was wearing the Bible necklace around her neck. He also noticed a heavy smell of cigarette smoke. Quaid shook all thoughts away as he placed steady hands on Sydney's shaking shoulders.

"I don't think he's on the island yet. That's why we need to move now." Lifting eyes to Maria standing nearby, he asked, "Are you ladies ready?"

"Yes, sir, we are. We're just taking the readied suitcases."

"Good. The plan is—"

Quaid broke off as Paul entered through the kitchen, stating, "Jake and Neal are patrolling the place. The pilot will be ready to leave in twenty minutes. How do you want to handle this?"

For a second, Quaid eyed his two main people with pride. They were both calm and ready. Nodding in quiet approval, he stated, "Jake and Neal will stay behind, load up our remaining stuff from the two houses, and catch the afternoon ferry. They'll leave the TV and various lights on. That won't hurt for a couple days, and hopefully it will buy us more time. I've instructed Jake to pick up some needed things at headquarters; then they will join us with Maria's car." Here he paused to verify Maria's consent.

"Whatever's needed," was all she said.

Still having his hands on Sydney, Quaid brought his attention back to her. He was pleased to note that she had visibly calmed as he had spoken. Smiling, he gave her shoulders a gentle squeeze then let his hands drop. "You're doing fine, Sydney, but now we need to get going. If you have further questions, they'll have to wait until we're in the car or in the helicopter."

Her eyes suddenly grew large once more. "A helicopter? I've never flown in one before!"

"Relax. It's a six-passenger beauty. Like the ferry, this adventure we're on is introducing you to a lot of firsts." At that he turned to head toward his bedroom while stating, "Okay, let's get cracking!"

"An adventure he says. That's what he thinks!" Sydney mumbled as she followed him to her own room. Her eyes fell on the crystal cross still on the nightstand. She quickly unzipped the emergency suitcase lying on the bed to tuck it inside along with the velvet necklace box.

A short ten minutes later, Sydney looked back at the beautiful log home and then sighed. Sliding her eyes to Quaid seated with her in the back, she started to ask something but stopped as her eyes fell on the pistol in his hands. She watched him expertly check the full load in his Glock and then pull a bullet into the chamber. A chill ran up Sydney's spine as she hugged the bundle of mail handed to her by Jake. She hadn't looked at it yet, but for now it was giving her a bit of security in this world of guns and danger. Oh, how she could use a cigarette, but Maria had adamantly stated, "Not in my car!"

Noting her anxious posture, Quaid surmised her problem and pulled a pack of gum from his pocket, offering her a piece. Sydney shortly stuffed it in her mouth with a thanks. Quaid studied her a bit more as she stared blindly ahead. *Is it my imagination, or is she wearing a little less makeup these days?*

Remembering the necklace, he casually said, "I noticed you're wearing the necklace." As he spoke, Sydney's hand flew to the charm, but she didn't comment. Right then, Paul stopped the car, so Quaid's speculations about why she chose now to wear it were interrupted. Handing Sydney the pack of gum, he jumped out to open and close the chained gate one last time.

After the gate was locked again, Quaid stepped out to survey the road both ways before signaling Paul to pull up beside him. Climbing into the car, within a couple minutes, the foursome drove into the road leading to the private airstrip. A short time later, Paul parked next to a helicopter stationed a distance from any buildings. Making sure no one but the pilot was near, Sydney's three protectors quickly ushered her into the new mode of travel. Once all had donned headsets to communicate over the noise and were securely in, the pilot started the large rotor. Maria sat in front with the pilot while Sydney sat behind with Quaid and Paul on each side.

As they lifted off, Quaid instructed the pilot to head west and then make a wide swing northward over Lake Michigan to the Upper Peninsula. "That way, if someone is watching, they'll think we're headed to Wisconsin or elsewhere. Then we'll head back to St. Ignace from the northwest."

As the helicopter's nose dipped and took off, Quaid felt Sydney stiffen. Her left hand lay clenched in a fist on her lap, and her knuckles were turning white while her right hand rubbed the pewter Bible like it was one of those worry stones. She jumped when his voice sounded in her ear. "Did you know Beaver Island is part of a group of fourteen islands? As we go higher, you should be able to see some of them." Sydney leaned over Quaid to look but quickly covered her eyes and sat back.

*Hmm. She must be scared of heights,* Quaid surmised. Knowing his voice was also being heard by his fellow officers, Quaid said, "Beaver Island has a bit of interesting history. In 1848 a split-off group of Mormons moved there from Wisconsin. They were led by James Strang. They founded the village of St. James after him and the King's Highway, which are both still on Beaver Island. They also started the first northern Michigan newspaper. It was called the *Northern Islander.*" Feeling Sydney's body start to relax beside him, Quaid warmed to his subject.

"Strang's power soon went to his head. In 1850 he proclaimed himself king of the island, thus the road—King's Highway. Liking the power, he soon started being very authoritative, which extended to anyone on the island, even those not in his religious group. That went on for about six years until two of his own followers assassinated him."

By now the helicopter was heading north toward the Upper Peninsula. A couple times Sydney turned her eyes to Quaid's showing interest in his words, but most of the time her gaze remained glued on the approaching land. He was further rewarded in his calming efforts when one time she turned fear-laced eyes to him. Leaning slightly closer, she admitted softly, "I'm afraid of the water. I don't know how to swim."

Hearing her words, everyone turned eyes her way. As Quaid nodded approval at his team's look of kindness, Sydney said in a strained voice, "Thanks for talking me through those last few minutes."

"No problem." Smiling warmly, Quaid almost reached for her hand. Rubbing the back of his neck instead, he assured, "I don't know about Maria, but Paul and I are excellent swimmers. You're safe."

Sydney gave him a smiling thanks before turning her eyes forward again.

Quaid studied her profile while thinking, *She is wearing less makeup!* It startled him how beautiful and expressive her eyes were. *I guess I never noticed before because the eye makeup got in my way.* Now he couldn't help but admit how pretty a woman she really was. Not liking the avenue his mind was heading down, Quaid reprimanded himself and directed his mind to ways he could reach her for Christ.

For a moment, the only sound was the loud *whop, whop* of the rotor. Then Paul asked in his ear, "So what happened after Strang was murdered?"

Pulling his mind from the woman beside him, Quaid said, "Umm, where was I? Oh yes, a group of mainland men came and drove the Mormons off the island. There were over 2,600 of them by then."

"How many people live full time on the island now?" Maria wondered.

"I would guess somewhere between three hundred and four hundred people."

"Wow! That gives a better idea of how large that group was, doesn't it?"

"Yes, it does. After they were gone, the island became somewhat lawless until the mid-1890s, when it was officially incorporated into Charlevoix County and their government."

All grew silent again as the helicopter made land and turned east. Then Paul spoke up again. "I heard the island referred to as America's Emerald Isle. As you seem to be our talking encyclopedia, do you know why that is, Quaid?"

Quaid leaned forward to give his partner a thumbs-up. "Thanks for finally acknowledging which of us is the wiser."

"Knowledge doesn't make you wise, smarty; it's how you use the knowledge that does that," he shot back.

As the two men bantered back and forth, Maria spoke up, cutting them off. "Out of curiosity, I looked up Beaver Island on the

Internet. I read the same things Quaid just told us about. The one thing he didn't mention was that the Mormon homes and buildings are all gone, except one. The print shop remains. It's now a museum. I think it would be interesting to go through it sometime."

All grew silent as they thought about Beaver Island and its history.

Then Paul piped up with, "So, Sir Quaid, oh Learned One. Why is it called America's Emerald Isle?"

Quaid replied theatrically in an old English voice, "Oh, Lowly One, after the Mormons left, Irish people began moving to the island. Many of the current residents are from Irish descent. If we'd been able to explore the island, you'd have found many things with Irish names: stores, restaurants, etc."

During this time, Quaid thought Sydney seemed to be enjoying the interchange. That is until she let out a heavy sigh then said wistfully, "Exploring the island would have been fun."

Not hearing any sarcasm, Quaid replied, "Maybe we can come back sometime."

Immediately, Sydney's eyebrows went skyward as she swung eyes his way. Realizing how that must have sounded, Quaid quickly stated, "I mean...you; maybe, once all this is resolved...you can come back."

A disgusted frown knit her brows as she stiffened and turned her eyes forward. "Sure, Quaid. If I live, that's exactly what I'll rush to go do!"

Heavy sarcasm hung in the air.

Quaid studied her profile a second then looked out his window.

Sydney broke the silence. "If you know all about the killer's men back on Beaver Island, how come you don't arrest them?"

"For what?" Paul asked. "They haven't done anything wrong."

"But..."

"The chief does plan to pick them up for questioning but wants to wait until they're back on the mainland. Once they're brought in, we might be able to get some clues as to who they're working for and maybe where he is," Quaid added.

When he finished, Maria chimed in with her heavy Spanish

accent. "The fact we do know about these guys is to our advantage. If we take them out of the picture too soon, the killer will just bring in more, and we wouldn't know them." Turning in her seat to better see Quaid's face, Maria then asked, "What I don't understand is how they found us so quickly."

"That has the rest of us puzzled too."

Paul asked, "Sydney, have you received any kind of communication from anyone you know? You still have your cell phone, right?"

"I do, but I've not received anything. Besides, with Maria dogging my every step, I'm sure you'd know it if I had."

Maria turned back around in her seat as the group grew silent once more.

Out of the blue, Sydney calmly stated, "I did run into someone I knew on the ferry."

"What?" Quaid practically shouted into the headphones. Seeing everyone raise hands to their ears, he quickly apologized and then demanded, "When was this? You were with one of us all the time!"

"When Maria and I went to the bathroom…remember, Maria? We bumped into them as we came out."

"Them? Now you're saying there was more than one?" Quaid threw his next question to the front. "Maria, how come I'm just hearing about this?"

For the first time, Sydney saw Maria lose some of her composure as she stuttered, "But…but…I studied the couple. It was a man and woman. They mumbled their apologies then walked on. Neither even looked Sydney's way! I know because I watched as they walked across the room and sat down facing the outside." She then said to Sydney, "You never mentioned you knew them."

Sydney clarified, "I didn't know her, but I've seen him in the bars in Petoskey." Then with a degree of condescension, she added, "Not that I was interested in the likes of him. I was looking for bigger fish."

Before Quaid could reply, Paul said, "Regardless, obviously he did know you and passed the information on!" Out of frustration he added,

"Man, they've known our whereabouts since day one! I'm surprised they hadn't found us before now." In disgust, he turned his head away.

Taking a deep breath, Quaid too was frustrated. It was these seemingly little unimportant details that made their work so much harder. Controlling his voice, he said, "Okay, ladies. This is a setback but not the end of the world. But let me make myself perfectly clear! From this moment on, Paul and I need to hear *anything*—and I stress—anything that strikes you even the tiniest bit odd. Clear?"

"Yes, sir. I'm sorry. I honestly thought it was nothing. If she'd let me know he was someone she knew, I'd have told you right away."

"Maria, stop kissing up! It was an honest mistake! We're not perfect. Ease up, Quaid."

"Sydney, you still don't seem to understand how serious all of this is, or you don't care! Either way, if you don't start cooperating better with us, I'll contact headquarters and get a different team to protect you. I won't put my people in unnecessary danger. Do you understand me?"

"Okay, warden. Yes, sir!" Sydney saluted him then looked straight ahead out the front windshield.

*Lord, is she ever going to grow up? Please don't allow her foolishness to get any of my people killed.* As he turned his eyes back out the side window, Quaid wondered again how he could break through her callousness. *At times, she's so irritating!*

After about five minutes, Quaid broke the silence to explain, "Our new location will be St. Ignace."

Sydney started to ask where that was, but Quaid, still being a little miffed, cut her off. "Do you know where the Mackinac Bridge is connecting Upper and Lower Michigan?"

"I've never been there, but yes."

"St. Ignace is the small city just north of the bridge. A friend owns a private helipad on property near his home. We'll be landing there. It's only a couple miles from there to the safe house."

"If we're flying in, how are we getting there?"

Quaid was impressed that Sydney was calm enough to think through what he was saying. She actually blushed when he praised her and added, "My friend is loaning us a vehicle until the guys arrive tomorrow."

A few minutes later, Sydney let out a loud exclamation when the bridge came into view. Quaid smiled, for her first sight was more impressive than most people ever get to experience. The pilot swung out to give all a better view.

This time, it was Paul who spoke up. "Did you know the Mackinac is the longest suspension bridge in the world?"

To which Quaid quickly replied, "No, it's not! There's one in Japan that's longer."

With a smug voice, Paul stated, "That depends, partner. It depends on what you're measuring."

"Okay, in that case, explain yourself," Quaid insisted.

"Sydney, do you see the two towers?"

"I do."

"If you measure the distance between them, then this bridge ranks as the twelfth longest in the world. But, if you measure from land to land, then it's the longest. What you're looking at is almost five miles across there."

"Really? It doesn't seem that far across."

"It is. The longest between towers is a bridge in Japan, but its overall length is only 2.4 miles." Paul shot Quaid an I-knew-more-than-you-on-this-one look and then leaned back in his seat.

Not being outdone, Quaid asked, "If you're so smart, when did the first car drive across the Mackinac Bridge?"

Paul didn't even bother gloating at Quaid as he replied, "November 1, 1957."

Still staring forward, Sydney asked, "So how did people get to the Upper Peninsula before that time?"

Both men leaned forward expecting the other to answer.

In the silence, Maria piped up. "They had to take a ferry. I imagine like the one we used for Beaver Island, or maybe even larger."

Ten minutes later, the helicopter sat down on a pad near a large three-storied cement block home with a pillared front located on a bluff above St. Ignace.

Later that night, three men on Beaver Island drove past the airport and a golf course toward the gated driveway. Having the road to themselves, they cut the lights and parked a distance away. Dressed totally in black, the threesome made their way to the gate; it then occurred to them that the fence could be electric. A small argument ensued as to who would touch it to see. After finally doing rock, paper, and scissors, it fell to Jerry. He grabbed it, and immediately his body started convulsing.

Letting out an exclamation, Buddy ran forward to fling Jerry's body away when Jerry started laughing. "Just kidding."

An irritated Buddy grabbed the top wire and vaulted over. The other two soon followed. They walked the two-track a good distance before seeing the trees thinning ahead. Veering into the woods, the men took exaggerated care to miss sticks and dried leaves as they progressed closer to the house beyond. They constantly checked for outside movement but saw none.

Finding a clear break in the brush and trees, they had a direct view of a well lit-up house. Giving each other a high five, they inched forward. One of the curtains was partially open. They easily saw a lit-up television screen. Pete nudged Buddy. "Is that *Mash*? I love *Mash*! It's one of my most favorite things to watch!"

"Shh!"

Convinced everyone was still there, the three made their way back to their car. Once inside, Jerry called the boss.

After hearing the report, Corey instructed Pete to concentrate on his island job and for the other two to take the ferry home the following morning. Warning them to keep their mouths shut or else, he hung up.

Their work now done, the three men were excited about the amount of money they'd soon be receiving. Turning the car around, they headed to the store, bought chips and beer, and then went to their motel to celebrate.

# Chapter 19

Things weren't going well for Pierce Matthews and Hope Montgomery. Pierce had come to Hope's cabin after work as usual. But instead of a prolonged hug, Pierce had startled Hope on the porch by stating he'd like to take Sarah to his cabin for the evening. "Lately, we haven't had any one-on-one time, and I think it's important."

"Okay." It was a reasonable request but had come so out of the blue that Hope was speechless.

"So, if you'll pack her diaper bag, we'll be going."

"Right this second? I thought we could visit a little." Laying her hand on his arm, Hope stepped closer. "Is something wrong, Pierce?

You didn't greet me with our usual hug. And you've not been yourself lately. Please tell me what's wrong."

Running his free hand through his dark wavy hair, Pierce grew frustrated. "I have things on my mind, okay? Give me some space!"

As if slapped, Hope dropped her hand and stepped back. Allowing her hurt feelings to the front, she lashed out with, "I wondered when this Pierce was going to appear!"

Pierce narrowed his eyes to demand, "What's that supposed to mean?"

"Only that over the past months, I'd almost forgotten why I had initially built up resentment toward you." Hope knew she should stop, but he'd hurt her feelings; so she plowed ahead. "I'm finally seeing the side of you who so easily tossed aside his newborn daughter!" As soon as the words were out, Hope regretted them. Putting one hand to her mouth, she stretched the other toward Pierce, but he stiffened and stepped back.

"I'd like my daughter now." Looking around with exaggerated care, he then asked, "Where is she anyway? I hope she's safe. After all, you have been standing here talking to me quite a while!" He too knew he'd regret his words, but Hope's had stabbed him in an already hurting heart.

With fire in her eyes, Hope doubled her fist. She experienced a strong desire to hit him. With her eyes still on his face, Hope watched Pierce's one eyebrow go up and a smirk appear.

Her body filled with frustrated rage. Not wanting him to see the tears that were also building, she turned to go inside the cabin. Through gritted teeth, she stated, "Silly me! I had envisioned a few moments of cuddle time, so I had placed her with some toys *safely* in her crib to play!"

The door slammed, almost connecting with the beagle pup trying to exit the house.

As Pierce stared at the door, the pup ran up eagerly wanting some attention. It took a moment for Pierce to reel himself back from the angry exchange that had just taken place. Dropping onto the nearby porch swing, he absently petted the dog now seated in his lap. *Oh Lord, how did this happen? In times like this, it's so easy to accept the fact that we're sinners saved by your grace. Attitudes get out of control so quickly!*

Pierce's thoughts turned dismal as he blindly stared out at the white picket fence surrounding the pond he'd put in for the girls that summer.

A few minutes later, Hope came storming onto the porch. She had baby Sarah in one hand and a bulging bag with clothes hanging out in the other. At their entrance, the puppy launched off Pierce's lap to greet them.

Pierce came to a stand and immediately said, "Hope, I'm so sorry."

She froze at his words. Lowering her eyes, she stared at the floor a moment and then squared her shoulders. With a challenge of conviction in her eyes, she stated, "I think we may be rushing things. Maybe… maybe this engagement is too soon." She stopped, waiting for his response.

Pierce didn't move or speak.

Hope saw conflicting emotions running rapidly over his face. Then, not saying a word, he stepped forward to take Sarah into his arms.

"Dada, dada," she said while hugging him around the neck.

He tried to maintain eye contact, but Hope switched hers to the same pond he'd been studying a moment earlier.

The awkward moment was interrupted when he asked, "Isn't there something you'd like to say?"

Slowly bringing her vivid blue eyes back to his hazel ones, she asked, "Like?"

He shrugged and then replied sarcastically, "I don't know. Maybe something like, 'I'm sorry too, Pierce!' Unless your hearing's going, I did just apologize."

Hope's anger flared again. Dropping the diaper bag at his feet, she said, "You of all people aren't in a position to teach me how to act like a Christian!"

The two glared at each other while Hope's heart ached over what was happening. As their moods penetrated to the baby, she began to whimper and then burst into tears. Picking up the bag, Pierce looked sadly at Hope, whose eyes were fixed on baby Sarah. He gazed at her reddened cheeks for one long minute more. Seeing no other words were coming, he turned and walked to his truck.

As soon as Pierce left the porch, Hope sagged backwards against the front door with her arms crossed protectively up front. Tears spilled over as she watched the two she loved most in the world drive away. Then she whispered, "Lord, what have we done? We love each other! How can we also be so cruel? Maybe this is a mistake. Please help us, Lord."

Hope watched them pull up to their cabin a short distance away. As they walked onto their much larger front deck, she hoped Pierce would look her way, but he didn't. Turning away, Hope went inside. The empty cabin shouted of loneliness.

She walked to baby Sarah's room and leaned against the doorframe. Tears began dripping off her chin and nose as Hope pushed herself to a straight position and walked into her own bedroom. Flinging herself across the bed, the tears continued to flow as she whispered, "I said terrible things to him!" Her sadness slowly morphed into grief for her dead husband, Dean, and unborn baby girl, who were now with the Lord Jesus in heaven. As her sobs drew to an end then stopped altogether, Hope's pride finally admitted she should have apologized too. Entertaining that thought, she soon grabbed for a tissue as a new batch of tears pushed their way out of already swollen eyes.

A long time later, she fell asleep.

The phone beside her bed rang. Taking a moment to get oriented, Hope started to reach for it but decided she really didn't want to talk to anyone. Instead, she let the answering machine get it. Hearing Pierce's voice, Hope flung herself off the bed and raced to the kitchen. Her hand was on the receiver but froze when she heard his next words. "Hope, would you please grow up and answer the phone? I know you're there!" Holding her breath, she heard an exasperated sigh, and then in a sad, resigned voice, he said, "I just called to say that Sarah fell asleep in the play yard, so I'm keeping her for the night. I'll drop her off on my way to work in the morning." There was a pause then, "Good night. I hope you can sleep well. I doubt I will."

After he hung up, Hope replayed the message several times trying to detect a tone of accusation, but it wasn't there. All she heard was the voice of someone feeling every bit as sad and sorry as she felt. Having missed the supper hour, Hope decided that food didn't sound good. Instead she drew a hot bath and took a long soak. A little later, she crawled into bed to cry herself to sleep once more.

The next morning, Hope woke to the sounds of music filling her room. She stretched to shut off the alarm clock but refrained when the words of a chorus floated through the air right into her heart.

> Let me be a little kinder, let me be a little blinder,
> To the faults of those around me let me praise a little more.
> Let me be when I am weary just a little bit more cheery.
> Think a little more of others and a little less of me.

The words prompted Hope's mind. *Was I kind to Pierce last night? I know he's probably struggling with the first anniversary of Vicki's death. I'm sure it doesn't help that he's trying to be excited about Sarah's first birthday at the same time. Lord, is it so wrong for me to want him sharing his hurts and pain?*

Hope's heart ached as she threw the covers back to grab her robe. Realizing Pierce could be coming any minute, she shut the radio off and flew to get ready. The words of the chorus remained on her mind as she began humming the catchy tune.

A little while later, a fully dressed Hope found herself cheerfully singing the words as she prepared a bowl of instant oatmeal in the microwave. Staring into the machine, she said to the Lord, "Please give me the kinder words with Pierce this morning." As the bell dinged that breakfast was ready, Hope frowned at the kitchen wall clock. Pierce was running late. He should have been there with Sarah already. Now that her mind was in the right place, she was anxious to talk with him.

About a half hour later, Hope finally saw the truck coming. As she'd been watching out the front window, the door was close at hand. Flinging it open, Hope watched them approach. A slightly disheveled Pierce rushed up the steps and across the porch to her.

Even in an uncombed state, Pierce was a very attractive man. Hope's pulse quickened as he stood before her. Smiling warmly, she started to greet him when Pierce interrupted. "I am really running late." He then handed her the baby and hurried off the porch.

"But Pierce, we need to talk."

Already opening the truck door, Pierce yelled back, "It'll have to wait."

An exasperated and disappointed Hope dropped the bag, hiked Sarah higher on her hip, and raised a hand of farewell to the rapidly departing truck. She stared after it until Sarah tried sticking her finger in Hope's eye, which brought her attention back to the baby. Cuddling her close, Hope nuzzled Sarah's neck. "I missed you, baby girl! The house is too quiet when you're gone."

Turning to look one more time up the now empty lane, Hope sighed heavily. "So much for telling your daddy how sorry I am." Picking up the bag, she walked into the cabin, nearly tripping over the puppy in a hurry to get inside too.

Corey Drake was happy. He'd been able to charter a private jet the night before and was at that moment signing the rental car paperwork the Beaver Island airport manager had kindly provided for him. With a great flourish he signed in a clear hand—Damien Cooper. Displaying a good fake ID for the manager, he was handed the keys and soon was out of the office. Not wanting people to focus too much attention on his arrival and departure, Corey kept his words short. He wanted to be in the air before 10:00 a.m. Hopefully, the hired guys would already be heading off the island.

As he moved to leave the airport building, Corey started running through his plan of eliminating Detective Williams and his partner, Paul Statham. His adrenaline surged but checked when he overheard two men talking. They were seated at a small table located below a large aerial map of Northern and Upper Michigan. They were staring intently at the map, but his ears picked up the words, "Helicopter leaving in a hurry yesterday afternoon." Corey decided to stay a while longer.

"It sure was a pretty bird."

"Yeah, and the pilot wasn't a local guy; that's for sure. He flew in with it about ten days ago. He had three passengers, two men and his wife."

Corey's radar beacon was practically screaming in his ear. Changing directions, he began pretending interest in photos of pilots decorating the walls around the large room. Inching his way closer, he listened.

"Did you have a chance to talk to him? I didn't see the helicopter on the pad, so I assumed he left."

"He kept pretty much to himself when he was here. Charlie told me he and his wife were staying at the hotel. The two of them flew out early this morning."

The two guys grew silent as one pulled out his pipe. Pausing with the pipe midair, he grew thoughtful then commented. "He definitely was here for some special purpose, for he kept that helicopter ready to leave at a moment's notice. I tried striking up a conversation one day, but he wasn't chatty; that's for sure."

"Yesterday, I was with the mechanics when he walked in. A short time later, his cell phone rang. I heard him say he'd be ready to go in less than half an hour. He then called his wife saying he was leaving and would be back for her later."

The men grew silent again as Corey drew closer. The pipe man pulled out a bag of cherry-blend tobacco. Tamping some in the bowl of his pipe, he then struck a match to it and drew in deeply. After letting out a couple smoke rings, he added, "After he did his pre-flight check, he started that bird and moved her to the run-up pad out near the end of the runway then shut her down."

Corey was close enough to observe the other man knit his brow. "That was odd, wasn't it?"

"It got my interest! I made a point to watch who was flying out. Sure enough, a car soon pulled right up to the helicopter. All I can say, it must have been someone real important! Three people got out, and then a while later, they hustled someone else out of the car into the bird. It happened so fast I couldn't tell if it was a man or woman."

Taking a couple more puffs and blowing them toward the ceiling, the pipe man turned his attention back to the map before adding, "I'll tell you something else that was strange. When they lifted off, they were heading due west; but a couple hours later, the pilot came flying in from the east, and ... he was empty."

"Where do you suppose he left his passengers?"

"Well, given the time frame, I would guess Mackinac Island or maybe the Sault. I don't rightly know."

At that point, Corey was close and made a decision. "Good morning, gentlemen. I wonder if I could have a word with you."

The men focused their attention on the stranger. They seemed surprised they hadn't heard him walk up.

Corey put on a professional voice and mannerism as he rapidly flipped the wallet in his hand open. He left it open just long enough for them to be impressed with the badge clipped inside. Then, looking quickly around, he lowered his voice. "I'm here on official business and wonder if I might ask you men a couple questions."

Positive they were being involved in something really important, the men eagerly agreed.

Before long, Corey heard all he needed to know about the helicopter. Standing taller, he thanked the men for their cooperation. Staring at the map above their heads, Corey had no doubt the passengers were Sydney and at least part of her protection team. Controlling his frustration and anger at the obvious slip-up from his so-called hired help, he thanked the men then returned the rental key to the airport manager. Not wanting any further questions, Corey walked rapidly out of the building to the nearby jet. He was soon on board, barking the orders, "We need to leave now!"

As the pilot did his preflight checks, Corey angrily strapped himself in. He had to figure out where they'd gone. It was intriguing that the chopper had left going west yet returned from the east. *Clever, Quaid Williams. Very clever! Too bad people noticed. You've not lost me yet!* He was thoroughly irked that Williams had gotten a step ahead of him once more. He knew he'd have to do better in the future and not underestimate the two men again.

As the jet headed south, Corey tried to think of his next move. "How can I contact you, Sydney? How did Vince contact you?" He figured a strategically placed call just might yield the info he needed and allow Corey opportunities to frighten and intimidate her. As various ideas turned over and over in his mind, a solid one suddenly took seed. Groaning at his stupidity, Corey stated out loud, "Of course! We always tend to make things harder than they really are!" What he remembered was that Vince had repeatedly stated he'd purchased a cell phone specifically for Sydney so he could have a private line to her.

Growing excited, Corey unbuckled himself and walked to the cockpit. Shortly after, the jet banked steeply to head for Petoskey's airport. About three hours later, a smiling Corey was back in the air with Sydney's cell phone number in his hand.

Meanwhile, no sooner had the jet lifted off Beaver Island when Detective Paul Statham received a call from the airport manager. The stranger's sudden lingering had caught the manager's attention. His eyes then narrowed with suspicion when he saw the stranger flip his wallet open. Shortly after he'd walked out, the manager quizzed the two men and then went straight to his office. He remembered clearly Detective Statham's words asking him to call if anything suspicious happened at the airport. Finding Paul's contact card tucked in the middle drawer, he soon was telling the detective what had just transpired.

All morning, Pierce struggled with a bad mood. Even his foreman started giving him a wide berth after Pierce unjustly railed on him for forgetting shingling nails that Pierce was supposed to get. Finally at noon, he made a decision.

Locating his foreman, Pierce apologized for being so unreasonable and said he was taking the rest of the day off. A short while later, Pierce stood beside Vicki's gravestone. Squatting, Pierce wiped debris away with his glove and then pulled the glove off. Tracing her name with his finger, he slowly began voicing words out loud. "Vicki, I miss you terribly. With Sarah's birthday being the same day of your death, I'll probably always have memory moments on that day."

He went quiet a long time and then said, "Vicki, in spite of planning to marry Hope, my desire is to teach baby Sarah a rich knowledge of you, her true mother." His words stopped again.

After a long moment, he continued. "I didn't plan to love Hope, but I thank God for bringing her into our lives. She's wonderful with Sarah. She has such a giving heart and gentle ways about her. Although at times, her tongue can be rather sharp, and she can be stubborn as a mule!" A slow smile spread across his face. "I guess we all can, huh? We had our moments too, didn't we?"

A heavy sigh escaped his lips. "All these things about Hope are wrapped up into a package that I've learned to love."

Again, Pierce paused as thoughts of Hope and Vicki mingled together. "She reminds me a lot of you, and yet... she's very different."

Another heavy sigh escaped. "We had a terrible fight, and now I fear she may want to break up with me. She may think it's too soon."

*Go talk to her. Take her flowers and apologize again.*

*Peace I leave with you, my peace I give unto you. Not as the world giveth, give I unto you. Let not your heart be troubled.*

The two thoughts came almost simultaneously out of the blue but seemed as if they were spoken directly into his ear. Glancing skyward, Pierce contemplated the words. As he did, a sense of God's presence warmed Pierce's hurting heart. As natural as rain sliding off a leaf, Pierce's thoughts moved toward his heavenly Father as he slid to his knees on the cold cement pad.

"Lord, help me, please. Help me talk to Hope and be enthused about Sarah's upcoming birthday. Help me be the man you'd have me to be, the father you'd have me to be, and the... future husband." As Pierce prayed by Vicki's gravestone, the crisp November air faded to the background as a warm peace—one that surpasses all understanding—started seeping into Pierce's troubled heart and soul.

Finally, acknowledging the fact that Vicki's memories would forever be with him but didn't need to overwhelm him, Pierce stood. Patting her granite stone with the bronze roses attached, Pierce turned to leave while whispering, "Thank you, Lord."

After lunch, Hope tried to chase away her sad mood by turning the radio to the oldies. Cranking it up, she grabbed the mop, preparing to wash the kitchen floor. Instead, Hope had a sudden urge to move with the music. Sarah, sitting in the middle of the living room, began clapping her hands while Hope spun with her broom partner. In the midst of this, Pierce arrived.

The music being as loud as it was, Hope didn't hear Pierce's knock. She also didn't know the unheard knock had prompted him to open the door in time to watch Hope in the middle of dipping her mop.

Catching movement out of the corner of her eye, she started losing her balance. Pierce quickly moved forward to right her with his arm.

A totally embarrassed Hope slid her eyes toward his warm hazel ones and smiled sheepishly. "I…um…I was trying to lift my spirits with music."

With one raised eyebrow directed her way, he observed dryly, "By the looks of it, it was working."

*There's that eyebrow I love and those wonderful hazel eyes.* Hope became lost in his eyes until a new song started, and she remembered the radio. Pulling her thoughts together, she eased away from his hand to shut the blaring radio off. As she walked to the kitchen, Hope paused as she heard the words, "I woke up this morning, you were on my m-i-i-ind. You were on my mind. I've got troubles, whoa-oh."

Switching the radio off, she stepped back into the living room. It was then she noticed roses in Pierce's hand.

Trying to get her blush under control and her thoughts in order, Hope nervously straightened her sweatshirt. She hoped she didn't have baby food down her front. Lately, Sarah was getting great pleasure out of flicking her spoon loaded with food.

After smiling a greeting to his baby daughter, who was intent on standing by the coffee table, Pierce turned to extend the roses Hope's way. "I'm sorry for my moodiness and sharp words. Will you forgive me?"

Relief and emotion played across Hope's face as she threw her arms around Pierce's waist, nearly crushing the roses between them. Raising the roses safely to the right, Pierce held her close with his left arm as she cried, "I'm sorry too! I've been so miserable today!"

Pierce kissed her head as he swung her gently around. He then suddenly exclaimed, "Hope, quick! Grab the camera! I think Sarah's going to take her first steps."

Hope ran to the kitchen, for she knew babies didn't wait for cameras. The camera was on and set for video before she'd fully turned back to the living room.

Pierce had laid the roses safely in the nearest chair and was squatting down when Hope pushed the record button. Baby Sarah was centered on her screen and was standing near the coffee table. Hope recorded her turning toward her daddy.

With hands extended, Pierce coaxed, "Come on, baby. Come to Daddy."

A huge smile spread over her little face as Sarah took one step toward Pierce. She tottered a moment and then gained her balance with one hand still firmly on the table.

"Come on, Sarah. You can do it! Come to Daddy."

With a determined look, Sarah pushed off the table and tottered two steps into Pierce's waiting arms.

Standing, a jubilant Pierce tossed her into the air and deftly caught her while exclaiming, "Vicki, our baby took her first steps!"

Pierce froze at the sound of the camera whirring shut. Turning to Hope, he hurriedly said, "I'm sorry, Hope. I wasn't thinking."

Hope slowly lowered the camera as she struggled with sadness and a touch of jealousy. Praying for strength and wisdom, she took a deep breath and exhaled. Walking to her family-to-be, Hope placed her hand on his arm. Looking intently into his eyes, she softly declared, "Pierce, I struggle with times of jealousy about what you and Vicki had together. As I suspect, you may about Dean and me, but please believe me when I say that I want Sarah to know about her real mommy." With a catch, she added over the lump forming in her throat, "If I'd have died instead of my baby girl, I'd like to think someone would make sure she knew all about me."

Pierce shifted Sarah to his right arm while drawing Hope close with his left. Kissing her forehead then nose, he stated, "I love you, Hope Montgomery."

"I love you too."

"From now on, let's try really hard to communicate with each other about our times of overwhelming memories." Seeing her nod in agreement, he then added, "And may we not be threatened if sometimes one of us needs a little alone time with those memories."

Hope moved in closer as her arms wrapped around the two.

At that moment, baby Sarah grabbed a fistful of Hope's hair while loudly declaring, "Momma, Momma."

# Chapter 20

As soon as Detective Paul Statham got off the phone with the airport manager, he paged Quaid on his cell phone. As the two detectives weren't getting help from Jake and Neal until mid-afternoon, they'd split up. Paul patrolled the parking area and covered stairs leading up to the front door. Quaid had the beach side facing Lake Huron. When his cell phone hummed, he was in the middle of talking to his friend, Pierce Matthews.

"Pierce, Paul's buzzing me. Can you hold a moment?"

"Sure."

He hit the appropriate button and then asked, "What's up?"

Briefly Paul filled him in and then stated, "Looks like we left at the right time." As he talked, Paul surveyed the string of connected three-storied condos. His main interest fell on the middle one of the five, but he was very aware of any comings and goings of the neighboring condos. Fortunately, these were mainly used during the summer months by people who had other homes, so only one besides theirs was occupied. Studying the identical layouts, Paul smiled. Once again Quaid had chosen an easy place to secure.

The condos were accessible through the garage or covered stairs on this side and two sliders on the beach side. The garage entrance was ideal for loading and unloading Sydney in private. A slanted roof covered the garage and sloped up to the top of the second floor, which housed the kitchen, dining room, living room, laundry, and one bathroom. Immediately under the living area was a large family room opening into a cemented, walled patio with sandy beach beyond. This room also had stairs to the back; halfway up, one had the choice to follow on up to the laundry room or head down to the garage.

Two spacious bedrooms with private baths comprised the third floor. Each bedroom had one dormer window; one looked out over the garage while the other had a view of the beach and lake. This was the bedroom Sydney was placed in, as her dormer had an attached metal ladder that could be rolled out the window connecting her to the deck below. This gave her an escape route if upstairs during a breach of security.

Paul's attention was drawn back to Quaid's voice. "It amazes me how this guy stumbles on to our information! At least we still have the advantage. He doesn't know exactly where we are."

"True, but the manager said the men he talked to speculated we had to be somewhere on this side of the state. That does narrow it down considerably!"

The men grew silent, and then Quaid asked, "Any speculation on whether the badge he showed was real or not?"

"I asked the manager if the men had gotten a good look at it. He said they only got a glimpse before he flipped it shut."

Again the two men grew thoughtful. Quaid made up his mind to ask the chief about running that glass print with the current law enforcement people. It rankled to do it, but he had to rule out whether or not the badge was a fake. Out loud he said, "Well, the way I see it, we have two choices. Either we keep moving, or we take a stand here."

Surveying the layout once more, Paul said, "I vote we stay here. This time she's behind bulletproof glass. Plus, there aren't trees around this sandy beach and parking lot for anyone to hide."

"I agree. This is a good spot. So we hunker in and wait for our man to show. Once Jake and Neal arrive this afternoon, I'll feel a whole lot better. Plus, I plan to run Sydney through some ways to escape."

The two men talked a bit longer; then Quaid switched back to Pierce. "Are you still there?"

"Yeah. I switched you to speakerphone so I could keep working on this house draft."

"Could you take it off now?"

"Done."

"So, as I was saying, Pierce, you have more resources than I do. I hoped you'd be willing to use them to help me find the whereabouts of Sydney's sister. If she's still alive, I think she's her only living relative."

Quaid heard the sounds of scribbling as he filled Pierce in with more details.

After a moment, Pierce said, "I'll get my lawyer to contact a detective agency right away."

"Thanks, buddy. If everything goes according to plan and Sydney survives all of this, I have an idea finding her sister could be a powerful statement of Christ's love for her. Let's pray her sister's still alive."

"And that she wants to reconnect with Sydney. She may not."

It didn't take Sydney and Maria long to settle into their new place. But the stress of being hunted was taking its toll. Sydney seemed glad when the men decided to spend the first night in the condo with the women. Paul had slept on one of the sofas in the downstairs family room while Quaid slept in the living room. Now that morning had come and sunshine was glistening off Lake Huron, Sydney appeared relaxed.

Paul moved to a nearby single-level motel that housed only eight rooms; four connected on each side of a paved parking lot. All doors opened toward the parking area. The department had rented the four sitting closest to the condos. Three would be used by Paul, Jake, and Neal, with the fourth being set up as a command center.

After all that had been explained to Sydney, Quaid went on to say, "Once Jake and Neal arrive this afternoon, you and I will run through various escape routes leading to the command center." Noting Sydney shiver, Quaid was satisfied that she finally seemed to understand the danger she was in.

"Okay, well... just let me know when you want to do it," Sydney responded.

Before returning back outside, Quaid exchanged a few quiet instructions with Maria then headed to the sliding door off the dining room. Opening it, he turned to Sydney, who hadn't moved from the center of the living room. "By the way, your softer makeup makes you look much better." Seeing Sydney's startled blush, he quickly focused on Maria. "Lock up after me!"

He then crossed to the steps leading down to the patio and beach. Pausing at the halfway landing, Quaid took a moment to critically survey the beach area and lake beyond. His eyes stayed on Mackinac Island, which was very visible this morning. He knew it was a unique island. It didn't have any cars on it and was only accessible by water or air. Sighing, he made a mental note to sometime visit the island and then continued his survey.

Satisfied all was well, he walked on down the steps and clicked on his wrist stopwatch. Heading to the left, he shortened his stride to what he thought Sydney's would be. It took him a minute to reach the small stream separating the condo properties from the small motel. Lining

## Out of the Snare

the stream were some old, straggly pine trees, but Quaid saw they were too tall to be a hiding place for anyone. Stopping to scan the beach and lake once more, Quaid then searched the stream for the smallest possible crossing area. If Sydney needed to run this way, she would have to jump the stream. Spying the most likely spot off to his right, Quaid tried it. The distance was little more than a large step for his long legs.

Once across, he was about thirty yards from the back of the motel. Starting the watch again, Quaid angled down and around the motel to the room being set up for the command center. He knew that would be the one room with an officer in it at all times. He frowned at how much the sand had hindered his progress. It was softer on this side of the stream. It took him almost two minutes to reach the door he needed. Not wanting to be out of sight from the condo for long, he turned and trotted back to the stream.

Jumping it, he paused to once again survey the area. His mind did the math as he studied a couple of boats now bobbing about a mile offshore. It had taken him almost three minutes from the bottom of the steps to the motel door. He still needed to factor in where she could be in the house, crossing the deck and down the stairs. It could take up to four minutes, which was a long time if someone was after her with a gun. The only good thought was that he doubted Sydney would be walking in that situation.

Quaid spoke to himself as he reasoned it out while walking toward the condo. "Of course, it will take even more time if she's up in the bedroom." He figured it would probably take her a full two minutes to open the window, lower the ladder, and climb down to the deck. Rubbing his chin, Quaid prayed if that were the case Maria would be able to give Sydney time to get cleanly away.

With all the excitement of the move, Sydney had dropped the mail down in her bedroom and forgotten it until that next morning. Finding it, she emptied the bag on the open counter separating the kitchen and living room. Maria and Quaid stood near as she went through the contents. To everyone's disappointment, the papers still hadn't come.

Sydney was beginning to wonder what Vince had done with them. The thought of the third partner getting a hold of her and not believing the papers weren't in her possession caused her pulse to leap.

Sydney's thoughts then strayed back to her restless last night. Being in another strange bed with foreign sounds all around, she'd found it hard to sleep. After tossing and turning for what seemed like hours, Sydney's tired mind landed for the first time on Vince's family. It occurred to her that his wife probably now knew all the sordid details of what she and Vince had done, including their affair.

For the second time in just a few days, Sydney felt shame. But this time it was mixed with guilt over the sorrow the other woman must be experiencing. Not only had she lost her husband, she'd also found out he'd been untrue to her. Sydney sat up in bed as the thought occurred that his family might be in danger just like she was. The seed grew in her mind. It so unsettled her that she had decided to ask Quaid about it in the morning.

When she did, he assured her the Louisville police were patrolling Vince's home but hadn't noticed any undue attention.

Quaid's words relieved Sydney, but the shame and guilt still gnawed at her insides. *I've ruined their lives!* Those words kept playing over and over in her mind. She didn't know what to do with the guilt. A part of her said Quaid would know, but pride kept her from asking him.

Deep in thought, Sydney went to her bedroom and sat on the bed while holding the necklace around her neck. Since leaving Beaver Island, she only took it off to shower. The feel of the little Bible against her skin gave Sydney comfort. Having memorized the verse etched in it, she often said it almost as a talisman. "Be strong and of good courage; do not be afraid, nor be dismayed, for the Lord your God is with you wherever you go."

As Sydney swept the room with her eyes, she softly asked, "Are you with me, God? Are you here?" Shaking her head, she then said, "Of course you're not. Why would you waste time on me after all I've done?"

A feeling of hopelessness threatened to consume her when suddenly the snare verses started flowing through her mind. In the haste to leave Beaver Island, Sydney had forgotten about the piece of paper with the verses and the little booklet. They were still tucked in the borrowed Bible on the dresser. Now, thinking there might be a Bible in this new place, Sydney went in search of one. She couldn't remember what the references were but decided reading anything could be a comfort. But after a thorough search yielded nothing and after ignoring Maria's repeated questions about what she was looking for, Sydney went back upstairs.

That afternoon Jake and Neal arrived with news that there weren't any hits from running the glass print through former law enforcement and that someone had broken into Sydney's home.

Quaid asked with a frown, "Could you tell if anything was taken?"

"By the way the house looked, especially a desk in the spare bedroom, I'd say whoever it was, was looking for the paperwork," Jake replied.

Then Neal added, "Since we've been getting her mail every day, there's no way he got it before us unless it was delivered some other way and we missed it."

As Neal talked, Jake walked back to Maria's car, which the two officers had just driven up in. Pulling out two plastic bags, he handed them to Quaid. "Here's Sydney's mail for the last couple days and the other things you requested."

Quaid studied the new sets of miniature shoulder two-way radios in the other bag. He wasn't sure why he felt prompted to have them on hand, but Quaid had learned long ago to go with his gut on things. A grim look covered his face as he studied the two men standing attentively by.

"Okay, men. Get yourselves settled in the motel. Afterward, Jake, you report to Paul. He's patrolling the beach, but we're switching now. So come back here. Neal, you come to me on the beach. Paul and I will fill you in on your duties when we see you."

The men grabbed their gear and walked to the motel. A short time later, Jake was stationed in the parking lot while Neal combed the beach. Paul went to get some shut-eye before taking over for the evening while Quaid headed indoors with Sydney's mail. It was time to do some practice runs with her. He was determined to have all angles covered in case she needed to flee the premises.

"Quaid! We've gone over this four times! Not to mention, you've made me run it twice! I've got it!"

"This is the last time, Sydney. What do you do if Maria says the word *run* and you're in the laundry room?"

"I go down the stairs to the family room, out the slider, and run to the command center."

"And if you're in the kitchen or living room?"

While rolling her eyes, Sydney impatiently replied, "Out the slider by the dining room, across the deck, down the steps, and run to the command center."

"You're upstairs somewhere."

Heaving a heavy sigh, Sydney stated, "Open the window in my bedroom, roll the ladder out, climb down to the deck, and run to the command center." Here she stopped. "If the papers come, do I grab them before running?"

"No! Just run! Unless it's me or Paul, you don't stop for anything or anyone, no matter what you hear or see. Can you do that?"

"I think so."

Quaid grabbed her shoulders. "Sydney, you have to know! This needs to be so ingrained in your head that you don't even stop to think. You just move! If any of us, especially Maria, holler, "Run!" you do it!"

## Out of the Snare

He briefly tightened his grip then dropped his hands. Stepping back, he said, "Sydney, I know you can do this. You have to trust me. These drills could save your life."

As Sydney studied Quaid's expressive brown eyes, her pulse jumped at the concern she saw there. Willing him to say something personal, Sydney was disappointed when he lowered his eyes to the little Bible nestled against her throat. Then he started quoting Joshua 1:9 while raising his eyes back to hers.

As he slowly said the verse, Sydney felt a foreign feeling of strength seep into her body. A new conviction that she really could do what was needed prompted her mind toward God. *I don't know if you're really here, God, but I think I'm starting to believe you could be.*

With wonder in her voice and all boredom gone, Sydney looked intently into Quaid's eyes. "I'll do whatever I need to do."

"Sir, will you come in here? Over."

Pulling the COM link from his belt, Quaid replied, "On my way. Over." It was getting dark. He and Neal were preparing to exchange places for the night, but now he asked Neal to remain while he checked out what was wrong inside.

As soon as Quaid stepped on the deck, a very irritated Maria came out the door gesturing with her hands and speaking in Spanish. "Yo sera muy feliz cuando este trabajo por la mujer adentro es terminado!"

"Whoa, whoa, Maria!" Taking her arm, Quaid turned her around to head back inside. Once there, he found clothes strewn all over the living room floor and an equally angry Sydney pacing back and forth.

"Get her away from me before I knock her flat!" Maria stated.

To which Sydney irrationally replied, "You and whose army?"

As Maria stepped forward, Quaid moved between the two women.

Both started speaking at once, so Quaid held up his hands. "Ladies, take a seat!" For a moment, he wondered if they would comply, but soon they were seated in the tall stools at the counter. Quaid stood nearby with arms crossed. "Now, Maria, what's going on?"

Immediately, Sydney jumped to her feet. "Why are you asking her first?" She whirled to leave the room but didn't get far when a steel hand gripped her arm. Stopped in her tracks, Sydney jerked her arm but was held fast.

Slowly leveling his eyes at her, Quaid heard Sydney continue mumbling under her breath as he asked again, "Maria?"

"I'm tired of her bossing me around! I'm not here to be her personal maid!"

"True," Quaid readily agreed. "What did she do?"

Again, Sydney resisted his grip. Instead of breaking free, she found her body drawn in tightly to Quaid's body. "Go on, Maria."

"I was reading a book when she came downstairs with an armload of clothes, which she promptly dropped in my lap!"

"I asked you to come with me to the laundry room, but you ignored me!"

"Sydney! I'll get your side in a moment!" Quaid said close to her ear.

Sydney turned in his arm to blurt, "But she totally ignored me!"

Quaid stared Sydney to silence. Not taking his eyes away, he asked, "Maria, what happened next?"

Maria faltered as she said, "Well...um, I threw the clothes off while telling her to do them herself."

"You forgot to mention tossing in a few choice words!"

With his focus fully on Maria, Quaid raised his eyebrows. He didn't blame her for not wanting Sydney to boss her. He'd witnessed Sydney's attitude several times himself, but Quaid drew the line at Maria losing her professionalism. Swearing at Sydney was out of line.

Maria grew defensive as she came to her feet. "Sir, I know I shouldn't have sworn at her, but she's pushed me to the limit with her rudeness and bossiness. I'm here to protect her and try to make her somewhat comfortable, but does that include doing her laundry and cooking every meal? She doesn't lift a finger to help!"

Sydney started to respond, but Quaid raised his free hand. Releasing her from his side, he said, "Sydney, would you please pick up your clothes while I have a few words with Maria?"

Throwing Maria a smug look, Sydney walked to gather up her clothes and take them to the laundry room.

Quaid waited until he heard water going into the machine before walking around the counter and leaning forward on his elbows. A low serious talk followed, which came to a conclusion when Sydney stepped back into the room. Standing straight, Quaid stated, "Sydney, there's going to be a change of plans for tonight. I think you two need a break. I'll be staying indoors with you while Maria takes duty outside for a few hours. For the next fifteen minutes or so, can the two of you manage to get along?"

Not sure that he liked the look of interest and sly smile that crossed Sydney's face, Quaid studied the two women. Feeling like he'd just refereed two teenagers, he shook his head then turned to leave. He paused as a thought entered his head. Going to the hall closet, he opened the door to pull out his duffle bag. Quaid retrieved his Bible, rezipped the bag, pushed it back with his foot and then shut the door. Without explanation, he handed Sydney the Bible. He then walked out the slider and down the steps.

# Chapter 21

"Sir, can you come in here? Over."

Quaid's talk with Neal about him staying on outside duty a while longer had taken more time than anticipated, but he still couldn't believe the women were already having trouble again. Exasperated, he replied, "Coming. Over."

Neal had recalled more details about the break-in at Sydney's house. His bringing the subject up again reminded Quaid that he'd forgotten to mention the incident to Sydney. His focus on practicing escape routes had completely wiped it from his mind. Quaid's patience with the women was running thin as he stepped through the door. Ready to launch into a lecture, Quaid paused when his eyes caught sight of Sydney's face. It was white as a ghost.

With wide eyes, she didn't say a word, just extended her shaking arm his way. It wasn't until Quaid stepped closer that he saw her hand held a cell phone. Pulling his eyes from Sydney's large brown ones, he said, "Maria, what's going on?"

"Sir, we heard a beep coming from upstairs. Investigating, we found it was coming from her phone. There's a message on it, sir. I believe it's our man."

Taking the phone, he punched the voice mail button. He soon heard an obviously muffled voice come over the line.

"Hello, Syd baby! Remember me?" An ugly chuckle filled Quaid's ear, and his muscles tightened. "By now you know I'm not far behind. It's just a matter of time before I pinpoint your whereabouts; then you and I will take care of some unfinished business. I'm sure you must have the papers by now."

As Quaid listened, his senses came alert to any possible telltale background noises, but he heard none. Seeing Sydney's whole body start to shake, he motioned for Maria to seat her in the living room as the voice continued. "By the way, sorry for the mess at your house." Another sinister laugh then, "Oh, one more thing. Since Quaid Williams and possibly even Paul Statham will be hearing this, I just want to say how much I'm looking forward to meeting you two!"

The line went dead.

For a long moment Quaid stood still. *He knows our names!* The conviction that this person had access to law enforcement information solidified in his mind. As that thought and the message played over and over in his mind, a change of plans began presenting itself.

"What mess?"

Sydney's words interrupted his thoughts. "What?"

"He said he was sorry for the mess. What mess is he talking about?"

Stepping closer, Quaid replied, "I found out this afternoon that someone broke into your house and rifled through a desk. We figured it was our man. Now we know for sure."

As Sydney started to shake, Quaid's voice calmly demanded, "Sydney, I need you to pull yourself together. I also need to know if those papers came and you never told us."

She shook her head while replying, "I don't know where they are. I haven't seen them."

With COM link to his mouth, Quaid said, "Paul, I need you to come here. Over." Knowing Neal and Jake were also listening, he added, "Stay alert, men! Over."

He waited until hearing the men respond with two clicks each and then turned back to Sydney and Maria. "Sydney, has this man called you before?"

"Never. If it's our partner, he only had contact with Vince."

"He may have broken in to search for the papers, but no doubt he was also looking for a way to communicate with you."

"Should I shut the phone off?"

"No. We want to keep him talking to us. It may help us catch him."

At that moment three knocks came at the front door, with pauses between each one. "There's Paul."

Maria went to let him in as Sydney stood. She seemed uncertain as to what she should do now. Seeing her so vulnerable, Quaid felt compassion and...something else. Squelching a sudden urge to wrap his arms around her, he turned to Paul. Taking him aside, Quaid quickly explained the situation.

"What time did he call?"

"According to the phone, 4:45 this afternoon." Checking his watch, Quaid added, "That was little over an hour ago."

"So the chances are he still doesn't know where we are."

"That's the way I figure it, but I think it's time we brought in some help."

"What are you thinking?"

"I'd like you to take the phone to Petoskey to see if our people

## Out of the Snare

can clean up the voice. Maybe we can get his real one. En route, call the chief and ask him to call in a favor to his buddy with the U.S. Marshal's office."

"And you?"

Quaid looked back at the still shaking and uncertain Sydney. "I plan to stay in here with Sydney. We'll have the other three on patrol until you return. Then we'll see where we stand." Turning back to his partner, he added, "Since it's only about a one-and-a-half-hour drive home, I figure you could be back in say four hours. That makes it before 11:00 p.m. How does that sound to you?"

"I think it's a good idea. I'll press the chief to try getting the help here before morning or there after."

Placing a hand on his longtime friend's shoulder, Quaid said, "Take care, buddy."

"Sure thing. Besides, we both know if speed is required I'm your man!" A warm camaraderie passed between the men.

As they turned toward the women, Quaid said, "Maria, we need to use your car again." She dug the keys from her purse and then tossed them to Paul, who was soon heading out the door.

Now that part of the plan was in motion, Quaid turned his attention to Maria and Sydney. He wanted to make sure they both remembered the knock signals set up for the team. "Ladies, remember, no one comes in here except one of my team." Getting an affirming nod from both, he then rehearsed the knocks. "I'm one, pause, then two; Paul is one, pause, one, pause, one; Neal is two, pause, then two; and Jake is three, pause, then three. Any questions?" They didn't have any, so he continued. "None of us will ever use the doorbell. If it rings, don't answer it. And Maria, you call me immediately! Again, don't open the door for anyone but one of us four."

While Quaid spoke, he was pleased to see Sydney stop shaking.

When he finished, Sydney asked, "What's Maria's signal?"

"Good question. She is going out. Let's see, how about...four, pause, one."

Nodding affirmative, Maria checked her gun clip. Snapping it back in her gun, she racked one in the chamber then headed for the front door. Before starting her walking patrol, she was to touch base with Jake in the parking area. With her hand on the knob, Maria paused. The two standing inside watched her stare at the door then slowly turn around. Walking back to Sydney, she said, "I'm sorry I swore at you earlier. Everything's going to be all right. We won't let this man near you if we can help it."

Without waiting for a reply, she swung around and left.

Quaid followed to do the deadbolt then returned to Sydney. It was obvious Maria's words had greatly affected her, as she started shaking again. Walking to the kitchen, Quaid said, "How does a cup of coffee or tea sound?"

"It... it sounds good. I prefer coffee, please."

A short while later with steaming cups in hand, the two walked into the living room and took a seat. Taking a sip of coffee, Quaid studied Sydney over the cup. He was pleased to see her visibly calming. All in all, she'd had quite a shock. He knew the man on the phone had made her feel within his reach, which would make anyone feel vulnerable. Wanting to get her mind elsewhere, he asked, "Did you read anything from my Bible?"

Sydney stared at him blankly before absently replying, "No, not really. I did sit down with it. Not knowing where to read, I started flipping through it. I noticed you'd written notes in the margins. I hope you don't mind because I started reading them. Your comments were interesting, but I'd only read a couple when we heard the beeping above our heads." Here she softly asked, "You had underlined verses. Why?"

"I underline the ones that speak to me." He found the Bible and sat down closer to her. "Where were you reading?"

Sydney was staring at the floor and didn't seem to hear him, so Quaid said, "Sydney?" He waited until she looked his way before asking again, "Where were you reading?"

"Um, it was the first chapter of Romans."

Soon at the spot, Quaid noted several verses underlined. Leaning forward, he handed her the Bible. "Which one in particular?"

Sydney's eyes roamed his face as if searching for some meaning to all that was happening before lowering them to the pages in front of her. "Let's see... I think it was... yes, it was verse twenty." She raised her eyes back to his.

Trying to guide her senses and mind back to a safe place, Quaid gently asked, "Will you read it to me?"

Sydney said sure and started reading. "For since the creation of the world His invisible attributes are clearly seen, being understood by the things that are made, even His eternal power and Godhead, so that they are without excuse." Looking up, she asked, "What does it mean, *Godhead*?"

Quaid was surprised she'd asked such a complicated question. Gathering his thoughts, he said, "The Bible teaches that God is three parts: Father, Son and Holy Spirit, yet they are one God."

Sensitive to her obvious confusion, Quaid raised his hand and said, "This is a very simplified example, but see my finger?"

He held it up for her to inspect.

"Like yours, it has three joints yet is one finger. That's how God is. He's three distinct personalities yet one God." He let her mull that over a while.

Sydney then asked, "And what does *without excuse* mean?"

"Even if there weren't any churches, Christians, Christian TV, or radio stations, people would still be able to see God in nature."

"How?"

"Through the wonder of a flower! Or the beauty of birds or the sun during daytime and moon at nighttime." Warming to his subject, he added, "Do you know if you look at snowflakes under a microscope that no two are alike? I find that absolutely incredible!"

At that point, Quaid's mind momentarily traveled to a wintry wonderland of snowflakes.

Hearing a heavy sigh, he glanced at Sydney in time to catch a look of sadness in her eyes before she turned away. Wondering what had brought it on, Quaid asked, "Was there something else on your mind?"

Instead of opening up like he'd hoped, Sydney changed the subject. "Did the police do anything with the men at Beaver Island?"

Smoothly changing gears with her, Quaid replied, "They were brought in for questioning but didn't know much. They never had direct contact with their boss. He always called them by cell phone. The contact number he'd given them was to another cell phone, which is now not in service. As for their pay, somehow he paid them in cash by an envelope left in their mailbox." With grudging admiration, Quaid added, "The man is smart."

As Quaid spoke, he watched despair settle on Sydney's face. Wanting to reassure her, he quickly added, "But Paul and I are smarter! We'll catch him." Not seeing a convinced Sydney, Quaid impulsively reached over to place a hand on hers.

Instantly, a small spark of warm electricity passed between them. Jerking abruptly back, Quaid stood. Bringing his mind back to the business at hand, he rubbed the back of his neck while asking, "Did you go through the mail Jake and Neal brought today?"

Sydney slowly closed the Bible then sat it on the end table. Standing, she replied in a stiff voice, "No, I forgot all about it." She then headed up the stairs.

Wondering what had brought on the mood change, a stymied Quaid watched her go.

Returning a few minutes later, Sydney avoided eye contact as she dumped the contents of the bag on the table. Quaid stepped forward, and the two began sorting through it.

"All I see is junk mail and bills." In frustration, Sydney went to knock it away when her eye caught a letter. Picking it up, she looked at Quaid in wonder. "It's from Hope."

Quaid expected her to open it, but instead she kept staring at it.

## Out of the Snare

*Now what's going on?* he wondered before asking, "Are you going to open it?"

"Yes, but... well." Sydney stopped. Lifting her eyes from the envelope, she softly stated, "It's the first letter I've ever received."

Not fully comprehending what that kind of life must be like, Quaid covered by pulling a switchblade from his pocket. Flicking it open with his wrist, he reached for the letter, saying, "May I?"

Reluctantly Sydney let it go. Inserting the knife tip at the corner, Quaid expertly slit it open and handed it back.

Pulling a chair out, Sydney sat down. The envelope contained a letter and photos. Excited, she held one up. "Look! She sent photos of baby Sarah!"

Quaid smiled then turned back to the mail. All of it did appear to be either advertising or bills, but then one in particular caught his attention. Picking up the large white envelope stamped "Catalog," he read the return label: Brovont Brothers Church Supplies. Immediately alarms went off.

"Sydney, can you think of any reason why you'd be getting a catalog of church supplies?"

Concentrating on her letter, she mumbled, "No."

"May I open it?"

"Sure."

Within seconds, Quaid had it open and pulled out not a catalog but a folder. Inside the lumpy folder were documents, lots of them! Investigating the lumps, Quaid pulled out two small cassettes like the type used in specialized answering machines. He studied them a minute then turned back to the documents while saying, "We've hit the jackpot, Sydney!"

Sydney frowned in confusion at Quaid's words. Seeing what was in his hands, she straightened in the chair as he handed her the folder.

Quaid picked up the envelope to peer inside; he then pulled out a single sheet of paper. Noting who it was from, he handed it to Sydney while stating, "It's from Vince."

Sydney froze at his words.

Staring wide-eyed at the paper, she raised frightened eyes Quaid's way.

With a gentle voice, Quaid asked her to read it out loud. She stared deeply into his eyes before looking back at the paper. Sydney began reading:

> Dear Syd,
>
> If you're reading this, it means I'm dead and you're in danger! Sydney, in an attempt to protect us, I put your name as the sole owner of the dummy corporation. I should have told you. I'm sorry. Our "partner" called the other night wanting to meet with me. Therefore, I'm sending these documents and tapes to a friend with instructions to wait a couple weeks before mailing them.
>
> Please tell the authorities that I hid a voice-activated recorder in the picture frame on my desk. I'm hoping our partner doesn't find it first.
>
> One last thing. Sydney, I can't begin to express how much I regret stealing this money and ruining my family's life. If you're smart, you'll sign all the paperwork over to the police. There's still a chance for you. Take it! Don't stay caught in the mess we're in. Break free!
>
> I'm sorry there's nothing else I can give you to help discover who our partner is.
>
> Not everyone is given a second chance with their life. Do the right thing!
>
> —Vince

"Susie, will you ask Duke to come in here?"

A few minutes later, a tall, well-built, dark-haired man stepped into the Louisville, Kentucky, U.S. Marshal's office.

"You asked for me, Chief?"

"Yes. A friend of mine up in Michigan needs some help. Since you and a couple of your men are between jobs, I said you'd go."

"Sure, Chief. What's going down?"

"Some skirt got in trouble with the law, and an unknown third partner is looking for her. He already killed the other partner."

As the chief talked, Duke's interest grew, and he leaned forward intently. "If she doesn't know who he is, why's the unknown partner after her?"

"Apparently, he found out the killed man had put all their embezzled funds in an offshore account under the woman's name. The papers have disappeared, and he thinks somehow they were sent to her. He's looking for them and her signature."

"Do they think he's getting close?"

"I guess so. That's why they're asking for our help."

"When do you want us there?"

"Susie's making arrangements for three of you to be there by early tomorrow morning."

"Okay, Chief."

Duke rose.

The chief observed Duke deep in thought as he moved toward the door.

Pausing with his hand on the knob, Duke turned back. "Hey, Chief, can Luke and Matt go ahead of me? I just remembered there's something personal I need to take care of first."

The chief considered that a moment. He thought about denying the request but then remembered Duke had been dealing with personal stuff a lot lately. Thinking there were probably problems at home, he relented. "Okay, but make sure you're there sometime tomorrow! Give Susie a heads-up about your new arrangements. Then tell Luke and Matt to pick up their tickets and info from her too."

Heading out the door smiling, Duke said, "Sure thing, Chief!"

# Chapter 22

After Quaid and Sydney finished looking over the missing documents, Quaid placed a call to the chief. Quaid learned Paul had already phoned in, and the chief had contacted his friend with the U.S. Marshals. "Three of them will be arriving sometime early tomorrow morning. Their names are Luke, Matt, and Duke."

"Duke? That's actually his first name?"

"No, but I don't know what his first name is. This guy comes highly praised though by my friend. He says Duke is one of his best and is the lead man of his team."

Pleased more men were coming, Quaid then told of the documents and Vince's letter. "There's not much to go on. If you remember, I'd already found the tape recorder in Vince's office, but so far it's not done us any good." Quaid grew silent. More than anything, right now his main desire was to find the identity of Sydney's elusive third partner.

"I take it you've decided to stay put and let him come to you?"

"Paul and I agree that it seems the best plan. With three marshals helping us five, I don't see how he can get near Sydney. But... my instincts tell me he's going to try."

"Once Paul gets here, we'll see about getting a clear voice sample from the phone and then run it through our database. You never know, something may turn up."

While the chief talked, Quaid grew increasingly uneasy, which prompted him to silently pray. "Lord, help me relax. I need to think clearly, and I need some wisdom here. Something is bothering me, but I can't put my finger on it. Please help me." As the Lord filled him with calm assurance, Quaid notified the chief he'd be in touch.

Throughout the conversation, Sydney had gathered up the junk mail and tossed it in the trash. Returning, she eyed Quaid still talking while she bent to pick up the white envelope. Quaid had placed the documents and cassettes back inside. As she reached forward, Sydney caught sight of Quaid vigorously shaking his head for her to leave it alone. Letting her hand settle on it a moment, Sydney took a deep breath then picked up the remaining mail, which included Hope's letter and pictures. She then took them upstairs to her bedroom. When she returned, the envelope was no longer on the table, and Quaid was standing in the living room with the TV remote. His cell phone was back on his belt.

Sydney walked up to him and paused as he said, "I thought we'd watch a movie tonight." Pointing at the nearby cabinet, he added, "Under there are some DVDs."

Shrugging her shoulders, Sydney knelt in front of the TV. Opening the door, she began reading titles of movies stacked inside.

Pleased she wasn't going to argue about the movie or the white envelope, Quaid sat the remote down and headed to the kitchen.

Knowing the refrigerator was fully stocked, he hollered, "What kind of pop do you want?"

"Is there anything stronger?"

"Nope." Quaid heard Sydney sigh then say with disgust, "Of course not!" Louder, she replied, "In that case, anything cold!"

Soon the sound of popping corn, followed by ice being dropped in glasses, echoed through the condo.

Quaid entered the room with his hands holding a tray with full glasses, popcorn, and bowls. He even thought to grab napkins. Seeing Sydney holding the remote, he paused. Knowing most men had trouble yielding control of the remote, Quaid figured Sydney expected him to make a big deal about it, so he decided to do otherwise. Pointedly staring at the remote in Sydney's hand, Quaid raised his eyebrows and then set the tray on the coffee table. Eyeing the movies, he said, "Either we're having an all-nighter, or someone couldn't make up her mind."

She took a long drink from the nearest glass and then wiped her mouth before replying. "You choose."

Quaid scanned the titles then chuckled. "My! We are in a mood, aren't we? Here's a Western, a Disney, a sci-fi, and a feel-good movie." Lifting eyes her way, he further said, "I expected a chick flick." He was surprised by the hardness that entered her eyes.

"Vince's letter was enough to wipe romance from my mind!" Sydney reached for the popcorn bag and poured some in a bowl. Pausing, she then poured one for Quaid too.

Quaid studied the titles again. "I've decided we'll watch this feel-good one with James Garner."

Not commenting, Sydney settled back while Quaid put the movie in the player. Pointedly reminding her she had the remote, he then picked up his drink and full bowl of popcorn. Sitting in the recliner, his feet were soon up, and he sighed. "Man, this is nice. I'm actually glad you and Maria had a tiff. It's been a while since I've been able to relax like this."

# Out of the Snare

Pointedly staring at Quaid's holstered gun and COM link on his belt, Sydney's face conveyed doubt that he was totally relaxed.

As the movie began its opening, she said with a hesitant voice, "Thanks, Quaid."

He tilted his head and studied her face. It pleased him that she was going lighter on the makeup, but it still didn't hide the many emotions playing across her face. He saw traces of vulnerability, fear, and yet he also detected a measure of confidence in his ability to protect her. All the time he quietly studied her, Sydney's attention was on the TV as if she hadn't expected a reply.

"You're welcome, Sydney."

For a brief moment, her eyes slid to his then back to the TV. They soon became engrossed in the storyline unfolding before them. Quaid had heard about this movie but hadn't been able to watch it yet. Knowing it contained strong life messages, he wondered how it would affect Sydney. James Garner played a billionaire who died. He'd never developed a good relationship with his children, and now they were fighting over his money, all except one grandson who Garner specifically had chosen to receive a video. This video was narrated by his grandfather and contained several tasks he wanted the young man to perform. As the movie played on, the self-centered grandson began turning into a person that cared about the needs of others.

Throughout the movie, Quaid glanced Sydney's way. He was pleased to note her attitude changing. She had started out slouched in the overstuffed chair, but now she was sitting on the edge with elbows on her knees and hands supporting her chin.

At an especially poignant part, she paused the movie then turned sad eyes Quaid's way. With tears rolling down her cheeks, she asked, "Why did God let that happen?"

His first thought was to remind her it was just a movie, but then he reconsidered. "Sydney, there's one sure thing in this life. If we're born, we die. That's a given. We just don't know when or how. In this movie, the writer wanted it to be her time. She'd accomplished what she was supposed to."

"You mean by being his friend, his true friend?" Letting her eyes go back to the still picture on the screen, she said to herself, "She didn't care about his money. She cared about him!"

"That's right." Quaid gently added, "Sydney, money never truly makes us happy, and it can't buy us friends either, at least the kind that stick through good times and bad."

Lowering her eyes to the empty popcorn bowl still in her lap, Sydney grew silent. Quaid allowed her time to sort out how his words might apply to her.

Sighing heavily, Sydney avoided Quaid's penetrating eyes as she started the movie. When the credits rolled at the end, Sydney came to her feet and handed Quaid the remote. Scuffing her toe in the carpet, she stared at the floor while asking, "Will you be staying in here tonight?"

"Yes. While we're here, when I'm off duty, I'll be sleeping in the family room downstairs."

"Good," drifted down the stairs as Sydney headed up them.

After shutting the machines off, a thoughtful Quaid carried the tray into the kitchen then checked his watch. Flipping open his cell phone, he decided to check on Paul's current location. Learning he was at that moment crossing the big bridge, Quaid asked him about Sydney's phone.

"They were able to get a clear voice. It's being run through the database as we speak. Now we sit and wait."

*Now we sit and wait. Now we sit and wait.* Those words kept running through Quaid's mind as he set his alarm for 5:00 a.m. and tried getting comfortable on the sofa downstairs.

The marshals arrived by rental car about seven that next morning. Quaid and Paul were surprised when only two climbed out. When questioned as to where Duke was, Luke quickly supplied that he'd had personal stuff to attend to. "Our chief let him go with the understanding that he'd show up no later than this afternoon."

Exchanging glances with Paul, Quaid briefed the new men on the setup and then sent them to get some sleep. Jake took his turn in the command center while Quaid and Neal patrolled. As they made their rounds, Paul finished setting up freestanding camouflaged surveillance cameras. He took great care to place them in specific blind spots. The feed was monitored in the command center. Plus, there was a large radio keyed to the men's COM links, so an instant message could be relayed to all. There also was a separate two-way directly linked to local police. The final measure of protection was done by the chief. He had contacted the Coast Guard asking them to do periodic patrols off the coast for any suspicious looking boats in the area.

Even though Quaid was bothered by the missing Duke, he felt they had all bases covered to the best of their ability. But when 5:00 p.m. rolled around and Duke still hadn't made an appearance, Quaid started getting antsy. It occurred to him Vince's murderer could have found out their plan and had waylaid Duke. Since Quaid's team didn't know what Duke looked like, the suspect could easily infiltrate the group while avoiding the marshals. Duke's lateness was fueling Quaid's thoughts, so he went to find the now patrolling Matt.

"I don't know what to tell you, sir. He should have been here by now."

"My concern is him coming in after dark without letting us know. None of my people know him."

"Maybe we should call my chief and find out if he knows something."

Quaid stood by as Matt pulled his cell phone to call. Hearing for himself that Duke was en route and should arrive any time, Quaid sent Matt back to patrolling. After he left, Quaid still had a strong foreboding about Duke's no-show. Staring out over the lake toward Mackinac Island, he decided to bounce his concern off his longtime partner. "Paul, meet me in the family room. We need to talk. Over."

A short while later, the partners dissected the situation from every angle. As they talked, the feeling of uneasiness grew in Quaid.

"I've worked with you too long not to pay attention when these things hit you, Quaid. Are you thinking our guy is somehow going to slip in here after dark, posing as Duke?"

"Why not? None of us have met him! Matt's description was, 'He's tall, in good physical shape, and he has dark hair.' That description fits hundreds of men! Besides that, we already know it describes our murderer, and … Luke for that matter."

"I see a plan brewing in your head. What do you propose?"

From a bag, Quaid lifted out five mini shoulder two-ways. "I want to use these with our team—only! I've already set them to the same channel, which is different from the COM links we share with the marshals. If any of us suspect one of the marshals, we'll give each other three clicks. That will be the signal to move in closer to Sydney … with guns pulled!"

"Have you thought about running the print from Sydney's glass against these three?"

"I have, but it doesn't sit well. I hate thinking our murderer could be one of us!" Quaid then added, "Besides, what are the odds that of all the agencies we could have asked help from, we'd call the one with our murderer? That's so incredibly high it's ridiculous!"

"That's true. But your gut's telling you something." Paul then added thoughtfully, "Or it's the Holy Spirit trying to warn and direct you."

Quaid studied his longtime friend intently before replying, "If Duke isn't here in the next hour, say by 8:00 p.m., I'm going to ask the chief to run a check on any connection between these three and Vince."

"While you're at it, have them also run their prints with the one from the glass," Paul suggested. "Let's cover all our bases."

As it was, Duke didn't arrive by 8:00 p.m., so Quaid placed the call to his chief.

# Chapter 23

A little before 9:00 p.m., Quaid's fear of an impostor infiltrating the group was laid to rest when Matt's voice came over the COM link announcing Duke's arrival.

Luke was manning the command center; Neal and Paul were in the process of switching places on the beach. Jake and Matt would soon be doing the same in the parking area. Quaid had just entered the condo to let Maria step outside for a bit of fresh air before she'd be in for the rest of the night. The original plan had been for Luke to later change places with Matt, and then Quaid would be a roamer.

Now that the missing Duke had arrived, Quaid changed his mind. Figuring Duke needed daylight in order to know his surroundings well enough to patrol, Quaid decided to put him in the command center, Matt would stay at the covered stairs area, Luke would handle the beach, and Paul would be a roamer with Quaid. That way, Jake and Neal could get rested for the morning shift.

Liking the change, Quaid clicked his COM link and relayed the plan to everyone. He then specifically instructed Matt to tell Duke directions to the command center and where to stow his gear at the motel.

Before heading to the command center, Duke decided to do some recon of his own. So, once his gear was stowed at the motel, he took a walk.

Keeping to the shadows, he moved quietly around while getting the layout. There were a series of five connected condos, and from what he understood, the woman they were protecting was in the middle one. Detective Williams had chosen well, for the place wouldn't be easy for anyone to breach.

In a crouch, Duke stopped to watch a Hispanic woman exit the covered stairway at the third condo. He observed a hand on her holstered pistol as she scanned the lit parking lot and beyond. Duke involuntarily stepped deeper into the shadows. It was a matter of pride to him regarding his stealth abilities. When her eyes skimmed right past him, Duke smiled.

Apparently satisfied all was well, the woman turned to speak with someone at her left. This person wasn't in Duke's line of vision, so he moved closer. The man was well concealed yet had a good position to see most of the parking lot, outbuildings, dumpsters, and road beyond. Moving ever closer, Duke had expected it to be Luke, one of his own men, but instead saw someone he didn't know.

He hesitated where he was then inched closer until he could hear the conversation. He heard the woman call the man Jake. Staying put, he reveled in the fact of his undetected nearness.

Duke scanned the area for any possible roamers. The last thing he wanted was for Detective Williams or his partner to sneak up on him. Although Duke had to admit the odds of that happening were slim. He temporarily forgot the two talking as his mind mapped out the job ahead. He wondered how long he and his two men would be at this assignment.

Suddenly, his thoughts were interrupted. Coming to attention, he listened intently.

"Maria, Lieutenant Quaid told you my knock signal, right?"

"He told me everyone's. Let's see... yours is three knocks, a pause, and then three more knocks. Right?"

"You've got it. Don't forget them! I don't want you shooting me because you think it's the wrong signal."

Maria bristled and then relaxed, apparently deciding Jake was teasing.

Duke was making a mental note of the words when the two suddenly turned to their left with guns drawn. He was impressed with their speed and thought the woman had been a hair faster.

Out of habit, Duke had laid a hand on his own pistol and then relaxed when his man, Matt, stepped into view near the two officers.

Duke watched him smile and then heard him say, "Sorry if I startled you. I actually thought you were too engrossed in talking to notice my approach." Showing a genuine look of respect on his face, Matt admitted, "Guess I was wrong." Extending his hand, he introduced himself to Maria.

The two men then fell into conversation, which Duke listened to with his head bent. He didn't see Maria walk away. Finding he was getting bored with their chitchat, Duke started making his way back toward the command center. He was halfway back when he heard an ominous click and a female voice close at hand. "Going somewhere?"

As he went to move, she commanded, "Keep your hands away from your sides and turn around slowly!"

Duke did as directed and stared into the barrel of Maria's pistol.

He tried to detect nervousness but saw none. Her hand was steady as she said, "Step out into the light."

As he did, Duke glanced back toward the men. They were out of sight. By the look in her eyes, Duke knew this woman wasn't a rookie, so he did as he was told.

"Who are you?"

"I'm Duke with the U.S. Marshals. I'm supposed to be helping you with this assignment, so I'd appreciate you lowering your gun."

Maria studied the handsome dark-haired man standing before her. "Not so fast! Do you have ID?"

As he started to pull it out, he paused to state with an edge to his voice, "I thought you people were informed of our coming."

"We were, but in my opinion there's no harm in being cautious. Now, since the safety's off on my gun *and* a bullet's in the chamber, I'll ask again; do you have ID?"

Duke slowly unzipped his coat with one hand then pulled one side open revealing a badge clipped to his shirt pocket.

Lowering her gun, Maria extended a hand. "I'm Maria Lopez. I'm a member of Detective Williams' team."

Taking her hand, Duke smiled. "Nice to meet you, Maria. I'm Duke. I must say, you're impressive. Not many get the drop on me. In fact, you're the first woman to do so! Good job! If you ever want to work with the marshals, I hope you give our office a call."

Not interested in getting too friendly, Maria let his comments go. Instead she asked, "Aren't you supposed to be in the command center?"

"I am. So, if you'll excuse me, I'll be on my way."

As he turned to leave, the overhead light revealed a scar at the corner of his eye. Maria was momentarily struck by the fact that it didn't hinder his good looks at all. She thoughtfully contemplated his suggestion of working with the marshals as she watched his broad back round the corner of the motel. "It's a tempting idea if I could work with the likes of him," she said to herself while walking around the parking lot before heading back to the other two men. Jake had turned over his position to Matt and was walking toward her.

When they met partway, he asked, "Were you talking to someone?"

"It was the new guy, Duke."

"I thought he was supposed to be at the command center."

"He was." Shrugging, she added, "I guess he wanted to get a feel of the place first, or maybe he just needed to stretch his legs. Who knows?"

"Well, I'm off to bed. See you in the morning."

"Good night, Jake." Turning, Maria walked to Matt's position. They exchanged a few words, and then she headed up the stairs to take over while Quaid returned outside.

At 12:20 a.m. Sydney's phone rang, waking her. Quaid had instructed her to let the voice mail answer, so as the phone kept sounding its tune, she went to wake Maria. The two of them paged Quaid and then made their way downstairs. Within minutes, he rapped on the sliding door near the dining room table. Maria let him in and then backed up to stand near Sydney.

Quaid observed them standing in robes and slippers. Seeing Maria's protective mode with Sydney and their overall agitated state, he asked, "What happened?"

Sydney handed him the phone. "Another call came."

"Did you answer it?"

Defensively she retorted, "You told me not to!"

"I was just checking; that's all. Have you listened to it?"

The women shook their heads in the negative as Quaid stepped forward to take the cell phone and punch the voice mail button.

A muffled voice soon came over the phone. The women leaned in to hear.

"Well, well, well! How come you're not answering your phone, Syd? Actually, it doesn't matter. I have a feeling we'll be talking face to face real soon! Um…Quaid…do you really think bringing in

U.S. Marshals is going to help?" At this point his voice grew angry. "You can make me go away by having Sydney sign the papers! Leave me a message on this number callback, and we'll work a drop place out." There was a long pause then a sneer. "But I don't suppose you're going to make this easy, are you? By the way, you could have chosen a warmer spot. St. Ignace is cold this time of year!"

The trio heard an evil laugh as the call ended. No one spoke.

Sydney started gasping for air, saying in a panic, "I...can't... breathe!"

"Maria, quick! Find a paper bag or something for her to breathe in!" Quaid ordered as he sat Sydney on a dining room chair. He gently pushed her head down between her knees.

Maria opened various cupboards until she found a lunch bag and brought it back to Quaid.

"Here, Sydney. Put this over your mouth. Take slow, deep breaths."

"I...can't...get...air!"

"Try to relax, Sydney," Maria said in a soothing voice.

As Quaid massaged the muscles in her neck and Maria patted her arm, Sydney slowly began relaxing until she soon was breathing normally. Sitting up straight, Sydney pulled the bag away. Looking up into Quaid's steady eyes, she said in a harsh whisper, "He knows where I am!"

"We don't know that for sure. All we know is that he's aware you're in St. Ignace. That doesn't mean he knows you're here in this condo. St. Ignace has lots of people and houses."

Turning in the chair, she clasped both hands around Quaid's left forearm. "Tell me you'll protect me! Tell me he won't get me!"

In a strong, commanding voice, Quaid said, "Sydney, look me in the eyes." When she did, he continued. "I promise you. I will protect you with my life! No one will get to you as long as I'm still alive."

"The same goes for me!" Maria assured.

Tears began streaming down Sydney's cheeks as she looked from one to the other. Quaid and Maria stood patiently by. Slowly the tears stopped, and Sydney asked, "What do we do now?"

"Well, he knows about St. Ignace and the marshals, so I'll alert everyone. But Sydney, in my experience, the fact he called means he's not ready to act yet. So, even though this will be hard, I'd go back to bed and try getting some sleep. For a while, I'll stay in the house. Okay?"

While Quaid watched, Maria escorted Sydney back upstairs. He then began pacing. More and more the conviction grew that their man was somehow connected with the marshals or had access to police files. The thought filled Quaid with anger. Pacing back and forth, he prayed the chief would call soon with confirmation regarding a fingerprint match or connection with Vince.

Around six the next morning, Quaid was dismayed to see fog rolling in off the two large lakes surrounding St. Ignace. It didn't help that daylight wouldn't show for another hour or so.

Before long, the fog turned thicker than pea soup. Quaid had trouble seeing more than a couple feet in front of him. Picking up the COM link, he gave instructions to the group. "Jake, you relieve Matt near the covered steps near the front door. Neal, you take Duke's place in the command center so he can get some sleep. Luke, you're on the beach; Paul and I will roam. Stay close, men. This fog is thick!"

After hearing all the verbal affirmatives, Quaid went to the family room to get his own Kevlar vest on.

It had taken Sydney a long time to fall asleep the night before. She'd expected to sleep in but woke to use the bathroom. Harboring bothersome thoughts, she decided sleep was over, so she stayed up. At 7:15 a.m., Sydney came downstairs. She was dressed but still wore slippers, had no makeup, and her hair was a mess.

Maria already had coffee going, and to Sydney's nose, it smelled great. With her steaming cup, Sydney went to the dining room table.

Setting the cup down, she pulled Hope's letter from her sweater pocket and then sat down. Sydney pulled the photos out of the envelope to lay them out before her. She was lazily looking them over while sipping her coffee when Maria joined her.

"What do you have there?"

"Photos from a friend. They're of her, her soon-to-be husband, and his baby, Sarah."

A fully-clothed Maria sat down next to her at the table. She too sipped a cup of coffee as she stared out the door at the fog.

"Would you like to see them?"

Maria replied, "Sure. Why not?"

Sydney picked up one photo, studied it, and then handed it over. "This is my friend Hope with baby Sarah."

Maria smiled at the baby. "She's a little doll!"

"She sure is. I guess she looks a lot like her mother."

"What happened to her?"

"She died giving birth to Sarah."

"Oh."

Sydney handed her another one. "This is baby Sarah by herself."

The last photo held Sydney's attention the longest. Then, letting out a long sigh, she said, "And this one is Sarah and her dad, Pierce."

Maria looked at the photo. As she did, Sydney saw her body stiffen as Maria leaned closer and pointed with her finger. "Did you say this was Pierce?"

"Yes, he's good friends with Quaid. They go to the same church. Why?"

A frowning Maria stared at the photo.

Suddenly, Maria's chair went toppling as she stood and said with conviction, "I have to tell Lieutenant Quaid!"

# Chapter 24

Quaid and Paul had come together for a quick talk near the stream and then separated. Quaid worked the beach area and south while Paul was to head west then south through the parking lot. Quaid hung close to the buildings, for visibility was bad. When he pulled even with their condo and patio, Quaid's cell phone vibrated on his belt.

It was the chief.

"Quaid, we found a connection with Vince and Corey Drake. The corporation security guard identified a photo of him. The guard said Vince had cleared Corey through the same night he was killed. He had called him Mr. Clark. We also matched the print from Miss Turner's glass to his on file. He's our man all right! Has he gotten there yet?"

"I hope not, Chief! The fog here is thick this morning. We can't see farther than an arm's length in front of us. But...who is this Corey Drake? Should I know him?"

"Yes...he's..."

At that point, Quaid's cell phone buzzed that another call was coming in.

Maria held the phone to her ear while instructing Sydney to get her shoes on.

Not understanding, Sydney asked, "What's going on?"

Quaid chose that moment to answer his phone, so all Maria had time to do was furrow her brows and point toward the stairs. She was pleased it did the trick, for Sydney started moving as Maria said in the phone, "He's here!"

At the same moment Quaid stated, "I was talking to the chief, so this better be important!"

Maria barely let him finish the sentence before saying again urgently, "He's here! The man looking like Pierce Matthews is here!"

Quaid froze. "Where? Where did you see him?"

"I saw him last night! It's Duke!"

"Duke?"

Growing impatient, Maria almost yelled, "I'm telling you, it's Duke!"

"Maria, we have to be sure about this. Why do you think it's him?"

"I just saw a picture of Pierce with his baby. He looks exactly like the man I ran into last night near the parking lot, except Duke has a scar by his eye."

Quaid's thoughts jumped into high gear. "You saw Duke last night? Never mind, we'll talk about that later! Maria, I'll call our team while you get Sydney up and dressed!"

## Out of the Snare

Totally forgetting the chief, Quaid called Paul on the private two-way. He then got Neal, but Jake didn't respond. Knowing he was supposed to be stationed right outside the covered stairway to the front door, a sick feeling hit the pit of Quaid's stomach. He started moving toward the front door. En route he called Paul back with the same instructions. Unfortunately, Paul had swung wide near the motel and front road so wasn't any closer to Jake's position than Quaid was.

On top of that, the men were further frustrated as the fog seriously hindered their progress.

Jake didn't like the fog. He couldn't see a thing. Stepping to the edge of the covered stairway, he leaned against it facing the parking lot. Staring up, he hoped the sun would burn it away soon, for every sound was a potential threat in the fog.

Hearing a crunch to his left, Jake pushed away from the wall and pulled his pistol. Suddenly a man materialized out of the fog a couple feet from Jake. He tensed as the man extended his empty hand, saying, "I'm Duke, one of the marshals."

A feeling of relief washed over Jake as he lowered his gun. Smiling, he peered closer and then frowned. *He looks a lot like Pierce.* Right then the two-way chirped at his shoulder then came alive with Quaid's voice.

As Quaid's voice came over the mike, Duke lunged. Within seconds, he'd wrapped his arm in a strangle hold around Jake's neck. With the other one, he quickly snapped his neck. Before Jake's body was fully settled on the pavement, Duke was heading up the stairs.

Finally gaining the corner of the condos, Quaid didn't stop to massage the sore shins he'd acquired from running into steps and railings along the way. He'd repeatedly called Jake on the two-way with no response. Rounding the end, Quaid could move a little faster, for there weren't any stairs. Within minutes, he came around the next corner that placed him on the parking lot side. He knew only two condo widths separated him and Jake, but in the fog, it seemed a mile.

Quaid felt his way along the first covered stairwell attached to a garage. Passing that one, he noticed the fog starting to lift. He could clearly see his feet and pavement. Thanking the Lord, he moved forward until he touched the next set of stairs. *Only one more to go. Lord, please let Jake be all right*, he prayed while trying to pick up speed.

Maria had her holster strapped in place and Kevlar vest on. The loaded pistol rested in her hand. Racking a bullet into the chamber, she took the safety off. Hearing Sydney moving around upstairs, Maria began pacing the area between the front foyer and the living room. All her nerves and muscles were tensed for possible action as she waited for further orders from Quaid.

It irked her that she actually had Sydney's third partner in her sights but didn't know who he was. There wasn't any doubt in her mind that he'd try somehow to use the fog to his advantage. Kicking the wall, she scowled then walked to the window. The fog was thick, very thick. She couldn't see the outer railing of the large deck.

Sydney was upset and confused. Something was happening. Something had upset Maria. After putting her shoes on, Sydney went to the bathroom. She turned on the vent fan and then lit a cigarette before making some kind of order with her hair and makeup.

She had just finished the hair when a knock came at the front door below. Three knocks, pause, then three more. It was Jake. Relieved that a man would be inside with them, Sydney picked up her mascara.

As she leaned in to the mirror, Sydney heard Maria turn the

deadbolt and open the door. The next second Sydney froze, for Maria yelled, "Run!"

Adrenaline and fear ran through Sydney's body as she dropped the mascara brush in the sink and ran across the hall to her bedroom. Not allowing herself time to think, Sydney unlocked the dormer window and pushed it open. She could hear scuffling and things being knocked over as she flipped out the attached metal ladder to let it snake down the side of the building. Before hearing it settle on the deck, Sydney was out the window and started down.

The moment the front door was open a couple inches, Maria knew her mistake. Throwing her weight against the door, she tried getting it closed, but Duke was stronger. Within seconds he was inside and had knocked her pistol away. Maria knew she had to buy Sydney time, so she began throwing defensive punches and kicks, all the while hoping that Sydney had moved when she yelled.

As Maria stumbled back, her hand touched a bronze vase sitting on a stand near the front door. Grabbing it, she swung it forward with all her might. It was Duke's turn to stumble back, and Maria took that moment to locate her weapon.

He soon was coming at her again. Reverting to an age-old maneuver, she raised her knee and jammed it in his groin. As he bent over, she clasped her hands together and brought them down on his head. She was sure he would go down, but the man was fit and angry. He recovered quickly. Gaining his balance, he charged forward once again. Throughout the struggle, Maria repeatedly tried to accomplish two things: find her gun and avoid his fists. She knew from past experience that she was no match for a man's strength. Her only advantage was her size and speed. She fended off blow after blow, but in the end, she didn't accomplish her goals.

Backed up against the counter separating the hall from the

kitchen, Duke got her cornered. With one savage swing, he landed his fist against her temple, and she wilted to the floor.

When Sydney's feet touched the deck, she paused, trying to figure what angle to move toward the stairs in the fog. Deciding, she moved forward. While her mind was shouting, "Hurry," her eyes were saying, "You can't see! You have to go slow!" Bile built in her stomach, shooting up her throat as Sydney progressed across the deck. Fearing she might find the opening to the stairs first, Sydney groped the air in front of her.

Convinced her enemy was right on her tail, she pressed forward. Reward came when her knuckles rapped against the railing. Stifling a cry of pain, she went hand over hand while sticking her foot out, all the while hoping she was headed toward the opening. After a few steps, her foot tipped forward into air. *The stairwell!*

Relieved yet still not able to see, Sydney started down.

Paul and Quaid converged on the middle condo about the same time. As Quaid reached the covered stairway, he paused to lean his ear against it. He thought he heard the sliding door pulled open. About the same time, Paul tripped over something. A couple seconds later, he quietly stated, "I found Jake."

Bending down, Paul was able to see most of Jake's body as the fog kept slowly rising. He searched for a pulse. Finding none, he said in a low voice, "Quaid, he's dead."

In a tight voice, Quaid kept to the business at hand. "Paul, the fog is starting to lift. I can see above my knees now. You call Neal about Jake then head north toward the stream. If Sydney got away, that's where she's headed. I'll go up the stairs." Already moving, Quaid softly said over his shoulder, "The Lord is with you, buddy."

# Out of the Snare

Paul stared a moment longer at Jake's body before replying, "You too, Quaid."

Duke couldn't believe how much time he'd wasted on the Spanish woman. She'd been surprisingly quick and strong. After she went down, he figured Sydney was gone but did a quick search in case. He soon found the open bedroom window and cursed. The fog prevented him from seeing where the ladder led to. Figuring he'd be faster through the house, he flew down the stairs two at a time and headed for the slider. The woman still lay where she fell. He wondered briefly if he'd killed her too but then brushed it from his mind.

Throwing the sliding door open, Duke paused to listen. Behind him, he heard sounds coming through the house. Surprised that the detectives seemed to be already on to him, Duke turned his attention forward. Ahead, he heard nothing. Sure that Sydney had to be somewhere in front of him, he cursed the fog and moved forward.

It seemed to Sydney she was moving down the stairs at a snail's pace. She kept imagining her killer gaining on her. Then something strange happened. One of the snare verses came to her mind. It was one she hadn't memorized. That realization so unsettled her that Sydney missed a step and almost lost her footing. Tightening her hold on the railing, she was able to stay upright. Reaching the halfway landing, Sydney experienced another surprise. The fog was rising! At that same moment, she heard the sliding door open above. Fear threatened to paralyze her, but then the verse went through her mind again.

"The fear of man brings a snare, but whoever trusts in the Lord shall be safe."

Sydney's mind whispered, *Is that what you want me to do? Trust you? How do I do that?*

*Keep moving,* were the only words that kept playing over in her mind.

As if God had covered her ears with his hands, the sounds above stopped. Plus, instead of fear, newfound strength got Sydney's feet moving again. As she sped down the stairs, Sydney went so quietly she felt like she was floating. As she moved down, the fog continued to thin. At the bottom, she paused to glance back up the stairs she'd just descended. The sight reminded her of a painting she'd seen once in a store front. It pictured stairs leading to heaven. Like the painting, the stairs disappeared into the clouds, except here it was fog. Marveling, she turned toward the stream and was happy to see the fog was above her eye level now.

Realizing no one could see her fleeing, Sydney kept thinking, *Thank you, God,* as she ran. She headed the direction Quaid had made her practice so many times as the stream came into sight.

As Quaid hurried up the stairs, he noted the door was open. His Glock was poised and ready as he stopped a couple steps from the top. Pressing his body against the right side, he inched upward and forward while peering inside. Seeing a foot, he silently moved to the opposite side to better see down the hall.

It was Maria, and she wasn't moving. He couldn't tell if she was dead or not.

Moving fast and low, Quaid rolled in and up to one knee then froze. While listening for signs of movement, he noticed the rise and fall of Maria's chest. Thankful that she wasn't dead, Quaid moved up beside her. As he peered toward the living room, he saw the slider open to his right. At that moment, he heard the sounds of falling and cursing on the stairs. Knowing Duke's approximate position, Quaid didn't waste time with being stealthy. He knew that if Duke was headed down the stairs it was because he was in pursuit of Sydney.

Before heading out the door, Quaid took a moment to look at Maria's face. He saw an ugly swelling on the left side. Taking time to click the two-way at his shoulder, he called Neal, who was locked inside the command center. In a whisper he said, "Neal, the bird's in flight! I repeat! The bird's in flight! Also, we need medical help for Maria. Over."

After Neal triple-clicked the affirmation, Quaid headed out the slider and across the deck.

Sydney reached the stream. At the same time, she was pleased to see thin slits of sunshine breaking through the fog. Between that and the verse repeating itself in her heart and soul, Sydney started to believe she'd be all right.

She found what she thought was her jumping over spot but misjudged the distance. Upon landing on the other side, her foot slipped, and she nearly fell backwards into the water. Cursing, she grabbed for some pine branches hanging down and was able to pull herself forward. Falling on her stomach, Sydney lay there to catch her breath. Her foot was wet and very cold. She began shivering.

Then she heard a shot.

For a moment she was afraid to move, for Sydney was acutely conscious of the noise she'd made. Then reason took over. Thinking it might not have been directed her way, she began crawling toward the motel. Suddenly, she heard her name spoken behind her, and Sydney's heart jumped into her throat.

Frightened, she did something out of character. Instead of stopping, Sydney hauled herself up and ran with all her might around the end of the motel. All the while she kept thinking, *I'm sorry I cursed your name, God. Please protect me!*

As she rounded the front corner, more shots rang out.

Finally locating the command room door, Sydney pounded frantically.

Due to the lifting fog, Paul misjudged the distance to the end of the condos. He came around the north corner faster than anticipated. He spotted Duke a second too late. Duke's bullet hit Paul's gun arm in the right shoulder. In a defensive move, Paul ignored the pain searing through his arm as he fell to the ground and rolled onto his stomach. Using the ground to stabilize himself, he tried taking aim but had trouble getting his arm to move.

Certain that Paul was down for good, Duke focused his attention on the stream ahead where he'd heard splashes. Limping rapidly forward, he cursed the fog for causing his fall. Clearly able to see Sydney crawling on the other side of the stream, he stopped, took aim, and called her name.

As Quaid moved, the fog seemed to lift before him, making a clearer path. The lower he went down the steps, the better he could see, and the faster he moved. His heart nearly stopped when he heard the shot. The report told him it wasn't Paul's gun. Not allowing himself to dwell on who might have gotten shot, Quaid moved faster. He soon saw a limping Duke in front of him, heading toward the stream.

In a full run now, Quaid got close when Duke stopped to aim his gun toward the stream. Walking slowly closer, Quaid got Duke in his sights while demanding, "Give it up, Duke, or should I say, Corey Drake! Drop your gun!"

Quaid knew Duke had no intentions of complying when he turned with his gun still raised. Squeezing the trigger, Quaid heard two more reports as a bullet whizzed past his head.

With Duke's body now on the ground, Quaid ran forward. One look told him he was dead, so he lowered his gun. Seeing Paul down to his left, his heart nearly stopped, but then he remembered the two

## Out of the Snare

other reports. Kneeling close to Duke's head, Quaid saw evidence of two bullet holes, one in the throat and one in the temple.

A subdued Quaid went to join his partner, who was now lying on his back. As Quaid knelt beside him, he heard sirens in the distance. A couple seconds later, Luke and Matt ran up. They stared at Paul and then walked to the body of their superior.

Watching them, Quaid and Paul saw disgust register on Luke's face, but Matt's was full of sadness. He kept shaking his head as if attempting to understand how his boss could have strayed so far from the law.

After a moment, Luke turned away. Walking to Quaid, he said, "I'm sorry, sir.

We didn't know." He studied the ground a second and then asked, "Is there something I should do?"

As he was the ranking man in charge, Quaid said, "Yes. Direct the EMTs to Jake's body by the front stairway."

"Yes, sir." He turned and trotted off.

Quaid turned his attention to Matt but withheld any instructions. He was still standing over Duke's body with a shocked look on his face. Deciding to give him a minute, Quaid focused his attention back on Luke, who was waving at the EMT driver pulling into the parking lot. "Hey, Luke!"

Immediately, he swung around. "Yes, sir?"

"Tell the EMTs an officer's down inside the condo. She's the priority!"

Luke nodded his agreement and then spoke to the ambulance driver. They soon disappeared out of sight.

Quaid turned his attention back to his partner.

With a frown, Paul groaned then stated, "Took you long enough to show up! For a moment there, I thought you'd stopped for coffee or something."

Quaid smiled. He knew his partner was going to be fine. Clicking his two-way, he asked, "Neal, is Sydney safe?"

"Yes, sir. Safe and sound." He then added, "Although a bit hysterical. Over."

"She's entitled. Over."

Quaid told Neal to bring Sydney then signed off.

While speaking, Quaid had noticed blood seeping from Paul's right shoulder. Now, helping him to a sitting position, Quaid pulled a clean handkerchief from his back pocket. He gently pushed it inside Paul's coat sleeve to help stop the flow. He then sat down next to him.

The two partners watched another ambulance pull in. Neither spoke. After a long moment, Quaid randomly stated, "I guess the fog must have held the ambulances up."

Another silence; then Paul asked, "Is Maria all right?"

"I'm not sure. She was unconscious when I left the room, but praise God, she was breathing!"

# Chapter 25

A day later, Hope rang Sydney's doorbell.

Even though Sydney had sprayed an aerosol freshener, Hope's nose picked up the scent of cigarette the moment she opened the door. The other thing she noticed were dark circles visible under Sydney's eyes. Swallowing her pity, Hope smiled and stepped in. There'd been flurries that morning, so she handed Sydney her coat then took off her wet shoes. Stocking-footed, Hope waited until Sydney hung up the coat then gave her a big hug. "Welcome home! Thank God you're okay!"

"Yeah, well...Jake isn't! The Lord let him die!"

Startled by Sydney's sudden outburst, Hope silently asked the

Lord for wisdom. She badly wanted to soothe Sydney's hurts, but before she could respond, Sydney asked, "Where's Sarah? I thought you'd bring her."

"Pierce is watching her this morning. We both thought a quiet visit was in order today." Hope smiled, adding, "Now that she's walking, Sarah requires, let's say... more hands-on attention." Scanning the living room, Hope spied a comfortable looking chair and sat down. "This way, we can chat uninterrupted."

Sydney shrugged her shoulders. "Would you like some coffee or tea? I have hot water already in the pot on the stove."

"Tea sounds nice." As Sydney moved to go make it, Hope said, "Looks like winter's just around the corner."

From the nearby kitchen, Sydney replied, "I hope not. Winter is so dreary! I could use some days of sunshine. It cheers me." Sydney finished her statement in front of Hope, along with her cup. "Here you go. I have a variety of flavors to choose from."

Hope chose blueberry and pulled it from the wrapper. She started dunking it up and down while waiting for Sydney to return with her own cup. Satisfied the color looked right, she squeezed the bag with her spoon and laid it on a saucer. Taking a sip, she sighed and leaned back.

Hope studied Sydney now seated on the sofa. A hot cup steamed in her hands, but Sydney's mind was obviously elsewhere as she stared at the floor. A haunted, sad look was openly displayed on her face. Hope gave her a few moments and then ventured, "Do you want to tell me about it?"

As Sydney raised her head, the cup in her hand began to shake. She carefully sat it down before turning tear-filled eyes Hope's way. "Jake died because of me. It's all my fault!"

Sydney buried her face in her hands as great sobs tore through her body.

Hope set her teacup down and went to the sofa. Sitting on the edge, she rubbed Sydney's shoulder. "That's not true, Sydney. Jake was killed by a merciless, cold-blooded man, the same one they believe killed your friend Vince. Jake's death was his fault, not yours." As she spoke, Sydney turned toward her and collapsed in Hope's arms. Holding her close, Hope prayed God would ease Sydney's distress and give Hope an opportunity to help.

Eventually the sobs stopped, and Hope went in search of tissues. She found a box in the back bathroom. By the time she returned, Sydney was wiping her eyes with her sleeve and was somewhat composed. Hope handed her the box and then sat nearby to wait until Sydney felt ready to talk.

Sydney hiccupped and then said, "Jake was a nice guy." She turned red-rimmed eyes Hope's way. "Did you know him?"

"No, we never met."

Sydney's hand was touching a tiny pewter Bible hanging on a silver chain around her neck. Upon entering, Hope had noticed it but refrained from asking. Instead, she waited.

Hope watched Sydney's eyes travel to the front picture window. Then she pulled herself out of the chair, and Sydney walked over and flung the drapes wide open.

Being a cloudy day, Hope noticed it didn't bring any more brightness into the room.

With her back toward Hope, Sydney stated with hesitant words, "He...was...only...in...his...mid-twenties. He was...about my age." Another hiccup escaped as she finished.

Not sure what to say, Hope remained silent.

"Did you know Paul and Maria were hurt too?"

"Yes, Quaid called us from the hospital yesterday afternoon."

At the mention of Quaid's name, Sydney peered down at the pewter Bible still being held by one of her hands.

Hope wondered if Quaid had given her the necklace. That thought came as a total surprise. The woman in Hope was intrigued. She wanted to ask, but instead, something else came out. "Have you heard how Maria and Paul are?"

"Detective Neal called this morning. They spent the night in the hospital. After driving me home, he went back up to the hospital. The four of them will be returning sometime today." Sydney paused a moment then added, "I guess Maria has a bad bruise and concussion. She'll be off work a few weeks. Detective Statham's arm will be fine. The bullet didn't do any major muscle damage." For the first time, she looked Hope's way. "They both got injured trying to protect me."

"Yes. It was their job. That's why they were there, Sydney."

"I know. I know." Hope saw the struggle going on in her expressive face. Then Sydney did something bizarre under the circumstances. She smiled a big Cheshire cat smile, but Hope noticed it didn't quite reach her eyes. "Detective Neal said Paul's grumbling about having desk duty for the next few weeks. Like Quaid, they both prefer action. Have you met Detective Paul Statham?"

"Yes. The day you three came and I gave you the crystal. Remember?"

"Oh, yes... the crystal." Sydney turned back to the window.

Hope picked up her cooling tea, took a couple sips, and waited.

"Thank you for the letter and photos. It was the first one I'd ever received. In fact, the picture of Pierce with Sarah helped solve the identity of Vince's murderer." A hollow laugh followed her words. "Would you believe I also got a letter from Vince that same day?"

Hope watched Sydney quickly put a hand over her mouth to muffle a sob threatening to escape.

At that moment, Hope came to a decision. She set her cup down and stood. Squaring her shoulders, she walked up behind Sydney. "I'm glad you liked the letter, but I'm sad it was your very first one." Here she took a deep breath then placed a hand on Sydney's shoulder. She felt her flinch but maintained the hold while gently saying, "Why don't you tell me what's really on your mind."

Sydney hung her head then choked out, "Why did God let Jake die?" Turning her body slightly, Sydney looked Hope's way. "I've heard repeatedly from you Christian people that God loves us! How can that be true if he let Jake die for no reason?"

"Come back and sit down, Sydney. We need to talk."

Hope led her to the sofa and sat down beside her.

"When my husband, Dean, died and then a couple months later I miscarried our baby, I was angry at God. I wanted to know the same things you do. How could a loving God let this happen? Or was he looking the other way?"

"Exactly! Jake was trying to protect me! Me! Of all people to die for, it shouldn't have been for me! I'm not worth it!"

"But you are worth it! Please look at me, Sydney." Hope angled herself toward Sydney and waited for her to turn. Once she did, Hope saw her brows knit together outlining tortured eyes beneath.

She reached for her hand. "Sydney, you think you're not worth Jake losing his life for?"

She nodded her head but didn't speak.

"Sydney, there's so much I want to say. But... first of all I need you to understand a couple things. Jake knew what he was doing." She felt Sydney's hand tighten in hers. "He knew the risks involved. Sydney, he chose this profession because he wanted to help people just like you."

Sydney stiffened and pulled her hand away.

Hope watched her a moment then repeated in a firmer voice, "Sydney, he wanted to be an officer of the law to protect people just... like... you."

Hope let that sink in. She could see the doubt but also that Sydney was mulling the idea around. "If he's anything like Quaid and Paul, Jake probably hated what men like Corey Drake do all for the sake of money. Quaid said he probably didn't even bat an eye when he killed Jake or Vince for that matter! He was an evil man, and Jake wanted to help stop him. Which in a way, he did!"

"How? How did Jake help stop Duke?"

"By giving his life! I guess we'll never know for sure, but he may have been able to hinder Duke's progress enough to give you more of a chance." Unbidden, tears came to Hope's eyes as she added with conviction, "I'm sorry Jake died, but he died a hero! There's no greater honor of sacrifice then to lay down our lives for someone else."

"But why did Jake have to die? God could have protected him like he did Detective Statham. That bullet could have hit his head, but instead it went into his arm!"

"Yes, God could have protected Jake, but it wasn't his plan. Just like it wasn't his plan to protect his own Son, Jesus, from the torture of the cross." Leaning forward, Hope asked, "Sydney, do you know why Christ stayed up on that cross and died?"

"No, not really."

"He died for you and me. And he did it willingly, just like Jake did! Ever since Adam and Eve in the garden, Christ knew there wasn't any way for us to be brought back to God; so he made a way for us to have access. The Bible says Jesus could have called legions of angels down from heaven to free him from the cross, but he chose not to."

"Why? Why did he stay up there? Why would he willingly suffer like that?"

"Because that's how much he loves us. That's how much he loves you."

"Me! I'm not worth it! He didn't stay up there for me!"

"But he did, Sydney! If you'd been the only person left on this earth, he would have still stayed up there and died willingly."

Tears flowed down Sydney's cheeks as she tried to understand that kind of love. "No one on this earth has ever loved me like that, not even those who knew me! Why would Jesus?"

"Because he made you and knew you before you were even formed in your mother's womb. The Bible says we are 'fearfully and wonderfully made.' And you know what else?"

Sydney shook her head.

"God doesn't make junk or mistakes! Nothing takes him by surprise either. If it did, he couldn't be God, could he?"

"No, I guess not."

Hope picked up her purse nearby and pulled out a little booklet.

She then asked, "Sydney, has anyone ever taken the time to show you how you can have eternal life with God?"

"No."

"Would you mind if I did now?" Hope held up the booklet. "This will help make things clearer if you'll let me."

Sydney's eyes landed on the booklet and widened. She whispered, "I've seen this before!" Lifting eyes Hope's way, she explained. "On Beaver Island, Quaid gave me a Bible and this booklet to read. Shortly after that, we found out Vince's killer knew where I was, so we had to leave in a hurry. I left the booklet behind." With wonder, she reached for it. "May I?"

Hope smiled and handed it over.

"I never actually opened it, but I'm sure it was this same cover."

Hope was pleased to hear Quaid was reaching out to Sydney on spiritual matters. "Sydney, let's read the booklet together."

"Yes! Yes, I'd like that."

Moving closer, Hope suggested, "You read, and I'll explain if you have questions."

Sydney read the front cover, "May I Ask You a Question?" then turned the page. Inside was a picture of an open Bible. She read, "Has anyone ever taken a Bible and shown you how you can know for sure that you're going to heaven? The Bible contains both Bad News and Good News. The bad news is something about you. The good news is something about God. Let's look at the bad news first."

She paused before turning the page.

Sydney took a deep breath and began reading.

"'Bad News #1—*You are a sinner*. Romans 3:23 says, "For all have sinned and fall short of the glory of God." Sinned means that we have missed the mark. When we lie, hate, lust, or gossip, we have missed the standard God has set.'"

Sydney stopped to study the picture of a bull's-eye. An arrow was stuck to the side, not in the middle.

Hope watched her mind go elsewhere a moment then come back to the present. Sydney read on.

"'Suppose you and I were each to throw a rock and try to hit the North Pole. You might throw farther than me, but neither of us would hit it. When the Bible says, "All have sinned and fall short," it means that we have all come short of God's standard of perfection. In thoughts, words, and deeds, we have not been perfect.'"

Hope sensed Sydney was seriously thinking about the booklet's two examples. Before Sydney read on, Hope asked her, "Do you have any questions? Do you understand about how we miss the mark? How we're all sinners?"

"Yes. I understand. Being a sinner is probably one of the easiest things for me to understand about myself."

"As long as you remember that Romans 3:23 says the word *all*. You're not the only sinner in this world. We're all in the same boat."

"Okay, I get that."

"Let's read on then."

"But it says here at the bottom that the bad news gets worse!"

"That's true, but then we get to move on to the good news."

Sydney turned the page.

"'Bad News #2—*The penalty for sin is death*. Romans 6:23 says, "For the wages of sin is death." Suppose you worked for me, and I paid you $50. That $50 was your wages. That's what you earned. The Bible says that by sinning we have earned death. That means we deserve to die and be separated from God forever.'"

Sydney's head tilted slightly as she studied the picture on this page. There was a man standing by a great, gaping divide with the word *God* in a cloud on the other side.

As Sydney studied the picture, Hope saw a look of hopelessness begin to appear in her eyes, so she pushed Sydney to read on.

"'But ... since there was no way you could come to God, the Bible says that God decided to come to you! Good News # 1—*Christ died for you*. Romans 5:8 tells us, "But God demonstrates His own love toward us, in that while we were still sinners, Christ died for us." Suppose you are in a hospital dying of cancer. I come to you and say, "Let's take the cancer cells from your body and put them into my body.""''

Hope stopped her here. "If that really were possible, what would happen to me?"

"If you took my cancer cells into your body? Why...you'd die!"

"So then what would happen to you?"

Sydney answered in a soft, timid voice, "I'd live." She hurried on to say, "But no one would ever do that for me!"

Hope smiled. "Read on, Sydney."

"'The Bible says Christ took the penalty that we deserved for sin, placed it upon Himself, and died in our place. Three days later Christ came back to life to prove that sin and death had been conquered and that His claims to be God were true.'"

"Is that true? Did Christ come back alive after three days? I always thought that was a fairy tale like Easter bunnies and Santa Claus."

"Sydney, can you get the Bible Pierce and I gave you?"

Sydney stood to get it.

When she returned with the maroon Bible, Hope stated, "Before I leave here, I'll write down some verses for you to read in the Bible that tell about Christ's resurrection and all the people who saw him. But getting back to where we were. Let's read on."

"'Just as the bad news got worse, the good news gets better. Good News # 2—*You can be saved through faith in Christ.* Ephesians 2:8, 9 says, "For by grace (undeserved favor) you have been saved (delivered from sin's penalty) through faith, and that not of yourselves; it is the gift of God, not of works, lest anyone should boast." Faith means trust.'"

"What must you trust, Sydney?"

"I must depend on him alone to forgive me and to give me eternal life."

"That's right! When you sat down on the sofa, did you test it first to make sure it would hold you?"

"No."

"Why not?"

"I trusted it would hold me. It has every other time I sat on it."

"Exactly! But lots of people try to trust other things to get them to heaven. Read what the page says."

"'Just as you trust a chair to hold you through no effort of your own, so you must trust Jesus Christ to get you to heaven through no effort of your own. But, you may say, "I'm religious." "I go to church." "I don't steal." "I'm a good person." "I help the poor." These are all good, but good living, going to church, helping the poor or any other good thing you might do cannot get you to heaven. You must trust in Jesus Christ alone, and God will give you eternal life as a gift. Does this make sense to you?'"

Hope paused her again. "Sydney, does this say any of those other ways can get you to heaven?"

"No. It says it's a gift that God gives, not anything I can do on my own."

"That's right. We must trust in Jesus Christ and him alone. If we do, God promises us eternal life. Do you have any questions about that?"

Sydney turned back to the first page of the booklet and worked her way through the bad and good news again. Suddenly, a wonder hit her face as she looked up at Hope. "No, I don't! It makes sense!"

Hope smiled. In a gentle voice, she said, "Let's turn the page."

Sydney read the first sentence and stopped. "'Is there anything keeping you from trusting Christ right now?'" Tears filled her eyes. Softly she read on. "'Think carefully. There is nothing more important than your need to trust Christ. Would you like to tell God you are trusting Jesus Christ as your Savior? If you would, why not pray right now and tell God you are trusting his Son?'"

Tears were freely streaming down her cheeks as she pleaded with Hope. "Does God really want me? Me?"

"Of course he does. His arms are waiting wide open."

"Can you pray with me?"

## Out of the Snare

"Sure." Sliding off the sofa, Hope turned and went to her knees. With elbows propped on the sofa, she clasped her hands together and waited for Sydney to join her. Hope began praying aloud and then paused as Sydney soon joined in.

With halting yet sincere words, she asked the Lord Jesus to forgive her and to make her into a new person. "God, I'd like to be someone your Son, Jesus, could be proud of. I'm tired of doing things my own way. All I do is screw it up! Hope said Jesus died for me too on that cross. Help me be more like Hope, and Pierce, and... even Quaid."

Hope almost chuckled at the way she mentioned Quaid.

Sydney grew silent, and Hope thought she might be done. But then she heard Sydney speaking almost in a whisper. Leaning closer, Hope heard her say, "May I live worthy of what Jesus and Jake did for me."

Hope realized Sydney was unable to say more, so she finished with, "Thank you for the gift of your Son, Jesus Christ, and the forgiveness of our sins. In Jesus' name. Amen."

With tears in her eyes, Hope lifted her head and smiled. Sydney had laid her sins and burden of guilt at Jesus' feet, and he took them! Hope could see the evidence shining out of Sydney's eyes. The two women stood and hugged.

A short while later, they turned to the booklet once more. Together, they read the last two pages describing what had just happened and how to grow in the knowledge of Christ's love. When they were done, Hope gave her the booklet. "I recommend you keep reading it over, especially the last two pages. Also, I encourage you to memorize John 5:24 like it suggests." She then asked for a slip of paper and wrote verses down for Sydney to look up about Christ's resurrection.

While Hope did that, Sydney studied the little booklet and then read the back cover. At the bottom was a Web site address of www.evantell.org plus a toll free number: 1–800–947–7359.

The women soon drifted into normal chatter, and the time flew. Glancing at the kitchen clock, Hope realized it was time to leave.

"I promised Pierce I'd be back by noon so he could go to work this afternoon." She soon had on her coat and now dry shoes. Buttoning the coat, she paused. "Sydney, you're a new creature in Christ now, and ... you're my sister in the Lord. If you have any further questions about the booklet or the Bible, please call me."

Sydney then walked up and surprised Hope with a hug. She said shyly, "I think I'm going to like having you as my Christian sister." Stepping back, she grew a little embarrassed and then said, "I do have a question though."

"Sure, Sydney. Anything."

Sydney touched the little pewter Bible and then asked, "Do ... do you think Quaid blames me for Jake's death?"

Hope frowned and quickly assured, "Of course not! Why do you feel that way?"

Sydney studied the floor. "I haven't seen or heard from him since he left in the ambulance with Paul. I thought he'd call to give me an update, but Neal did instead. I think he's avoiding me."

"If I remember right, Quaid told Pierce he had business in another state. I don't think he's even in town. Besides, I'm sure he has lots to do with tying up loose ends so the case can be closed."

Doubt still played in Sydney's eyes as she raised them back to Hope.

Hope's eyes landed on the necklace Sydney was still touching. "May I ask you a question?"

Sydney nodded, so Hope asked, "Did Quaid, by chance, give you that necklace?"

A soft blush spread up Sydney's cheeks. "Yes, he did. But it doesn't mean anything. Why do you ask?"

"Whenever his name was mentioned this morning, you touched it. I just wondered."

The sun chose that moment to break through the clouds and shine through the front window. Its beam hit the crystal cross, sending a rainbow of colors dancing around the room.

"Look at that, Sydney!"

The two women oohed and aahed over the various colors, and then just that quickly, the sun moved on and the colors disappeared.

Sydney looked back at Hope. "Do you think that was God's way of letting me know he's here and to trust him?"

"Absolutely!"

# Chapter 26

Before leaving town, Quaid had gotten permission for Sydney to attend Jake's funeral in the company of Pierce and Hope. He asked Hope to let Sydney know, so the night before, Hope had called to say she and Pierce would be picking her up that next morning around ten. Sydney was hesitant about attending, but Hope thought it would be good for her; so Sydney reluctantly agreed.

At their arrival, the trio found the funeral home already packed so were seated in the side overflow room. A big-screen TV was set up so they could watch the ceremony. The camera often scanned the main room, which was mostly a sea of law enforcement people. Sydney searched the screen for Quaid. She found him sitting up

## Out of the Snare

front with Paul and Neal. Not seeing Maria with them, Sydney figured it was because she wasn't well enough yet to attend.

As they had arrived, Pierce asked Sydney if she wanted to walk up and view Jake, but she declined. She asked him then if it would be okay to leave during the last prayer. Sydney didn't want any officers giving her a critical stare. Since he and Hope agreed, the three of them left before Quaid's group exited the main room.

On the way home, Sydney stared blindly out the car window. When they pulled into her driveway, she asked Hope to go with her before the judge that afternoon.

Hope glanced Pierce's way as he replied, "I can work it out to watch Sarah if you want to go with her." Since Hope already knew that one of the detectives needed to escort Sydney, she agreed to meet Sydney at the courthouse.

When the time came to leave for the courthouse, Sydney's heart fluttered. She expected Quaid to take her, but when she opened the door, it was Detective Statham standing there. Sydney unconsciously smoothed the loose fitting slacks she had on. It had taken much thinking on her part as to what would be appropriate to wear.

The last time she'd stood before the judge, Sydney hadn't cared what she wore, but now she was different. Even though it had only been a few days since asking Jesus to forgive her and be her Savior, Sydney looked at her clothes in a different way. This morning she'd chosen to wear a loose fitting pullover top with complimenting slacks. She even styled her hair differently and wore more feminine earrings. The detective's raised eyebrows of approval at her new appearance did much to soothe raw nerves over Quaid's continued absence in her life.

Sydney sat at a low table between Paul and Hope in the courtroom waiting for the judge. Since Jake's funeral had been that morning, everyone was in a somber mood.

The three stood as the judge entered. He was the same one who weeks earlier had warned Sydney about putting his men in jeopardy.

As the fresh reminder of Jake's death tormented her mind, Sydney groaned inwardly as the judge instructed. "You may be seated."

As they complied, he eyed Paul's arm in a sling. "How are you, Detective Statham?"

Paul stood back up. "I'm doing well, Your Honor. I will be pushing paper for a few weeks. But the doctor says there wasn't any permanent damage, so I'm thanking the Lord."

"And Officer Lopez?"

"Maria's got a concussion and bad temple bruise, but it looks like no long-term repercussions for her either. She's gone down state to spend time with her family, Judge."

The judge nodded and then indicated Paul could take his seat before looking at Sydney. His eyebrows rose as he commented, "It appears these last weeks have had their effect on you, Miss Turner. To the better, I might add."

Sydney slowly rose. "Yes, Your Honor." Glancing briefly down at Hope seated on her other side, she added, "I'm a different person now."

"Good!" His eyes slid to Hope. "And you are?"

The women changed places standing as Hope replied, "My name is Hope Montgomery. I'm Sydney's friend, Your Honor."

"Friend, huh?"

"Yes, Your Honor. I guess you could say I'm mainly here for moral support."

The judge noted the woman's quiet confidence and mannerisms. Nodding his approval, he invited her to take a seat. He then scanned some papers in front of him before saying, "Since this is a relatively informal meeting, you may remain seated unless otherwise instructed by me."

"Yes, Your Honor," the three responded in unison.

The judge's eyes settled on Sydney. She tried to remain calm under their intense stare.

"Miss Turner, much has happened since you last appeared before me."

## Out of the Snare

"Yes, Your Honor."

"As you know, due to your going into protective custody, the house arrest and monetary penalty due were both suspended."

Sydney started to respond, but the judge stopped her. "Let me finish."

"Yes, Your Honor."

"Upon being notified the situation was resolved and you were returning to Petoskey, I had every intention of having the ankle tether put back on." He paused to narrow his eyes. "But then I received two calls: one from Detective Williams, another from his chief. They've asked me to reconsider. Detective Williams was especially adamant that you wouldn't be a flight risk."

Here he stopped. Speaking in a harder voice, he slowly stated, "I'll have you know, Miss Turner, that Detective Williams even went so far as to say he'd take responsibility if you left the state."

Sydney's eyes widened. *Quaid did that?*

Her look of surprise drew a thoughtful frown from the judge, and then he continued. "I'm setting aside the house arrest issue for the moment. We'll come back to it later. I understand the documents concerning the embezzlement scheme have been recovered."

Paul held up the large white envelope. "That's correct, Your Honor."

A clerk stepped forward to take the envelope and then walked it to the judge, who pulled out the contents.

"Your Honor, Sydney has already signed them. I'd like it noted that she's willingly turning them over to the court."

"Miss Turner, is that correct?"

"Yes, Your Honor."

"So noted."

All was silent as the judge studied the documents. Sydney had a strong urge for a cigarette, so she fidgeted. Hope and Paul calmly kept their eyes on the judge.

"Everything looks in order here. We'll expedite the funds' return to the Louisville corporation from which they were taken. Now, the issue of your financial debt to society. Miss Turner, you still owe the State of Michigan the amount of $100,000."

A groan escaped Sydney's lips. Since she signed the papers and the embezzled money was being returned, Sydney had hoped the judge would drop the amount. For the first time, a feeling of resistance surged, and she started to speak.

But before she could, Paul came to his feet. "Your Honor, if I may speak?"

"Proceed, Detective."

"Your Honor, an auction of donated items was held on Miss Turner's behalf. I have a check here in the amount of $72,400."

Again the clerk stepped forward, retrieved the check, and laid it on the bench in front of the judge.

"Detective, that's a big start, but she still owes $27,600."

This time, Hope came to her feet. "Your Honor, if I may speak also?"

Wondering what Hope was up to, Sydney stared at her.

Intrigued at Hope's request, the judge signaled for Paul to take his seat. "What's on your mind, Ms. Montgomery?"

"Your Honor, I too have a check."

At Hope's mention of another check, Sydney was shocked.

The judge registered the fact Miss Turner had not been aware of the second check. He prompted Hope to continue.

"Your Honor, our church took up a special offering for Miss Turner over the past few weeks. Their desire was to show Sydney… um, Miss Turner, our love and support. The check I hold is for $23,000."

Sydney gasped and then choked beside Hope.

Momentarily forgetting the judge, Hope reached for a pitcher of water sitting on the corner of the table and poured her a glass. She then turned back to the judge. "Sorry, Judge. Anyway, in addition to this check, I also had an individual approach me. This person is prepared to make up any difference the judge still deems necessary." She then lowered herself to the seat.

## Out of the Snare

Unsure what to do, the clerk waited until the judge indicated he should bring up the second check. After studying Hope's demeanor and grace, the judge summoned the check. Once the other check was before him, he stared at them a long time and then raised his eyes to Sydney. She grew nervous under his stare. Finally he said, "Miss Turner, please stand."

With shaky knees, Sydney obeyed.

"Miss Turner, you've been in our fair city less than a year, and from all reports, you've not been a good woman. Yet here are a group of people willing to give you these large amounts of money. I'm concerned you're going to abuse this show of love and trust."

"Your Honor—"

"Young lady, I'm not finished! You will remain silent until I ask you to respond!"

A subdued Sydney said timidly, "Yes, Your Honor."

"Over the last few years, you've made some bad decisions that culminated into bad results. People died! I'm not saying you're directly to blame for Detective Jake's death or Mr. Edgar's. They were murdered by a cold-blooded, trained killer. It's unfortunate he was one of our own. I'm sure the Louisville Marshal's office is still reeling under the discovery and deceit. But Miss Turner, even though you didn't pull the trigger, it was partly your greed that helped get your partner Mr. Edgar killed."

As the judge spoke, Sydney's vision bleared, and her head started to bend down under the load he was heaping on her.

"I want eye contact, Miss Turner! I want to be sure you thoroughly understand my words!"

Sydney's head popped up. "Yes, Your Honor. I'm sorry."

"For what, Miss Turner? What are you sorry for?"

A sob escaped as she blurted, "For everything!" A trembling hand came up to cover her mouth. Hope reached up to give Sydney's other hand a quick squeeze.

Hope's encouraging gesture sent warmth spreading through

Sydney. Calmness unlike any she'd ever experienced filled her being. Ever since praying to give her life to Christ, in that moment, Sydney realized she was slowly changing into a different person. This included having feelings of gratefulness that now flowed from her heart toward Hope. A part of her wanted to focus on this strange yet good feeling, but the judge began speaking again.

"In regards to threats to our society, it's my responsibility to do what's right in the eyes of the law. I must say, the drastic change of your appearance and behavior between now and a few weeks ago is marked. It goes a long way toward helping me make this decision. Is your friend here the cause of these changes?"

"Partly, Your Honor. You see…um…a few days ago, I…um… became a Christian. That is, I…um…prayed to God…and…" Growing a little frustrated, she ended with a rush. "Judge, I'm just different now from the inside out!"

"That's commendable, Miss Turner. But I've learned that people will tell me just about anything to get off." Before she could protest, he raised a hand. "I'm not saying you're lying. I'd be one of the first people to applaud your being a changed, better person whether it be by a religious experience or whatever. At this point, I don't know if it's true. My best advice to you is prove it! Prove you're a different person!"

A feeling of boldness prompted Sydney to reply, "I intend to, Judge."

At her words, he grew silent. The judge thoughtfully stared at Sydney and her companions. He then read some notes lying before him and looked at the checks once more. After what seemed a long time to the still-standing Sydney, he came to a decision.

"Miss Turner, I've taken into account the words of Chief Bishop and Detective Williams plus the statements that these two checks say to me. They tell me there are people out there willing to invest in you to help make you a better human being. Only time will tell if they've made a wise investment. I hope you never take these people for granted on what they're risking for your behalf. Having said all that, I've decided you will remain under three years' probation. I've also decided the debt to society will be considered paid by these two checks. I've further decided the house arrest will be rescinded."

At the look of puzzlement crossing Sydney's face, the judge clarified. "In other words, Miss Turner, you're a free person. If I were you, I'd do all I could to become the person these individuals think you can be. And I don't want to see you in my court again as a lawbreaker!"

"Thank you, Judge. You won't! Thank you so much!"

The judge nodded Sydney's direction, gathered his papers, and stood. "You're free to go, Miss Turner." Having said that, the judge then left the room.

Instantly, Hope was to her feet. "You're free, Sydney! And the debt is paid! You don't owe anything more! Praise the Lord!"

A numb Sydney was enclosed in Hope's arms, and then she was handed over to Detective Paul, who also gave her a brief one armed hug. "I know this isn't a professional thing for me to do, but I'm pleased to hear you've accepted Christ as your personal Savior. The hug is welcoming you into the family of God."

"Thank you, Detective." Not sure how she felt about everything that had just been said by the judge, Sydney was a little dazed.

Detective Paul stepped in to take over. "Come on, ladies; let's leave this room and get Sydney back to her freedom."

With his good arm, he helped the women on with their coats then escorted them out of the building.

# Chapter 27

The next afternoon Sydney was restless. Her job at the clothing store had informed her of the decrease from full to part time. Her first day back didn't start until the following Monday, so she had time on her hands.

Sydney was now free but had nothing to do. The house was clean. She had even contemplated getting Christmas decorations out, but Thanksgiving hadn't come yet. After smoking several cigarettes, Sydney decided a drive sounded good. Once in the car, another idea emerged, so she called Hope and asked if she could come for a visit. "I'm going to drive around the lake a bit first, so I won't be there until sometime after lunch."

## Out of the Snare

"That works out good. I should have Sarah down for her nap by then."

A little after 1:00 p.m., Sydney pulled up to Hope's cabin. She took one last draw on her cigarette before stubbing it out in the ashtray. Upon exiting the car, the fresh country air filled her lungs, causing a cough. Sydney took a moment to look around her before climbing the steps. Once at the top, she paused at sight of the swing swaying back and forth with the cold winter breeze. The motion reminded her of how nasty she'd been to Hope weeks earlier.

As Sydney thought about the words she'd spoken, a smiling Hope opened the front door. "Hi. Did you have a nice drive?"

"I did. It's like I'm seeing the world through new eyes! How could I not have seen God's handiwork before?"

"I guess you weren't looking. But come in. It's cold out here."

After the door was closed and her coat hung on the oak coat tree, Sydney said, "Hope, I want to apologize for the things I said to you about… well, about Pierce being my man. I was mean and obviously very foolish. Since you're the one engaged to him now, I guess I didn't know what I was talking about."

"That's okay. It seems that was a long time ago, and I forgive you. In fact, that meeting helped me see you in a different light that eventually led me to listen when I felt prompted by the Holy Spirit to give you the crystal."

"I didn't deserve your kindness, but thank you."

"You're more than welcome. Now let's forget it. How does hot chocolate sound?"

Sydney rubbed her cold hands together. "With marshmallows?"

"Of course! What would it be without them?" Moving toward the kitchen, she added, "What do you say if we sit at the kitchen table and chat? I just put Sarah down with soft music playing, and she's not quite to sleep yet. That way, she won't be so apt to hear us and may fall asleep faster."

"Sure. That's fine."

Unlike the first time Sydney had paid Hope a visit, the two women conversed freely. Even so, Sydney got the distinct impression that Hope had something else on her mind.

Sydney shrugged the thought away and went on to tell Hope that her job at the clothing store was now only part time. She watched Hope take that in then come to some kind of decision.

"Sydney, did you know Pierce bought a large three-story turreted home in Petoskey? We're going to turn it into a bed and breakfast."

"No, I didn't know that. I suppose it makes sense with his remodeling and house building skills." She grew thoughtful then said, "That's really nice, Hope. Will you be moving there after you're married?"

"No. Pierce and I plan to stay out here. We both love it here so much. At some time, our plans are to add on to his larger cabin. We'll use this one for family when they visit."

Hope's words were suddenly interrupted by barks at the back door. Rising, she said, "That's Ellie. She's been off chasing some imaginary foe in the woods." Hope grabbed a towel hanging near the door before opening it. Moving fast, she caught the squirming beagle to dry her feet off.

Sydney enjoyed the sight. Being a poor city girl, she'd never had any pets. For the first time, the idea of getting one began to take root.

"There you go, Ellie." Hope handed the dog a chewy. Wagging her tail with delight, she carried it to her doggy bed.

Hope took her seat. With a frown she asked, "What were we talking about?"

"The bed and breakfast. Do you have a name picked out?"

"We're thinking Hope's Serene Haven, but that's not decided yet." Sitting straighter in her chair, Hope said, "The reason I mentioned it is … we're wondering if you'd consider being the manager/hostess?"

Sydney was in the middle of a sip when Hope delivered her question. She nearly choked. "Me? You want me to be the manager?"

"Yes, we do. Pierce and I have talked about it and prayed. We think you'd be great! Besides that, you'd be able to help me redecorate! I'd love to have you involved." In her enthusiasm, Hope leaned forward. "Wouldn't that be fun? Pierce said I could decorate however I want!"

Catching a look on Sydney's face, Hope curbed her excitement and forced herself to silence.

Sydney was too shocked to think. *Did I hear her right? She's offering me a job and wants me to help decorate? Me, from the poor side of Louisville?* As she thought about the idea, Sydney's mouth dropped open, and her eyes grew wider. Realizing Hope was watching her, Sydney managed to clamp her mouth shut.

Finally finding some words, she stuttered, "You...you want me to work for you? You want me to manage your bed and breakfast?"

"That's right, Sydney. You don't have to give me an answer right now. All I'm asking you to do is prayerfully think about it."

"Well...um...sure. I can do that." Sydney reached across the table and shyly squeezed Hope's hand. "Thanks, Hope. I will think and pray about it. The idea sounds too good to be true!"

"It's true. Believe me. I'd like an answer within a couple weeks though, for we need to get busy on it."

"Okay. I can do that."

The two women fell silent as thoughts absorbed their minds.

Sydney spoke up first. "I've been thinking about being a new person in Christ. I know I'm brand new at this Christian-living thing, but I'm thinking of going back to my real name. You know, kind of a symbolic thing. What I mean is...so much of what's been bad is associated with the name Sydney. I'd like to get away from that old person, and I think asking people to call me by my real name would help."

"What a wonderful idea! A new way of life deserves a new name. So from now on I'll call you Abigail."

"If you think that's too formal, you're welcome to call me Abby...if you'd like," she added shyly.

"Hmm, Abigail...Abby." Hope let the names roll around her tongue then declared, "I think I prefer calling you Abigail. I once told you a story about Abigail. Do you remember that?"

"Yes, I do. You said she was a woman who tried to do what was right and good." Sydney paused then added, "That's what I would like—to do what is right and good."

"The biblical Abigail is a wonderful person for you to strive to be like!"

"I had a dream about her once. Actually, it started out as a dream but ended up being scary!" The memory started to invade Sydney's mind, but she shook it off by changing the subject. "Have you heard from Quaid today?"

"No, I haven't. Is there something wrong?"

Sydney hesitated and then blurted, "I still think he's avoiding me! I know he was out of town for a while, but he's back now. Remember? We saw him on the screen at Jake's funeral."

"He still hasn't called you?"

"No." Sydney's shoulders slumped. "I don't know why I think he should. It's just that … he's been constantly in my life for weeks, and now I don't see him at all."

"And I imagine during that time under his protection, it was probably a safe feeling having him around. Wasn't it?"

Sydney glanced up at Hope and then admitted, "Yes. Yes, it was. Now I feel kind of cast away or forgotten, I guess."

"Don't give up on him, Sydney. I'm sure there are lots—"

They were interrupted by the sound of a vehicle stopping out front and a door shutting.

As Ellie started barking, Hope moved to quiet her while saying, "Now who could that be?" Checking her watch, she added, "It's too early for Pierce."

Footsteps crossed the deck; then a knock sounded at the door. As Hope moved to answer it, Sydney peeked around the corner out of curiosity.

When the front door swung open, there stood Quaid. He was dressed casually and seemed at ease. From where she was standing, Sydney could see him but didn't think he'd noticed her yet. Her face turned red while Hope said, "Well, hi, Quaid. What brings you out here?"

He stepped into the cabin while saying, "I'm looking for Sydney. She wasn't home, so I took a chance she might be here." Seeing her off to the side, he stopped speaking.

That morning, Sydney had considered wearing her usual tight clothes but found they didn't appeal anymore. Instead, she chose loose fitting blue jeans with a soft-flowing button down blouse. The colors complimented her eyes and blonde hair.

Now Quaid's eyes traveled up and down surveying her new appearance. He paused then stated, "Well, look at you. Sydney, you look great!"

Sydney was pleased at his words but hadn't expected the sudden flutter that hit her heart and stomach. Catching her breath, she took a step back. "Thank you, Quaid." Gaining some composure, she said, "You were looking for me?"

"Yes, I was. It's the first moment I've had to tie up some loose ends about this case for you." He turned to Hope. "May I take my coat off?"

"Of course! Where are my manners? Please forgive me. Would you like something hot to drink?"

"Coffee would be nice. It's nippy outside." Noticing the Bible necklace around Sydney's neck, Quaid smiled broadly at the two women and then followed them into the kitchen. After a short while, the three of them sat around the table with hot drinks.

"How are you doing, Sydney?"

"I'm good." She glanced Hope's way then added in a flurry of words, "Actually, I'm great! I don't know if Paul told you or even if you've talked since he found out. That is—what I'm trying to say is—I prayed to receive Christ as my Savior." *There! I said it!*

"I know. Paul told me. I'm very pleased."

*He's very pleased!* The words stuck in Sydney's mind as she breathlessly added, "Um... Quaid, there's something else new about me."

"There is! What's that?"

"Well... since I'm a Christian now and not the same Sydney, I thought I'd go back to using my real name. Sydney was the old me. So I'm asking everyone to call me either Abigail or Abby."

Quaid looked at her a long moment before replying, "That might not be so easy for me. In my mind, you're Sydney. That's the name that fits you!"

"Sydney is the name that used to fit me; that's my whole point. I'm not that person anymore! I want people to think of me differently. The only way I see that happening is if they call me Abigail or Abby."

Quaid studied her face intently then said, "Okay, Syd...I mean Abigail. If that's what you want, I'll try to remember. Just don't get impatient with me if I slip up every once and a while."

Abigail's face lit up with dimples showing. "Deal. Thanks, Quaid."

In that moment, Sydney had no idea how appealing she looked to Quaid. The two were lost in each other's eyes, until Hope loudly cleared her throat.

Quaid recovered first by stating, "It looks like you're getting off to a good start by working on a friendship with Hope here."

"I am. She's been great!"

Hope instantly replied, "You're sweet...Abigail." Then turning to Quaid, she said, "You mentioned telling Sydney more about the case. Is it all right for me to hear, or should I leave the room?"

Quaid assured Hope she could stay and then began his narrative.

"After Paul and Maria were discharged from the hospital in St. Ignace, we all returned home, and then I headed to Louisville. Syd...Abigail, do you remember telling me about the day you came across Vince in the mall? You said you had been upset because Vince wouldn't give you a larger chunk of the embezzled money. You also told me the two of you had argued loudly."

"I remember telling you that."

"Well, apparently Drake had been at a table close enough to overhear you. Then, when Vince walked back to work, he must have followed him and got all the information he needed to become involved. Shortly after that is when he contacted Vince by phone and became your silent third partner."

"That sounds reasonable." Sydney's forehead knit into a frown as a new thought occurred. "Not long after the third partner came on board, Vince approached me about signing some papers. He said it was to get me on the checkbook. Was that true?"

"No, it wasn't. My guess is Drake made him nervous, so to protect the money, Vince had put everything in your name. Neither he nor Drake could touch the money without your being involved. Our guess is Drake found that out just before killing Vince. He probably thought he could forge your signature but couldn't find the paperwork. Figuring Vince had somehow gotten them to you, he came to pay you a visit."

He paused to ask if there were any questions. When they both shook their heads no, he went on.

"Shortly after Drake came on board, Vince was told his company was having an audit. Fearing they might find out what he'd been doing, Vince had the bogus company declare bankruptcy and close."

"I remember that! He had contacted me that no more money was being squirreled away. He also said that if I was patient within a few months I'd be getting a substantial amount of the money."

Picking up the story, Quaid continued.

"The Louisville police discovered that Drake had a gambling problem. At the same time, he was also in the middle of a messy divorce. Between those two things, he owed a lot of money that he didn't seem to have. Anyway, before I left Louisville, the police believed they'd found two other unsolved cases that will link to Drake. Apparently, to help his financial problems, he also became a paid assassin."

Quaid paused as Hope made rounds with the coffeepot.

Seated once again, Hope asked, "How could someone be on both sides of the law at the same time?"

"I don't know. He was one messed up man! We have the necessary evidence that Drake was undoubtedly Vince's killer."

He looked with sadness at Sydney before going on. "He was good at clearing away evidence but didn't know Vince had hidden a recorder on his desk. Drake hadn't planned on leaving any witnesses, so he didn't disguise his voice. For a long time, that recording was no help, at least not until we started doing voice matches with law enforcement people. The final verification came from Drake's own chief."

Here Quaid paused, shaking his head. The women exchanged glances. It was obvious to them how hard it was for Quaid to reconcile the idea that Corey Drake had been a veteran U.S. Marshal.

"Syd…um…Abigail, you know how he found out about our run to Beaver Island?" It was more a statement than a question.

With her face turning red over the memory of not telling anyone about the man she knew on the ferry, Abigail nodded yes.

"The morning after we left Beaver Island, he landed there in a chartered jet. We believe his intention was to render my team and me useless then convince you to sign the documents. He had no way of knowing you still didn't have them."

Sydney shuddered at how close he'd come to catching them and at Quaid's calm usage of the words *render us useless*. She knew exactly what he meant!

"For your sake, I'm thankful we were already gone. Anyway, before leaving the airport terminal, Drake got into a discussion with some local men and found out we'd already left. He got back in the jet and had the pilot fly to Petoskey, where he had rented a car under a false name and managed to break into your home."

A lot of what Quaid was saying Sydney already knew bits and pieces of. Now he was filling in the blanks. To Hope, however, this was all new. Several times, her expressive face showed various emotions, or she would let out a gasp.

"I think he still hoped to find the documents in your home but was disappointed. What he did find was a cell phone bill. That's when the calls started coming."

During his narrative, Hope brought Quaid a glass of water and opened a package of cookies. After taking a long drink, he then paused to eat a couple of them before continuing.

"Ironically, it was my chief and I who led him to our next location when we called in help from the U.S. Marshals. Normally we'd have found someone in Michigan. But that particular branch chief is friends with my supervisor, so we went with them. I'm not sure that Drake knew of his likeness to Pierce, but I'm sure he figured Sydney had given us a good description. This must have prompted the excuse that he'd arrive after dark in hopes that he could evade us. His plan actually worked. I unknowingly helped it along when I assigned him to the command center. My thinking had been that since he was arriving after dark the area around the condos wouldn't be familiar. Drake's last call was actually made from within our own command center!"

Here he shook his head again and looked down, his mind obviously on another scene. In a quiet voice, he stated, "Drake being right there with us—Jake never had a chance."

Hope immediately placed a hand over his. "Quaid, Jake's death wasn't your fault!"

"He was a rookie and my responsibility. I unwittingly invited the killer right into our camp!" He ended with disgust.

"That may be, but Jake knew the risks of his job. This Corey was a trained lawman gone bad!"

Sydney was surprised by Quaid's words. She'd believed Quaid's absence from her life was because he'd blamed her for Jake's death. *He blames himself!*

Out loud, she softly agreed. "Hope's right, Quaid. Corey or Duke or whatever his name, he's the one who killed Jake! It was a senseless, evil murder!"

Quaid studied Sydney's face as a couple of tears escaped to roll down her cheeks.

Taking a deep breath, Quaid went on with his story.

"We believe Drake was so pleased with the new job assignment that he became even more arrogant. Arrogant people always make mistakes! His partners told me he was a man driven to outsmart the bad guy. In his mind, that's probably how he saw Paul and me. We were the ones he needed to outsmart. He hurt Maria, but from what I could gather, she put up a good fight."

"She did! I heard some of it as I ran to the bedroom and then out the window."

At mention of the window, Quaid and Hope saw a look of wonder cross Sydney's face. With excitement and awe, she said, "Quaid, you know I'm afraid of heights, right? We didn't practice the ladder escape because of that fear. You just talked me through it. I truly believed that once I threw out the ladder and saw the distance down to the deck I'd freeze up, but you kept telling me the adrenaline would keep me moving. But even that didn't happen! It was God! He sent the fog! I couldn't see how far the bottom was, so I climbed right out and down!"

Sydney's realization of Christ's care for her touched Hope and Quaid. Sharing a smile, they remained silent as Sydney mulled that over in her head. "I hadn't even come to him yet, and he was protecting me." It was more than she could fathom.

Quaid seemed to be nearing the end of his story, but Sydney still needed to know the answer to something. "Quaid, I asked you once how you knew about me before Vince. At that time, you said you weren't able to discuss it with me. Can you now? How did you know about me first?"

"Well...when you came to town and began attending church, something about you just didn't add up. In church you acted like a Christian, but I kept hearing you were popular at the bars. My gut reaction was that you were putting up a front, so I ran a check on your Kentucky plates. Sydney Larsen didn't come up, but Abigail Turner did. I then started running other checks. The interesting thing is I did it after Vince had put your name on everything. The bogus company came up with your name only, which gave me plenty of red flags. It was just a matter of time before I put two and two together."

# Out of the Snare

Silence hung in the air as Sydney and Hope absorbed all he had said.

Quaid was growing tired of the whole subject, so he concluded with, "Well, that about sums it up. Paul and I think Drake's plan was to kidnap you, Sydney—Abigail, in exchange for the papers and your signature. I can only imagine what his plan after that would have been!"

The room grew silent once more.

Sydney's mind dwelt on what could have happened to Quaid or Paul. Sorrow for Jake flowed through her body as she fought back more tears. Raising sad eyes, she looked at Hope then Quaid. She noted that since his story was done, he'd moved into a relaxed mode. He was leaned back in the kitchen chair, with his hands in his pockets.

Suddenly, he sat up. In one hand was a folded piece of paper. "Sydney, I almost forgot. Due to Duke's other murders, the state of Kentucky had a reward out for his capture."

Handing her the paper, he stated, "I talked to my team. We know you're without a steady income right now. So we voted to have the reward check made out to you."

A flabbergasted Sydney stared at the folded check.

With a shaky hand, she took the check and opened it. The amount was $5,000. Unable to handle any more blessings, she placed her arm on the table, laid her head down, and wept.

A long while later, Sydney became aware of muffled voices in the living room. Raising her head, she found a box of tissues close at hand so used lots of them to mop up the mess on her face and arms. She knew her eyes had to be red and puffy, but she was beyond caring. *Quaid's seen me worse.*

Sydney sat straighter as a wonder began to fill her. She felt good inside, and... she felt loved. *Loved by people who really don't know me.* The thought was humbling and sweet.

Sydney blew her nose and stood up.

A moment later, Quaid walked into the kitchen.

Hope followed soon after with Sarah in her arms.

With a shaky smile, Sydney asked Quaid to tell everyone thanks as he joined her again at the table. He assured her they'd be told and then picked up the box of tissues. "Here. I have a feeling you're going to need more."

Confused, Sydney's eyes searched his.

"I don't know if you realized this, but I was gone for almost a week."

Remembering what she and Hope had been talking about before Quaid's arrival, Sydney almost chuckled. *Didn't realize? I've been pouting and stewing about it!*

"After Louisville, I went somewhere else."

She wondered what was going on but became sidetracked when he took her hand in his warm, capable one.

"Sydney, through a private detective that Pierce knows, we've located your sister."

Sydney stiffened. *Found my sister?* Her eyes roamed Quaid's face.

"She lives in northern Indiana, and I went to see her."

She finally found her voice. "She's still alive? You really found her? How is she? Can I go see her? No, that's right; I can't. I have to stay in Michigan unless I get the judge's permission to leave." Her words came out so fast they tumbled over one another.

Quaid let her questions wind down, and then he said, "She's a third grade schoolteacher, and from what I can find out, she's married to a good man. She also has two children, a girl ten years old, and an eight-year-old son."

*My sister's alive and she's a teacher? My sister's a teacher!* It then occurred to her that she was an aunt. The revelations were almost more than Sydney could take in, but surprisingly, she didn't cry. She just stared at him while clinging to his hand, wanting more information.

"Sydney, there's something else. I brought her back to Michigan with me. She's here."

## Out of the Snare

"Here? She's here?" Sydney started to rise when Quaid tightened the hold on her hand.

"Not here at the cabin. She's staying in Petoskey at the inn downtown."

Sydney's body began to shake. Then fear set in at the thought of seeing a sister who'd not been in her life for eighteen years. They weren't children anymore. A lot of life had happened during those years.

Unknowing, Sydney's emotions played across her face for Quaid and Hope to read.

Tightening his grip, Quaid gently asked, "Would you like to go see her? I'm sure Hope won't mind if you leave your car here a while and ride with me."

Sydney's eyes slid to Hope, where she received a teary smile and nod.

With a heart full of new possibilities and hope, Sydney turned smiling eyes back to Quaid. "Let's go. My sister and I have a lot of catching up to do."

# Epilogue

The moment Abigail entered the sanctuary and she saw the sea of people, her feet stopped. *Am I crazy? What am I doing?* Panic flowed down her throat, causing flutters in her stomach.

Then her eyes landed on Quaid Williams standing tall and sure near the groom, Pierce Matthews. All it took was a smile and slight nod from his ruggedly handsome face, and her feet started moving again. Keeping time with the music, Abby made her way down the long aisle.

The date was February 15, and almost three months had passed since that terrible, foggy morning in St. Ignace. Abby found it ironic that it was about this time last year that she'd moved from Louisville to Petoskey under the alias of Sydney Larsen. Much had changed since then.

The truly big change had culminated with Jake's untimely death on her behalf. His death had helped her finally understand Christ's sacrifice on the cross not only for her but for the whole world.

Through Hope Montgomery, Abby understood what needed to be done, and she'd surrendered her life to Christ. Since then, she'd grown in love with God's Word, the Bible, and enjoyed spending time with fellow believers in Christ.

Her mind naturally flowed back to Quaid. She'd thought they would become a couple, but he had other ideas. Abigail had been honestly hurt and confused when Quaid insisted they just be friends. Now she was beginning to understand why. There was much to learn about being a new person in Christ and a sister.

As she progressed closer to the front, Abby's eyes found her sister and family seated on the left. Her heart warmed and feet slowed.

Quaid saw Abigail slowing down and looked to see what caused it. Spying her sister, he smiled. *It was nice of Hope to invite them.* Quaid remembered back to the day he'd brought the two sisters together after being eighteen years apart. Now as he watched them, Quaid knew the decision to temporarily keep Abigail as a friend had been a good one. *She not only needed time to learn what being a Christian meant; she also had a long lost sister to get to know.*

Glancing at his fidgety friend standing nearby, Quaid studied Pierce's profile. He knew Pierce and Hope had experienced more tragedies then most people ever would. Yet they'd grown in their faith and closer to each other. They helped each other be stronger.

His eyes flowed back to Abby making her way closer to the front. When she first asked everyone to call her Abigail or Abby, it had been difficult. She was Sydney in his mind. But over time, that had changed. The old Sydney was almost gone. In her place was a woman Quaid was learning to care about. Now, as he stood by Pierce as his best man, Quaid acknowledged that he was ready to take the next step with her. In that moment, plans evolved to ask Abby out for their first official dinner date. The thought brought a smile to his face.

Abby felt Quaid's eyes on her, so she focused back on the front. His warm brown eyes brought a smile to her face. She stayed focused on him as she reached the end of the aisle. Abigail only had three steps to navigate before taking her position as Maid of Honor. Before reaching the top, Quaid's eye lowered in a quick wink. Abby had no idea the beautiful picture she presented to Quaid as a blush played across her cheeks.

When she came to a stop and turned forward, the organist started playing *Endless Love*. Everyone came to their feet.

As Abigail watched Hope coming down the aisle, she marveled at the Christian love she was witnessing. At the last minute, Hope's only brother had been unable to walk her down the aisle, so Frank had stepped in. To Abby's amazement, she found out Frank was Pierce's first wife's father. Frank and his wife, Helen, were Hope's friends back when she lived in Grand Rapids. They had been instrumental in leading Hope and her husband, Dean, to the Lord. After Dean's untimely death, God used Frank and Helen to bring Hope and Pierce together over the common cause of baby Sarah. And now these two dear people of God were showing their love once again.

For a moment, Abigail's mind traveled to the love God had shown through the sacrificial giving of his only Son. She knew that Jesus and the Holy Spirit of God were motivating factors behind the kind of love she was witnessing right now in the church. Bringing her eyes back to Pierce, Abigail could easily see godly love flowing from him as he watched his approaching bride. From conversations with Hope, Abigail knew these two were so committed to God that they'd remained sexually pure until their wedding night. This kind of love was still foreign to Abigail, but she had a growing desire to learn it.

## Out of the Snare

When Frank placed Hope's hand in Pierce's and stepped back, Abby's eyes found Quaid's once more. For the first time, she thought she detected something deeper coming from his eyes, and it startled her. Bringing her attention back to the couple saying their vows, Abigail tried to calm her beating heart.

A short time later, Hope handed Abby the bridal bouquet, and then Pierce helped her kneel before the pastor. Abby's eyes wandered to the large illuminated cross in front of them.

As the pastor talked and then prayed over the two people, he mentioned the need to always keep Christ in the center of their marriage. He also mentioned they weren't really two becoming one, but three—Christ, Pierce, and Hope. He then petitioned God to bless their union, their raising of Sarah, and any other children they might be granted.

When he talked about Christ, Pierce, and Hope being three-in-one, Abby remembered having asked Quaid what the *Godhead* meant. He'd used his finger as a simple explanation—three joints, one finger.

Opening her eyes, she peeked his way only to find his eyes were already on her. They held each other's gaze. In that moment, Abigail knew another new beginning was about to start.

Smiling shyly, she again turned her attention forward to consider the cross.

*Thank you, Jesus. Thank you for having patience with me and accepting me into your family. Thank you for bringing my sister back into my life and that her husband is working a job transfer into this area. Thank you for helping me to quit smoking and swearing. And thank you for friends like Quaid, Hope, Pierce, and Paul.*

Abigail knew her journey of living a new life in Christ was just beginning, but she wasn't afraid. She'd been delivered from Satan's snare, and she was thankful for that too.

As Abby's thoughts drew to a close, the pastor finished his prayer over Pierce and Hope. "In the name of Jesus. Amen."

Agreeing, Abigail said in her mind, *In the name of Jesus. Amen.*

## Pamela Bush

Our soul has escaped as a bird from the snare of the fowlers;
The snare is broken, and we have escaped.
Our help is in the name of the Lord,
who made heaven and earth.

Psalm 124:7–8 NKJV

Out of the Snare

Please turn the page for an exciting preview of
*Out of the Whirlwind*
The first book in the
Out of the Whirlwind Series
*This book can be purchased at*
*www.pamelabush.com*
*www.amazon.com*
*Or ordered through your local bookstore*

*From*
*Out of the Whirlwind*
*By Pamela Bush*

# Chapter One

"Something borrowed, something blue." A friend was getting married soon, so Hope was rummaging in the back of the closet looking for her memorabilia chest. The words kept softly repeating themselves as the search continued. The chest in question had belonged to her grandmother and was full of important documents plus old photos and coins among other things. It also held Hope's lacey marriage garter which happened to be blue.

"There you are!" Hefting a few boxes aside, Hope grabbed the wooden box and pulled it to daylight. Dropping to her knees, she pulled a little key from her pants pocket to unlock the old clasp.

For a few moments, she took time to read the top few certificates and then came across the garter nestled on top a red velvet box. Seeing the box, her hand stilled as past memories flashed across her mind. "It's been a long time little box," she murmured. Taking a deep breath and exhaling heavily, Hope picked up the garter. Setting it on the carpeted floor, she then lifted out the hand-sized velvet box. A picture of its contents came steaming to the front of her mind. Along with it—oodles of memories! Memories she had valiantly suppressed but were now screaming to be let out!

She seriously contemplated not opening the box. *Hope, just set it back in the chest. Lock the clasp and walk away.* The thoughts were very strong, but then the Spirit of God gently whispered to Hope's heart. *It's time, Hope. It's time to face the past and heal the remaining scars.*

Hanging tentatively between the past and the present, she found the strength to make a decision. *You're right, Lord. It is time.*

Slowly lowering the chest lid with her free hand, Hope closed the little lock and rose to her feet; temporarily forgetting the garter still lying on the floor. Still clutching the unopened box to her bosom, she walked downstairs to the kitchen. Spying the hot pot of coffee, she dumped the contents of her now cold cup sitting on the counter and refilled it. All the while, the box stayed at the spot near her heart. With the now steaming cup in her free hand, she slowly spun in a circle trying to decide where best to open the little box. In the process, a breeze floated in the open window above the sink. Turning towards the air, Hope caught a delightful scent of fresh spring lilacs wafting in the room.

They beckoned her. Before losing her nerve, she walked to the back screened door. Letting out a heavy sigh, she nudged it open with her shoulder and walked to the swing suspended from the porch roof. Taking a seat, she surrendered the red box to the seat beside her and thoughtfully sipped her coffee all the while running her fingers softly over the velvety top. Unconsciously, she began gently rocking the swing back and forth, back and forth, while absorbing all the sounds around her. Above her head was the creak of metal against metal with the sway of the swing. It blended with the song of a red winged blackbird coming from a backyard tree and car tires echoing on the pavement from the not too distant main road.

She calmly swung until the last dregs of her cup were gone and then she set it on the nearby deck table. Taking the box in both hands, she unconsciously set the swing moving faster as she slowly raised the lid. There nestled in the satin lining was a pair of turtles exquisitely crafted of lead crystal and gold. The mommy and baby turtle were one piece, and as the memories started to come, the present sights and sounds began receding into the background. The lilac scent grew fainter. The bird songs grew quieter. All she seemed able to focus on was the crystal piece. There was a time when she had loved collecting rare crystal pieces.

Hope continued staring at the turtles for a long, long moment and then slowly lifted the piece into her hand. The sun chose that moment to send a beam chasing across the porch which struck the crystal turtles. Instantly, rainbows danced around, mesmerizing her. The beautiful sight hypnotically pulled more and more of Hope's mind to the past.

She felt her heart leap just like it had that day long ago.

Hope's heart surged with pure joy.

*I'm going to have a baby! I have to rush home and tell Dean the good news!*

She was now no longer in the present. Her mind was fully engulfed in the past back to a chilly, snow threatening November day.

# listen|imagine|view|experience

## AUDIO BOOK DOWNLOAD INCLUDED WITH THIS BOOK!

In your hands you hold a complete digital entertainment package. Besides purchasing the paper version of this book, this book includes a free download of the audio version of this book. Simply use the code listed below when visiting our website. Once downloaded to your computer, you can listen to the book through your computer's speakers, burn it to an audio CD or save the file to your portable music device (such as Apple's popular iPod) and listen on the go!

How to get your free audio book digital download:

1. Visit www.tatepublishing.com and click on the e|LIVE logo on the home page.
2. Enter the following coupon code:
   081b-2e30-cff4-6dbb-6b6e-11fd-57df-aed6
3. Download the audio book from your e|LIVE digital locker and begin enjoying your new digital entertainment package today!